P9-DDI-362

A Simple Autumn

BALLANTINE BOOKS TRADE PAPERBACKS
NEW YORK

A Simple Autumn

A Seasons of Lancaster Novel

Rosalind Lauer

Copyright © 2012 by Rosalind Lauer

Published in the United States by Ballantine Books, an imprint of The Random House Publishing Group, a division of Random House, Inc., New York.

BALLANTINE and colophon are registered trademarks of Random House, Inc.

All scripture taken from *The Zondervan KJV Study Bible.* Copyright © 2002 by Zondervan. Used by permission of Zondervan Publishing House.

ISBN 978-0-345-52675-5

eBook ISBN: 978-0-345-52676-2

Lauer, Rosalind.
A simple autumn: a seasons of Lancaster novel / Rosalind Lauer.
p.   cm.
ISBN 978-0-345-52675-5 (pbk. : acid-free paper) —
ISBN 978-0-345-52676-2 (ebook)
1. Amish—Fiction.   2. Lancaster County (Pa.)—Fiction.   I. Title.
PS3612.A94276S53 2012
813'.6—dc23
2012027601

Printed in the United States of America on acid-free paper

www.ballantinebooks.com

2   4   6   8   9   7   5   3   1

First Edition

Text design by Christopher Zucker

For my mother,
Susan Lauer Noonan,
Who managed a large family with poise and good humor
And kept us all close in spirit.
We love you.

PART ONE

Secrets

Ask, and it shall be given you;
Seek, and ye shall find;
Knock, and it shall be opened unto you.

—Matthew 7:7

ONE

A lull covered the congregation like a warm blanket. The preacher had been talking about faith for so long that his voice was now a gentle hum in the back of Jonah's mind.

Now was the time.

Jonah King knew that church wasn't meant for ogling people, but it wasn't often these days that he was under the same roof as Annie Stoltzfus. He turned his head, just a few inches, to find her among the women seated on the other side of the barn.

There she was. . . .

Her face was framed by golden hair twisted back and tucked under her *Kapp.* Her blue eyes flashed his way, quick as lightning, and he looked away. All it took was one brief glance to get hope frolicking in his chest. Ya, he had it bad. Here he was, a grown man, and his heart got to racing at the sight of a girl.

But there had always been something special about Annie. She wasn't quiet and agreeable like most Amish girls. Annie was stubborn and spirited and willful. She loved to laugh, and she would stand face-to-face with a player twice her size in a volleyball game. Annie could hang tough; he knew that from years of skating with her on the pond or playing board games with his sister Mary and her. But when it came to children, Annie melted like butter. The little ones were her soft spot, the true way to her heart.

Ya, Annie Stoltzfus was no ordinary Amish girl, and it was all the things that made her so different that pulled Jonah to her time and again.

Of course, he never spoke about it. No one in his family knew that Annie Stoltzfus had hooked him ever since they were kids.

How many years had he watched her and waited, hoping she'd notice him? They had learned their lessons together in the one-room schoolhouse, and when they were children she'd come to their house countless times to visit with his sister.

And all those years, she only had eyes for Jonah's brother Adam. Ya, Adam had been the name on Annie's lips. She'd baked many a pie for him, and she'd fretted about him when he'd gone away during his *Rumspringa,* the time when Amish youth were given some freedom to date while their parents looked the other way. Adam had taken his rumspringa to extremes, leaving home for three years.

Jonah glanced to his left, where Adam sat with that squinty-eyed look he got when he was thinking. Adam surely had a lot to think about. He was the oldest, and now the head of their family, a big responsibility for a man so young. Even with sister Sadie gone to Philadelphia, there were still ten of them at home—eleven if you counted their grandmother, Mammi Nell, a widow who lived in the Doddy house just behind the vegetable garden. Seated here on the men's side, with Jonah, were Simon, Gabe, and Adam. Five-year-old Sam sat over in the women's section with little Katie, who was only two. Mary, the oldest King girl, kept them under her watchful eye with help from twins Leah and Susie and twelve-year-old

Ruthie. In Amish families, no child was too young to learn a chore, so there were usually plenty of brothers and sisters to mind the little ones.

When Adam had returned to head up the family after their parents' deaths, some folks had expected him and Annie to wed. But Adam had chosen to marry someone else, an Englisher girl with a yearning for a loving family and a heart big enough to help him raise the King children here in Halfway. Now that Adam was out of the running, Jonah wondered if Annie would finally see him in a new light. The Bible said that there was a time for every purpose under heaven. Maybe fall was the season that Gott might answer his prayers and plant a seed of love in Annie's heart.

He could always hope; nothing wrong with that.

Jonah turned his attention back to Preacher Dave, who was still talking about the Bible passage "Judge not that ye be not judged."

"Judgment is a chore for the Heavenly Father to take care of," Dave was saying. "It's not our task to look at our neighbor, our brother or sister, and judge them. Isn't that a wonderful thing? One less chore on my list for the day. We must let Gott be the judge. It's not our place to look to the man or woman beside us and decide whether the things they do are right or wrong. . . ."

Jonah straightened on the wooden bench, pressing his hands flat on his thighs. As his palms brushed the coarse broadcloth of his Sunday trousers he saw the truth in Preacher Dave's sermon. Ya, everyone knew they shouldn't judge their neighbor. It was a lesson taught among the Amish all the time. Jonah took a deep breath, wishing folks could take it to heart and stop passing judgment on him and his brothers and sisters.

The congregation seemed equally restless. Someone coughed. Little Matthew Eicher came toddling toward the men's section, crossing from his mother to his father. A child fussed over in the women's section, and in front of him the Zook boys nudged each other.

Everyone's itching to file out of the barn and catch the tail end of summer, Jonah thought as specks of dust glimmered in a shaft of sunlight from the hay-mow. Although they were more than halfway through the service, there was more to come.

It was a fine September morning, one of those days that wasn't sure whether it wanted to hold on to summer's heat or let the trees and barns begin to cool from the breeze sweeping over the hills. The morning had been crisp and cold, but now, with so many people filling the barn, there was enough body heat to bring to mind a summer day.

Rubbing his clean-shaven chin, Jonah frowned as the Zook boys stirred again.

Eli Zook leaned into his younger brother John and whispered in his ear. John was brother Simon's age, nine or so, and Eli had all the vinegar of a boy pushing into the teen years. Eli proved himself a bully, pinching his brother's arm. That brought a glare from their father, Abe, though none of the other men sitting nearby was paying him any mind.

The weight of Simon sinking against him told Jonah that the boy was falling asleep. Jonah slid an arm around his brother's shoulders, boosting him up.

Simon's heavy lids lifted.

Can't let the boy doze off during Preacher Dave's sermon, Jonah thought as his younger brother looked up at him with sleepy eyes, then took a deep breath.

Big John Eicher watched from the bench off to the side. And Jonah noticed that Big John wasn't the only one. Other men had their eyes on him and his brothers.

Always watching. And judging? Even though the preacher had

hammered away at them not to judge, Jonah felt disapproval heavy on his shoulders.

A cloak of self-consciousness had hung over the King family these past two years. When their parents were killed, people had rallied to give them support. Casseroles and baked goods had appeared on their table and jars of beets and peaches had stocked their pantry. Nearby Amish families had invited the children over after school to distract them from their grief and give the older family members like Jonah, Adam, and Mary time to get the household chores done. Neighbors had helped with the spring tilling and planting. The whole community had turned out to raise the new milking barn.

The good folks of Halfway, Amish and Englisher, had been more than generous with their help during the Kings' time of need. But the farm was running smoothly now, better than ever with the new automatic milking equipment and the larger herd. Thanks to Gott, the family no longer needed assistance. Jonah had been relieved when folks were able to start greeting him without a veil of pity over their eyes.

And just when things seemed to settle back to an even pace, Remy McCallister, Adam's Englisher girl, had come along and turned everyone's heads again. And then there was sister Sadie, who was *hoch gange*—gone high. Over the summer she had left home to sing with a group of Englisher musicians. He suspected tongues were still wagging over the King family.

Jonah didn't like the extra attention. It was like a splinter stuck under the skin. The skin healed over it, but the dull ache lingered. That was the problem now with his family. So many folks saw the Kings as different from other Amish families, and it wasn't going to change anytime soon with Adam about to marry an Englisher girl, an *Aussenseiter*. Ya, Remy was working hard to learn their ways, but good and kind though she was, she was still Englisher inside.

As one of the other ministers spoke about the evils of gossip that came from judging others, Jonah recited a silent prayer in his heart. Gott knew the Kings were a good, obedient family that followed the Ordnung, the rules and regulations of their church district. If only the people here could see that. "Help them see us with fair and honest eyes."

TWO

After the service, Jonah pitched in with the other men to move the church benches from the barn to the tables outside, where they would be used as seating for the light lunch. The weather was holding, so the meal would be taken out in the sunshine.

"Right over there," one of the older women instructed as Jonah and his brother Gabe toted a long wooden bench. "Over by the beech trees. They're in need of seating over there."

Jonah and Gabe followed her directions, clearing the crowd outside the barn and maneuvering around the rows of parked carriages.

"Just put it over there in the state of Ohio," Gabe said, making Jonah laugh as they traipsed through the grass. Gabe had a cutting sense of humor that often remained hidden.

"Not that far. Just carry it to Bird-in-Hand," Jonah said, referring to a town a few miles away in Lancaster County.

"If we've carried it this far, I think we could make it to the next town," Gabe muttered. Usually the tables were grouped in one spot, but the layout of the Eichers' yard didn't allow that, especially with the many carriages and buggies parked there today.

When Jonah saw Annie over at one of the tables with his sister Mary, his fingers nearly lost their grip on the bench.

This would be a good chance to talk to her. Some smart comment . . . Something funny to make her laugh. Annie's laugh made everyone smile.

But what could he say? Talking with girls had never been his strength. He kept quiet, and Annie didn't pay any mind to Gabe and him.

"They've already started packing," Annie said as she set each place with a knife, cup, and saucer. Mary followed her down the table, pouring water into each cup. "They'll be staying in Lowville with Perry's cousin till they get on their feet. It's an Old Order Amish group in upstate New York."

"Annie, what will you do without your sister?" Mary asked sympathetically.

"And little Mark," Annie added.

From his time spent doing repairs at the Stoltzfuses' house, Jonah knew Annie was attached to her nephews Mark and Levi. Mark was just a toddler, but Levi was around brother Sam's age—a time when small chores could be turned into play.

"It breaks my heart to see them packing up their little family," Annie said.

Jonah kept his eyes on the bench as he drank in the conversation. So Perry and Sarah Fisher were moving to New York. He'd heard some talk of Perry pursuing an opportunity there, but wasn't sure the young family would be willing to pick up and leave Halfway.

"I'm going to miss them so much." Annie's voice was laced with sadness. "But Sarah says I should come join them after they're settled."

A chill curled up Jonah's spine. Would Annie really think of leaving?

"Annie, no!" Mary gave voice to his concern. "Could you just up and leave us in the blink of an eye?"

"It wouldn't be all that soon, and . . ." Annie's voice trailed off as she noticed Gabe and Jonah nearby. "Anyway, let's finish up here so we can help Lizbeth with the second shift."

Jonah lingered, listening. Annie couldn't leave Halfway. She wouldn't.

"Come on." Gabe clapped a hand on his back. "The sooner these tables get set up, the sooner we can eat. And the way I'm feeling, I could tuck away half the church spread."

As he followed Gabe, Jonah turned back to steal a look at Annie, who had drawn close to Mary for private words.

Jonah lifted his straw hat to rake his dark hair back. A few overheard words from Annie and his heart had clouded over.

Was Annie really going to leave Halfway?

He was plodding back to the barn when he heard someone calling to him.

"Jonah? Jonah King. Come."

He glanced up and saw two bearded men beckoning him from the porch. Uncle Nate stood beside a squat man with black eyeglasses—Jacob Yoder.

Squaring his shoulders, Jonah tamped down his worries and climbed the porch steps. "The sunshine is back," he said, tipping his hat.

"After five days of rain, it's good to know there's still a sun to shine down on us," Nate said with a wry smile.

"But it got a little warm in the barn during the services." Jacob's brown eyes were magnified by his glasses. "I noticed that young Simon was dozing off in there. Everything okay? Is the boy sick?"

"A boy needs his sleep, and we know our Simon has his problems with that," Uncle Nate said. "Is he having the bad dreams again? I remember when he was sleepwalking through the night. That was a terrible thing."

"Night terrors," Jacob said, wanting to set them straight. "That's what Dr. Trueherz says they're called. But the doc thinks they were caused by trauma."

And Simon had been through more than his share of pain. The only witness to their parents' murder, Simon had suffered deeply during those dark days. Some nights the boy had paced the halls with a crazy look in his eyes and a panic in his heart.

But not anymore. Many things had been resolved when the police had arrested the man who killed Levi and Esther King. And when the puzzle pieces had fallen into place, Simon settled into an easier peace.

"I don't think Simon has had a nightmare for a long time," Jonah said, glancing over at the paddock where Simon was tossing a football with other boys his age. "And the night terrors ended in the winter."

"Good! That's good to hear." Jacob nodded, his head bobbing on his broad shoulders.

"No more sleepwalking?" Uncle Nate asked.

"No more. I think he's just tired today," Jonah said. "Probably because he's been staying late in the stable with his horse."

"I'm counting on you to make sure Simon gets the sleep he needs," Nate told Jonah. Their uncle did his best to look out for the family, Jonah knew that, but he felt himself bristling over the warning. Simon was a good boy.

And Jonah didn't notice anyone asking about why Eli Zook was pinching his brother during the service.

Thankfully, Jacob Yoder turned the talk to Ira and Rose Miller, the banned couple who had attended the service today to confess their sins to the community.

"Such a pickle Ira got into, all over that Jeep." Nate touched his beard lightly.

"No driving means no driving." Jacob pushed his glasses up on his nose.

Jonah knew that Jacob was right, but knowing the rules didn't make shunning any less painful. His gaze skimmed past the tables where the ministers and older members were sitting down to full plates—the first shift of lunch.

A small table, barely bigger than a sewing table, had been set off to the side near the rose trellis. Not the most desirable spot, with fat bumblebees buzzing over the late blooms. Old Ira Miller sat there with his wife, Rose, but they had no food yet. They would have to wait until every member in good standing had eaten, and a member could not take a plate from their hands.

A person in the *Bann* had to be separated from the rest of the community. There was a reason for the rules, and yet Jonah felt a pang of sympathy for the older couple. How miserable it would feel to be shunned.

"Where did that car come from, anyway?" Uncle Nate asked.

"It belongs to his son," Jonah offered. "Ira's Zed left it behind when he left the community. It's sitting on the side of the road with a 'For Sale' sign in the window now. I pass it every time I take the covered bridge into Paradise." He stopped himself, not wanting to be one of the gossips.

"Bishop Samuel warned him many times to put it up, but Ira did nothing." Jacob shrugged. "What else could the bishop do but bring on the bann?"

"Mmm." Uncle Nate's lips curled to one side. "Cars have tempted many a good man. Didn't you and your brother drive a Ford back in your rumspringa?" he asked, squinting at Jacob.

Jacob's cheeks flushed red above his beard, but he smiled. "That was a very good car. When you pressed the gas, it could really gallop. Faster than any horse I ever knew."

"Fast, but you can't feed a car hay and oats."

The two older men chuckled.

"Those days are far behind us now," Jacob said with a sigh.

Nate nodded. "Ah, but sometimes it seems like yesterday."

Seeing the smile on his uncle's face, Jonah wondered if his own father had ever learned to drive a car. Dat had never spoken of it, but Jonah knew it was something most young men tried.

Even Jonah. He was embarrassed to admit it now, but he had driven the very Jeep that had gotten Ira in trouble. Zed had taught Jonah everything about the vehicle. How many times had they climbed dusty hills and plunged through the low part of the river in that Jeep? He remembered gripping the stick shift, the pattern of the gears like a road map in his mind. He'd been a good driver, but he'd known that driving wasn't going to be a part of his life. Jonah would never stray far from the path of the Amish.

"Time marches on," Jacob said wistfully. "Now we have our own boys in rumspringa. Hard to believe. And you and Betsy have an Englisher girl living with you." He tipped his hat back, squinting at Nate.

"We do. But Remy's living Plain now. She's been going to the classes. Going to get baptized."

"Is she learning the language?"

"She's getting better at it," Nate said.

"The little ones love to teach her words," Jonah said. Remy's arrival had overturned the applecart for his family, but Jonah had to admit, she was trying to fit in.

Jacob pushed his glasses up on his nose. "She seems like a nice girl, but do you think she'll really stay? Some Englishers like to dabble with Amish life, but they never stick with it."

"I think Remy is a special one." Nate's brown eyes scanned the gathering on the lawn.

Jonah followed his uncle's gaze to the girl in the purple dress, her bright orange hair framing the edge of her kapp. She was helping the women serve the meal. For an Englisher, she was a hard worker.

"All I know is that Remy is quick to pitch in, and Betsy likes her sunny outlook," Nate added. "I think she'll stick around."

Jonah nodded in agreement, but Jacob shook his head doubtfully. "You can't make a Jersey into a Holstein."

Uncle Nate laughed. "That's true."

Jonah held his tongue, though he was bothered by the small-mindedness of some people in the district. To compare a young girl to a cow?

It was a relief when the older men were called to sit for the meal. Saved by the lunch bell.

THREE

As Annie poured water at the men's table, she tried not to stare at the girl serving potato salad. Ever since the Englisher girl had come along, Annie had kept her distance. In her mind she pictured Remy McCallister as a sneaky spider who'd gotten her venom into Adam. A fiery red spider!

At first, her face had burned with embarrassment whenever she saw Remy with Adam at a singing, the two of them looking so in love. Bad enough that he'd chosen someone else. Annie also wondered what people thought of her now that the man she had hoped to marry was with an Englisher girl.

And it hadn't been easy these last two weeks, having Adam and his brother Jonah around the house, helping Dat fix the section of the roof that had blown off in a storm. To walk out the door and see him carting shingles or swinging a hammer on the roof—that was uncomfortable.

Annie had done her best to stay away from Adam and his girlfriend. But now, with Remy standing right in front of her, well, a person had to look somewhere. Her gaze caught on the tight bun under the Amish kapp Remy wore. Such an unusual color of hair, orange and bright as the setting sun.

Watching her now, Annie saw that Remy didn't resemble a spider at all. No, she was really just a girl, not much older than Annie. Remy was learning Pennsylvania Dutch, as well as pitching in with the cooking and the cleaning. The girl was already dressing Plain, though she would always stand out among the Amish with that hair the color of fire.

As she filled another cup with water, Annie tasted bitterness on the back of her tongue. Disappointment was sour. Her path had seemed straight and clear once, but now she was tangled in a thicket of thorns.

Twenty and without a beau.

Annie lifted her pitcher—almost empty—and looked back at Remy, who was now over at a smaller table near the rosebushes. Her smile was sweet as warm honey as she leaned forward and let the people there help themselves to potato salad. And the man and woman smiled right back at her in appreciation.

Annie's jaw dropped open. Oh, no! That was Ira Miller and his wife, and the couple was still in the bann!

Quick as a butterfly, Annie hurried over to the small table set off by the side of the yard. Remy was heading over to the men's table with the big bowl.

"You can't do that," Annie said breathlessly. She put her hands on the plastic bowl and nudged it from Remy's grip. "You can't serve this to anyone else now that they've dipped into it."

Remy's green eyes opened wide. "I don't think anyone will really mind." She lifted the spoon from the bowl Annie was now holding and covered up the missing portions. "See? No one will notice."

"That doesn't matter. It's just not allowed." Annie felt her face growing warm. She didn't want to make a big scene, but she couldn't let this bowl be passed around. "Don't you know that Ira and Rose Miller are being shunned?" she asked in a lowered voice.

"I saw them confess, but . . ." She glanced back at the table where the couple was eating quietly. "The bishop let them attend church today. Isn't the shunning over?"

"Not yet. There's one more week. And while they're being shunned, the rest of the district can't be eating food that's been dipped in by them."

Remy frowned. "It's just a bowl of potato salad. . . ."

What would it take to make the girl understand? "It's the rules when someone is in the bann," Annie said emphatically. "It's always been this way."

"Annie's right." Annie's mother, Lovina, was suddenly at her side. "We must *meide* them. You see? That's why they're seated at their own table."

"I didn't realize that—" Remy's face grew pale as the truth set in. "I didn't think they'd even be allowed here if they were shunned."

"The rules of shunning can be complicated," Lovina said.

"I'm so sorry." Tears glistened in Remy's eyes. "I didn't mean to break any rules."

For the first time, Annie felt a tug of sympathy for the girl. She couldn't help it if she was an outsider.

Lovina patted Remy's shoulder. "This is just a pebble on the path. Now tell me, is that the bowl?" When Annie nodded, her mother took it from her hands. "Don't worry. I'll take care of this. We'll give it to Ira and Rose to take home with them." She cocked her head as she eyed the bowl. "Though it is quite a lot of potato salad for two people."

Just as quickly as Mamm had popped up beside them, she disappeared around the side of the house, and Annie found herself alone with this girl she barely knew. A girl on the verge of tears.

Remy swiped at her eyes with the back of one hand, then pressed a fist to her heart. "I feel just awful. What a stupid mistake! And it could have been worse if you hadn't stopped me."

"You were only trying to help." Annie's words were sincere. She couldn't bear to see more tears from this young woman.

Remy pressed a hand to her pale cheeks. "I feel like a fool."

"You didn't know," Annie said. So many things this girl didn't yet know, and it wasn't her fault. In just a few months she was trying to learn everything Annie had been taught since she was a little one. "No need to fret over it. And look, the first shift is all done, and I'm hungry for a peanut butter and marshmallow sandwich. How about you?"

Remy sniffed. "I am sort of hungry."

"Let's get some food." Without a second of hesitation Annie put a hand on Remy's shoulder and led her over to the tables of sandwiches, salads, and desserts. Annie's smile felt as easy as the breeze combing the grass. When she and Remy sat down together at a table, not a smidge of jealousy remained.

Soon after they sat down they were joined by Mary King and her younger sisters, teen twins Leah and Susie, and wise little Ruthie.

"It's wonderful good to be out here in the sunshine," Susie said brightly. "On days like this, I think summer might stay forever."

"It's a trick of nature," Mary said. "One day it's summer, the next day we're huddling by the stove before dawn."

"I like the changing seasons," Ruthie said. "I'm always looking forward to the next one. It's hard to pick a favorite." She paused with a pickle halfway to her mouth. "Remy? You're white as a pastry board. What happened?"

"I made a stupid mistake," Remy said. "But Annie here saved me from making it worse."

Annie felt a blush of warmth as Remy recalled the incident over the potato salad and the shunned couple. Adam's Englisher girl had a good heart.

"And you didn't know about dipping," Mary said sympathetically.

"Once a shunned person serves himself from community food, members in good standing can't eat from that bowl or platter."

Remy rubbed the back of her neck. "That's one lesson I'll never forget. But the couple is so sweet. It's hard to believe they were shunned."

"I know." Ruthie nodded. "Rose Miller taught me how to embroider flowers at Mamm's quilting bees. She was so very kind."

"Good folks are put in the bann sometimes," Mary said. "It's got to be done so that people obey the rules."

Annie could see the confusion shadowing the young faces of the girls at the table. "I know it's hard to understand, but I've never seen our bishop put a member under the bann without giving the person lots of chances. It's a last resort that usually comes only after many warnings."

Ruthie seemed lost in thought as she pulled the crust from her bread. "I'll be glad when the shunning is over. I'd like to learn some more embroidery from Rose. Maybe she'll come to our next quilting."

"That would be wonderful good." Mary nodded at her younger sister.

"Maybe I can glean a few shortcuts from Rose," Remy said. "I have a lot of catching up to do."

"You'll get there," Annie said encouragingly.

"You haven't seen me sew," Remy said. "It's quite a challenge for me. Leah and Susie have been helping me, but I'm all thumbs."

Leah and Susie exchanged a mischievous look, then bubbled over with laughter. "Remember the time you were embroidering a patch and you accidentally sewed it onto your dress?" Leah asked.

Remy pressed a hand to her mouth to cover her grin. "I don't think anyone is going to let me forget that little mishap."

"I've already forgotten it," Ruthie said. "Your quilting is getting better and better every time you pick up a needle."

"That's sweet of you to say, Ruthie, but I can accept my limitations. I'll keep to the kitchen while you and your sisters manage the quilt business." Like most Amish women, Esther King had started her girls quilting at a young age. Selling the quilts at markets had become one of the family's side businesses.

"But you're going to be our sister soon." Ruthie's eyes were round with mirth as she bit into her sandwich.

Remy's face softened with pleasure, and Annie felt a twinge of longing. Her heart ached to have a beau, a man she loved. Someone to start a life and a family with . . . a baby in her arms and a toddler hanging on her skirt. Wasn't that the dream of every Amish girl?

"Ya, time to learn the family business," Susie teased Remy.

"I'll keep trying," Remy said, "but honestly, I think I'd have better luck learning to milk a cow."

The King girls burst out laughing.

"What's that about?" Annie asked.

Remy rolled her eyes. "I think they're remembering the time I tried to help milk the cows in my nightgown. Let's just say, I don't have dairy skills either."

"But you always try to pitch in," Susie said. "You're a helper."

"And a good worker," Mary added.

Annie nibbled on delicious apple *Schnitz,* enjoying the banter between Remy and the King girls. What a difference a day could make! Only a few hours ago she had thought very mean thoughts about Remy. Ya, she had judged her, just as Preacher Dave had spoken of today. And to think, she had pictured Remy as an orange spider who'd attacked Adam. This girl was gentle as a lamb.

Laughter bubbled from her throat. How silly she'd been.

"What are you laughing at?" Mary asked.

Annie hesitated, noticing the expectant faces of Remy and the King girls. "I'm laughing at my own addled brain," Annie said.

FOUR

"Are you sure no one will see us?" Gabriel King asked his cousin Ben as his horse Mercury trotted the buggy down the road. Anyone passing them would think they were just out for a quiet ride on a Sunday afternoon. That was how it looked—and Gabe wanted to keep it that way.

"I told you, Blake and his father have built a whole maze of trails on their property. It's way off the road, and it backs up to the woods. No one will ever know we're there." Ben pointed up to the road ahead. "See that blue mailbox on the right? Turn there."

Gabe shifted the reins so that Mercury turned down the paved lane that split off from the main road. "And Blake won't mind me coming along?"

"He said that I should bring my friends. The more the merrier— that's what he said." Ben gave his shoulder a shove. "Don't be such a nervous Nellie."

"I'm not nervous." Gabe cocked his hat back on his head. "I just don't want to get caught doing things that are against the Ordnung."

Ben gestured toward the land and trees around them—the red maples, the whispering leaves of the birch trees, the stubby fields, golden in the late-afternoon sunlight. "Who's around to catch us?"

"I'm just saying there'd be a price to pay with the bishop." And with his brother Adam, too. Adam wasn't so easy about looking the other way during rumspringa like most Amish parents.

"Take it easy." Ben slapped his knee. "We're just doing some friendly socializing on a Sunday afternoon."

"I'm not worried about that," Gabe said. "And it's not what I came here for."

It was fine for Amish youth to socialize with friends on the Sabbath, but the sort of activity they were about to take on would be frowned upon any day of the week. Gabe knew that, but still, he couldn't resist the excitement of what Blake Gooden had to offer.

Gabe had never met Blake. He'd never really been friends with an Englisher before Remy McCallister had come along, and she was more a family friend. But ever since Cousin Ben had met Blake, the Englisher boy and his collection of dirt bikes were all that Ben wanted to talk about when the older folk weren't around. Ben had met Blake at a horse auction with his father. They had talked for a while, and Blake had invited Ben over to check out "some real horse-power." At least, that was how Ben had told the story. All that Gabe knew for sure was that this guy had some fast motorbikes, something Gabe had always wanted to try.

When they pulled around to the back of the sprawling house surrounded by porches and tall poplar trees, an older man paced on the back deck, talking on his cell phone.

"That's not Blake." Ben looked toward the scattered hay bales and trails on the other side of the fence and cupped his ear. A high whining sound pealed from the back acres. "Hear that? That's Blake."

The man on the phone waved at them, then turned away to finish his conversation. As Gabe hopped down from the buggy and tied

Mercury up to a hitching post near water, he hoped his cousin was right about this Blake fella. It wasn't often that Gabe went out of his way to meet someone, especially an Englisher.

"This had better be good," Gabe muttered under his breath.

"You'll see." Ben nodded, his lips banded together smugly as the bike whined closer, appearing on the path that wound around the barn. Once it was in sight, the bike closed the distance fast. It shot toward them, then skidded to a stop, spraying dust. The rider was cool and mysterious behind a full helmet with smoky glass covering his face.

Blake was tall and thin—a similar build to Gabe's, though he didn't seem to have a lot of muscle on him. Gabe held his breath until the rider took off his helmet, revealing just a tall boy. The short, pale curls cut close to his head reminded Gabe of one of the neighbor's sheep.

Ben did the talking on their end, and Blake nodded at Gabe, saying, "Cool." He led them over to an outbuilding that had been turned into a garage. Inside, half a dozen shiny bikes were lined up, tilting casually to rest on their metal pokers. Kickstands, Ben called them.

"Very nice," Gabe said, taking in the glimmering silver and parts painted in crazy lime green, orange, and blue brighter than a bolt of lightning. He hadn't seen anything so tempting since his *Grossmammi* had taken him into a candy store in Paradise when he was just a boy.

As Gabe listened to Blake's explanation, he learned that the bikes had funny names like Rupp and Taco, Arctic Cat and Yamaha. He didn't understand what made them different from one another, but he didn't care. He just wanted to give one a try.

"You'll want to start with a minibike," Blake said. "For newbies, they're easier to handle than a full motorcycle. They all give a differ-ent ride. Depends on what you like."

Gabe swung one leg over a small blue bike and planted his hands on the handlebars. The grips fit his fingers like a glove. He pressed his shoes to the ground, testing. Would he be able to balance?

"This is great," Gabe said. "But why do you have so many?" A guy could only ride one at a time.

"My father is into toys," Blake said. "Besides, there isn't a whole lot else to do out here. But we ride all the time. Dad and I built a dirt bike track out in the back pasture. And sometimes, when I get bored, I take the trails through the woods. Have you ridden a bike before?" he asked.

"This is his first time," Ben answered for Gabe. "But I told him it's not that hard to do."

"Let me show you how it works." Blake grinned. "Knowing how to stop is key." Gabe got a lesson on how to switch gears with the kick pedal so that the bike could go faster.

It didn't seem so hard to learn, though some of Blake's words floated off in the air. In his mind, Gabe was already flying down the path a mile from here.

"But you gotta wear a helmet. It's my dad's rule." Blake took two gleaming helmets from the rack and handed them out. "Try these on."

Gabe tossed his hat to Ben, who hung both of their hats on the empty pegs. The helmet squeezed his head as he pulled it on, but once there it felt okay. Gabe flipped the visor down and the journey was complete.

He had entered another world.

Gabe snapped the kickstand up and turned the key. So easy.

Beside him, Ben straddled the orange bike. "I'll lead the way," he said. His visor was still up so Gabe could see his face, but his voice was a faraway sound from inside the helmet.

The helmet was heavy on his head as Gabe nodded slightly, then gave him a thumbs-up.

"They call it the need for speed." Ben revved the engine, dropped his visor. With a shrill whine his bike shot out of the garage.

Gabe followed the steps Blake had told him—what he remembered—and suddenly the bike was galloping forward. A wonderful good ride . . . much smoother than a horse.

He kept his speed slow and steady, testing his balance, leaning a little to the side as he curved around a fence post.

Not bad.

The bikes were low to the ground—and fast! Ben was speeding down the lane like a fleeing stag.

Gabe slowed to watch his cousin loop through some turns in the course made out of hay bales. The rear tire of Ben's bike shifted in the dirt, fanning out to the left. The skid sent Ben's bike toppling sideways. Ben went down into a pile of loose hay.

"Whoa." Gabe steered over to help his cousin, but Ben was already back on his feet, swinging onto his bike.

In a flurry of motion to his right, Blake whipped down a path beside them on a yellow bike.

Gabe grinned at the three of them, buzzing like mad bees in a race.

He soared down the straight path, then shifted to a lower gear to slow on the curve to avoid the electric fence. The tires slipped on the sand as he turned, but he kept his balance and sped ahead.

The bike bumped over a tree root and he went flying through the air.

Gabe laughed as he landed, juggling balance with the machine that ate up the earth like a hungry beast.

This was living. This was the way a man should travel God's earth.

FIVE

That night, Jonah sipped his grape juice and wondered if he would grow old waiting for Annie to notice him. He imagined himself here at the family table in ten years, having a light supper of popcorn and grape juice before the singing.

Ten years. Leah and Susie would probably be married by then.

And in twenty years, would he be combing his gray hairs before he hitched Jigsaw up to a buggy?

By then most of his siblings would be married off and settled with families of their own. But here at the table would be old brother Jonah, still pining for a secret love. His throat tightened over a kernel stuck in his throat. If he waited much longer to let Annie know how he felt, he'd be a wrinkled old man.

"So who's going to watch the little ones tonight?" Adam looked across the supper table, his brows knit in concern. "Who's going to the singing?"

"I'll be going," Jonah said.

Gabe grabbed a handful of popcorn. "Me, too."

"If you're going, you'd best beat the dust off your clothes," Mary said. "What were you and Ben doing to get so dirty in your church clothes?" she asked Gabe.

"Just riding around."

"Hmm. Well, you know I won't miss the singing," Mary said. "I haven't seen Five all week." Five was the nickname of John Beiler, Mary's beau.

Poor Mary, Jonah thought. With their sister Sadie gone off to the city, most of the household chores fell on Mary's shoulders. She barely had a spare moment to spend with Five.

"I promised Remy a ride," Adam said, rubbing his chin. "Seems that half the house is going."

"I'll make sure Katie and Sam get tucked into bed," Ruthie said. She put a handful of popcorn in front of Katie, adding, "We can read a book in bed, right, Katie?"

"The purple crayon," Katie said.

"Okay." Ruthie smiled. "I like *Harold and the Purple Crayon,* too."

"I like that book, too," Leah said, her eyes bright behind her glasses. "I'll help you, Ruthie."

"And I can make sure Sam gets a bath," Simon said. "How long has it been, Sam?"

Sam swiped at his mouth, but his upper lip remained stained purple from the juice. "I don't know."

"You know, Leah and I are fifteen now," Susie said. "When will we be allowed to start going to singings?"

Adam grunted. "You just turned fifteen. I think you should wait another year. Sixteen is a good age for rumspringa."

"It's too hard to wait that long!" Susie said dramatically.

Jonah grinned. "Is there a boy you're looking to court, Susie bug?"

Susie's cheeks flamed a rosy color. "No. There's no boy, but . . . I just like to go out and be with people. I'm a social butterfly."

Jonah noticed the spark of amusement in Mary's eyes, though Adam kept a straight face.

"Well, you'll have to be a social butterfly here on the farm for a bit longer," Adam said. "I don't see you two in the kitchen much. You must help Mary with the chores. Adult privileges are for those who take on adult responsibilities."

"I want to learn how to cook more dishes," Susie said. "And Leah isn't lazy. She just gets lost in her books."

"I pitch in, too," Leah said. "And what about all those weeks at the end of the summer when we detasseled corn for Tom Kraybill?"

"That was hard work," Mary agreed. "You girls were so spent at the end of each day. It's the only time I've seen Leah fall asleep without a book in her hand."

"I just want to go to the singings," Susie said.

"Because you're a social butterfly," Jonah teased her. He could imagine his younger sister flitting from one group to another like a butterfly in the garden. While her twin, Leah, was a quiet bookworm who liked to view the world through stories, Susie wanted to be in the world, talking and laughing. In some ways Susie reminded Jonah of Annie. Such sunny personalities.

"I just can't wait to go to a singing," Susie said. "How I miss the singing that used to go on here with Sadie in the house! Every night while we washed the dishes, we would sing together. And all over the farm, you could always find Sadie. You just had to listen for her beautiful voice."

The family grew silent for a moment, and there was only the clatter of forks on plates as they all thought of their eighteen-year-old sister, who had left home for Philadelphia this summer.

Everyone missed Sadie. Sometimes, when the wind whistled through narrow outbuildings by the silo or stirred the leaves of the beech trees, Jonah was reminded of his sister's music. There was always music on the land, a song that changed with each new season, but somehow Sadie had managed to give voice to Gott's earth in songs that could steal your breath away.

Ya, he missed her, too.

Although the younger ones kept hoping she'd return and get right with the church, Jonah had seen the look in Sadie's eyes when she was with her boyfriend, Mike. Sadie had fallen for an Englisher boy and Englisher music, and though Jonah loved his sister, he feared she was lost to them.

The last time she had visited here, Sadie had seemed happy. But Jonah couldn't imagine leaving his family or the life that he knew to chase a dream. He knew a thing or two about the world out there, the world that the Amish stayed separate from. It had its temptations, but it also had sharp teeth and the bite of a wolf. Jonah preferred to chase his dreams right here in Halfway.

As he chewed another mouthful of popcorn, he wondered if maybe tonight would be the night that Annie Stoltzfus finally looked him in the eye. "Ask, and it shall be given you. Seek, and ye shall find." The Bible verse came to him unexpectedly, and he now understood it. He was going to have to find the words to talk with Annie.

He flashed back over his years of longing for Annie. He remembered every moment, whether she was just serving him coffee at a barn raising or brushing past him while ice-skating on the pond. He remembered her words, her laugh, the pattern of freckles on her nose. And all along, she never noticed him. He wondered what it would take to get her attention. To look up and see those blue eyes watching him. To press his palm to one of her creamy cheeks . . .

Lately he'd spent some time at the Stoltzfus house, helping to fix storm damage. Annie had a way of looking right through him as if he wasn't there, but he'd gotten a closer look at her daily comings and goings. Fixing the shingles on the damaged roof, he'd gotten a bird's-eye view of her life.

From the roof he'd watched her go off to the henhouse or out to the yard to hang clothes. There was something soothing about watching her fingers clip clothes up so quickly and systematically. Shake, clip, shake, clip, clip . . . Dresses and pants and shirts went on the outside line and undergarments inside so that they couldn't be seen from the road. He knew the routine from home, but there was something wonderful about watching Annie do it.

He didn't mean to spy, but it was hard to look away. He had memorized the way she walked, and he was a sucker for anything she cooked. He knew her well, but he didn't know how to talk to her. He couldn't find the words to talk to any females outside his sisters or grandmother. And that was a painful thing for a twenty-two-year-old man to face.

At the supper table, Sam broke the uncomfortable silence. "I have many things to show Sadie," he said. "When is she coming home?"

"We don't know, dear one," Mary said quietly.

"She wants to come in November for the weddings," Ruthie said. "She told me that in her last letter. She'll even stay a few days to help with the cleanup."

"But we don't know if the bishop will allow it," Adam said.

"Ya." Ruthie lowered her gaze to the table. "Sadie is afraid he'll give her a talking-to if he sees her here."

"And he will," Mary said. "It's not an easy place Sadie's gotten herself into, what with falling in love with her music and an Englisher man." Although her words were harsh, there was only sadness in her voice. "I don't think she'll ever come back to us."

"I want her to come back and see my boat. It's almost done," Sam said, his eyes shiny with hope. Sam had been building a toy boat in the woodshop with Adam, and Jonah had been glad to see the youngest King boy bonding with the oldest. "I hope it will float," Sam added.

"You'd best finish up before the weather turns," Jonah said. "People are saying it will be a wet fall."

"I like fall," Simon said. "It's school that's the problem. I barely have any time to train Shadow now that I have to go study reading and writing all day."

"But I miss school," Leah said. She and Susie had finished their eight years of schooling last spring. "I miss hearing Teacher Emma's voice while I'm working quietly. And reading, writing, and arithmetic are a lot easier than washing down milking stalls and cleaning house."

"What if we got real jobs?" Susie asked, turning to her twin. "Yesterday at the market I heard that Lovina Stoltzfus needs help at the tea shop. One of her daughters is moving away with her husband to an Old Order settlement up north."

So it was true; Annie's sister was really leaving Halfway. Over a mouthful of juice, Jonah considered what it might mean.

"I'd like to work in the tea shop," Leah said.

"Ye Olde Tea Shop." Susie smiled. "That would be the most exciting thing that ever happened in our lives! We would meet people from far and wide."

"Tourists," Adam said glumly. "Englishers. It's not the same as being social at a singing."

"Still . . . I would enjoy working there. It would be like setting up a tea party every day." She turned pleading eyes to Mary. "Will you ask Annie about it? Ask if her mamm might hire us?"

"And who is going to mind your chores around here while you're in town?" asked Mary.

"We'll do both," Leah said.

Susie nodded. "We'll do double the work."

Jonah kept quiet, but he decided to ask for them. It would give him something to talk to Annie about.

As the meal finished, Jonah asked Mary about the renovations going on at the Beilers' farm.

"Oh, it's coming along. They've put in a small kitchen and they're working on the bathroom."

"Have you seen it?" Adam asked.

Mary nodded. "It's nice and new. More than enough space for two people starting out."

The plan was for Mary and Five to live in the new apartment over the carriage house after they were married.

"It's funny that Five's dat had all those boys," Gabe said. "He gave the older ones land when they got married, but then he ran out."

Jonah nodded. The Beilers' story was not an unusual situation among the Amish. Five's father had set the older Beiler men up with parcels of land, but now he had no more left to give without cutting the farm too small.

Someday, it'll be the same problem for me, Jonah thought as he fetched his hat and headed out to the barn to hitch up his horse. There'd be no stake in this farm for him. After Adam married in November, he and Remy would be in charge of the King family farm.

But when Jonah was ready to wed, he'd be looking for a place to live and land to farm. If he managed to get married before he was an old, withered man. He laughed at himself as he got Jigsaw's harness from the tack room.

God willing, Annie would notice him one of these days . . . before he was sent off to rock in a chair at the Doddy house.

SIX

At the Stoltzfus dinner table, everyone was laughing at Dan Esh's stories of his fishing capers. Annie's last bite of panfried walleye melted in her mouth as her brother-in-law finished telling how he and Perry had caught the fish on the nearby river that afternoon.

"Nothing was biting," Dan said. "Three hours, we were waiting. So Perry broke out the cooler Sarah had packed for him. Gave me half of his sandwich, which was nice. *Denki,* Perry."

Across the table, Perry touched his short beard and grinned. "Ya, but I thought you'd be eating it yourself."

"I *was* eating it when I remembered something my father had told me. How he once had baited a hook with bread and caught a whopper. I figured it was worth a try."

"And that's how you caught these fish?" Annie asked.

"Not exactly," Perry said.

"The problem was, that bread wouldn't stay on our hooks," Dan said. "I don't know how my dat did it. But I was getting frustrated. I pulled a piece of ham from my sandwich and stuck that on the hook." He paused, his gray eyes twinkling. "Next thing I knew, I had a tug on my line. A heavy pull! It didn't come in easy, but I finally landed that big fish."

Laughter rose from the family.

Dat roared with amusement. "With ham? I've never heard of that." He pressed one hand to his chest and laughed some more.

Dat's laughter lightened Annie's heart. Aaron Stoltzfus had always been warm and good-natured, but lately the stress of the farm had been wearing him down. It showed in his pale complexion and his lack of energy at the end of each day. With a small farm to run and no sons to help him run it, Aaron had relied on the help of his two sons-in-law, Perry and Dan, to keep things going. But Perry would be leaving soon, and the Eshes' harness shop in Halfway was demanding more and more of Dan's time lately.

Annie and her mother kept telling Dat that he should hire some local help, but Dat said no. "We've managed all these years on our own; I don't want strangers running the farm."

"It wouldn't be strangers," Mamm always reminded him. "Some of our Amish neighbors could use the work. And with the money from the shop, we'd have no trouble paying them." Ye Olde Tea Shop, which had started as Mamm's side business, had gotten popular with more and more tourists coming to Halfway these days. The shop was bringing in money for the family, but it also pulled Lovina and her daughters away from the farm.

Annie's older sister Sarah rose and started clearing away plates. "So that's how you caught one fish," she said. "How did you come home with four?"

"Are you kidding me?" Perry's dark brows rose. "I know something good when I see it. I started baiting my hook with the ham, too. Four pieces of ham and we brought in four fish."

"We would have caught more," Dan added, "but it was getting dark and we were running out of ham."

"Mmm." Dan's wife, Rebecca, pressed a napkin to her mouth. "That's why the walleye was so good and smoky. Tastes just like ham."

Everyone laughed again.

"I'm glad to see my wife shares my sense of humor." Dan handed his plate to Rebecca, and Annie caught the unmistakable look of love between them. How her heart ached to know that sort of love.

Annie brought a washcloth over to Mark in the high chair. She loved tending to her little nephews. "I think you're wearing more fish than you ate." She wiped little Mark's face and hands before releasing him to toddle around.

"I don't need a wiping," said five-year-old Levi. "I'm not a baby."

"Hmm." Annie squinted at him. "You look fishy to me."

"I'll wash at the sink, then." He scooted off the bench and went to the sink.

"Now I know how to get him to the sink," Rebecca, Levi's mother, said, smiling at Annie. "Set *you* on him."

Annie smiled. "If you need me, just send him down the lane." Rebecca, Dan, and Levi lived in a cottage on the property, so Levi spent most days on the farm.

"Perry and Dan, denki for the fish," said Annie's mother, Lovina. "Your walleyes made a delicious meal for us."

"And a good surprise on a Sunday when we usually just have a small snack for dinner." Annie's father folded his napkin and dropped it onto the table. "Next time you go fishing, I'll supply the ham."

"Next time will be a long ways off, Dat," Sarah reminded him. "We're heading off Friday. Perry ordered the driver already."

Sarah's words drained the smile from Annie's face. In all the laughter and joking, Annie had let the dreaded day slip from her mind. But it was coming, this Friday. In a way, tonight had been a farewell dinner for Sarah, Perry, and little Mark. They would be leaving Lancaster County . . . leaving the state of Pennsylvania.

Aaron rose from the table and put a hand on his daughter's shoulder. Were those tears shining in his blue eyes? Annie wondered.

"You don't need to say it again," Dat said softly. "Your move up north has been heavy on my mind ever since you and Perry announced it. You know your mamm and I are sad to see you go."

"It wasn't an easy choice." Sarah paused, her arms full of stacked dishes, her smile a bit shaky. "But, Dat, you know how hard it is to find land in Lancaster County." The young couple had moved in to one of the upstairs bedrooms when they married, and though they'd been saving money, they didn't see a way that they could buy property here anytime soon.

"I know that, Sarah. You and Perry have made a good choice. But it's like castor oil; it doesn't go down too easy."

Sarah looked to her husband. "Perry thinks it's the best thing for us, and I know my husband will do his best to provide for his family."

Perry nodded at Sarah with such a look of love in his eyes that Annie thought her heart would melt. She had always wondered at the quiet bond between her sister and Perry Fisher. Mutual respect, admiration, and a willingness to work side by side.

Sarah didn't even notice as Annie took the plates from her and set them beside the sink. Her oldest sister, Rebecca, was already rinsing forks in a pot of clear water, so Annie grabbed a towel and got to work.

"We're all going to miss you," said Hannah. "Mamm, who's going to take Sarah's work at the shop?" Eighteen-year-old Hannah was the youngest of Annie's sisters, and though she looked like she was barely a teenager, she'd been meeting with the bishop to be baptized this month.

"I'll need to hire some help at the tea shop," Lovina said. "Same with Dat here on the farm."

"I can manage without a hired hand," Dat said. "I've always said, we've got to keep this a family farm."

"The choice is yours," Lovina said, "but I'm going to ask around for help at the shop. And it wouldn't hurt to hire an Amish man to work here. A hearty young man who wants to learn how to work the land."

Dat waved his hand as if swatting a gnat. "Pshaw! An old man like me can work the land, too."

"You're not old, Dat," Annie said.

"But you're going to need help, Aaron," Perry said. "With Dan taking over the harness shop and me gone, there's going to be more work around here than any one man could handle."

"Everyone will pitch in," Aaron said. "We'll make do."

Hannah blew a wisp of hair out of her face. "Sounds like Annie and I are going to be spending more time out in the barn."

"At the end of the day, the chores will be done," Lovina said. "Important thing is that Perry and Sarah get a good start. What grows in that part of New York? Is the land the same as ours? I want to imagine you there in the months ahead."

"There's a lot of dairy farming. Three years ago my cousin moved up there, and last fall he was able to build a house," Perry said. "There's opportunity up north that we don't have here. More open land. Cheaper land, and a lot of it can be tilled. We've almost got enough saved to buy forty acres. In the meantime, Cousin Gideon needs help on his farm. That'll give us work right away, and a place to stay."

"I'll miss you all so!" Lovina's voice was as warm as a familiar quilt on the bed. "You will always be welcome here."

Dropping some forks into the drawer, Annie saw her mother gather Sarah into her arms. The knot in Annie's throat grew thick. Another minute of this and she would be crying.

"You've shared your fine home with us for too long," Perry said. "We're grateful for all you've done for us. But we've talked and prayed about making this move. I think it's time."

"Bishop Sam has given us a letter for the clergy up in Lowville, saying that we're baptized members in good standing," Sarah said.

"And it's an Old Order group?" asked Dat.

"It's the Byler Amish," Perry said. "More conservative than we are. No gas lamps or indoor plumbing."

"Do you remember the days when we had the outhouse in the back?" Lovina asked her daughters. "It wasn't so bad. You'll be used to it in no time."

Annie wondered if she would fit in among the Byler Amish. Not that she had made up her mind on moving to New York, but she had to ask herself how she'd feel about following a stricter Ordnung.

"We'll be near a lake, and close enough to take a ride to Lake Erie," Sarah said. "They say that lake is so big, you can't even see the other side."

"That would be such a wonderful sight!" Mamm said. "We'll have to go there when we visit, Aaron. Take a look at the great lake Gott created."

"It is a Great Lake," Perry said, "one of five."

"Oh, you're a smart one." Lovina clapped him on the back as everyone laughed.

The men moved into the front room to talk and relax with the little ones while kitchen cleanup was in progress. Annie brought some table scraps out to the porch to feed Sunny, their border collie. When she returned to the kitchen, talk of the big move was still in the air. Sarah was explaining that the Lowville Amish didn't allow phone shanties that were shared by neighbors.

"So we can't even talk to you on the phone?" Hannah asked as she wiped down the table covering. "How will we share news?"

"We're going to do a circle letter," Rebecca said. "And we're counting on you to write about everyone here, Annie. You're the writer."

"Me?" Annie pressed the paper plates down into the trash. "I don't mind writing, but I don't think a true circle letter will work. I can't bear to wait for other people to write and keep the chain going."

"You can send your letter straight to me, anytime," Sarah assured her.

Annie wanted to say that a letter was no comfort at all, not like having her sister nearby. Nothing was turning out as Annie had planned. She had always thought she'd be married to Adam King by the time she turned twenty. Married and living a stone's throw from her sisters.

And here she was, not a prospect in sight, and she was losing part of her family. Her throat felt thick, squeezed tight by worry, and her eyes stung.

Don't cry. Do not cry! She clamped her teeth over her lower lip to keep it from wobbling. She didn't want to be a Gloomy Gussy. Sarah deserved better.

When she looked up to find a place in the cabinet for the glass she'd been drying, Sarah stood beside her, her blue eyes watchful. Annie had never been able to fool her.

"Be happy for me, Annie." Sarah grabbed her arm and pulled her to the side of the big kitchen, away from the commotion of dishwashing. "Perry and I are going off on an adventure. There's good opportunity for him there, and a chance for us to farm our own land someday."

Annie twisted the dish towel around one hand. "But you'll be so far from home."

"Ya, but Perry has some family there. And you can come visit us anytime. It's not like you to see the bad in things. Look at all the good that might come of this. Now smile for me."

Swallowing, Annie forced a smile. "You know I want the best for you. I pray that Gott has good things waiting for you in New York."

"I know that." Sarah rubbed Annie's arm fondly. "And think about what I said before. New York might be your chance to start over. Even if you and Adam weren't right and proper beaus, that doesn't make it hurt any less to have your dreams crushed."

Annie took a deep, calming breath. "How did you get so smart about things like that?"

"When it comes to my sisters, I've had a lifetime of experience," Sarah said. "I can read you all like a book."

"Ya?" Rebecca called from the sink. "If you can read me now, you'll know that someone needs to serve coffee and apple schnitz while I finish scrubbing these fry pans."

Sarah laughed as she led Annie back to the heart of the kitchen. "I'll make the coffee. Where's Hannah gone off to?"

"She's getting washed up for the singing," Lovina said as she returned from the front room. "Though I don't know how much more washing that girl can do. With the time she spends in the shower, she's going to scrub clear through the skin." She turned to Annie. "Are you going to the singing, too?"

When Annie nodded, her mamm shooed her along.

"You'd better get along, then. Go hitch Dapple to the buggy. We'll get the kitchen spic-and-span."

"I don't mind helping," Annie said.

But Lovina wouldn't hear of it. "You'll have double chores on your shoulders after your sister leaves," Mamm said. "Best to make hay while the sun shines. Off to the singing you go!"

SEVEN

*O*utside the barn, a cool wind swept over the stubby golden fields, making the leaves on the trees shimmer in bunches of gold and red and orange. The sun was an orange ball over the hills—a harvest sky that promised cooler days ahead. It would be a perfect night to give Annie a ride home—just cool enough to make two people want to huddle together for warmth.

When Jonah led Jigsaw over to the buggies lined up beside the barn, he saw Adam there, hitching Thunder up to the open carriage on the end.

"I like this cooler weather," Adam said.

Jonah nodded, stroking the withers of his horse. Jigsaw nickered in appreciation.

A second later, Gabe trotted over bareback on Mercury.

"A traffic jam and we're not even on the road yet," Jonah said. Though all three brothers were going to the same place, by courting tradition each wanted to take his own buggy, in the hope of leaving with a girl. "It's a good thing we have more than one buggy."

"Ya. Otherwise you two would have to sit in the back of mine." Gabe hopped off his horse and led it over to the buggy he had "fixed up." A few weeks ago he had come home with a big plastic machine that played music CDs. "I got it for just five dollars at an Englisher's garage sale," Gabe had told Jonah. They had talked about how their sister Sadie would have enjoyed it, though Gabe only had five of the shiny CDs to play. Sadie was always singing on the farm. Mamm used to say she was born with a song in her heart.

"But you know we can't ride with you in that thing." Adam snickered. "Jonah and I are baptized members. We can't be riding in a buggy with music playing all night from that boom box you have."

"I like to call it a party machine," Gabe said.

Adam shook his head, but Jonah laughed. "What happened to the quiet Gabe who was devoted to our animals?"

"One word," Gabe said. "Rumspringa."

"Mmm." Jonah tightened a strap. "If only we'd had milking machines during my rumspringa. I remember being too tired to go out some Sundays after the chores and the milking."

"It's true!" Gabe agreed. "I didn't think it was a good idea at first, but you were right, Adam. The machines were a good thing. Look at us—all three of us going off. Mary, too. Before the milking machines, I didn't have much time to think about going to the singings."

"And now?" Adam clapped Gabe on the back. "Got your eye on a nice Amish girl?"

"Maybe I do. But I never kiss and tell."

Jonah laughed along with his brothers, but he wondered at the change in Gabriel. Like a bird that'd left the flock, he seemed to be flying in his own direction without a lick of fear. It surprised Jonah, and he wondered if it concerned Adam. Among the Amish, it wasn't necessarily a good thing to stand out from the crowd.

Good meant following the rules and obeying the Ordnung. Good Amish didn't have *Hochmut,* the pride that might fill their heads with foolishness and let them believe they were better than their neighbors. Good Amish moved with humility. They filed into church in an orderly way. They dressed the same. Good Amish lived Plain.

No boom boxes.

Inside the Eichers' barn, Jonah moved his mouth to the songs, but no sound came out. He had a terrible singing voice. Sadie used to say he sounded like a wounded animal—so he kept it to himself. Even with a bad voice, he never missed a singing.

Tonight he had managed to get a seat right across the table from Annie. He could have spent the whole night watching her red lips form the words to the songs. Those lips—they were as bright as the red maple trees that glowed this time of year. Her blue eyes danced with each fast song, a wild swirl of crisp leaves in the autumn wind.

That was how she haunted his heart. Every season, every corner of Gott's good land, he saw Annie there.

But to keep from staring at her like a *verhuddelt* man, he let his gaze slide down to the table and over the other girls, too. Annie sat sandwiched between his sister Mary and her sister Hannah, a young girl as sweet as a sugar cookie, but to Jonah a paler version of Annie. Emma Lapp, the schoolteacher, had a fair voice, and she never missed a note or a single word of a song. The three Mast sisters helped carry the tunes, but poor Nellie Zook had a voice worse than Jonah's—only she didn't know it.

Beside him, Gabe's voice boomed.

"Joy, joy, joy!"

Gabe's voice had a lot of power for a kid without a lot of meat on his bones. John Raber was a good song leader, and fellas like Adam and Five could follow along.

Jonah liked to filter out single voices and listen to the whole roomful of song, wide and open as a September sky at sunset. When all the young people sang and their voices blended together, you could feel Gott's grace.

> *"How great my joy.*
> *Great my joy.*
> *Joy, joy, joy!*
> *Joy, joy, joy!*
> *Praise we the Lord in Heav'n on high."*

Pressing his knuckles to the edge of the table, Jonah could feel the vibration of sound in the wood. A singing could really wake up the soul!

When they took a break from the singing, Jonah forced himself to head over to Annie, driven by the fact that he had something to say tonight. He was looking out for his younger sisters. At least, that was what he told himself.

Standing next to Mary, Annie looked much younger, mostly because she was a head shorter. Her summer blue eyes seemed to peer right through him, but he pressed ahead.

"Annie." He nodded. "Leah and Susie have been wondering about your mamm's tea shop in town."

"That's right." Mary tapped Jonah's arm gently. "They wanted me to ask you about it."

"Is it true Lovina's looking to hire some help?" Jonah asked.

"Ya, it's true," Annie said.

"The twins are hoping to be apprentices," Jonah said. "Some-where off the farm, I think." He threw this last bit in to make the conversation less businesslike, but it didn't work too well.

"Then they should talk to Mamm," Annie said. "With Sarah and Perry leaving, we're going to need some help. Maybe on the farm, too, though you know how Dat is about that."

"Mmm." Jonah grunted. He knew that Aaron didn't want to hire anyone on the farm. After a storm had torn off part of the Stoltzfuses' roof, word had gotten around that they needed help to fix it before the rain got in. Jonah had been quick to volunteer, along with Adam, who had good carpentry skills. They had gotten a tarp on the roof right away, and this week they planned to finish up with the new shingles.

Jonah wanted to continue the conversation, but he couldn't think of another thing to say. Had he just grunted? He wanted to kick himself.

There was an awkward silence. Well, awkward for him. Annie was gazing off in the distance, and Mary was smiling at Five, her eyes the color of warm honey.

What a fool I am, Jonah thought. He was a grown man in his twenties and still he didn't know how to talk to a girl. He had no clue how you get a girl to like you. *How do you even know what to say to her?*

Annie was looking over his shoulder, already distracted. "They're setting up for volleyball." She looked up at the sky. "We'd best begin now, before it gets dark. Soon it'll be too cold for outside activities."

"Let's get on a team together," Mary told her best friend.

When the two girls headed over to the net, Jonah could only follow and hope that his skills in volleyball would help Annie see him as a man with strength instead of a bumbling fool.

The teams were already forming. Quickly, Jonah moved to the side of the net where Annie and sister Mary stood, so that he'd be on their team. Volleyball was his game. Although pride was a sin, he liked to think that his patience and accuracy were a blessing here. Gott had made him good at waiting for the ball and popping it over to the right spot.

He rubbed his hands together, trying to push down the nervousness that boiled from having Annie just off to his left.

The game was off to a good start when the ball came to Jonah. He popped it up gently, and Annie moved in to smack it over the net.

"Good one," he said.

Her casual smile made his insides melt, but there was no time to bask in the feeling. The second serve was heading his way.

The ball passed back and forth over the net, and Jonah had a few chances to knock it into the right spot. Some of his teammates complimented him on making good shots. Did Annie notice?

When he jumped high to send a hard-hit ball back over the net, she looked up at him with eyes of wonder. "Wow, Jonah."

He bit back a grin, trying to shrug it off, though he felt sure he'd never forget those words.

Wow, Jonah.

He was still smiling down at her when the ball sailed over the net, right toward them. Annie held up her fists as Jonah, desiring to protect her, lunged toward the ball. He jumped up and smacked the ball back.

But as he landed he crashed into Annie. She was such a little thing compared with him, and the force of his weight knocked her over.

With a little cry of anguish, she fell.

By the time Jonah had regained his footing, she was on the ground beside him, crumpled in a heap like a sack of potatoes.

It was a game-stopper. All the girls rushed in to help Annie to her feet. They sat her on a chair and gathered round her, coddling and soothing and lending her a handkerchief to dry her tears.

Arms folded, Jonah hung back with the other young men. "Is she all right?" he called to the cluster of girls.

"She'll live," Mary reported, "but she's going to have a fat lip."

"I'm sorry," Jonah called. "Sorry, Annie." He looked down at the ground, wishing that he could be the one to pat her back and soothe her.

Surrounded by Mary and the other girls, Annie went over the

crash. "How did that happen? I was just reaching up to hit the ball, and something barreled into me like a charging bull!"

"Oh, dear Annie!" one of the girls cooed. "That was Jonah King who banged into you."

"The game is not fun with one who's so competitive," someone else said.

Jonah's ears burned. Competition was frowned upon in Amish groups. Competitors were out to prove that they were better, and that was a sign of pride . . . hochmut. It was not a good thing.

"It was an accident," Remy pointed out in Jonah's defense.

"But it's always the men who fight too fiercely to win," Annie said.

Jonah frowned. Of all people to say that—Annie was a tough competitor in any game.

"Sometimes I think it's too dangerous to play with the men," Annie added.

Did other people agree with what she was saying? He looked around, but found that the guys had lost interest in what the girls were saying. They were already lobbing the ball back and forth, talking about how it was getting hard to see in the gathering dark.

Jonah's heart sank. At last, Annie had noticed him, but in all the wrong ways.

"Let's go back inside and do some more singing," Adam suggested. "It's getting too dark out here for more games."

The girls surrounding Annie began to move, a slow herd. At their center, he could see Annie holding on to Mary's arm.

"Sorry about that, Annie," he said, making sure to meet her eyes for this second apology.

"Ya." She waved a hand at him, as if swatting a pesky gnat. "I think we'd best keep our distance, Jonah. You and me, we'd best stay far, far away from each other."

"That might be safer for both of us." Jonah rubbed his elbow, trying to make a little joke of it.

Annie winced as she pressed her fingers to her swollen lip. "It's going to hurt when I try to sing." Although she didn't say the words, Jonah knew she was thinking: *And it's all your fault.*

Sick inside, he stopped walking. Quickly he dropped to the back of the crowd as he wondered how he could bungle such a simple thing as a volleyball game.

As night fell, most young people wandered back into the barn for some more singing. Some couples, like Remy and Adam, stayed outside to talk in the privacy of the gathering dark.

Wounded in spirit, Jonah sat on a hay bale outside the door. How many singings had he come to with high hopes, only to have them crash to the ground?

This love for Annie bordered on crazy. But the Bible said love was God's greatest gift. Wouldn't it be a sin to ignore the love that God had planted in his heart?

The night air cooled his burning face as he leaned forward and let the song from inside wash over him.

"Good Lord," the group sang out, their voices big and bold, "show me the way."

Good Lord, he thought, *show me the way.* Jonah sat alone, thinking that he should just go home now. Once again, he would be leaving the singing without Annie beside him in the buggy.

"Jonah?" He felt a hand on his arm. His sister Mary sat down beside him. "Can't you just tell her you're sweet on her?" she asked.

Jonah sat upright, staring at his sister. "I was hoping no one noticed."

"I always knew you were sweet on someone," she said. "I didn't know who until tonight."

"Can you keep quiet about it?"

"Sure. Gossip is a sin. But, Jonah, this is Annie we're talking about. She's like a sister to me, and you know her well."

"Ya." Maybe he knew her too well. "All those years we played together as kids . . . ice-skating and horseback riding. Singing around a bonfire and picking apples. Sometimes I wonder if she thinks of me as a brother."

"Just talk to her."

"No," he answered flatly. "I've felt this way for a long time, but I don't have the gift of gab she has. I can't say the first word to her, even about the simplest things like the weather."

Mary nodded sympathetically. "You've always been the Quiet One."

He winced, as if burned by the old nickname.

"Well, I think you and Annie would make a very good couple."

"Didn't you hear her just now? She hates me."

"She's upset. And acting stubborn as a mule, if you ask me."

"Stubborn or not . . . she doesn't see me as a beau." He drew in a breath, forcing himself to face the truth. "She probably never will."

"Maybe she just needs a little push." Mary touched his arm. "I could drop a few hints."

"Don't say anything," Jonah warned.

"I won't give you up. But I am going to say something about her fit of temper. It's not like Annie to be so downright mean."

"She's just upset because she got hurt," he said.

"Even so, that's no excuse for snapping at you that way."

"She's upset," he said. "I can forgive her."

"Dear Jonah." Mary squinted at him, shaking her head. "There you go sticking up for her again." She squeezed his arm. "You've got it bad."

That was the truth. Leave it to Mary to hit the nail on the head.

And sometimes the truth was a very heavy hammer.

EIGHT

*W*hat were those fellas saying to Emma?

Gabe King twisted away from his cousins Ben and Abe King to get a look. Emma was over by the line of buggies, talking with David Fisher and Ruben Zook. Both boys were older than Gabe, and neither one of them had a steady girl.

They'd better not set their sights on Emma, Gabe thought as he leaned against the cart of hay that the horses were feeding from, to get a better view of what was going on outside the barn.

People were starting to leave the singing. Adam and Remy were pulling out in a buggy. Lizzy Mast was climbing into an open carriage with Amos Lapp.

"Now, that's a new one—Amos and Lizzy," Ben said, scraping a toe through the dirt. "But I don't think it will last."

"Are you feeling bad because she's not riding home with you?" Abe teased his brother.

"I didn't even ask her!" Ben protested.

Abe shrugged. "Your loss."

As his cousins teased each other, Gabe shot another look back at Emma. Still there. He wanted to leave, but he didn't want to get too far ahead of Emma. He would have to pull off to the side of the road ahead and wait for her, and it wouldn't do to have everyone from the singing pass him by, stopping to ask if he was okay.

If only they could leave together like a normal couple. But no ... he had to be dating the schoolteacher, a girl who was stern about her reputation. "I have to be a model for my students," she always said. They had to court in secret. Sometimes Gabe wondered why he didn't go for a normal girl who worked on the family farm, scraping honeycomb or baking pies.

What would Emma do if one of them asked if she wanted a ride home? There was a good chance of that. With her bright eyes and smooth skin, Emma Lapp was a beauty, and she had a smart way about her. And not just smart like a roomful of books. Emma saw the light burning inside other people. She had a quick way of figuring out the things a student could do well. She helped build up the good aspects of a person.

No one could make a person warm up inside the way that Emma did. Gabe understood why fellas gathered around her at singings. They were on her like honeybees on a flower, and he didn't like that one bit.

He had known Emma Lapp since her family moved here. He'd been in the third grade when she came to the one-room school-house for the first time, with a tooth missing from her smile and a quiet manner. Back then Emma and her brother Caleb didn't get much attention because their sister Elsie took it all. The small girl had a very big personality that made the other children want to play with her.

But that first day he had watched Emma as she finished her work in the blink of an eye. A smart one. But instead of showing off to the teacher, she had turned to help Sadie with her arithmetic.

He had seen that she was good at heart, but he'd always thought she was too prim for the likes of him. She would be lost in a book, while Gabe would be looking out the window, longing to be home to do real work like cleaning the horses' hooves or mending the fence.

When he thought about it, it was surprising that he and Emma had gotten together at all. For Gabe, math was for keeping records on the milk cows. And reading and writing? He'd learned just enough to manage the farm if he needed to. But for Emma, every day was about words and arithmetic problems and teaching children to read from the primer.

There couldn't be two more different people under Gott's big heaven. Even so, she was the one girl who stuck in his mind.

It was his parents' death that had brought them close.

It had happened during a cold spell in winter; those short, dark days when everyone wants to sleep more. Even the cows.

A local man they trusted had turned on Levi and Esther King, killed them just like that. Gabe didn't like to think on those days much. The grief that fell over his family was like a winter that refused to end, a coat of sadness heavy on the whole community.

Through it all, Gabe remembered Emma there, her brown hair pulled back neatly under her kapp, her eyes shining silver as the moon during their darkest hours. She had stood with the children in the cemetery as the simple funeral prayers had been said. She had visited the house, bringing a covered dish and showering Leah and Susie and Ruthie with attention. She had been especially good with Simon, talking to him even when the terrible memories stole his voice and sent him sleepwalking through the house at night like a verhuddelt person.

And when Simon wanted to believe that bears had killed their parents because it made more sense than the terrible truth, Emma had bought him a book about bears. "So he can have the facts," she'd said. Sometimes the things she said made her sound wise like Mammi Nell instead of a young girl not yet nineteen.

"We best get going," Abe said, drawing Gabe back to the present. Abe untied his horse from the cart of hay that had been nearly emptied by the grazing animals. At singings most couples tied their horse up to graze and left it hitched to the buggy because it was too hard to hitch up a buggy in the dark.

Ben tipped his head closer to Gabe's face. "You're daydreaming. Thinking about the need for speed?"

"What? No." Gabe saw that Emma and the guys were gone, and his pulse beat a little faster. Had she taken a ride? No . . . she wouldn't have. But where was she?

Ben checked the harness on his horse. "Are you going to stick around here and hold up that fence post all night?"

Gabe pushed away from the fence and found his buggy. "I'm right behind you." He turned on the boom box and a song filled the night. "Born in the USA!" the man's voice crooned.

"Nice." Ben tipped his hat back, listening for a moment. "Just mind you don't wake up the Eichers' cows."

Gabe smiled, turning down the volume. "Or the Eichers," he said under his breath. He waited until Ben rolled down the lane. *Let the others go first, so they won't see me stopping.*

At last, the lane was clear and only a few stray buggies were left behind. Gabe turned off the music—not wanting to call attention to their secret meeting. He signaled Mercury and they started in a slow trot so that Gabe could watch for Emma on the side of the road.

In the pitch-black night, lit only by scattered stars, he felt that pulse of tension. It wasn't safe for a young girl to be walking alone in the dark, especially with all these buggies passing her by. He had learned the terrible things that could happen along the side of a road. Sure, Amish youth walked and scootered these country roads all the time, often after dark.

But thinking of Emma out here alone reminded Gabe of the dangers the night held. He wanted her by his side. Safe in his arms.

A dark form by the side of the road made hope leap in his chest, but it turned out to be nothing more than a lonely tree.

"Emma," he called desperately. "Where are you?"

NINE

*A*nnie shivered and tugged her sweater closed as Dapple pulled the open carriage away from the singing. The night was dark, but ahead of them a line of half a dozen red triangles seemed to float up the hill: the warning reflectors on the backs of buggies.

Annie knew that most of those buggies were heading home with courting couples inside.

She shivered again. "It's cold. A sure sign that fall is really here."

"Where's the blanket?" Hannah turned in the seat beside her, squirming to reach into the back of the buggy. "Got it." Hannah unfolded the blanket and tucked it over their legs. "Is that better?"

"Much better. Denki." The buggy in front of them turned off to the right at the fork in the road. "There goes Mary and Five."

Hannah pulled the blanket up to her chin as she turned to watch them. "But that's not the way to the Kings' farm."

"They'll take the long way home," Annie said. "Courting couples like to ride around for a while. Gives them a chance to talk."

"I wish I had a beau." There was a sad note in Hannah's voice.

"It will happen for you, Hannah. Sooner or later."

"It's already later." Hannah sighed. "I'm eighteen and I've never courted anyone. I'm sure to be an *Alt Maedel*."

Annie laughed out loud. "You can't be an old maid so young! You're just beginning to court. If you were an old maid, then tongues would surely be wagging about me, with no prospects in sight and even older than you."

"You heard them?" Hannah's voice was a whimper nearly drowned out by the clip-clop of horses' hooves.

Annie's jaw dropped. "You mean . . ." She'd been joking, but now the joke was on her. Her good mood began to fade. Were people really talking about her because she didn't have a beau? "Do folks say I'm going to be an old maid?"

Hannah pressed her palms to her cheeks. "I shouldn't have told you! I'm sorry. And now I have to close my eyes for the bridge. It always scares me." She lifted the rough blanket and ducked her head underneath.

Hannah had always been afraid to go over the Halfway Mill Covered Bridge. The echoing noises and darkness inside the wood structure had spooked her since she was a child.

"I'll tell you when it's over." Annie had always found the old wooden bridge to be comforting. The cozy wood overhead and the sound bouncing around made her feel like she was attending a singing in a barn.

Tonight she was grateful to have a minute to sort through her thoughts. With her eyes on Dapple's bobbing head, she mulled over her childhood dreams. Maybe it was her fault for pinning her hopes on Adam. They had never courted—not really—but she had spent a lot of time with him. Mary King was her best friend, and in their younger years the two girls had spent every spare moment with each other, playing games or running the summer produce stand or baking cookies and pies.

Annie had always admired Mary's brother Adam. From the time he was a boy he could build things—birdhouses and boxes in the beginning, then cabinets and chairs. She had liked his shiny black hair and had always wondered what was going on behind those smoky brown eyes. Then came the time when Annie and Mary came upon Adam building a hope chest in the woodshop.

"Are you going to sell it?" Mary had asked her older brother.

"I don't want to," Adam had answered. "I'd like to keep it."

"What for?" Mary had asked.

"Maybe for the girl I marry." At that moment Adam's eyes had landed on Annie . . . and she'd been sure he was talking about her.

That was the day Annie had started to plan. Annie loved planning, and she realized if she married Adam, she and Mary could remain close friends forever.

But it was not to be.

The air grew light around them and echoes faded as they emerged from the covered bridge. "You can come out now, scaredy-cat."

Hannah's face peeked out from the blanket. "I wish they would take the cover off that bridge."

"Tourists love it," Annie said, still stuck on her worries. "Those girls who are talking about me . . . What exactly are they saying?"

"One of the girls in the group getting baptized said— Oh, I don't want to gossip, Annie. I won't tell you her name, but she said she hopes she doesn't end up twenty years old with no beau in sight."

Annie's cheeks blazed with embarrassment, a fire that no amount of wind could cool. "No beau in sight . . . that much is true," she admitted.

Hannah touched her arm. "I shouldn't have said anything."

"No, I'm glad you told me, even if the truth hurts."

"Well, the best way to make them stop talking that way is to start courting someone."

"I don't know about that." Annie swallowed over the lump in her throat. She couldn't think of a single young man in their district who she'd take a ride with. And certainly there was no one she would kiss.

Maybe she would be an alt maedel.

"There must be someone you've got your eye on," Hannah prodded.

Annie shook her head. "No. Honestly, there's no one who sparks my heart." None of the young men even came close. "For me, the right man isn't just looking for a wife. He's looking to fall in love." That was the thing holding Annie back from young fellas like Ruben Zook or David Fisher. She wouldn't settle for just a man.

She was waiting to fall in love.

Hannah turned to face her sister, her round face pale as a moon. "Ach! I just got goose bumps. You make it sound so wonderful good. I want to fall in love, too." Hannah looped an arm through Annie's. "Help me find a beau, Annie. You know so much about how to talk to a fella and I don't know where to start. Won't you help me?"

Annie smiled. "It's not like learning to bake a pie."

"But you're a good teacher." Hannah's features still seemed child-like though she was only two years younger than Annie. "You taught me how to make the best piecrust in the world."

Annie watched the road, moved by the sweet girl gripping her arm. How she would love to help her sister. "It's not like learning to bake a piecrust. But it wouldn't hurt for you to hone your kitchen skills. Dat always says that Mamm melted his heart with her venison stew, and I almost won Adam with my flaky piecrust."

"I'll be having lots of chances to cook once Sarah is gone,"

Hannah said. "And I promise, I'll do whatever you say. Will you help me, Annie?" Hannah's hopeful eyes made her shine like an angel in the darkness.

At that moment Annie decided to do everything she could to help Hannah find her way to love. It would be an act of goodwill. Besides, it would help take her mind off her own worries.

"If you want to find a beau, there are three things to remember. Good cooking. Good humor. And enough conversation to make a young fella feel comfortable."

"I never know what to say to a boy," Hannah told her.

"That's the thing. The small talk has to flow, smooth as cake batter." Annie had no problem talking to young men. She flitted from one group to another, chatting with everyone. But Hannah was shy. She hung in the corner of a room, quiet as a moth.

"Then you'll help me?" Hannah's voice soared with hope.

"I'll do my best. I can help smooth out your social skills. And I'll even keep my eyes open for a good match for you." None of the young men in the district appealed to Annie, but that didn't mean she couldn't find someone for Hannah.

"Oh, sister Annie! Denki!" Hannah gave her a quick hug, mindful of the horse's reins.

Annie patted her sister's arm, feeling a sense of satisfaction for the first time in months. She was going to be a matchmaker. She was going to help two people find love and happiness. And what was it Mamm always said?

Happiness was like jam. You couldn't spread it without getting some on yourself.

TEN

*E*mma pulled her sweater tight around her and jogged in place to ward off the cool night. A coat would have served her better than a sweater, but who would think to bring out a coat this early in September? Hers was tucked into a cedar chest in Dat and her stepmother Fanny's room.

Out here on the roadside, deep black night surrounded her. The croak of frogs rose from the field behind her, a chorus of song to rival the singing her group had just done in the Eichers' barn. Emma had been careful to keep to the roadside and move out of the way of passing buggies and any cars that might happen this way on a Sunday night, but the ruts and lumps and thistles on the ground made for bumpy walking in the dark.

Where was Gabe? She had seen him talking with his cousins when she headed out. He couldn't be far behind.

She pursed her lips, then smiled. No need to worry. Gabe was a strong, capable young man, and she felt perfectly safe here in the inky darkness at the edge of the Eichers' mowed fields. Emma liked the soft quiet of night. Nothing could surround you with barely a whisper against your skin the way that darkness did. Her sister Elsie couldn't understand why Emma wasn't afraid of the dark.

"But don't you know that Gott created the dark, too?" Emma told her. "I think He wanted to remind us how wondrous warm and bright the day is, and He does that. Every night and every day."

Elsie had liked Emma's answer so much that she had taken to asking the question over and over again, and the story of Gott creating night and day had become a family tale that brought them both comfort.

Emma rubbed her arms briskly as she imagined Elsie at home, snug as a bug under her quilt in bed. The thought of Elsie with her pink lips and button nose, cozy under the covers, warmed her. And as she hugged herself, there came the gentle clip-clop of a horse's hooves on the pavement.

Gabe? Oh, she hoped so. She held her spot on the shoulder of the road and waited.

"Emma? Emma, where are you?"

"I'm here!" She stepped out, her heart lifting at the approaching sound.

Gabe called to his horse, halting the buggy. "I heard a voice, but I don't see the pretty schoolteacher who likes to hide out in cornfields."

Emma laughed as she stepped onto the paved road. "You make it sound like a game I play." She stopped to pat Mercury before she moved to the buggy.

"I figured one of us must like it, because I sure don't." Gabe sat still and tall as she climbed in beside him. A tower of will, he was. She squinted through the darkness, hoping to see the handsome planes of his face and the little smile that he reserved just for her. No one would ever call Gabe happy-go-lucky, but when he was with Emma she always found a way to crack that aloof shell and get a peek at the emotions that glimmered inside.

"What do you mean?" she teased. "I think it's exciting to have a secret that no one else knows about."

"I think you're exciting." He slid a hand around her waist and pulled her close. The warmth of his body was welcome in the cool night, and the smell of wood smoke and soap filled her senses. "The secret? I could do without that."

When she looked up at him he moved closer and pressed his lips to hers. She closed her eyes, enjoying the sensation of warm sparks flying in the night. His kiss took her breath away. It always did.

These moments with him were rare, but she cherished being close to him.

When the kiss ended, she took a deep breath and opened her eyes to drink in the sight of him. Such a handsome boy! Gott had truly blessed her to find him.

"We'd best get off the main road before a car comes along and blinds poor Mercury with its lights." Despite his words, he was holding tight to her, and she didn't want him to let go.

She ran her hand over his shoulder and held tight to the muscles of his arm. "Denki for waiting. I thought maybe you gave up on me and rode off in the other direction."

"Mmm." He grunted, turning away. "I would never do that. But I saw you talking with David and Ruben."

"We were talking, that's all." She watched as he unwrapped the reins and urged Mercury forward. Was he jealous? "You know I only have eyes for you."

"But you won't let anyone else know about it," he said. "When will you leave a singing with me, Emma? I'm tired of leaving in an empty buggy and meeting you down the road."

"Gabe . . . we've talked about this before."

"And we need to talk again. I started going to singings just to see you, but you spend most of the night talking with other fellas. It's not right, Emma."

"But I can't be rude to them."

"They wouldn't be coming up to you if they knew about us. That's the unspoken rule: You leave a fella's girl alone. But since this is all a *secret*—you and me—half the young men in Halfway think they have a chance with you."

"But they don't." She looked over at him. In the darkness she was barely able to see the bold features that she always studied by the light of lanterns at each singing or youth event. "And you know how careful I have to be."

She had explained her position a dozen times.

"It's so very important for me to set a good example for my schol- ars," she said. "An Amish teacher must teach with her whole life, and I have to take care to stay on the right path." A proper teacher had to be well-grounded in her faith and in her community.

"Oh, you're a straight arrow," Gabe said. "No one could argue with that. You're about as straight as they come."

She folded her arms. "And how did I end up with a crooked arrow like you?"

"I'm not so crooked," he said. "Just a touch wild."

"That's for sure," Emma teased, though in truth she thought Gabe was probably just an average teenaged boy. Wild, but most people didn't know what he was up to because they were looking the other way during rumspringa.

But she had known Gabe a long time, and he'd always had a wild streak. Stubborn, too. Once, when they were very little, Emma had cried when they were playing market and Gabe refused to sell her his corn because his cows needed it.

Then there was that raft he and his cousin Ben built to fish down the river. That became quite an adventure when the raft started to fall apart and slipped under the covered bridge.

A few summers ago when Emma had been visiting Sadie on a hot summer day, all the King boys stripped down to their underwear before her eyes and jumped into the pond. Gabe's mamm had corralled the girls into the side porch for cookies and lemonade—but mostly to get them out of sight of the boys. The girls had giggled and whispered, but the boys—they hadn't even cared!

After school Gabe had always tried to organize baseball games in the spring or hockey games in the winter. He played hard, but he worked hard, too. Sadie said that no one knew their milk cows quite as well as Gabe.

That wildness made her heart catch.

She didn't want to admit it, but it was a part of Gabe that made her pulse race. If only he could strike a balance between wild excitement and obedient Amish—then he'd be the perfect beau.

He called out to Mercury to head down the lane, then turned to catch her staring up at him. "What's on your mind, Miss Straight Arrow?"

"I'm just wondering how a straight arrow like me and a wild one like you ever got together."

"Mmm. But we are together. And I say if we're courting, we should be able to spend some time together." Gabe steered the buggy onto the side of the road by her house. "You're a schoolteacher, Emma. Not an angel."

"I'd like to be both," she said defiantly.

He reached for her, his hands circling her waist as he pulled her close. "A tiny waist. A back with a spine and muscles and shoulders under a dark sweater."

She smiled as he recited her features, as if taking inventory.

"No, Emma, you're no angel. Just a flesh-and-blood girl."

"You're right about that." Her blood was warmed by the closeness of him. She held her breath as he moved close to kiss her. Such a wondrous thing, Gabe's kiss! Like a starburst on her lips.

She ended the kiss and pressed her cheek to his chest, the broadcloth of his jacket, his Sunday clothes, so familiar now. They'd been courting for so long now. Like Gabe, she longed to share the news that they were a couple with all their friends and families.

Whenever they were close like this, she wondered why she worried so much about what others would think about their courtship. They were a wonderful good match.

But when they were apart, the truth bothered her like a hangnail. Gabe's family had been through so much, and now with his older brother marrying an Englisher and his sister off on rumspringa . . .

Oh, why did she have to fall for a boy from a family that was causing the ministers so much worry?

She didn't like to think about it; she had been friends with Sadie, and it was not her place to judge another. But she knew Bishop Samuel was talking about taking measures against Sadie for leaving the community a second time to live among the Englishers.

And then there was Adam King about to marry the Englisher girl. Adam and Remy had gotten approval from the church leaders. From what Emma had heard, if Remy was truly committed to becoming a baptized member and living the Amish life, the church would let Adam marry her.

Church approval was a very good thing. But the situation was unusual. Most Seekers, English who wanted to try living Amish, didn't last more than a few weeks, and very few took the time to learn the language and the laws of the community.

Remy McCallister was a special girl. But the fact that an Englisher was marrying into the King family was an odd thing that would make them stand out for generations to come.

A three-horned sheep.

As much as people pretended that the three-horned sheep was no different, when you looked out to the pasture, there it was with three horns. And as Emma often told her young students, three did not equal two.

PART TWO

When Your Heart Aches

A man's heart deviseth his way:
But the Lord directeth his steps.
—Proverbs 16:9

ELEVEN

I'll take mine sunny-side up, just like the day," Dat said the next morning when Annie asked him how he wanted his eggs.

"It's good to see the sunshine," Lovina said. She handed a piece of biscuit to little Mark, who sat content in the high chair. "Will you be able to make hay today?"

Dat nodded. "We need to do as much as we can this week, before Perry has to go."

Annie tousled one of the golden ringlets of Mark's hair. She had missed tucking him in last night because of the singing. Normally it wouldn't matter, but now Mark's nights in the house were running out. There were but a handful of days until the departure on Friday.

She leaned forward and pressed her cheek to his. "I'm going to miss you, little one."

She was rewarded by an applesauce hand on her nose. "Hey, that's my nose!"

The little boy grinned as she swung around to face him.

"Where's your nose?" she asked, and he pressed a finger to his button nose.

"You're delicious." She planted a kiss on his forehead, then turned away toward the stove, feeling weepy. She still could not believe that the Fishers would be leaving on Friday. She cracked two eggs on the edge of the skillet and tended the sizzling edges.

The morning air was chilly, but the sun was strong, and Annie seized the chance to get some clothes washed and hung. The family's collie trotted over and stared suspiciously when she saw Annie fussing with the machine. The gas-powered washer made a clamor that frightened the dog.

"I know it's not wash day," Annie told the dog, "but with all the rain we've been having, we're falling behind."

Seeing that Annie meant business, Sunny nosed the screen door open and scuttled away.

The clatter of the washing machine on the porch matched the noise of the men hammering on the roof. Dat said they were almost finished with the repairs. The beat reminded Annie of a tune they had sung at the singing last night. She sang aloud as she swept the porch, knowing no one would hear her over the din.

The late-morning sun warmed through her prayer kapp as she shook out a dress and hung it with two clothespins. At the end of the line she paused to move her basket and glance up at the sky. Still no clouds. Wonderful good.

Her gaze skimmed the roof of the farmhouse. A tall, handsome man hammering into the roof came into view.

Adam . . .

Her heart sank in regret. When was she going to stop pining for a man who was about to marry someone else?

But her annoyance faded quickly when she realized that she was wrong. It was Jonah King. He and his brother were both tall, with broad shoulders that seemed to test their shirts. And Jonah's dark hair and eyes beneath his straw hat were so like his brother's.

Her sister Sarah's words came back to her. She did need to move on.

Annie uttered a quick prayer to Gott, asking Him to free her heart.

She glanced back at the roof. Of course Adam wouldn't be here. They wouldn't be able to spare him with everyone trying to finish up the harvest.

Just then Jonah King lifted his head and waved to her. She swallowed hard. He'd caught her staring. She nodded primly, turning back to the clothesline.

"How's your lip?" he called down.

Annie pressed her fingers to her mouth. "Much better, denki," she called before ducking behind the wall of a damp sheet. The swelling must have gone down overnight. It didn't hurt at all.

Odd how the body could heal quickly, but the heart took its good old time.

TWELVE

*G*uitar music floated from the boom box behind him as Gabe drove his buggy toward town. He had decided to combine his run into town with a trip to the school to see Emma. Of course, everyone thought he was stopping by the school to drop his brother and sister off. No one knew he had been out late last night, driving down dark roads with Emma beside him.

He knew there would be students there this morning. No chance to kiss or pull her into his arms. But it would be enough, just looking in her eyes for a bit. That smart, steady flicker in her eyes always made him feel good. He could see the love in Emma's eyes, and on a cold September morning, there was nothing quite like that.

The hum of an engine over the music let him know that a vehicle was creeping up behind him.

Gabe slowed the buggy and directed Mercury to the far right of the road to let the vehicle behind him pass.

The yellow bus's engine grumbled as it slowly moved around their open carriage, taking Englisher children to their school.

"I wonder what it's like to ride a bus to school every day," Ruthie said.

"I want to drive a school bus," Simon said. "No one on the road would be bigger than me. And if a bad person came along, I could close the door and drive away."

Gabe kept quiet. Simon had a fear of evil bred from the trauma of witnessing their parents' murder, but he'd gotten much better in the last year. Gabe smiled at the notion of Simon driving a yellow bus. The boy would get his chance to drive a vehicle soon enough, and Ruthie . . . well, Ruthie was a girl. She might live her whole life without hearing of a boy's rumspringa antics.

Squinting, Gabe measured the bus with his eyes. He had never driven anything that big, but he had been behind the wheel of a car before. It had been fun to drive a car, but nothing like the thrill of racing over bumps and taking tight turns on a motorbike.

He was itching to get back on a motorbike. Now that he'd had a taste, it was just like Ben had said. He felt the need for speed.

To hit the throttle and have the bike surge ahead, that was power. And the way the brakes responded when you wanted . . . that was control. Two things that Amish life lacked . . . power and control. The pace of life was slow, and someone else was always making decisions for you.

Gabe liked being in command, and the bikes gave him that.

As their buggy approached, he spotted Emma on the front porch of the schoolhouse, sitting beside a student. He hoped she wouldn't be mad at him for stopping by. Emma was always careful about their relationship. She didn't want folks seeing them together, but he figured the students wouldn't think anything of Gabe dropping off his brother and sister.

"We'd better turn off the music," Gabe told his siblings, who were sitting in the cramped backseat area. "Do you know how to do it, Simon?"

"I got it," Simon said, and the music faded.

"Denki. Teacher Emma doesn't like loud buggies pulling up to the school."

"How do you know?" Ruthie asked.

Gabe shrugged. "I just know. Teachers don't like anything that breaks the rules."

"Teachers like rules," Simon agreed.

The schoolhouse was a simple wood structure. Painted a buttery yellow, it had a concrete porch where an old-fashioned school bell hung, its rope dangling in easy reach. Gabe hadn't liked the place much when he was a student here, but now that Emma was the teacher, it seemed warm and cheerful.

He pulled up in front and reined in his horse.

"Good morning, Teacher Emma!" Ruthie called as she climbed out of the buggy with her plastic lunch cooler in one hand.

"Good morning," Emma called from the porch. Her smile froze when she saw Gabe in the buggy.

Was she going to be cross, just because he wanted to see her for a bit? School wouldn't begin for another fifteen minutes.

Simon dropped down beside his sister in silence.

A man of few words, like me, Gabe thought. He shifted in his seat and saw that Emma was still sitting on the porch with a little boy.

He would have to get out and go to her.

He secured the buggy and climbed out.

"You make two rabbit ears." Emma leaned over the little boy's shoes and folded his laces. "Like that."

"Good morning, teacher," Gabe said.

She looked up and tried to hide her smile. "Good morning."

"Can I talk to you for a minute?" He nodded toward the fence. "Just over there."

She hesitated a second, then lifted her head. "All right. Amanda, will you help Luke with his shoelaces?"

An older girl with pink lips who reminded Gabe of a mouse came up to the porch, and Emma followed him across the tidy lawn of the school.

"You shouldn't come here, Gabe," she warned. "During school time, I have to focus on my scholars."

"It's not school time yet." He turned around to face her, relieved to see that steady light in her eyes. Her prayer kapp was crisp and white. Of course, all the kapps around here were the same. But when Gabe looked at Emma, he saw her pure heart in that kapp. A pure heart and a starchy sense of order. Some of the other guys thought she was a priss, but Gabe loved that about her. She truly wanted to do things the right way, and she tried with all her heart.

She folded her hands and pressed her knuckles to her chin. "You shouldn't be here, Gabe."

"And you're beautiful when you get mad."

"I'm not mad, I'm . . . serious. That's how I have to be. The education of those children is my responsibility, and—"

"I know. It's all on your shoulders. But you're still an eighteen-year-old girl who's allowed to court. If you told people about us, we wouldn't have to wait for two weeks to see each other. Or sneak around like this."

"I'm not sneaking around. This is my job."

"You know what I mean." He put one hand up to lean on the fence post. "I want to see you, and I don't care who knows about it. And I know you feel the same way, Teacher Emma. Let me teach you how to go courting, the right way."

"Oh, Gabe . . ." Her stern expression gave way to a small smile. "I'd like that. But I'm not ready to shout it out over the hills yet."

"You don't have to do that, but I would like you to tell your family about me. If our families know, it won't be such a big secret anymore."

"It would be a good way to break the ice. . . ." She crossed her arms, considering.

Gabe smiled. He could watch her think for hours.

He had thought of the idea last night on the ride home. If Emma's parents accepted him, he figured the rest of the community wouldn't be too far behind.

"Let me think about it," she said.

Before he could answer, a swell of noise came from the lane in front of the school. "Thank God I'm a country boy!" came the friendly voice of the singer from the boom box. Gabe swung around to see Simon hunched in the back of his buggy.

"Oh, no!" Emma turned quickly, then took off running toward the sound.

Gabe raced ahead of her, his long legs covering the distance quickly. "Simon! Turn it off."

Simon ducked down, and within seconds the blare of music stopped.

"What are you doing?" Gabe jogged to a stop beside the buggy, where Mercury twisted his head back and nudged him, as if he was impatient to get going.

"I didn't turn it on!" Simon insisted. "I didn't do it. I just climbed up here to turn it off after . . ."

"After some other boy left it on." Emma turned toward the cluster of boys who were Simon's age. "Who did this?"

No one raised a hand.

"All right, then. Let me just say that it was not the right thing to do." She crossed her arms and paced in front of the group of boys before turning to them. "We don't use electronic things here at school." She turned to Gabe with a scorching look. "Good Amish do not have electricity or Englisher music in our homes . . . or at school."

Gabe winced as he tipped back his hat. Ouch. This wasn't going to help him persuade Emma that she should let people know they were courting. Emma had been disappointed that he had decided not to get baptized with her this month. He understood her disappointment, but he'd made his choice for a reason. He wasn't ready. It was as simple as that.

Months ago the bishop had ordered the young people who were getting baptized to get rid of their cell phones and stereos and iPods. Remy had traveled back to Philadelphia to give away her Englisher things. "They make you give up the fun," Ben had told him. Gabe agreed on that. He knew the rules, and he wasn't ready to buckle down and follow them just yet.

"Let's go into the classroom and get our primers out," Emma said.

Although her voice was calm, her words held power. The children picked up their lunch coolers and headed in the front door.

Simon paused in front of Emma, his brows hard lines of worry. "Sorry, Emma."

"It's not your concern." She stood, arms folded into her bulky sweater, watching as another carriage came down the lane, before looking up at Gabe. "But I'll thank you to take that noisemaker far away from my students."

"Yes, teacher." He followed her gaze to the approaching carriage and recognized Preacher Dave with his youngest children.

Emma waited on the porch to greet Dave and the children.

"Good morning," Dave said. He stood by the carriage as, one by one, each child hopped out and accepted a cooler.

"Come." Emma smiled as the children filed past her on the porch.

"Think the rain will hold?" Dave asked.

"I'd like enough dry weather to make hay," Gabe said.

Dave touched his beard as his pale eyes rose to the sky. The sun was shining, but the west held murky clouds, like a skim floating on soup. "The way those clouds are moving, I don't think you'll be doing that today."

Gabe shrugged. "I'll go with the weather." He looked toward Emma, but she was already crossing the porch, on her way into the schoolhouse.

Storms ahead, Gabe thought. But he could wait out the rain. The sunshine on the other side of the clouds was always worth the wait.

THIRTEEN

With two lambs born that morning and Perry and Sarah about to leave, the Stoltzfus farm was a very busy place. Annie was helping her sister pack that afternoon when Levi announced that a carriage was coming.

"Visitors!" Sarah said cheerfully, swinging her son's hand.

When Annie hurried out, she wasn't surprised to see her good friend Mary King. Mary had told her she would stop by to say good-bye to Sarah.

"*Kumm,*" Mary called as she climbed out of the carriage.

Annie hurried over to help her carry the heavy basket. "You brought strawberry jam?"

"For Sarah and Perry. Pickled beets and apple butter, too. A little bit of home to take along with them."

"That's so kind of you," Sarah called from the open kitchen door. She accepted the hamper with one arm and hugged Mary with the other.

They unloaded the colorful jars onto the table, and Levi made a show of counting and re-sorting them. Mary had also brought a sampler with the words HOME IS WHERE THE HEART IS.

"It will be wonderful for your new home," Annie told her sister as she filled the kettle for tea.

"All the girls in our house pitched in, except for Katie," Mary said.

"There's so much love in the needlework." Sarah ran her fingertips over the smooth yarns. "Denki, Mary."

"I wanted you to remember that your home is wherever you and Perry and little Mark are," Mary said. "Gott will follow you to New York."

"I know that." Sarah bit her lower lip. "I know this is the right thing, but it's a bit scary to be moving so far from my family."

Levi looked up from the table and crossed his arms. "I don't want you to go."

Sarah patted his shoulder. "I know, dear, but we have an exciting trip ahead of us, going to a new place. We want to build a wonderful good house there."

"With horses and chickens?" Levi asked.

Sarah's blue eyes sparkled with tears as she nodded.

"Okay, then."

Annie had to look away as emotion welled up inside her. She was sick about her sister's departure, but everyone knew an Amish wife had to follow her husband's decision. Besides, Perry had listened to Sarah's opinions, too. It had been wonderful having them here in the house, but Annie understood the young couple's desire not to live under her parents' roof forever.

When Sarah left the kitchen to put Mark down for his nap, Levi followed along. He was a bit old for a nap, but sometimes he would doze off while telling his little cousin a story.

"Poor Levi is going to be lost without his cousin." Annie put her mug into the sink. "He's like a little shepherd watching over Mark."

"I reckon it will be hard for everyone," Mary said, her hazel eyes shining with sympathy. "But I'm glad we have a moment, just the two of us. I wanted to talk to you about my brother."

"Adam?" Annie felt her cheeks grow warm.

"No . . . Jonah. That burst of temper you unleashed on him last night was frightful." Mary folded her hands on the table. "I'm saying this because I'm your friend, Annie. I know you meant no harm, but it was cruel to put the blame on Jonah."

"But he knocked me down," Annie defended herself.

"It was an accident. And what happened to forgiveness, Annie? You're not usually one to hold a grudge. 'Forgive us our trespasses.' "

A breeze pressed in from outside, stirring the curtains at the window and cooling the kernel of annoyance that had been burning inside of Annie. How right of Mary to remind her of the Lord's Prayer. She'd made such a fuss about having a swollen lip. And now, this morning, it was as if it had never happened.

"I was being silly, holding that against Jonah," she admitted. To hold anger against anyone was wrong, she knew that.

"You won't find a kinder, gentler man than him."

Annie nodded absently, not wanting to admit that she'd been edgy with Jonah because he was Adam's brother.

That was wrong, too.

"I'll be sure to set things straight with Jonah," Annie promised as she went to the window. Was he still working on the roof? She hoped he hadn't left for the day yet.

"I know you meant no harm." Mary nodded. "And did you have a chance to ask your mamm about the tea shop?"

"I did." Annie had talked to Lovina that morning before she and Rebecca left for the shop. "Mamm said she'd love to hire Leah and Susie. If it works out, it will be a wonderful good apprenticeship for them, don't you think?"

Mary's face brightened. "It's a good way to learn about business, and Lovina will be a good teacher. Strict but kind."

"Mamm is happy to take them under her wing. You know how she likes to mother young people."

"Denki," Mary said. "I think the twins could use some mothering right now. There's a bit of worry about me leaving after Five and I get married."

"Are they worried?" Annie pouted. "Poor dears. I wish I could sweep them all into my arms and hug them till their eyes pop." The desire to help Mary's younger siblings tugged at her. She'd been struck by that feeling a lot in the past few months . . . wanting to help Hannah, wanting to hold people's babies. Now more than ever she enjoyed her time with Mark and Levi. She had been coaxing Rebecca to have another little one, telling her that sometimes her arms felt so empty without a baby.

Mary laughed. "Next time Sam and Katie are misbehaving, I'll bring them right over for one of those hugs."

They laughed together, but Annie stopped short of telling Mary about the deep desire that was beginning to worry her. So far she had told no one, not even her sisters, and she thought it might be best to keep it that way.

Sarah returned, and she talked with Mary about how the Byler Amish were different from their district. Annie tried to listen, but her mind wandered off to Jonah King. He was a kind person. It had been unfair of her to blame him for her feelings about Adam. How could she make up for being mean to him?

Working the pin on her apron, she stared outside, following the dance of leaves as the wind swirled them in a circle. Someone stood up from weeding in the garden.

Hannah.

Dear, sweet Hannah. Annie twirled the straight pin under her fingertips as an idea popped into her head.

As soon as Mary left, Annie went outside to find Jonah. Moving away from the house, she shielded her eyes from the sun and gazed up. There he was, still working on the roof.

"Jonah! I've gotten so used to seeing you up there, like a bird perched in a tree," she called up to him, trying to sound friendly.

He lifted his head and tipped back his hat. "A very large bird."

She smiled. She hadn't realized he had a sense of humor. "I thought you might be gone. It's been a while since I heard hammering."

"I'm just finishing the flashing. Your roof is almost done."

"Oh." She had wanted him to be around for her plan. She smoothed her apron as he came down the ladder. "That's good. With Perry leaving, Dat would have never been able to make hay and get the roof fixed during this busy harvest."

He was on the ground now, standing taller than she'd remembered—a bit taller than Adam.

"Your lip looks much better," he said.

"Ya." She pressed her fingers to her mouth. "All better. I'm sorry I snapped at you when it happened. I was wrong to be cross with you."

"It's all water under the bridge." His eyes looked like Adam's—a deep brown, like Mamm's chocolate fudge. "So when is the day? When are they leaving?"

"Friday. They've got a driver and a big van booked. I can't imagine what it will be like around here without Sarah and Perry and little Mark. Our dinner table will seem empty."

"I know Levi will miss his cousin; I've seen those two playing in the barn. Levi chases little Mark like a mother hen."

"They are good together," Annie said, turning to glance over at the clothes flapping in the breeze. She could see Hannah's shoes and the bottom of her dress beneath a row of clothes. Perfect.

"Levi reminds me of my brother Sam. They're around the same age. And he takes care of his little sister that way."

"I keep telling Rebecca that Levi needs a little brother or sister to take care of," she said.

"You're right. A child learns a lot from taking care of his brothers and sisters."

She started backing away. "Do you think the roof will hold up through the winter?" she asked, trying to lure him toward the clothesline.

"It should." He pushed his hat back. "Where are you going?"

"Just over to help my sister take in the clothes," she said, "but I have some more questions about that roof. Why don't you come over and talk?"

He squinted at her, but nodded.

Annie grinned as she turned toward the clothesline. He'd gone for the bait!

She asked him a few more silly questions about how he'd repaired the roof, and Jonah answered them patiently as she began to take down shirts and dresses.

Hannah peeked around a bedsheet, her blue eyes round with curiosity. Annie flashed a look that said: *Kumm, now!* But Hannah didn't seem to catch it.

My younger sister is going to need some lessons tonight when the lights are out, Annie thought as she dropped a folded dress into the laundry basket. *She should be right here beside me, chatting merrily.*

"Now, look at this over here." Annie led Jonah over to a quilt hanging on its own. "Isn't that nice? It was hand-stitched by my sisters and me."

"Beautiful. A Sunshine and Shadow quilt, isn't it?"

"You know your quilts."

"My sisters have taught me well. There's always quilting going on at our house, but then you know that. You've been to our quilting bees."

"I have." Annie ran her hand over the fold in the quilt. "Just about dry. You know my sister Hannah, don't you?"

The sheet dropped from the line into Hannah's arms, and Annie hurried over to take two corners.

"Hannah is handy with a needle and thread," Annie said. "And she's not so bad in the kitchen either."

Jonah nodded. "I know that you make a delicious pie, Annie. What's your favorite thing to make, Hannah?"

And just like that, the two of them were talking. Annie folded a shirt and watched with satisfaction as her sister answered politely that she liked to make stews. "Everything in one pot," Hannah said.

"Mmm. You're making me hungry," Jonah said, and they all shared a laugh.

Ya, this was a good match she was making. Who'd have thought it would be so easy?

When Jonah carried the laundry basket back to the house for them, Annie could barely contain the big, bright smile that started from inside her.

Once she and Hannah got into the house, she nudged her sister. "So, what do you think?"

"I think you're verhuddelt." Hannah rubbed her arm. "Why do you keep poking me?"

"Didn't you notice how Jonah King just came alive out there? It's because he's sweet on you. I can tell," Annie insisted.

Hannah's jaw dropped in surprise. "Do you really think so?"

"I know it. He carried the laundry basket. That's the action of a fella who likes a girl."

Hannah blinked in astonishment. "He's a nice enough fella, but a little old for me, don't you think?"

Annie waved off Hannah's concerns. "Wise and handsome, I'd say."

And probably ready to marry.

Annie bit her lower lip at the prospect of her sister marrying before her. That would be hard to watch, especially with the tug of motherhood she'd been feeling lately. How she craved the feel and smell of a little baby in her arms!

But really . . . it was foolish to think of such things when neither she nor Hannah had a beau yet. And she couldn't begrudge Hannah her happiness. Jonah King was a fine suitor . . . even if he did look a lot like his brother Adam.

Annie would get past that, for Hannah's sake.

There was no stopping her now.

FOURTEEN

*T*he flock of birds that crossed the sky, heading south for warmer weather, reminded Jonah of his dat. He whistled his father's favorite song, "His Eye Is on the Sparrow," as he walked the path to the Stoltzfus barn. Dat had loved wildlife—birds and insects and frogs and even the deer who chewed plants in the garden down to bare nubs.

"His eye is on the sparrow," Jonah hummed in his gravelly voice, "and I know He watches me."

Ya, Gott had shown His divine hand today. What a difference He had made in a single day!

In the days and weeks he'd worked on the roof, Jonah hadn't gotten any closer to Annie until this afternoon, when out of the blue she had talked to him as if he were a good friend. Was it because of the accident at the singing? He tipped his hat back and scratched under the brim. It was hard to say.

And now, with the roof repaired, this would be his last day here. It seemed like a cruel trick when he first realized that. But he had seen

Aaron and his sons-in-law struggling to cover all the chores on this farm. They could use some spare hands, and he was ready to volunteer.

Outside the barn he found Aaron leaning on a stall, looking into an empty pen with two walls.

"Are you feeling all right?" Jonah asked. "I don't think I've ever seen you standing still before."

Aaron chuckled, his face pale against his ruddy beard. "I'm checking over the new birthing pen; got a pregnant Dexter cow due to go into labor soon."

Jonah put his hand on the rail and nodded. "This is nice." He pointed to the wooden walls. "You've got your walls on the west and north side to protect against the wind. Open to the sunlight on the south side. I think your mother cow will be happy to make a visit here."

"Denki. But you don't know Buttercup. Last year when it was her time she broke through the fence and gave birth on the riverbank."

Jonah laughed. "For creatures with big brains, they're not the brightest," Jonah said.

"Ya. It was okay until the calf walked right into the river. I wasn't too happy hauling her out. The water was cold." Aaron went to a stack of hay bales and shifted one from the top. Jonah helped him load it into a wheelbarrow.

"So." Aaron looked up at him. "How's my roof?"

"All done." Jonah scratched his chin. "I did the flashing and put the gutters back on today."

"Very good. Thank you for your help." Aaron grimaced and leaned against the fence. "With the harvest going on, we could never have fixed the roof in time for the rain and snow."

Jonah nodded. "Adam and I were happy to do it. We've got more helping hands at our place, so I could be spared. But you're losing a good worker here when Perry leaves this week."

"Ach." Aaron lifted one hand in a gesture of dismay. "Perry does the work of three men."

"So do you," Jonah said. "But you'll need help, at least for a while. I'm happy to keep coming over, maybe just in the afternoon. There are still the chores at our farm to take care of."

Aaron's blue eyes, so like his daughter's, scrutinized Jonah. "I would have to pay you. The roof, I know you said you wouldn't take any money. But if it's regular work, you must accept pay."

"That's not why I'm offering. . . ." Jonah paused. What was he going to tell the man—that he was really hoping to work at the farm to court his daughter?

"If you want to work here, you'll be paid." Aaron pushed the wheelbarrow toward the pen for the sheep, calling over his shoulder, "You know I don't hire just anyone. I'm picky."

"That's what I heard." Jonah followed along. "I'm flattered."

"*Gut.* Now you can help me clean out the sheep pen."

Round the other side of the barn, the sheep were pressing against the gate of their pen, anxious for feed. The muscles in his shoulders tightened when he saw Annie there, sitting on a hay bale with Levi and a baby lamb, which the boy was trying to feed from a bottle. Mark hung on Annie's knees, watching intently.

"Now hold your head still," Levi spoke to the creature gently, cupping its muzzle so that he could get the nipple in.

"That's it," Annie said. "I think he's getting the hang of it."

"What've you got there, Levi?" Jonah asked. "Is that an orphan?"

"How did you know?" the little boy asked.

"You're giving him a bottle." Jonah cupped the curls at Mark's neck gently, thinking of his brother Simon's shiny hair. It wasn't so long ago that Simon was toddling around the barn, learning about all the animals like this. And now Simon was nine, turning ten soon, and he was their horse expert. "What happened to his mamm?"

"He's not a true orphan," Annie explained. "His mamm rejected him, probably because she had triplets. Too many to keep track of. So we had to take him out of the lambing jug. Isn't that sad?" Her eyes sparkled with rue. That look—it could tear a man's heart out.

"It happens," he said. He'd seen a mother sheep try to hurt her young when she turned them away. It didn't happen often, but you needed to take special care when you had a bummer, a lamb who tried to bum milk from other ewes because it couldn't get enough from its mother.

"How come you've got some ewes lambing in the fall?" Jonah asked. In Lancaster County, the usual lambing season was spring. You could plan your schedule around it.

"We had a hole in the fence, and some of the bucks got through." Annie shook her head. "By the time anyone noticed, we had a couple of pregnant ewes."

Jonah nodded. Every farmer understood the importance of keeping fences in good shape.

"I'm going to take good care of him." Levi turned to Annie. "Do you think he can sleep in my bed with me?"

Annie grinned. "I don't think your mamm and dat are going to allow that, but you can ask."

Jonah found a shovel and began to clear out the sheep pen. "Have you got a name for the bummer yet?"

"Do we get to name it?" Levi asked Annie.

"If your doddi says it's okay."

"That depends on the name," Aaron called from around the side of the shed.

"Then I will think of a very good name," Levi said.

Jonah shoveled manure into the bin. "Why don't you name it Peanut Butter?" he teased. "Patty Maker?"

"Nay." Levi grinned.

"How about Moon Egg?" Jonah prodded. "Or Picky Picky."

"Those are not names for a lamb!" Levi insisted. He giggled, and Annie joined him.

"I kind of like Moon Egg," she said. Then she laughed again.

The sound of her joy was music in Jonah's ears.

That night at the dinner table, the teasing came full circle when Jonah's sisters noticed his happy mood.

"You've been smiling ever since you got home from helping the Stoltzfuses," Ruthie said as she passed the string beans down the table. "Did someone tell you a funny joke?"

"I . . . I think I was the one who told the jokes," Jonah said, thinking of how he had made Annie and Levi laugh.

"You? The Quiet One?" Susie blinked in disbelief. "What was the joke?"

"Nay." Jonah tore a biscuit in half. "It's not so funny if you weren't there."

"Well, it's good to see you smiling." Mary grabbed Katie's cup of milk as it wobbled on the table. "I was beginning to think your face was stuck in a serious frown."

"I'm not serious. Quiet, ya. But inside I'm very funny."

The girls giggled.

"If that's so, you're keeping the jokes to yourself," Leah said.

Jonah let his eyes skim over their smiling faces as he cut his chicken. Even Simon was trying to hide a grin. "Are you ganging up on me? I think you are."

"I'm on your side, Jonah," Ruthie insisted.

"We all are," Mary said, "as long as you keep smiling."

He stabbed some beets with a fork. "And I finished the roof today. Another reason to smile."

"That's good, because we need you tomorrow," Adam said. "The hay baler isn't working right, and you're the mechanic around here."

"I'll take a look at it in the morning." Would it take long to fix? Jonah wanted to get over to the Stoltzfus farm tomorrow. "I saw that you made good progress on cutting today."

"Ya," Adam said, his eyes on his food. "Another week or two and we'll be putting up the harvester till next year."

"Then things will slow down for a while." Jonah ran his thumb over the drops on his water cup. "Even with the roof done, Aaron is going to need some help to keep his farm running. Perry is leaving this week, and Daniel's taking on more and more of the harness shop in town. I'd like to do some work for them, if you can spare me here."

Both Adam and Gabe looked up at him at the same time.

"I would keep working here, too. At least half a day."

"We'll need that," Adam said, "at least until everything is cut and stored."

"But this is our busiest time of year," Gabe said. "And I had plans for a job, too." He turned to Adam. "I was going to talk to you about it after the harvest. I want to try something outside the farm."

"Why would you do that?" Adam asked. "You're so good with the cows. It's a gift you've got, Gabe. A blessing."

Gabe frowned. "I'm in rumspringa, and I don't want to be here all the time. And it would be good to make some money of my own, the way Sadie did."

Now Jonah and Adam exchanged a look of concern. Was Gabe pulling away, feeling *Unzufriede,* a sense of discontent with Amish life?

"Are you looking to get a cell phone and a souped-up buggy?" Adam asked.

Gabe shrugged. "I already have that boom box, but I wouldn't mind a few more discs for it. But it's not about buying things. I just want to try something off the farm for a while."

Adam rubbed his chin, a gesture Jonah recognized. He did that when he was worried. "In another few weeks, when the harvest is in, we'll talk about you getting a job. What Jonah's doing is different. Aaron Stoltzfus needs our help."

Gabe nodded, but Jonah could see the disappointment in his frown.

"But we can still go to our jobs at the tea shop, right?" Susie had been bubbling with excitement since she'd heard that Lovina would be willing to train Leah and her.

"Part-time jobs," Adam said. "But you'll have to keep up with your chores here."

"We will. I'll sweep up every morning and make all the beds." Her eyes darted over to her twin sister. "As long as I can get Leah out of hers."

"I'm not a lazybones," Leah said.

"But every chance you get, you curl up with a book."

"Because I like to read." Leah's eyes were prim behind her glasses. "There's nothing wrong with that."

"Oh, snooze." Susie patted her open mouth, faking a yawn.

"Girls." Mary gave them a stern look. "I hope you won't be bickering at the tea shop. Lovina has enough to do. She shouldn't have to put up with the likes of this."

"We'll behave," Leah said.

"And I was just kidding." Susie turned to her twin. "You know I love you, sister dear. It would be a little scary to take on a job alone. But I don't have to worry, knowing you'll be beside me."

"Ya. I'll be there to mop up your spilled tea," Leah said.

Everyone laughed, including Susie.

Jonah found himself grinning as he reached for his water. This was the way Mamm and Dat had wanted their home to be. Peace in the family. Peace, and plenty of love.

FIFTEEN

*Y*ou've been awful quiet tonight, Emma." Elsie stood on a step stool at the sink, scrubbing and rinsing the dinner dishes. "Cat got your tongue?"

"I've got a lot on my mind." Emma tossed the towel over her shoulder as she reached up to store plates in the cabinet.

Elsie turned from the sink to face her, and Emma recognized her sister's thoughtful expression. Her short upper lip was pulled back to reveal her widely spaced teeth—a feature of dwarfism that had always bothered Elsie, though Emma was always reminded of little white pebbles worn smooth from a stream.

"A burden is always lighter when it's shared by two," Elsie said.

"I know that. But let's talk about your day first."

This was their usual evening routine: Elsie washed and Emma dried. Their stepmother, Fanny, got the rest of the brood bathed and up to bed, while Dat drove back into town to help brother Caleb close up the Country Store, the small shop the family owned. Emma liked the patterns of her life. She enjoyed morning coffee with Fanny and Dat before anyone else got up. She looked forward to seeing her students' smiling faces each day. And there was something to be savored in the quiet classroom at the end of the day.

But there was truly something special about this time of day, when she and her sister had a chance to talk. Sixteen-year-old Elsie was a good storyteller as well as a good listener. A wonderful sister, and a best friend, too.

"Rachel King stopped by the store today." Elsie ran the sponge over a plate. "She said she's got four paintings finished, and three more in the works."

"She's been busy." Gabe's cousin was a gifted artist. One day when church was held at her parents' dairy farm she had taken the girls to a storage shed that she'd been using to paint. She had covered canvases with beautiful golden hills, red barns, and patchwork quilts flapping in the breeze. The artwork showed Amish life, though Rachel had been careful not to include any Amish folk. That would be against the Ordnung, as the Bible cautioned against making a graven image.

"I told her I would ask Dat about it. I know he doesn't want to sell Amish things, but when he sees the paintings, I think he'll change his mind."

"Mmm." Emma hoped her sister was right. Their shop, the Country Store, had once sold novelty items, but Dat had taken all the crafts out of the store when the bishop told him he couldn't sell some plaques carved by an Amish artist. Bishop Samuel had said that they violated the Ordnung because they showed Amish children.

"Rachel's paintings really touch the heart," Emma said. "I'm sure they'd sell quickly. But I think you might be stepping into a marsh of trouble here."

"The bishop?"

Emma nodded. "Do you think he'll allow it?"

Elsie shrugged. "We'll cross that bridge when we come to it."

"My brave sister." Emma took a plate from the rinse water and began drying.

"Brave or foolish, I'm not sure which one." She added more hot water to the sink, a lacy swirl of steam rising before her face. "Tell me about the singing last night. Who was there?"

"It was a good turnout." Elsie didn't care to attend the youth events, but she always enjoyed hearing details of the night from her sister. Emma gave her an overview, including the story of Annie Stoltzfus colliding with Jonah King on the volleyball court and Mary Fisher breaking off her courtship with Abe King.

"That's too bad about Mary and Abe," she said. "But I don't think they were a very good match. He's going to need a wife who knows farming, and she grew up helping her family run the bakery. I don't think she'd be happy on a farm."

Emma smiled at her sister's gift for observation. "Listen to you, missy matchmaker. You figured that out from just seeing them at church?"

Elsie shrugged. "I have good eyes. When I'm at the shop, I get to watch people all day long. When you watch and listen, you learn their stories, and you know I love a good story."

"I know that." Emma sighed, staring at the bowl she was drying. It was time to tell her sister.

"I have a story of my own to tell you." She went to the wide doorway and looked out to be sure no one was in the living room. Empty. Dat was still in town, and Fanny was upstairs supervising baths. She could hear the water running through pipes to the bath-room.

"So much mystery!" Elsie's mouth dropped open as she watched her sister creep close again. "I'm all ears!"

"The truth is, I've got a fella that I've been seeing. But it's a secret."

"I knew it!" Suds splattered as Elsie clapped her gloved hands together. "I had a feeling, ever since that terrible tragedy with the

Kings. You always reach out to your scholars when they're hurting, but I knew there was more to it when you kept stopping over at the Kings' farm. This just warms my heart! There's a little flame of love in Gabe's eyes when he looks at you, and he looks at you an awful lot!"

"Elsie!" Emma gasped, clutching her sister's arm. "How did you know it's Gabe?"

"I just knew. All the signs have been there, but you never talked about it."

"I can't tell you how many times I almost slipped," Emma admitted. "I've wanted to tell you, especially when my heart feels like it's going to burst. Gabe is a wonderful fella. Funny and strong and smart, too. He knows everything there is to know about cows. You should hear him talk about his herd. They're like his children. It's always Daisy this and Maybelle that. He's worse than me and my scholars."

"Emma, I'm so happy for you." Joy shone in Elsie's eyes. "You know, you sound like a girl in love."

"It feels that way," Emma said. Although she wanted to tell her sister more, some things would have to wait for a later time. It would be hard to describe the warmth that swept through her when Gabe pulled her close and kissed her. And how she felt so loved and safe when Gabe held her in his arms. . . . When she found the words, these were things she would share with Elsie and no one else. She knew Elsie would understand and share her happiness. That was Elsie's way—to experience things through another person's story.

"Is it wonderful good to be in love?" Elsie asked.

"Ya. But it's hard to keep it a secret. I never thought there'd be so many ruts and holes on the road to love."

"Why is it a secret?"

"Because of . . ." Emma opened a cabinet and placed a stack of bowls inside. "I don't want to sound like I'm judging, but I'm worried about the direction his family is going in. If people find out I'm courting someone from a family that's straying from the community, I could get in trouble with the parents and the school board."

"But Gabe didn't do anything wrong," Elsie said. "None of that is his fault."

"I know. He's not like Sadie or Adam. I don't think he'd ever leave here. But Gabe is no angel. He's got a boom box now, and he's talking about getting a job in town to make money for lights and things in the buggy. And he's not at all afraid of Bishop Samuel."

Elsie grinned. "Neither am I. That doesn't mean I don't respect him."

"A healthy fear of authority is a good thing," Emma said.

"Sometimes, but it doesn't have to be that way. You're not afraid of Fanny and Dat, are you?" When Emma shook her head, Elsie nodded. "And I know you respect them."

Emma wrapped the dish towel around one hand. "Gabe isn't getting baptized this month. He says he's enjoying his rumspringa, and he's okay with it for at least another year. How am I going to keep courting a boy who wants to sow his wild oats? I don't think I can do it."

"Don't cut him off." Elsie turned to her with round, serious eyes. "You're a smart girl, Emma. You can find a way to work it out with Gabe. I know you can."

"It would break my heart in two to end our courtship." Emma swallowed back the knot of emotion in her throat. "Gabe and I are really good together. But I have to do the right thing. Church leaders and parents are watching me."

"And you can show them that you won't give up on a person because a few bad things have happened with his family."

Emma pressed her fists to her chest. "Is that how you see it?"

Elsie nodded, her eyes stern. "Show your students that you support and love people for who they are inside. The color of their hair, their size, their family business—those things don't really matter. You know that Gabe has a good heart. That's what people will see. The boom box will go away soon enough. But don't walk away from love because you're afraid of the bishop."

Emma let her hands drop to her sides as she took a deep breath. Maybe her sister was right.

She took a cup from the rinse water. "How did you get so wise?"

Lowering the skillet into the sink, Elsie smiled. "I have a very smart big sister."

SIXTEEN

Tuesday morning, Jonah left Gabe and Adam in the milking barn. His brothers didn't need him right now, and he wanted to get a look at that broken baler before the day wore on. He would have to be on top of his chores if he was going over to Annie's, and right now, he couldn't think of anything he wanted more than a few hours of backbreaking work at the Stoltzfus farm.

Outside the barn, he circled the machine, checking the connections. It didn't take long to discover that a clamp had broken off. Jonah rubbed the back of his neck as he mulled over the jagged steel clamp. It needed a good welding.

That was not a problem.

When he was a boy, Jonah had followed their dat around the farm, eager to learn a man's job. While Gabe had taken a liking to the cows in the milk barn and Adam could always be found in the woodshop, Jonah was interested in the mechanics of things. He wanted to know how everything worked, from birthing a calf to tilling the soil to repairing harnesses and equipment.

Dat had rewarded his curiosity with explanations and plenty of hands-on work. By the time he was eleven, Jonah couldn't wait for school to end so that he could spend the entire day working with Dat on the farm.

Jonah smiled, remembering his school days. Gabe had complained bitterly, telling Mamm that school was a waste of time. Jonah had agreed, but he had kept silent. Grin and bear it; that was his way.

Still, it had been torture sitting in class, reading and writing all day when he knew that more important things awaited him outside the window. Math came easy to him, but pencil work seemed silly when there were fields to be tilled, parts to be welded, seed to be scattered, horses' hooves to be picked, and so many animals to feed and tend.

Life on the farm had fed his soul since he was a child. He was ever grateful to Gott for giving him a chance to work the land and live by the seasons. It was a good life . . . but a lonely one for a man his age, a man too old to be living with his family.

He had never imagined that a man in love could be so lonely.

"But that is about to change," he said as he plunked the welding helmet over his face.

He worked methodically, tacking the far corner first, checking to make sure the joint was square, then tacking the other four corners into place. Sparks sizzled like hope.

He would be spending more time at Annie's house.

She had forgiven him for knocking her down in the volleyball game.

But more than that, she seemed to see him with new eyes yesterday.

Now that her eyes were open, he wanted to be there, in plain sight.

After lunch, Jonah hitched Jigsaw to a buggy and rode into Paradise. He needed to pick up some winter feed for the sheep, and the Stoltzfus farm would be an easy stop on his way back.

An hour later, gray clouds were rolling in from the west as he loaded his purchases into the buggy. Another storm brewing, and with these warm temperatures there might be thunder and lightning. He pulled a plastic tarp over his purchases in the back of the buggy, just in case.

Although Jigsaw wasn't usually spooked by thunder, Jonah knew he couldn't outrun a storm. If it blew in, it would be a miserable trip back. God willing, he'd be off the open road for the worst of it.

Once he had traveled beyond the town limits, the landscape opened wide to Gott's Lancaster countryside. Misty blue hills surrounded the fields, most of them cut down to neat rows of golden stubble. Here and there, trees flamed yellow, orange, and red—the changing leaves of autumn. Although he'd farmed this country his whole life, it was a land that could still take his breath away.

The rain held off until he was about to cross the river. He was approaching the covered bridge when two fat drops tapped his hat. A moment later, rain was falling around him, splattering on the road and casting a veil over his vision. At this rate, his jacket would be soaked in two minutes.

He was grateful to duck under the roof of the covered bridge. Although raindrops rattled overhead, it was dry and dark inside.

Built in the early 1800s, the covered bridge was a novelty. Tourists came to Halfway to photograph it and cross over it, as if they were journeying to the Promised Land instead of taking the road to Paradise. Jonah chuckled at the notion. You could say that the road to Paradise was the way to the Promised Land. The towns in Amish country did have unusual names, but he rarely gave it much thought.

When his buggy emerged into the fresh air and slapping rain,

Jonah knew it was only a mile or two to the Stoltzfus farm now—an easy stretch.

He adjusted his hat against the rain as he came to an old Jeep for sale. It sat on a hill, its headlights facing out like two eyes watching the road. Jonah recognized the vehicle he'd learned to drive in—Zed Miller's Jeep. The very same one that had gotten Ira and Rose shunned. Part of their penance was to put the auto up for sale and never climb inside it again. The bishop had even warned them against hiring a car service anytime soon. He had ruled that they needed to be broken of their attachment to worldly things.

Jonah grunted as he passed the Jeep. There were some good old memories in that vehicle. He would never do it now that he was baptized, but he was glad he had learned to drive during his rumspringa.

About a mile ahead he spotted a solitary figure walking down the road—a woman in Amish dress.

He watched her for a minute as Jigsaw trotted ahead. Her short height, her springy gait—these were movements he knew like the back of his own hand.

It was Annie.

He clicked his tongue and Jigsaw picked up the pace, closing the distance between them in no time.

Hearing the sound of hooves on pavement, Annie looked back, shielding her eyes from the rain.

"It's just me." He reined in the horse as he approached her, and Jigsaw slowed the buggy to a gentle stop.

He wondered what she was doing out here alone, but this was no time for small talk with rain coming down like crazy.

"Come," he said.

Her blue eyes flashed with surprise, but she didn't hesitate. She hitched up her skirt and climbed into the buggy beside him.

Face-to-face with him, she smiled. "The seat is wet," she said, "but no more wet than I am already."

Hope welled inside him. To have Annie so close, sitting beside him in his buggy—it was sweet torture. And the chance to take care of Annie, even if it was only a brief ride to get her out of the rain, it was the answer to his prayers.

"Where were you?" he asked when they were rolling ahead.

"Just at my aunt's farm down the road. She's been sick and I made some soup for her."

"You should have used a carriage."

"And how about you? Why the buggy?"

"I thought I'd make it back before the rain," he said.

"Mmm. That, and maybe that Amish men like their buggies."

Jonah grinned. She was never one to mince words. "There's that."

She laughed, the sweet sound underlined by thunder in the distance. "Uh-oh."

He shot a look at the western sky, a fierce shade of gray. Light flashed over the hills as a jagged line of lightning tore the sky. "If the lightning gets close, the last place we want to be is out on an open road." He didn't fancy making Annie get out of the buggy to wait out the storm huddled near a bush.

The storm could sweep in quickly, but Jigsaw was fast, too. "We'd better make a run for it. Ready?"

Annie pressed one hand to the covering on her head. "Let's go!"

Jonah couldn't help but grin as he urged his horse to full speed. Flying in the wind with Annie holding on beside him, he didn't care about the rain that pelted his face.

This was the life he had dreamed of!

As Jigsaw took command of the empty road, Jonah uttered a prayer of thanks that there were no cars to deal with in this dark, wet mess.

All too soon they were making the turn down the farm lane,

bouncing over a rut as they approached the barn. Jonah wasn't sure if the loud beat that thrummed through his body was his heart or the horse's pounding hooves or both, but he felt happy and alive. More alive than he'd been in years.

They reached the barn just as the sky lit up above them and thunder boomed nearby. Jonah halted the horse and dropped to the ground.

"The nick of time!" Annie gasped as she gracefully hopped down from the buggy.

Even soaked with rain, she was beautiful. The blue of her dress, like a summer sky, seemed to make her eyes brighter. It was still raining on his head, but he didn't mind. He could stand here in the mud for years, just watching Annie.

She smiled up at him, and his throat grew thick. What was he going to say now? He felt that familiar worry tighten his shoulders. Did his feelings show?

But she was smiling up at him, her blue eyes dancing as she swiped the rain from her forehead. "That storm came in fast! Denki for the ride."

"It's good that I was there," he said, and right away he wanted to take it back. That sounded like something a father would say.

Why couldn't he ever find the right words when he was face-to-face with Annie? He looked down, and water poured from the brim of his hat. With a sigh, he took it off and smacked it against one hip to get some of the water off.

"Well . . . I'd better get this unhitched."

To his surprise, she helped him, working from the other side of Jigsaw. "Jonah?"

He ran his hand along the horse's back and looked up at her. "Ya, Annie?"

"I'm glad we met on the road. There's something I've been wanting to ask you."

She had his full attention. He opened his eyes wide, trying to ignore the galloping beat of his pulse.

"If someone was sweet on you," she said, talking softly, "you'd want to know, wouldn't you?"

Would I want to know? He reached for a strap near the horse, trying to hide the embarrassment that warmed his face. Was this really happening? Annie was here, saying the words he'd always wanted to hear, and he had his head stuffed under a horse's belly.

He straightened and faced her again, feeling a jolt of awareness that was like a burst of sunlight in the dark.

"I reckon I'd like to know," he said.

But the truth was, it was the one thing he'd been waiting to know all his life—that Annie was sweet on him.

"Well, then I'll tell you." She tilted her head to the side, then put her hand to her mouth to hide a smile. "There's a girl here who's got her eyes on you. But sometimes . . . ach!" Her hand flew back to her mouth, and she shook her head. "It's hard to find the right words!"

"I hate when that happens," he said earnestly.

"And maybe I've said too much already."

"Don't say that." He understood how it felt to be at a loss for words. But right now, despite the thick beating of his heart, he was able to speak. Knowing that Annie cared for him, he found the words.

"It's okay. We'll talk about it later," he said, looking down at her and smiling from the heart.

Even Jigsaw gave a blustery snort of approval as Annie clapped her hands together and sighed. "Oh, Jonah, thank you! My heart is singing with joy."

Mine, too, he thought. And it was a beautiful song.

SEVENTEEN

*H*annah?" Annie called from the mud porch, letting the screen door slam behind her. The news of her talk with Jonah bubbled inside her, and she would have dashed right into the house if her shoes weren't caked in mud. She slipped off her muddy shoes, lined them up by the door, and raced into the kitchen.

Mamm stooped down at the oven, peering at a tray of biscuits. The table was covered with trays of cooling cookies. It was Lovina's baking day for the tea shop.

"Where's Hannah?" asked Annie, slipping off her wet sweater.

"She's upstairs, fetching Mark from his crib." Lovina straightened, hands on her hips. "And look at you, soaking wet. Don't drip on the floor." She took a dish towel from the counter and handed it to Annie.

"Denki. I—I just got caught in the rain on the way home from Beth's." Annie dabbed at her shoulders and legs with the small towel.

"I see that. And how is Beth?"

"She's feeling better. Out of bed." She squeezed moisture from her dress into the towel. "This is still soggy." Without looking at Mamm, she crossed the kitchen. "I'm going upstairs to change."

"Mind you and your sister head back down. I've got three dozen cookies to ice and only two hands."

Upstairs she found Hannah in the nursery, where Mark was toddling around carrying an armful of books while Levi sat on the floor, pretending to read to his cousin.

Hannah's brows shot up when she saw Annie. "You're soaking wet."

"Ya, but I just had the most interesting talk with Jonah King." With a grin, she bent over Levi and put her hands over his ears. "He seems very happy to hear that you're sweet on him."

"You didn't say that!" Hannah covered her mouth with one hand.

Levi shuddered, pushing away Annie's hands. "Your hands are cold," he complained.

"But my heart is warm," she teased, turning back to her sister. "It's wonderful news, isn't it? And now that he's going to be working for Dat, he'll be around nearly every day. You'll have time to get to know each other."

"It makes me a little jittery." Hannah pressed a hand to her chest. "What do I say? I've never done this before."

"That's why I'm here to help you." Annie touched her sister's shoulder reassuringly. "I've got to change, and Mamm wants us downstairs to help with the cookies. But tonight, we'll talk. I've got lots of good ideas."

Hannah smiled. "I'm so grateful that you're helping me, Annie. Maybe I won't be an alt maedel, after all."

"Of course you won't." Annie squatted down so that she was face-to-face with little Mark. "Time to go downstairs. Do you want to help decorate cookies?"

"Cookie, cookie," he babbled.

A pang of longing passed through her as she touched his smooth cheek. Would he remember his aunts after he was gone a year or so? It hurt her to think he'd be growing up without knowing this part of the family, but Gott had other plans for Sarah, Perry, and Mark.

She would have to put her mind on other things, like helping Hannah. That was Annie's gift. She enjoyed doing things for others, bringing soup to her aunt or keeping her little nephews occupied. She would put her mind on the good things that she could do, and trust Gott to heal the parts of her life that she couldn't fix.

That night, when everyone else was asleep, Hannah and Annie sat huddled together on Annie's twin bed by the dim light of a lowered lantern. They had shared this room for a little more than two years, ever since Sarah and Perry married and took the larger room down the hall that used to be Annie's bedroom.

"You know, there are a few little tricks that you can do to bring out your natural beauty." Annie reached over and tucked a stray hair behind her sister's ear. They both wore nightgowns, long braids of hair hanging down their backs. Their prayer kapps hung on a hook on the wall, and Hannah had a quilt over her shoulders.

"Like what?" Hannah asked. "Candy Eicher says you can pinch your cheeks to put roses in them. I tried, but it doesn't last long."

"That doesn't work," Annie said. "But when you wash up in the morning, finish by splashing cold water on your face. It makes your skin nice and shiny."

"Okay." Hannah pulled her braid over one shoulder and tugged it anxiously.

"And your eyes, they're such a beautiful shade of blue."

Hannah grinned, tapping Annie's knee. "Your eyes are the same color."

"I know. And I've seen that our blue dresses are a very good match. They bring out the color of our eyes like nothing else." Annie popped up from the bed and took the lantern to the closet. "Where's your blue dress? You should wear it all the time."

"I think it's down with the dirty laundry."

"Then we'll have to wash it first thing tomorrow. You can borrow mine for a day, if you want."

"Denki, but I don't mind wearing the green. Just for one day." Hannah brought her knees to her chin, the quilt a tent over her. "Is this a sin, Annie? To try to look pretty?"

"Of course not! We're just trying to take care of the gifts Gott gave us. We're not talking about painting you with makeup or anything. But you know, there's a trick you can do with water. If you drink eight glasses a day, those little red bumps on your skin will go away."

"Just from water?" Hannah touched her skin. "I can do that."

They talked until they were both yawning. Annie promised to help her sister take advantage of any chance for Hannah and Jonah to be together. "Maybe you'll just bring him lemonade. Or you can go out and groom one of the horses while he's working in the barn."

"I'll do as you say, Annie," Hannah said as she spread the quilt on her own bed and ducked under the covers.

"Don't worry. I'll help you every step of the way." Annie turned off the lantern, staring at the light as it flickered to darkness. If this matchmaking was the right thing to do, why did she feel so hollow inside?

She pulled the covers up to her chin, thinking that she was just feeling sad about Sarah's family leaving this week. Ya, that had to be it.

The next day, Annie didn't have as much time as she had hoped for Hannah. Mamm and Rebecca were at the tea shop, and Sarah needed help packing for her big move.

"This is a very strange feeling, to be putting my belongings in a tea box," Sarah said as she and Annie pressed down on the linens and quilts to make room for more.

Everything that didn't fit in Sarah's hope chest was going into cartons they had saved from the tea shop. Annie agreed that it seemed odd to see Mark's little black pants and white shirts disappearing in boxes marked "Earl Grey" and "English Breakfast."

As Annie rose to gather more items, she saw Jonah outside near the barn. What was he doing? She paused near the window, and saw that he was rolling a wheelbarrow full of potatoes. Most likely on his way to the storage cellar.

The man had to be working up a thirst. This would be a good time for Hannah to bring him a drink.

"I'll be right back," she said, ducking downstairs to find Hannah minding the little ones. When she explained her idea, Hannah filled a glass with lemonade from a cooler on the counter.

"Are you sure I won't be bothering him?" Hannah asked.

"Of course not."

"And what do I say? If he wants to talk or . . . what if he doesn't have anything to say either? They call him the Quiet One, you know."

"Talk about the weather." She put her hands on Hannah's shoulders and steered her toward the door.

"What about Mark and Levi? I need to watch them."

"Bring them along." Annie motioned the boys toward the door. "Kumm. Hannah's taking you outside for some fresh air."

Levi grabbed his hat from the low hook by the door, and Mark toddled after him.

"See? It's a piece of cake."

"I don't see a piece of cake," Levi said.

Annie smiled. How she longed to run after him and give him a squeeze!

Instead, she hurried back up the stairs. "Sorry! I just had to take care of—" She paused abruptly as she came upon Sarah standing against the dresser, a small object pressed to her chest. Tears ran down her cheeks.

"Sarah! What's wrong?"

"This clock . . ." She extended her hands to Annie, showing her the timepiece with a square marble base. "Perry gave this to me when we were courting. An engagement gift. I was so happy when I got it, Annie. So sure that he was the man Gott intended me to be with. I still believe that, only . . ." Her voice quavered, and she paused to take a breath. "When I got the clock, I never thought it would travel so many miles from our home. I never thought we'd leave Halfway."

A knot formed in Annie's throat, and she tried to think happy thoughts as she handed her sister a handkerchief from a pile that sat ready to be packed.

"Sarah, honey! You're going to make me cry, too." Annie frowned, then took the clock from her sister's hand. "Let me see this. How did Perry come up with the money to buy such a nice gift?"

"He saved for months." Sarah sniffed. "That made it so much more precious, to know he did that for me."

Annie nodded. "You got a fine man in Perry Fisher. I know it's hard to leave your home, but you'll make a home in New York, Sarah. Perry and Mark—that's all it takes. Your own little family."

"You're right. Look at me, such a crybaby." Sarah dabbed at her eyes with the hankie. "Don't think I'm sad, Annie, because that's not it. My heart is full of hope over this journey. Our little family is going to be together in this new place. It's a little scary, but I think it will make us a very strong family. In some ways, this feels more real than the day Perry and I got married."

Annie bit her lower lip to hold back her own tears. "This is a brave thing you're doing."

Sarah shook her head. "Not really. We've got family to go to. And we'll still be with Old Order Amish. It's the life we're committed to. Lots of things will be familiar."

"But your family won't be there."

"That's the hardest part."

"And I thought the hard part was getting all these things into boxes," Annie teased.

Sarah laughed through her tears, then opened her arms wide. Annie hugged her tight, feeling Sarah's strength and hope like a halo that surrounded her.

"Okay, then." Annie pulled back and looked around the scattered clothing. "This will do." She pulled out a pair of Perry's socks and stuffed the clock inside them. "How's that for padding?"

When the packing was under control, Annie carried a box down the stairs and went to the kitchen. Where were Hannah and the boys?

She peered out the window over the sink. Were they still outside? Maybe Hannah had struck up a good conversation with Jonah. She slipped on her boots and headed out to find them.

They weren't in front of the barn, so she wandered back past the silo and around to the storehouse.

"Watch this!" Levi shouted. "This potato will go right in. Ready?"

Annie rounded the corner just in time to see Levi throw something toward the storage cellar.

Mark stood by holding a potato, and Jonah was tossing them fist over fist, down into the cellar. The boys seemed to be enjoying the game, but where was Hannah?

"That looks like fun," she said, joining them.

"Annie . . ." Jonah tossed a potato straight up and snatched it out of the air. "We're pitching potatoes. Want to give it a try?"

She picked a potato from the wheelbarrow, squinted, and tossed it with all her might. It hit the wall of the storage shed with a clunk, then fell to the ground.

"That must be a bad potato," Jonah said.

"More likely a bad throw. You've seen me play volleyball. I'm not very skilled."

His dark eyes were different today. There was a glint of humor there. "Ah, but you have a lot of spunk."

"A lot of spunk, and a bruised potato." She picked up the potato from the ground and went to the edge of the shed to drop it into the bin. "Where's Hannah?"

"She went to find your dat."

"And she left the boys here?"

"I told her I didn't mind. They're helping me get the potatoes into storage."

"But wait . . ." She looked around. "Did she bring you a drink?"

"I sent her on to give it to Aaron. I saw him taking a break out by the woodpile, and he looked like he could use a little something."

Annie blinked. This wasn't at all what she'd planned. And here was Jonah King in a talkative mood, with a few jokes up his sleeve. Hannah should be here to see this side of him.

"Watch this!" Levi tossed a potato with his right hand, then another with his left. Both landed squarely in the underground bin.

"Nice arm," Jonah said. "This is good practice for baseball," he told Annie. "And it's good fun, too."

"Me throw!" Mark cried as he flung a potato in the air. It landed on the ground a few feet away.

"A good try." Jonah swept it up and lobbed it into the bin, and Mark ran to get another potato.

Annie put her hands on her hips as Jonah stood at the wheelbarrow, shooting potatoes into the bin, one after another. The boys giggled and tried to do the same.

"I think I should take the boys so you can finish your job," Annie said. "But I don't want to ruin your fun."

"They can stay," Jonah said. "I'll deliver them to the house when we're done." He paused, turning a potato in his hands. "Or you can stay. Practice your throw. We never did finish that talk yesterday."

"We didn't?" She thought of her sister's embarrassment that Annie might have revealed too much. Now poor Hannah was nervous. "Maybe I said too much yesterday. I hope you don't think I'm pushy."

Jonah cupped the potato. "Not pushy." He gave an easy toss and it landed in the bin. "But I hope you're better at cooking potatoes than throwing them."

Annie smiled. Why did that seem like a challenge? "That's for sure."

EIGHTEEN

*B*ells jingled as Emma opened the door of the Country Store, glad to step in out of the rainy Thursday afternoon. Since her position in the schoolhouse kept her busy all week, she rarely worked in the family shop, but today Elsie needed her help. Dat and Caleb were off on a short buying trip, and the store was too much for one person to mind all day long.

From the display window to the aisles of candy and fabric, the store was more dusty and gray than the original shop that had been opened by Emma's grandparents. When Mamm ran it, the lively shop was a hub for tourists wanting craft supplies as well as crafts made by local Amish artists. But their inventory of art had dwindled over the years, mostly due to a decision by Dat after the bishop had forbidden him to sell art depicting Amish folk. Now the shop catered more to Amish women in need of dress fabric and tourists looking to pick up a quick pack of candy and bottled water.

"Teacher Emma." Elsie's gap-toothed smile warmed her heart

after a day spent dealing with children restless from rainy-day activities. "How was your day?"

"Wonderful until a few little boys realized there would be no schoolyard activities after lunch." Emma slipped off her wet coat and hung it on a hook just inside the back room. "I felt bad for them. It's hard for children with so much energy to sit at a desk all day. Even when I break it up with activities, school doesn't compare with the freedom of riding a plow with Dat or picking berries in the back fields."

"You are a wonderful good teacher," Elsie said. "It's not your fault that discipline is another lesson to be learned."

"Mmm." Holding her canvas satchel to her chest, Emma took the stool beside Elsie. "That's true. Some lessons are harder to learn than others."

"Did you bring papers to grade?" Elsie asked. "It's been pretty quiet today, so you might get some work done."

"I have some student papers. And a project of my own that's turning into an essay."

Elsie squinted, curious.

"I'm writing a letter to Gabe. You were right, Elsie. It's not fair of me to keep him at a distance because of who he is. He's part of an Amish family in our district, and it's not up to me to judge their behavior. That was the preacher's message last Sunday, and I don't know why it took me all this time to get it through my thick skull."

"You're stubborn." Elsie's eyes sparkled as she reached out to touch Emma's wrist. "But don't forget the most important reason for that letter. You really care about Gabe and you want to be with him."

Emma sighed. "You have a way of getting to the heart of the matter."

Elsie shrugged. "When you see a flower bloom in the sun a dozen times, you figure out that sunshine helps a flower bloom."

Emma laughed at her sister's comparison. "Are you saying that Gabe is my sunshine?"

"I'm just glad you're giving him a chance. Have you finished the letter?"

"That's the problem. I keep changing it, and changing it again. It's become sort of like a poem and . . . well, that's not Gabe's style. He's a man of the earth, strong and willful. A doer, not a thinker."

"You're afraid he won't understand your letter?"

"I'm just afraid he won't like it. It's too flowery. And once I got started, I just couldn't stop. When I saw that I had five pages, I knew it was too much."

Elsie looked toward the door as the bells jingled. "Five pages is a lot. You want him to know you accept him. You can tell him your life story later."

"That's what I thought," Emma said. "So I'm rewriting it. Again."

They both looked up from the counter as the customer, an Englisher woman dressed in a bright red hat, peeked out from the fabric aisle. "Do you sell those little handmade dolls?" the woman asked.

"My sister and I used to make them," Elsie said, then explained how they no longer carried Amish crafts. "I would like to start selling things like that again, but I need to work it out with my father and our bishop."

"I've been looking everywhere for those dolls," the woman said. "My daughter runs a gift shop on the West Coast, and she's got me on a mission. She thinks she could sell a lot of them."

"Do you want to give me her name and address?" Elsie asked. "I could get you some in a few weeks."

"Really? That would be wonderful!"

Emma kept quiet as Elsie exchanged information with the woman. But once the door closed, she turned to her sister. "What was that about? Has Dat changed his mind?"

"He still doesn't want to have Amish crafts in the store. But that doesn't mean we can't sell some dolls to that woman directly."

Emma folded her arms. "Why, Elsie Lapp, I think you might be on to something. But you will tell Dat, won't you?"

"Ya, but if you haven't noticed, he's not so concerned about the store these days. I think he's worried about Fanny."

Fanny Lapp was expecting, but the midwife had some concerns about the way things were going. Fanny insisted that everything was fine, but she couldn't be on her feet in the store until the baby was born.

Elsie slid off her stool. "If you'll mind the register, I'm going to change the front window display. Dat doesn't like to fuss over it, but I can't stand to see dust swirling around the cans of soda pop sitting there."

"Do you want some help?" Emma offered. "I'm not exactly struggling to keep up with customers, considering there's no one in the store."

"I can do it. You finish that letter to Gabe."

As her sister lined the display window with white butcher's paper, Emma opened her satchel and took out the new letter she'd started that morning.

Dear Gabe was written at the top of an empty page. That was all she had so far. Now that she'd decided not to spill all her feelings, she had trouble figuring out what to say.

She stared down at the blank page, feeling like one of her students who couldn't find the words to begin an essay.

"How's it going?" Elsie called from the display window, a spot most people would have had to duck in, though Elsie was short enough to stand up straight.

"Not so good. This is a hard letter to write."

"It looks like you've been spared the chore." Elsie moved to the front plate glass and waved at someone on the street. "Gabe is here. He's outside, hitching up a carriage."

"What?" Emma shoved the letter in with her papers and raced to the door. There he was, lingering in the drizzling rain to check Mercury's bit and pat his withers. "What's he doing in town?"

"Why don't you go ask him?" Elsie said with a chuckle.

Emma flew out the door and nearly skidded to a stop on the sidewalk in front of the shop. "Gabe?"

He swung around, his amber eyes growing round with surprise. "Emma. What are you doing here?"

"Helping out at the shop. And you?"

"I came to pick up Leah and Susie." He pointed across the street. "They're apprentices at the tea shop."

Emma smiled. She'd taught Susie and Leah until they'd finished eighth grade just last spring. "Lovina is blessed to get such good girls. They'll work hard for her." She turned back to see Elsie watching from the shop window. "Do you have a minute to stop into the shop? I've been wanting to talk to you." This would save her the agony of getting the letter just right.

"Sure."

Gabe went first, and Emma noticed for the first time that his head nearly grazed the door frame. Had he always been that tall? They were close to the same height when they were sitting together in his buggy. But since she'd tried to keep her distance at social events, they had rarely stood side by side.

That would be changing.

"Do you know my sister Elsie?" Emma gestured toward the window. "This is Gabe King."

"Hi, Gabe." Elsie came to the edge of the shop window to meet him. "Is it still raining out there?"

"Just sprinkling." He took off his hat and hung it on the hook by the door. His eyes were cautious as he looked around the store. "Is your dat here?"

"He went on a buying trip with Caleb," Emma said.

Gabe nodded, walking past jars of licorice, pretzels, and gummi bears. "So you're just two kids in a candy store."

Elsie laughed, and Emma couldn't help but smile. That was the thing with Gabe; he made her feel like a carefree kid instead of a prim, stern schoolteacher.

"If you want to go in the back and talk, I'll mind the store," Elsie said.

Emma could have kissed her. "Denki. We'll just be a minute."

She motioned to Gabe to follow, and he shot Elsie a curious shrug before turning into the open doorway. He paused there, a puzzled look on his face. "What is going on here?"

Emma giggled and grabbed his hand, tugging him away from the doorway. "Elsie knows. I told her."

"You did?" He lifted her hand to his face and planted a kiss there. "Getting a bit daring, Teacher Emma."

"I guess I am."

"This is a new Emma. Spilling secrets and pulling me into the storage room." He wrapped his arms around her waist. "I think I like her."

"I thought you would." Emma wavered in the delicate rush of emotion that swelled inside whenever Gabe was near. She pressed her face to his chest, her cheek against the damp cloth of his jacket, which smelled of wood smoke and soap. The world seemed right when she was in Gabe's arms.

"Emma . . ." His voice was a whisper. "This was sure worth a ride in the rain." He held her close, his fingertips brushing her bare neck, just below the line of her prayer kapp. "You're full of surprises today."

"I guess I am." She looked up at his handsome face. "I think it's time, Gabe. We don't need to sneak around anymore."

"Really?" He threw his head back. "Yahoo!"

"But you can't go crazy now. No howling like a wolf."

He smiled down at her. "Teacher Emma, you're so strict."

She laughed at his teasing. "We can let people know we're courting. Elsie knows, and I'm going to tell Dat when he gets back."

"That is good news, Emma. I want folks to know. I'll stop and shout it from the hilltops on my way home."

"I think we should start by telling our families," she said. "Everyone else will figure it out when they see us together at the next singing."

"I like my plan better." With that, he lifted her off her feet and held her in his arms to place a kiss on her lips.

She closed her eyes and gave herself to the spark of love and the drumming of her heartbeat. His mouth moved over hers so tenderly. It was easy to lose herself in Gabe's kiss. How she loved him!

The jangle of the bells reminded her that they were in the shop.

Kissing in the afternoon.

In a very public place.

Had she lost all her common sense?

Gabe released her, and once her feet touched the ground she took his hand and pulled him to the back of the storage room.

"A customer?" he asked.

Emma put a finger to her lips, and they both pressed against the shelves to listen.

"I'll take two yards of the black organdy." The voice belonged to an older woman. "I'm sewing a dress for my niece. She's getting baptized next week."

"Lizzy Mast?" Elsie asked. "She's been taking the classes with my sister Emma."

"Ya, I heard the schoolteacher was getting baptized. She does a very good job with the children. . . ."

As they talked on, Emma turned to Gabe. "Elizabeth Mast's aunt?" she whispered.

A second later, they both blinked when they realized who it was. Lois Mast.

They both mouthed the words: "The bishop's wife . . ."

Emma covered her face with her hands.

This wasn't good.

If Bishop Samuel's wife found Emma back here, alone with Gabe . . . She closed her eyes as misery soaked through her good mood. Folks didn't expect to find their schoolteacher kissing a boy in the back room of a shop. Lois Mast wouldn't be saying such kind words about the schoolteacher if she knew what had been going on back here.

She edged toward the doorway to peer out. Lois had her back to the storeroom. Elsie stood at the counter cutting fabric, her face a sea of calm.

Emma scanned the shop. There was Gabe's damp hat, hanging by the door. Would Lois notice? She would want to know whom it belonged to. . . .

But black hats were not out of the ordinary, and people didn't usually come to the back room of the shop, and Elsie would do her best to steer Lois away from them. They were probably safe.

She looked at Gabe, who shrugged, as if apologizing. But it wasn't his fault. Emma was the one who had dragged him back here.

She was supposed to be a model of good behavior for her students. What had she been thinking?

"Maybe we should hide you," she whispered, eyeing the bolts of cloth stacked on one of the wide shelves. Thoughts of burying Gabe under a mound of fabric were going through her head when she heard the bells jingle again.

The shop was silent a moment, and then came Elsie's voice. "She's gone."

Emma peered out at the shop. Empty, but for Elsie. "That was a close call."

Elsie's head bobbed as she nodded vigorously. "She hasn't stopped in for months and now, today, she suddenly has a sewing project!"

"Nothing quite like hiding in a storeroom to make an afternoon exciting." Gabe strode straight to the door, pausing to put on his hat. "Maybe next time we can hide out in a toolshed," he said, winking at Emma.

"I've had enough of hiding." Emma pressed a hand to her chest. "I thought my heart was going to hammer clear out of my chest."

"Ya? And I thought that was because you were with me," Gabe teased.

She nudged his shoulder playfully. "I like the way you toss off a close call. Like you weren't even scared at all."

"I'm not afraid of the bishop's wife," he said. "But I didn't want to get you in trouble, Emma. Denki, Elsie. You got her out the door in good time."

Elsie smiled. "Someday we'll look back and laugh at this."

"I'm still too rattled to see the humor." Emma turned to Gabe, who had his hand on the door. "Before you leave, I wanted to invite you to Sunday dinner. It's an off Sunday, and Fanny and Dat will surely welcome you to our table. Dat's going to like you. Will you join us?"

"I want to come, but . . ." He squinted off into the distance. "But this Sunday . . . that's not a good day. There's plans already. . . ." He rubbed the back of his neck.

"I understand. Most families do visits on the off Sunday."

"But maybe the next Sunday?"

"That's a church day—the baptism."

"Right." He sucked in his lower lip. "How could I forget? We're hosting."

"That'll be a busy week for your family."

He reached for her hand, giving it a squeeze. Her hand felt so tiny in his! It made her feel feminine and protected. "I guess we'll have to wait a bit for the dinner."

"Just a few weeks," he said. "But we can spend time together at the singing. And I'll give you a ride home in my buggy."

Emma nodded, joy bubbling inside her. Soon everyone would know their secret. Emma loved Gabe, and she was finally ready to share it with the world.

NINETEEN

*I*t was nearly closing time at the tea shop, and Annie couldn't wait to get home to spend one last evening with Sarah, Perry, and Mark. Today was Thursday—their last night in Halfway—and she wanted to be home to help with the dinner preparation. But all the Stoltzfus women wanted to be home tomorrow to see their travelers off. That meant making sure that their new apprentices, Leah and Susie King, were adept at handling the tea shop on their own for most of the day.

Watching Susie deliver cookies to a group of Englisher mamms and their daughters, Annie decided that the King girls would do just fine. Susie was quick on her feet, and she seemed to enjoy chatting with customers. Like a hummingbird buzzing from one flower to the next, she merrily moved from table to table.

"You mean the Halfway Mill Covered Bridge?" she asked. "I knew it was old, but two hundred years old! That's older than Mammi Nell."

"I don't know your grandmother, but I'm pretty sure that's true."

Ed Kraybill, owner of the fish and game shop in town, was one of their regulars. He usually stopped for coffee to go in the morning, then stayed for a leisurely cup of tea just before closing.

"Would you like another cup?" Susie asked Mr. Kraybill politely.

"No, no. Any more to drink and I'll float away." He took a five-dollar bill from his wallet and handed it to Susie. "Keep the change."

"Denki." As the man rose, Susie cleared his empty cup and reminded him not to forget his overcoat on the hook by the door.

Wiping down the counter, Annie smiled. Susie was a very good fit for the shop. Anyone who could get a nice tip out of Mr. Kraybill had to be doing a good job. And although Leah was no match for Susie's bubbly personality, she was a hard worker, just what was needed in the back room, where the dishes had to be cleaned in steaming hot water.

Susie went over to the big table to tend to the women and girls, while Annie began to wash down the counter. The shop was almost empty, but she didn't want to rush the Englishers, and there was plenty of cleanup that could be done while they enjoyed their late tea and cookies.

She delivered a tray of dirty dishes to the back room, where Hannah and Leah were working together and talking. With the water running from the hose, they didn't hear her behind them.

"Sometimes, at the end of the day, I'm happy to rest my feet in bed and feel the quiet all around me," Hannah was telling Leah. "There's so much talking that goes on here. Some folks don't think the air is good unless it's filled with voices."

"I know what you mean." Leah stacked mugs in the rinse rack. "Sometimes quiet is a good thing."

Hannah dunked two dirty mugs in the soapy water. "I don't need to talk all the time."

"Me neither. I like quiet," Leah said. "Why do people think they have to yackety-yack all the time?"

Hannah sighed, leaning away from the steam. "I don't know. But Annie says I need to work on my conversation skills. I don't have the gift of gab. I'm trying to learn, but I don't really like it."

Poor Hannah. She didn't understand how important the art of conversation was in finding a beau. Especially with a quiet man like Jonah, who wasn't so good at filling in the silent spaces. Jonah had even been nicknamed the Quiet One, but when Annie had seen him with Hannah this week, she had realized that her sister was even more at a loss for words than he was.

In the past few days, Jonah had been talking more than ever before. What a sense of humor he had! He seemed to enjoy laughing, and he was a magnet for the little ones, who loved to watch him fix a pump or repair a broken door. Jonah could turn his chores into cheerful adventures that captured Levi's attention. Annie would never have guessed that such a wit had been hidden behind that wall of quiet. But whenever Jonah King had come up with a few clever things to say, dear Hannah had stood there looking at the ground!

What would it take to make Hannah come alive in a conversation? Her communications with customers were short and flat. One-word answers, with barely a smile. Earlier in the day, when Hannah had been waiting tables up front, Annie had pulled her sister aside and tried to get her to practice small talk.

"Listen to the talk that goes on in this shop," Annie had told Hannah. "Some folks have the gift of gab, and it can make a person warm up to you in no time. You should try it. Say something cheerful, and always be polite."

"I have good manners," Hannah had said. "But I don't like talking to strangers. I'm just not a chatterbox, and I don't know any of these people."

"You can get to know them by talking with them," Annie suggested. "Folks like to talk about their families or their pets. The tourists come with lots of questions, and you know all there is to know about Halfway."

A few minutes later, when Hannah asked a customer about the weather, Annie couldn't help but smile. Hannah was trying her best, but it would take time. The gift of gab was going to take a while, but patience was a virtue. If Hannah could learn how to make small talk, Annie could learn patience.

When Annie and Hannah got home from the tea shop that night the living room was filled with boxes and bags. Sarah and Perry were packing everything they could fit in the van—a dresser and a hope chest, and so many bags and boxes. Sunny kept barking at the suspicious piles of boxes.

"Does she think they're cows?" Perry joked.

"A fine watchdog we have," Annie said as she ushered the dog out the door. After that, she avoided that room, not wanting the reminder of what would happen tomorrow.

After dinner, Annie savored the chance to tuck little Mark in for the last time. Tonight he didn't want to go up, and she swept him into her arms to plant ticklish kisses on his neck until he surrendered.

When his dull whine gave way to giggles, and he stopped squirming, he looked up at her, his eyes twinkling with sleepiness. "A book?" he asked.

"We can read lots of books." Her heart was full as she carried him up the stairs, with Sunny following on her heels. She let Mark toddle around the room to pick out his favorite bedtime stories as she and Sunny sat by the crib, just watching. Such a busy boy. He opened each book and spoke a language that only he understood, but that was the beauty of being a child.

"All right, dear one." She picked him up, kissed his soft cheek, and lowered him into his crib. Mark lay on his side, watching her as she pulled the chair close and began to read.

She turned the pages, her eyes barely skimming the words.

I know these books by heart!

Of course she did. All these nights of reading to her nephews, the stories had become nighttime lullabies. Sunny yawned. Even the dog could have recited the stories if she knew how to talk.

Annie held the book up to the crib to show Mark a picture, but he had fallen asleep. A golden ringlet of hair fell over his forehead, and the lantern light caught the milky glow of his skin.

Sorrow was heavy on her heart. Not just the pain of saying goodbye. Watching little Mark sleep, she suddenly understood why Sarah's departure was hitting her so hard. Mark and Levi were the center of her life . . . but they weren't her children.

Her throat felt tight with emotion over her own sad state.

Oh, why had she wasted so much time waiting on Adam? She should be married by now, with children of her own. Instead, folks were calling her an old maid.

Twenty years old, and no marriage on the horizon.

A whimper escaped her throat, and she curled forward as warm tears flooded her eyes.

Dear Gott, in my heart I know You made me to be a mother . . . to have children. This is my gift. Why can't I find my way to the right path?

After having a good cry last night, Annie felt stronger when she got out of bed Friday morning. She was determined to make it through the good-bye without tears. Right now Sarah needed her support, and she didn't want to be the cause of more sadness for her sister.

If it weren't for the cartons blocking the living room, the day would have seemed like any other. Levi and Mark helped Annie fetch eggs and feed the chickens, then they headed over to bottle-feed the bummer lamb, who had taken to following around Sunny, the family dog.

"Your little lamb thinks it's a dog," Dat said, pausing in his chores. "When I went into the barn this morning, I found the lamb sleeping beside Sunny, nestled up in the crook of her belly." His eyes twinkled as he recalled the sight.

"Aw!" Levi's brows shot up as he cooed over the lamb. "Were you looking for your mamm? Don't you know you're not a dog?"

Mark leaned forward to stroke the lamb, mimicking his older cousin. "Not a dog," he echoed.

Annie took a deep breath, sure that Gott was making the children extra sweet today so she would have more moments to cherish in her memories.

When they returned to the house, the white van was parked out front, its doors hanging open. Boxes sat on the ground near the rear cargo area. Perry and the driver were trying to figure out what to load first, while Dat, Daniel, and Jonah carried more cartons and bags out of the house.

"Look at the big car!" Levi stared in wonder. "Can I have a ride in it?"

"Not today." Annie scooped up Mark and put a hand on Levi's shoulder to keep him away from the commotion. "That van is for Mark and his parents. They're going off to their new home in New York."

Levi frowned. "I don't want them to go."

"I don't either," Annie said, watching as the boxes disappeared into the back of the big van. She had thought she'd be upset by the sight of the vehicle, but there was too much excitement in the air to feel sad. "Let's go into the kitchen and get out of the men's way." She steered Levi around to the side door.

Sarah stood in the doorway, nervously watching the men, while Mamm fussed over a tin of cookies she was packing for the trip.

"Would you rather have chocolate-chip or cranberry-walnut?" Lovina asked.

"I don't know," Sarah said, still peeking into the living room.

"Mamm . . ." Rebecca looked up from her knitting. "I'm sure they have cookies in New York."

"But they have a long trip. Don says it's six and a half hours."

Annie shuddered at the thought. She couldn't imagine traveling so far from home. Six and a half hours by automobile would take days to travel by horse and carriage. She took a seat beside Rebecca and pulled Mark onto her lap for some last-minute cuddling.

"I wonder what kind of cookies Don likes," mused Lovina. Don was a local Mennonite man whom Annie's family hired to drive long distances.

"Well, if they're hungry, they'll be wanting more than cookies," Rebecca said dryly.

"That's why I packed them a cooler of sandwiches and apples." Mamm pressed the cover onto the tin and brought it to Sarah. "Do you have the sandwiches I made for you?"

"I put them on the seat of the van, so they'll be handy once we get going."

Lovina handed Sarah the tin. "Good thinking."

"That's it." Perry appeared in the doorway, his face flushed with excitement. "The van is packed. I guess it's good-bye for now."

Annie held tight to Mark, not wanting to let him go.

"Kumm, give me a hug." Lovina took Sarah into her arms. "I'm missing you already, but I'm excited for you, too."

"Denki, Mamm." Sarah was all smiles.

Suddenly, everyone was moving out the door, hugging and kissing, surrounding the van. Annie blinked, loving the excitement but feeling as if she were caught in a dream. This couldn't be real. Someone lifted Mark from her arms, and she lunged to kiss his cheek before he was buckled into a fancy padded child seat in the van.

When Sarah hugged her, Annie sank against her sister and held on tight. She wanted to hold on forever! But suddenly Sarah drew in a thin breath and leaned back. Her blue eyes caught Annie's in that no-nonsense way Sarah was known for.

"The offer is always open," Sarah said. "Come live with us in New York." Sarah lowered her voice and added, "We'll find you a proper beau there."

A proper beau . . .

Right now a husband was the answer to Annie's prayers, but she couldn't imagine giving up her home to find him. That would be like robbing Peter to pay Paul.

"Promise me you'll think about coming to Lowville," Sarah pleaded.

Unable to trust her voice, Annie could only nod. She would give it some thought.

Doors slammed. Sunny barked and circled the van, sensing that something was up. Last farewells rang out through open windows, and then the engine roared.

As the van rolled down the lane, Annie forced a smile. Tonight, after the lights were out, she would cry a river of tears in her bed. But for now it was best to be strong and try to look on the bright side. Mamm always said that joy came to those with a joyful heart. Well . . . she would try for joy.

The van was hidden by trees now, but no one turned away yet. Dat and Mamm stood side by side, as did Daniel and Rebecca.

In that moment Annie felt the strength of the two couples' love and commitment, and she ached with loneliness. She was next in line to marry, and she would probably be sewing her wedding dress now if she hadn't made such a foolish choice about Adam King. So many years of courtship wasted. After all this time it was no surprise that there were few unattached men her age in their district.

Angry with herself, she drew in a deep breath and turned to see Jonah with Levi hitched up on his shoulders. The little boy was waving madly from six feet in the sky.

She put her hands on her hips. "You grew up fast, Levi."

"I can see everything from up here," he said, his chipmunk voice full of awe. "Is this what God sees?"

Laughter broke the tension as Jonah hoisted Levi higher, then lowered him gently to the ground.

"That was fun." Levi adjusted his hat, looking up at Jonah. "I'd like to do that again sometime."

There was no match for the pure honesty of a child. With a surge of love, Annie swept toward the little boy. "Now that your cousin's gone, I'll have to get double the kisses from you."

"No!" Levi cried, dodging her. He ran in a circle and hid behind Jonah's legs.

Hands on hips, Annie faced the two of them. "I'm going to get you. I'm going to hug you and kiss you till your eyes bulge out!"

"No!" Levi giggled. "Save me, Jonah! Help me!"

Sunny barked, wanting in on the chasing game.

"Come on," Annie teased. "Just one little kiss?"

Jonah looked down at Levi, then at Annie, his face serious now. "I was hoping you were talking to me," he told Annie.

That stopped her. She blinked up at him, feeling unsure until he cracked a smile and everyone laughed.

She caught Levi, glad to turn away from everyone as she thought about what Jonah had just said. The man had some sense of humor! The Quiet One was clever once you got to know him.

And where was Hannah in all this?

Annie sighed as she hugged her nephew. When it came to matchmaking for those two, she had a lot of work ahead.

TWENTY

*D*isappointment clung to him. It was a bitter taste in the back of his throat that couldn't be washed down by all the lemonade Hannah Stoltzfus had tried to bring him.

Jonah reined in his horse at the top of the lane to check the main road for traffic. He let a truck and two cars go by before nudging Jigsaw ahead. The horse picked up his pace. Jonah figured he knew that home was the next stop, and he let him settle into an easy trot. Jigsaw had been a gift from Jonah's parents when he was sixteen, an age when most Amish parents let their son choose an animal to make his own. Now, all these years later, Jonah sometimes got the feeling that his horse could read his mind.

Unlike some people he knew.

All this week he'd thought that Annie knew just what he was thinking. But it seemed she thought he was thinking of her sister Hannah instead of her. He passed a row of trees in fiery colors. Beyond the trees, Aaron Stoltzfus's fields of mowed hay stretched out, gentle hills dotted by rectangular bales of hay.

One day next week Jonah would bring his brothers over, along with any other neighbor men willing to help, and they'd scour the fields, loading the horse-drawn cart with bales—forty or fifty at a time. It was hard work, but when they were done Aaron would have enough hay in storage to feed his horses through the winter. Now that Jonah had taken the job with Aaron he was committed to helping him, though it wouldn't be easy with Annie always nearby, always pushing Hannah toward him.

And just a few days ago, he'd had such high hopes.

He urged the horse into a gallop, wanting to escape the day, run from the past week of false hope and misunderstanding.

His first hint that he'd gotten it wrong with Annie was the fact that she kept darting away from him like a delicate butterfly. The few times she came close, she always made a point of telling him something about Hannah: how she had baked these cinnamon rolls that morning, that she was bringing him hot coffee, or that he could find her in the garden after lunch. Always, it was about Hannah.

He'd sensed that something was off early on, but it took him a few days to see her plan. She was pairing him off with Hannah, a sweet girl, but not the girl for him.

He came up on a slow-moving carriage, passed it, and flew ahead.

This morning, when he came out of the barn and saw the sun rising in the east, flaming gold over the bright trees and shining on the low-lying mist, he knew he had to tell Annie the truth. Even if she laughed in his face, it was better to put the truth out there than to live a lie.

He had wanted to tell her today. He'd been ready, but the look on her face when she saw the men loading the van had stopped him in his tracks. Although Annie had kept her chin up with a smile on her face, Jonah had seen the sorrow in her eyes. He could tell her heart was aching, and he couldn't bear to make her feel any worse.

While helping to load the van he had overheard Sarah talking with Annie. Sarah had said that she should come to New York to find a beau, and Annie had said she'd think about it.

That was salt on the wound. It was bad enough longing for Annie from nearby. Losing her to a settlement hundreds of miles away would shatter any hope of ever winning her heart.

They came to a four-way stop and Jigsaw slowed to a trot, then paused with barely a twitch of the reins. The horse seemed to understand traffic laws, but Jonah figured it was probably force of habit. They turned left and headed down the final stretch toward home.

Jonah sighed at the thought of telling Annie his feelings. He'd made a joke about it after the van left, hoping that Annie would pick up on it, but no, she hadn't. He would probably have to spell everything out very carefully. Open his heart. Brace himself for the answer she was bound to give.

A flat no.

He grunted. Tomorrow would be soon enough for that bad news.

When he rose over the last hill and looked at the two silos of their farm, he thanked Gott for the good feeling of coming home. Whatever the world handed him, he was grateful to have a good, loving family to return to.

The lawn needed mowing and weeds spilled over onto the lane. Next week, the whole family would pitch in to make the farm neat and tidy for Sunday's church service. Preparation would take a day or two, but it was always a good reason to make the house spic-and-span once a year.

On the side of the house, Mary had set a kitchen chair in the yard for haircuts. Sam sat there, bobbing like a pickle in a barrel. Jonah grinned. Mary had her work cut out for her with that one.

By the time he'd unsaddled Jigsaw and set him out to pasture, he saw that Mary had a new customer. Simon sat there, his lips pursed, a towel over his shoulders as she tried to even out the line of his hair.

"Stay still," Mary said softly. "We just need to cut over your eyes and then you're finished."

The scissors snipped along Simon's brow, sending glittery hairs into the air.

"It itches." He waited until she leaned back, then furiously rubbed his nose.

"That's one way to get it off." Mary slid the towel from Simon's shoulders and shook it out. "You're done. You can go back to training your horse."

Simon let out a sigh of relief. "I don't like haircuts."

"Then be glad yours is done." Mary turned to Jonah and patted the top of the chair. "You're next."

"I don't like haircuts either."

She frowned. "I don't like lima beans, but I eat them. Have a seat and don't complain about it. You need a trim. Or else you'll have to move to the stables."

Reluctantly, he sat in the chair and braced himself.

"Don't look so worried. So far I haven't taken an ear off anybody."

"So far." He frowned. "But that wouldn't be the worst thing that's happened to me lately."

"Why are you so glum?" Mary asked, the scissors whooshing at the back of his neck. "That's not like you, Jonah, especially after the smiles we've seen these past few days."

"Nothing is going right today," he admitted.

Mary came around to face him, hands on her hips. "Is this about Annie?"

He nodded.

"What is she doing now?"

"It's not really her fault. But it's a tangled mess, and I don't know how I walked right into it with my eyes open." He told Mary how Annie had come to him saying that someone was sweet on him. "I was sure it was Annie herself, and that's why I was walking on clouds a few days ago."

"But you found out it wasn't Annie?" Mary squinted at him. "Who is it?"

"Her sister Hannah. Annie has been trying to get us together. She's been playing matchmaker. Only I'm not sweet on Hannah. So now I've got to tell Annie that I'm not going to court her sister, and she's not going to like me at all once I dump that bit of bad news on her doorstep."

She laughed, but her dark eyes were full of sympathy. "Oh, Jonah! You've hit so many twists and turns on your path to find a good and fitting wife."

He grunted. "It's not a wife I want, and I won't settle for good and kind. I'm holding out for one girl. She's good and kind, all right. She's just not sweet on me." He turned to look up at his sister.

"You'd better hold still if you don't want your hair to look like it was cut with a handsaw."

He frowned, staring off at a section of yellow trees along the lane. It had probably been foolish to hold out for one girl. Foolish and stubborn. But Jonah just couldn't see it any other way. He closed his eyes as the scissors moved over his forehead. "Do you think I'm selfish?"

"Not selfish, but stubborn as a mule." Mary cut through a dense crop of hair. "And with Annie being stubborn in her own way, she's not likely to figure out her mistake. Do you want me to talk to her? I have a knack for saying things nice and gentle. I can set things right."

"No," Jonah insisted. "And don't say a word to anyone else, especially Adam. He doesn't have real fond memories of Annie."

Mary leaned back to scrutinize his hair. "You don't have to worry about Adam. He's put the past behind him. These days, he's able to see the good in everyone. That's the blessing of love."

The blessing of love . . .

Mary was right. Love was not something you earned, but a blessing from Gott in heaven. It was not a broken pipe he could weld together or a field he could till and tend and harvest. It was out of his hands. Jonah knew that was true, but he didn't like that at all.

TWENTY-ONE

*A*t last, he'd made it back.

Although it had been a week since he'd been on a bike, once Gabe swung his leg over and grabbed the handlebars, it all came back to him. The way his fingers slid into the molded grips, the curve of the seat—it all fit him perfectly.

"I feel like I was born on this bike," he told Blake.

"Yeah? Well, you look like you've been riding a long time. My dad and I built a lot of obstacles into the course, but you dominate out there. You got skill, man. I'm glad you're moving up to a bigger bike. I think you're ready."

Gabe grinned, warmed by the compliments. The dirt bike track had been in the back of his mind all week, calling to him like a coyote in the night. He was eager to get out there again, to fly through the wind and roar over the land.

"I've been thinking about this all week," Gabe said.

"You like it? Sounds like you caught the bug. That's cool."

Gabe got off the bike and went to the assortment of helmets on the rack. Sleek and shiny, they all looked good to Gabe. He chose a black one with orange and red flames painted around the visor, and wondered if he could get someone to paint flames on his buggy. He stowed his hat in the empty spot of the rack.

"I finally chose one." Ben rolled a third bike out of the big garage.

"Took you long enough," Blake said. "But that's one sweet ride. Little light in the rear."

"Is that a good thing?" Ben asked.

"It can be. Depends on how you ride it."

Gabe listened. He wanted to learn all there was about this motor biking, and Blake had been doing it for a long time.

Ben tipped his hat back. "Okay. I almost forgot—we brought you some money for gas." Ben set the kickstand and reached down to pull up a pant leg. He fished a rolled-up bill from his sock. "Twenty dollars." Ben had earned the money delivering milk and cheese for the family dairy.

"We'll bring more next time," Gabe said. He was annoyed that he had no way to earn his own money. Adam didn't understand that he was no longer a little child. He was a man now, and though he liked working on the family farm, it was time that he earned some money of his own.

"That's cool. Thanks." Blake pushed the money into a pocket of his blue jeans. "I'm glad you guys are coming out to ride. The bikes are no good when they're sitting here gathering dust. But the gas gets expensive. This'll help. So do you remember how to work the gears and stuff?"

"I remember how to crash into a hay bale," Ben joked.

"Yeah, I thought you got a little banged up that time." Blake glanced toward the obstacle course. "It's probably pretty muddy out there with the rain we've been having."

"A little mud never hurt anyone," Gabe said.

"But it'll be slippery. Just warning you. And if we get sick of the track, we can head back into the woods. There's some killer trails, but you got to watch for other people back there."

"Sounds good." Gabe couldn't imagine getting sick of riding the track. He could do that all day and all night. He raked his hair back and pulled the helmet on.

"Ben, you need a helmet, too," Blake called from the garage.

"Right." Ben hurried past Gabe, joking, "Got to have a shiny hat."

"Always gotta have a helmet, or Dad will freak."

Gabe slipped on his helmet and started the bike's engine. It rolled cleanly down the paved driveway, then bumped and twisted a bit when the tires hit the soft dirt of the trail. He gave a burst of throttle and the bike shot forward. This was what he'd been waiting all week for—the freedom and power of a bike with a roaring engine.

A cold, gray rain filled the air, but Gabe felt like he was riding a ball of fire through the now-familiar course. He took it easy the first time around, slowing for the turns. Blake had been right about the mud; it slowed the bike and sometimes the wheels spun wildly, spitting up muck behind them. He turned sharply to miss a fat tree, and the rear wheel slid. The bike wiggled and shook under him, like a crazed animal.

Gabe laughed, trying to regain his balance.

He pulled out of the skid and roared off with a yelp.

After an hour or so on the course, Blake suggested that they try the trail into the woods. Gabe wasn't so sure about leaving the privacy of Blake's property. What if someone saw them?

"We've got helmets that make us look like superheroes from comic books," Ben said. "Who can recognize us when we're wearing these?"

"He's right," Blake said.

Gabe looked down at the helmet with the flames curling around the sides. "Okay, then. Show us the way."

They followed Blake down the farm access road, past mown fields to a hilly area, too steep for good planting. Blake led them around to a narrow path through the tall weeds. Chaff and seed went flying when Gabe went off course, but he pulled back onto the trail as the bike dove into the damp darkness of trees.

Gabe grinned as he hit the throttle. These things that he saw every day—leaves and brambles, weeds and tree roots—everything seemed different when he was flying past it on a motorbike.

He gave a burst of throttle then lifted out of the seat to hop a twisted tree root—a trick Blake had shown him. His pulse raced with the effort of jumping with the bike, and he likened himself to a young buck, leaping and bounding through the forest.

A stone jutted out of the path ahead, and he hit the throttle to leap again. But this time, the tires slipped on the ground, and he couldn't get the bike up.

The rubber spun sickly against the ground, and before Gabe knew what was happening the bike skidded off to the side. It slipped out from under him, and he went down. Hard.

"Aarrrrr." He rested against the sodden ground for a minute, mentally checking. Two arms, two legs. He could still move, but his shoulder screamed with pain.

He pushed away from the ground, sat up a moment, then reached over to turn off the growling bike.

His shoulder still reeled. He'd have a good bruise, but nothing was broken.

The drone of another bike grew louder as Ben whirred up the path. He switched direction when he saw Gabe on the ground, heading straight for him, then skidding to a stop in the mud.

Ben flipped up his visor. "Gabe, are you hurt?"

"Not too bad." Gabe stood up and looked down at his pants. One side of his body was caked in mud. His black sleeve and pants leg were brown. Mary was going to wonder what he'd been doing on the Sabbath to get his church clothes so dirty.

"Gabe?" Ben's mouth dropped open. "You're bleeding." He got off the bike and moved behind Gabe to check it out. "Your jacket is cut clear through right up to the top."

More damage. "I'm going to have to hide these clothes."

"And you've got a cut here. Not so bad, but there's a nasty mark on your neck."

"I don't care about a mark." As soon as he said it, Gabe realized that other folks would notice it. Adam and Mary. And Emma . . .

How was he going to explain it?

"Good thing you had a helmet on," Ben said, still poking at Gabe's back. "I can't see much more."

"I must have hit that rock." Gabe looked down at the ground where he'd fallen. "Or the branch there." Suddenly he felt a pinch in the tender area.

"Does that hurt?" Ben asked.

"Ya. Don't touch it."

"Okay. I think you'll live." Ben stepped around to face him. "You want to go home?"

"No." Gabe wiped his muddy hands on his pants. "As long as I can hold on to the grips, I'm here to ride."

TWENTY-TWO

I can't wait until Gabe sees me in this dress.

The crisp, dark fabric, so unlike the gem-toned everyday dresses Amish girls wore, made Emma feel like a woman.

Mysterious and pretty.

She twirled, watching the skirt lift ever so slightly.

Her sister stood before her, trying to finish her task. "I can't pin the apron if you're going to keep spinning like a weather vane. But I'm glad you like it."

"This is the most wonderful surprise I've ever had," Emma said as she smoothed the black organdy gown over her hips. Emma had been asking around to borrow a black dress for her baptism, but the only one she'd found was small for her, and she had worried that it wasn't modest enough. "Too much leg," Fanny had said in agreement.

She had been thinking about tacking a new skirt on when Elsie had brought out this brand-new dress. It was a surprise gift, sewn by her sister's own hands. There were still some edges to be turned, but it covered her legs and fit her nicely.

"I can't believe you put this together without me knowing."

Elsie removed the straight pins from between her lips to say, "I wanted to surprise you."

"You did. Denki." Emma stooped down to give her sister a warm hug. "But how did you find the money for the fabric?" Even with Emma's teaching job and the shop, money was tight in their household. The store hadn't been doing so well in the last year.

"It wasn't so much. We sell the material, so I got the wholesale price. And I made a little extra last week from selling two cases of those lavender soaps that Mary Zook makes."

"What do you think?" Emma held out her arms.

Elsie stepped back for a better look. "It's a very good fit."

"You have a good eye for sewing projects," Emma told her sister. "I wish you would come to the next quilting bee with me. You'd enjoy it, and folks are always asking about you."

"But I'm always busy with the shop." Elsie handed her the material they'd cut for the apron and Emma held it to her waist. "How's that?"

Elsie squinted thoughtfully as she pinned two of the corners. "Be glad that our Order has us wear colors. Black isn't so good for you."

"It's a serious color for a serious occasion," Emma said as she smoothed down an edge of the apron.

"If you'll hold still, I'll pin the hem for you." Elsie took the pincushion and got down on her knees. "We'll keep it plenty long, in case one of our sisters ends up being taller than you," Elsie said.

"And what about you?" Emma asked. "You'll want to wear this when you get baptized."

Elsie folded over a section of the hem. "I'll borrow something from a short person like me. For me to wear this dress, there'd be too much sewing. Like trying to turn a chicken into a pig. At the end of the day, there'd be too many feathers flying."

Emma was looking forward to next week. The baptism was one of the things she had always watched with longing as a girl. It was a serious vow, the promise to obey the Ordnung for the rest of your life. But it was also an important crossing to the next part of her life. She was ready to cross over this bridge and become a member of the Amish community. She had been raised to be a good Amish woman, and she had always tried to make her life an example of good behavior for her students.

"You're such a big help," Fanny always told her when Emma helped with the chores or corralled her younger siblings for their mother. Good-natured Fanny had come along when Emma had worried that her dat might die of loneliness after their mother's death. And though it had felt a little odd watching her dat marry, Emma had welcomed Fanny into the house. Fanny and Tom had two children of their own now, and Emma had been glad to help with the household chores as each baby came along. Emma had always found joy in putting the kitchen in order, tidying up the bedrooms, sweeping and scrubbing. When she was little Mamm had taught her how to mend things, and she had whiled away many happy evenings mending clothes from the family's sewing bag.

Emma liked order. She engaged her scholars to help her keep the classroom tidy, and supplies of paper, pencils, and erasers were arranged in neat rows in her desk drawers. Order made sense to her, and she didn't understand how folks could think straight when their home was a tangled mess.

Once, while walking in Halfway, she had passed a parked automobile that was piled high with . . . things. Stacks of old newspapers, clothes, and shoes. Crumpled trash bags from fast-food restaurants. A tattered sweater, a tennis racket, and a torn book. Emma had stared at the car in alarm, wondering how that poor person could bear to be near such clutter.

Although the Amish way was to keep a tidy household, Emma

knew her strict sense of order wasn't shared by everyone. Folks like Gabe King saw things differently.

She closed her eyes and took a deep breath, imagining Gabe's arms around her. She and Gabe were so different, but there was no denying the strong attraction between them. Emma crossed her arms and ran her fingers along the edges of the stark white cape pinned over her dress.

Her new dress for the baptism.

How she wished Gabe had taken the classes with the ministers. Now he would have to wait another year to be baptized. Which meant that he wouldn't be allowed to marry in the Amish faith this year.

Another year to wait . . .

It would have been wonderful if Gabe was getting baptized in the group with her, but all the wishing in the world wouldn't make it so. Gabe said he wasn't ready, and most Amish folk respected a young person's choice to wait . . . as long as it was clear that he would eventually come around.

"Isn't it too bad that Gabe had to be with his family today?" Elsie pinned the back of the dress.

Emma smiled. "How did you know I was thinking of Gabe?"

"Aren't you always thinking of Gabe?" Elsie teased.

"Only . . . most of the time," Emma admitted.

"I wanted him to come to dinner tonight. I think he and Dat will hit it off. They're both interested in farming and cows."

Their dat had been raised on a dairy farm, and his stories of the farm always brought a smile to his face. Emma sensed that he missed the dairy business, but he couldn't afford a dairy farm of his own, and when he married Mamm he came into her family's business with the shop in town.

"It would have been nice to have Gabe here," Emma said, "but it's good that he's spending time with his family. A man needs to put his family first."

"That's true. I guess I just don't have your patience, Em. I want what I want when I want it."

Emma grinned down at her sister. Was there a heart more pure than Elsie's? "Your honesty is a virtue, but the bishop would remind you that you shouldn't want too much. We live on this earth, but not of it."

"I know that." Elsie shrugged. "I'm working on it."

TWENTY-THREE

*H*ow did it get to be so late?" Ben asked as they headed home, Mercury hitched to the small gray carriage.

"That's the only problem with dirt biking," Gabe said. "Once you start, it's very hard to stop."

"We're late now," Ben said. "Dinner is on the table already, and I'm sure that there's been some talk about the two of us being missing."

Gabe squinted at the rain that left drops running down the windshield. They just needed to come up with words that were truthful. "We'll tell them we were off riding and we lost track of time." He turned to his cousin, who was frowning, his face in a sour pucker. "What's wrong with saying that? It's true."

"A half-truth. Besides, you can't go in like that. There's blood on your shirt and your jacket's torn. Mamm won't even let you into the kitchen with so much mud on your pants."

Gabe growled. He was hungry for Betsy's good cooking, but Ben was right. He couldn't arrive for dinner at their house looking like this. "Why don't we go to my house first? I'll wash up and change clothes. You can wash up, too."

"That'll make us even later." Ben shook his head. "Blake said it's after five. We both have cows to milk."

"Ya." Gabe's mood was turning as dark and gray as the weather. "What can we do? Sneak into the barn?"

"You can drop me off at home. I'll go straight to the barn. You'd better go home and clean up that blood before your family gets back from visiting."

It was a good plan. "Isn't there some way I can get dinner from your mamm tonight?"

Ben shook his head. "Not unless you want to answer a hundred questions."

"Mmm. I really want dinner, but I don't like questions." Gabe decided to drop Ben off, then head home. When he arrived at the farm and pulled up beside the barn, he was relieved to see two carriages still gone. He would have the house to himself for now.

He stripped down to his underwear on the screened porch, but decided not to put his clothes in the laundry bin. His jacket had a tear clear through the fabric. The top of his shirt had a small hole, and it was covered in blood. He balled them up, carried them upstairs, and stuffed them under his bed.

Inside the bathroom, he couldn't see the wound in the clouded shaving mirror, but the spot was still tender and a scab was forming. Grateful no one was home, he stepped into the shower to get cleaned up.

Gabe was in the milking barn, leading Daisy to a stall, when he saw the gray carriage through the wide barn door. The family was back.

He tied Daisy to the stanchion, then leaned under the cow to quickly clean her teats. Then he attached the hoses and let the machine do the work.

Gabe straightened, ignoring the ache in his shoulder as he looked over the half-dozen cows that were already hooked up to machines. This was a good plan. Adam would be glad that Gabe had the milking going. That would keep him from being too mad about Gabe missing Sunday dinner and visits with the family.

A few minutes later Adam came into the milking barn, with Ruthie and Simon trailing behind him.

"We didn't mean to stay that late," Adam said, resting a hand on a steel post. "I see you've started."

"Ya. Once I knew I'd missed dinner, I figured I'd better get the milking going."

Ruthie and Simon started tending to the cows. Simon lugged a six-gallon container of milk to the big vat, while Ruthie released the hoses from another cow's teats.

Adam gave the stalls a quick look. "Do you need my help?" he asked Gabe.

"The three of us can handle it." The machines that Adam had recently installed had cut milking time down a lot. The process that used to take thirty minutes by hand now took only three minutes per cow. Such a difference!

"Then I'll go split some firewood. We're running low." Adam headed out, patting Gerta as he passed by. "And, Gabe, Betsy was worried about you. What happened to you and Ben?"

"It's a long story." *And I don't want to tell you all the details,* Gabe thought as he untied one of the cows from the stanchion and led her out of the pen. He had put on a clean shirt and a black vest that covered his shoulder well. "Ben and I got back too late and too wet to make it to dinner."

"You know how important it is to have the family together," Adam said.

"I do. And believe me, I was sorry to miss Betsy's good cooking."

Adam nodded. "It was good. Baked chicken."

As soon as he was gone, Gabe breathed a sigh of relief. He didn't like having trouble in the air, though sometimes he felt sure that a cloud hovered over his head. Now . . . he just needed to find a way to fix his jacket.

Simon moved the cows that were finished out to pasture, and Gabe let a handful of others in.

"Come on, find your places," Gabe told them. "You do this every day and every night."

Simon giggled. "I like to hear you talk to the cows. I think you talk to them more than you talk to people."

"I talk to people when I have something to say." Gabe patted Brownie's side. "I just have a lot more to say to the cows. Especially when they don't listen."

"That's most of the time." Simon picked up a container of fresh milk and lugged it down to the end of the barn. He was strong for a boy of nine, and a hard worker, too. It had been good to see Simon come out of his shell these past few months.

Ruthie was working nearby. "We missed you at dinner," she said. "Betsy was worried, but Nate said you and Ben were just boys being boys."

He brought the hoses over for her. "Nate's right."

"And Adam said he's worried that you don't talk much." Ruthie finished cleaning Clementine and turned to face Gabe. "He's afraid that you're going to go wild one day. Adam says the quiet ones are the ones to watch." She stifled a smile as she attached the milking machine. "Is it true?"

Gabe folded his arms as he thought about how much he could

tell Ruthie. He didn't want to say too much, but he liked talking to her. She always had a bright way about her, and she didn't judge. He leaned back against a stanchion, wincing when a post connected with the sore spot on his shoulder.

Ruthie's eyes opened wider. She never did miss much. "What's wrong?"

"It's nothing. I just got a cut on my neck. It's sore."

"Is it okay?"

"It's hard to tell. It's too far back for me to see."

She straightened up and moved out of the stall. Her face was pinched with worry now. "Let me look."

Gabe checked behind him. Simon was down at the other end. No one would notice. "Just tell me what you see." He opened his vest and shirt quickly and got down on one knee to get to Ruthie's eye level.

Her hands were gentle, but the wound still stung. "Oh, Gabe, that's a fierce cut. And the skin's turning black and blue. It must hurt."

"Sometimes." He started to stand up, but she pressed down on his good shoulder.

"Stay there. I'm going to get the first-aid kit. There's some ointment there to keep you from getting an infection."

She ran to the blue plastic box hanging on the wall. Watching her fetch the tube of antibiotic, Gabe wondered how she knew so much. Sometimes Ruthie seemed way too smart for her twelve years.

"Okay." She squeezed ointment onto a square of gauze and pushed his head down. "How did you do this?"

Gabe gritted his teeth as the cut tingled with cold. "Riding motorbikes. I took a spill and hit something on the ground."

"A bike accident? Oh, I'm glad you weren't hurt bad. It could have been so much worse."

"Don't worry. I always wear a helmet, and I'm a good driver."

She yanked his good shoulder back and swung around to face him as he rose. "A good driver? So this isn't the first time you were on a motorbike."

"No. And don't tell Mary or Adam. They'll only give me a talking to about how I'm going against the Ordnung."

"Well . . ." She closed up the first-aid kit. "It's true. But I'm more scared of you getting hurt bad."

"I'll be fine. Don't you worry."

She crossed her arms. "You know I will. But I won't tell. Nobody likes a tattletale." As she went to return the first-aid kit to the wall, he wondered if Ruthie could help him with his jacket. Had she learned to sew yet? He never paid much attention to what his sisters were doing.

"As long as you're helping me," he said, "would you mind taking a look at my jacket?" He'd rinsed all his clothes in the mud sink, but he'd been leery of putting his torn jacket in with the laundry.

"What's wrong with your jacket?"

"There's a big rip in the back. I know if I put it in with the washing, Mary's going to have a cow."

Ruthie let out a sigh. "You really are a wild one, just like Adam said."

He smiled. "So you'll mend it?"

"I'll give it a try. Put it in the sewing room, in the closet. Mary is so busy sewing her wedding dress, she won't be looking to do mending for a while."

"Denki." He removed the pump hoses from Tansy and smiled at his little sister. "And not a word to Mary and Adam."

"I won't tell them," she said, "but I hate to think of what Bishop Samuel's going to say when he hears about your wild bike rides."

Gabe shrugged. "If the wind blows my way, he'll never hear about it." He couldn't live his life worrying about what *might* happen. Besides, this was his rumspringa. It was his season to go wild.

TWENTY-FOUR

Monday morning, Emma arrived at school early. After being closed up for the weekend, the schoolhouse needed a little fresh air, and she enjoyed opening windows and wiping down the desks. The large windows allowed a full view of nature outside the window, as well as lots of natural sunlight.

Today the bursts of colorful trees in the schoolyard suggested an assignment about identifying trees. Perhaps her scholars could gather some of the orange, yellow, and red leaves that had fallen to the ground. They could do tracings and learn how to tell maple from oak, beech from sycamore. She would ask the students to do the tracings in the colors of autumn, and when they were complete they would cut them out and post them on the classroom wall—a colorful fall tree.

Smiling at the idea, Emma straightened the old-fashioned wooden desks, set in rows named after flowers, like Rose Road and Lily Lane. She was opening a window when a buggy came down the lane— someone delivering children to school. Was it Gabe?

She held her breath as she squinted to make out the figures in the open carriage. Three heads in white prayer kapps came into view—a mamm with her girls.

It was silly to be disappointed, but now that she had decided to share their secret, she wanted to see him more than ever. She was counting down the days until Sunday, when they would be together at the singing. How wonderful good it would be to sit right beside Gabe, to talk and joke with him all night and not have to pretend interest in what other boys were saying.

Students began coming into the classroom, and she greeted each one by name, then continued gathering supplies. Each child dropped off his or her lunch cooler and then returned to the schoolyard for a few last minutes of play.

"Good morning, Teacher Emma." Before she glanced up, Emma knew it was the cheerful voice of Ruthie King.

Emma greeted her, warmed by Ruthie's bright eyes and joyous smile. When Ruthie smiled, she seemed to glow from head to toe.

"I'm dropping off my lunch, and Simon's, too," Ruthie said, placing two coolers by the potbelly stove. "He's outside playing tag."

Emma gazed out the wide window facing the lane. "Did you get a ride from Gabe?"

"Not this morning. When we saw that it wasn't raining, we decided to walk," Ruthie said, taking a seat at her desk. Ruthie was one of Emma's most social pupils, and it wasn't unusual for her to break away from the other children for a very adult conversation. "And I'm so glad we walked because we ended up walking across a beautiful carpet of leaves. Such a pretty yellow, like golden pears! And when Simon and I walked across them, they stuck to our shoes. For a while we had yellow shoes!"

Emma smiled. "A sure sign that autumn is here." She gestured to the window. "I was just looking at those magnificent trees in the schoolyard, and I thought of a project the whole class might like."

Ruthie's eyes lit with excitement as Emma described the classroom tree. "I hope I can find a maple leaf. They're so fancy, with all the points. When you see them on the ground, they look like a thousand stars."

"Then we will have to find a nice maple," Emma said as she leaned over her large bin of classroom crayons. "Would you like to help me with this? I need to pick out fall colors for the project."

Ruthie joined her at the desk and peered into the box. "Orange, dark red, yellow," she murmured as she plucked each crayon from the box. "How about plum?"

"Plum is good. Keep going. We need twenty-eight." As Emma sat at her desk to fold and cut the papers for the project, she wondered how the Kings' family dinner had gone last night.

Would it be wrong to ask Ruthie? In a few days the girl would know her older brother was dating her teacher. Word would spread quickly. Emma didn't mind smoothing the way . . . and she was hungry even for a crumb about Gabe.

"How was your family dinner last night?" she asked.

"Wonderful good," Ruthie said, her eyes on the crayon box. "Betsy made roasted chicken with pumpkin pie for dessert."

"And how's Gabe? Did he enjoy it?"

Ruthie blinked. "He never made it on account of the accident."

An accident? Buggy accidents happened more often than anyone cared to know, but Emma hadn't heard of any incidents last night. She sat up straighter, instantly alert. "Is he all right?"

"He's going to be fine, but there's a cut on his neck and his shoulder is bruised bad. I was worried sick when I saw that cut, but I put some ointment on it for him."

Emma swallowed hard, tamping down surprise and alarm. "I'm glad it's getting better. How did it happen?"

"A motorbike crash," Ruthie said, shaking her head in disapproval.

A motorbike? Emma's face grew warm as anger swept through her.

"He crashed on one of his friend's motorbikes. It was an Englisher friend who has the bikes. Gabe says he'll be fine, but maybe you should talk to him about it. It's dangerous, and it's against the rules."

"Yes, it's against the Ordnung. I will talk to him about that." Emma strained to keep the anger from her voice. Ruthie was only the messenger; it would be wrong to upset the girl, who had a very clear picture of her brother's wrongdoing.

Children were streaming into the classroom. From the door, John Zook called, "Teacher Emma, can I ring the bell?"

She pressed a hand to her temple as she looked at the clock on the wall. It was time. "Yes, John. Give it a good ring, please."

Ruthie went back to her desk as the children took their assigned seats. Emma strode to the window, composing a letter in her mind. She would send a note home with Ruthie, a letter requesting that he come to the school to discuss an important matter.

Would he think she was talking about Simon or Ruthie? She didn't care if it was misleading. She had to talk to him; she needed to hear his side of this story.

The air blowing in did nothing to cool her hot temper, but she knew that would simmer down when she started teaching. Her scholars deserved a levelheaded, patient teacher, and she would be the teacher they needed.

Even when her heart was burning with anger over Gabe's antics.

A motorbike? How could he?

The next morning Emma waited for him on the schoolhouse porch. Her jaw felt stiff and her eyes were dry and sore. Not enough sleep and too much worry. She hadn't even told Elsie about what happened, knowing that Elsie would be disappointed. Besides, she felt like a fool to have trusted him. He'd lied to her. And he'd chosen a motorbike over her. That hurt.

Gabe King was not a suitable beau. She could not be connected with him and maintain her good reputation as Halfway's Amish schoolteacher.

Her heart ached at the sight of Gabe's buggy. Ruthie sat beside him, and Simon's dark hat bobbed in the back.

He got out of the carriage and she rose from the porch. She tried not to look at the eyes that could melt her heart. She stared down as she invited him into the classroom to chat.

Inside the schoolhouse she went to her desk, wanting the big wooden slab to keep Gabe at a distance.

"Emma?" Gabe's footsteps were heavy behind her. "What's wrong?"

"I heard that you got hurt Sunday." Standing behind her desk, she turned to face him. "In a motorbike accident." She didn't try to hide her disappointment. "A motorbike? Gabe, what are you doing?"

The color drained from his face. He pinched the brim of the hat in his hands. "How did you hear?"

"Ruthie mentioned it, but don't blame her. She's worried about you, Gabe, and I am, too. What are you thinking?"

He lifted one hand to stop her. "Take it easy. It's not the end of the world."

"You told me you had family plans and instead you went out riding motorbikes. How could you do that to me?"

"It's got nothing to do with you, Emma. It's just something Ben and I have been doing for fun."

"It's strictly forbidden, and you know that, Gabe King."

He glanced out the window and shrugged. "You make me feel like a bad student, Emma."

"Gabe, you're breaking the rules."

"Ya, but it's my rumspringa. I'm sowing my wild oats."

"Oats are sown in the soil. You are breaking the rules, and your bike racing has nothing to do with finding an Amish mate, the true purpose of rumspringa. You said it yourself. You're looking for fun, and going against the Order. It's wrong, Gabe."

"I'm not hurting anyone. I'm not breaking the Golden Rule. . . ."

"Ach." Emma sat down and folded her hands on her desk. "Tell that to Bishop Samuel."

"Why would I do that?"

Frustrated, she stared up at him. "So that you can ask for forgiveness."

Gabe shook his head. "I'm not ready to do that."

"But you must!"

"Don't ruin this for me, Emma." His eyes flashed, as if she was trying to hurt him. "It's the best thing that's happened to me in a long time."

"But . . ."

I thought I was the best thing that ever happened to you. She couldn't bring herself to say the words because now she knew how wrong she'd been.

She wasn't the most wondrous thing in Gabe's life.

He was in love with a motorbike.

"Don't you see?" she whispered, wary of children listening in from the schoolyard. "I can't court you if you're going to go off riding motorbikes."

"Emma . . ." Gabe's amber eyes were heavy with sorrow. "I'm not one of your scholars. I don't have to follow your rules. I have to do what's right for me." He shook his head. "I thought you'd understand."

Tears stung her eyes. She had always told him that he could tell her the truth. She had wanted him to feel free to share his sorrows and grief over his parents. But she had never expected this.

"You'd better go. It's time for the children to come in."

He nodded, then turned away.

Emma dashed away her tears so that she could watch him, black hat, broad shoulders, and long legs, a dark profile of the man she loved, walking out of her life. This couldn't be happening! She bit her lower lip, crushed by the thought of all the hope and joy and love going out that door with him.

TWENTY-FIVE

*I*t just doesn't seem right," Jonah said. "I'm here day after day, living a lie, and I never lied in the first place."

The Stoltzfus sheep blinked up at him, tucked its pointed chin, and chortled, "Mihihi." Sitting on its backside so that Jonah could take a look at its hoof, the sheep looked very human. A little bit like Bishop Samuel, but without the eyeglasses.

Was that why Jonah was telling the creature his problems? Or was he verhuddelt from walking around with this tangle of guilt and confusion inside?

"I need to clear my head," he told the sheep as he trimmed the hornlike nail that grew on the outer edges of the pad. Sheep were well-known for being prone to suffer from foot problems, and this fella had been limping around. "I can't keep this up."

The sheep bleated an answer and tried to scramble away.

"Hold on. You're not getting out of this so easy."

And neither would Jonah.

He had to tell Annie and Hannah the truth. He had never meant for anyone to think that he favored Hannah in the first place. That part had been a misunderstanding. And he'd fully intended to straighten things out with the truth, but everyone on the Stoltzfus farm had been on edge last week with the Fishers leaving for New York. Now, here it was Wednesday, and he was still tethered to Hannah—at least, in Annie's mind he was.

"What can I do?" he asked the sheep as he trimmed the ingrown ridge of nail. He had thought about asking Aaron if he could do without his help, but there were more chores here than any one man could handle. And today, when he had helped Aaron move some hay bales, the older man had complained that he was under the weather.

"Something's not sitting so good in there," Aaron had said, pressing a fist to his chest. "Indigestion. It happens whenever Hannah cooks the noon meal."

"Do you need an antacid?" Jonah had asked.

"Nay. I'd like a rest, but what can you do? Harvest is a busy time."

A very busy time. As Jonah cranked the winch to stack the bale high in the loft, he knew for certain that he would have to stay on here for a good while, even if Annie and Hannah soured on him when they learned the truth.

"And the truth shall set you free," Jonah said aloud as he brushed the hoof clean and took one last look.

The sheep's eyes softened. He seemed to be thinking over the words of scripture. Mmm. A good Amish sheep.

The high-pitched laugh of a child came to him on the wind, and he looked toward the outbuildings. Annie and Sunny were walking toward the sheep pens, Annie with a baby bottle in her hand. Levi was running in crazy circles, scrambling after the orphaned lamb that kept darting out of his reach. It was feeding time for the bummer lamb.

Annie said something he couldn't make out as she held up the bottle. That got the lamb's attention. It leaped in her direction, nearly collapsing as it landed on its spindly legs.

"And what am I supposed to do now?" Jonah asked the big sheep. "I have to return these clippers to that shed, right there where they're sitting."

The sheep gave a spastic shake.

"Ya, you're right. I could do that later, but I don't mind seeing Levi." He released the sheep, and the creature immediately scrambled to its feet and loped away, pausing only once to look back in scorn.

"Go." Jonah got to his feet, brushing grass from his pants. "Find green pastures." In truth, there wasn't much green grass left—mostly fields of gold and brown. Soon the sheep and cattle would need special feed to get them through the winter.

By the time Jonah came upon Annie and Levi, the boy was seated with the orphaned lamb in his lap. Sunny had scurried off to the edge of the fence to bark at a group of sheep, no doubt keeping them in line.

"Your lamb has taken to the bottle," Jonah said.

"She likes it!" Levi moved the bottle and the lamb's muzzle followed, sucking contentedly. "And she has a name now! We call her Fluffy."

"Ya?" Jonah rubbed his chin. "Some people don't name their sheep. They don't want the children to get too attached when . . ." Many sheep farmers, Amish and English alike, slaughtered their herds before the sheep were a year old. He turned to Annie. "Tell me you raise these sheep for their wool."

"Is that what you're getting at? Ya, we take their wool, and Dat sells some of them off." She patted the lamb in Levi's arms. "But he'll make an exception for little Fluffy."

"Gut." He lifted one side of his mouth in a half smile. "I'll sleep better tonight, knowing that."

She rolled her eyes, a gesture that tugged at his heart. It amazed him how Annie could be womanly and girlish at the same time. "You mean an experienced farmer like you would worry about one little lamb?"

"I work the land, but on our farm we never took a life. Dat believed in sharing the land with all Gott's creatures. He passed those ways on to all of us."

"I remember that about your dat," Annie said. "All those bird-houses he used to build. He would make sure they had seed in the winter. And he didn't believe in hunting, did he?"

Jonah nodded. He missed his parents, but he was glad to remember them by the good they had done in their lives instead of the terrible way they had died.

He went into the shed to return the clippers and get a rake. When he came out, the lamb was scrabbling to be released.

"Fluffy! Settle down," Levi ordered.

"Fluffy wants to run," Jonah said. "She's done with her milk. See?"

Levi noticed the empty bottle. "Oh." He helped the lamb onto the ground and she bowed at his feet, then circled around as if chasing her tail.

"Fluffy thinks she's a dog," Jonah observed as he started raking the pen.

Annie and Jonah laughed as Levi tried to pet her and she slipped away. The lamb seemed to enjoy playing tag.

"Levi's so good with her." Annie leaned on a post near Jonah. "And you're good with Levi. He likes having you around, Jonah. He's told me that."

"I've been thinking, it might be good to bring Sam around some-time when I'm working here. He and Levi could play together."

"That would be wonderful good," Annie said. "Levi misses Mark. Do you think Sam would like to help with Fluffy?"

"If Sam spends five minutes with Fluffy, he will be begging us to get some sheep on the farm."

Annie sighed. "You know the little ones well. Someday, you'll make a very good father."

He stopped raking, caught by her comment. Looking down into her sparkling blue eyes, he wanted to remember this moment in time. Annie could see him as a father . . . that lightened the weight on his shoulders.

"Hannah is blessed to have found you."

The hope that had been sizzling inside him now sputtered and went cold. He went back to raking. "Annie, we need to talk about that."

"No." She held up her hands. "You and Hannah need to talk. I don't want to butt in. But I will say I'm glad you're spending a lot more time here with us. It's been good for everyone. You've become a good friend, Jonah."

She wouldn't feel that way when he told her the truth. "Annie . . . I'm not coming here for Hannah."

"I know that. You're working for Dat, and we all appreciate that. He's feeling the burden of the farm right now, with Perry gone."

Jonah wiped the sweat from his brow. It wasn't a hot day, but the strain of trying to cut through to the truth was more work than any farm chore.

Stop raking and tell her. "I don't favor your sister. I favor you."

Why couldn't he wrench those words from his throat?

Because he didn't want to end this moment with Annie. Because he wanted to be her friend . . . and her beau, too. His time here on the farm had changed some things for the better. Now he didn't worry so much about talking to girls. He could find plenty to say to Hannah or Annie without his face heating up and his tongue getting twisted in his mouth.

He continued cleaning the pen. "Have you gotten word on how the Fishers are doing up there?"

"Sarah called from town! She called the tea shop, and Mamm

talked with her. They're settling in. Perry's cousin is putting them up in a little cottage on his dairy farm. She said it's very cozy. And Gideon has twins who are around Mark's age. Isn't that perfect? Gott has truly blessed them."

"He has." He didn't look up from his work as he asked, "And what about you, Annie? Are you still thinking of joining them in New York?" The words were tight in his throat, and he prayed that she would answer no.

"How did you know that?"

"My hearing works just fine . . . and you've made it no secret."

"It scares me to think of leaving my home. Not just my family, but everyone here. Halfway is all I've ever known, and I'm happy here." She leaned onto the post, watching him closely. "Do you ever think about leaving?"

"No. Halfway is where I belong." His family, this land, this community . . . He lived and breathed this small parcel of Lancaster County. Gott wanted him here; he was sure of that.

"I feel that way, too, except when I go to the singings and have a look around. While I was waiting on your brother, all the men my age found wives. There are no single men left!"

She said it as a joke, but it stung.

There's a single man who's waited for you all his life, he wanted to say. *A man who loves everything about you.*

But the words were locked inside, too delicate to wrench out. He spread fresh hay in the pen, angry with himself for shutting down.

"That's why I'm so torn," she added. "I feel like I belong here, but I know that Gott wants me to have a family. So what can I do? If I'm to have a family, I'll have to go somewhere else to find a husband. And that breaks my heart."

Mine, too, Jonah wanted to say. That would make two broken hearts.

TWENTY-SIX

*T*hat's it. Keep twisting," Gabe said.

Gabe stepped back from the fence as his younger brother used a set of pliers to twist the wires around, creating a braid that would hold. They were in the back acres, repairing a hole in the fence, and once Gabe had shown Simon how to attach the wires, his brother had stepped up to give it a try. It was Simon's first time mending a fence, but he was getting the hang of it.

Cold air was setting in over the land, and clouds of mist rolled in over the hills. Puffs of steam came from the nostrils of the waiting horses. Gabe tucked the spool of wire into his saddlebag and looked over the east hills, toward the town. They were too far away to see the town or any of the houses, but he knew that Emma's home was in that direction, on the outskirts of town.

Emma was there right now, probably grading papers or helping Fanny prepare dinner. He imagined her in the kitchen, punching dough. All the anger she had toward him now could go right into that fat wad of dough.

Or maybe it was worse than that. Maybe she didn't even care enough to be mad. She might have decided that a proper schoolteacher like her could never be seen courting a man like him. Someone who dared to break the rules.

He patted Mercury's withers, thinking that people should be as loyal as horses were. Emma had said that he could tell her anything. Her big beautiful eyes had never blinked when he'd talked to her about his parents' murders. She had understood his resentment toward Adam coming home to be the boss, and she had always listened when he told her stories about "the big girls," the cows that Gabe cared for and knew so well.

But Emma didn't want to hear about how it felt to ride a motorbike. All at once, her heart and mind had closed to Gabe. Just like that.

And he decided that he would do the same. He knew how to curl up inside himself like a beaver settled in to hibernate for the winter. He could dig into the mud and never, ever trust anyone again. That was fine with him.

"How's that?" Simon asked, stepping back.

Gabe leaned in for a closer look. Simon had twisted the wire into a nice, tight braid. "That'll hold it. Good work, Simon. Now you know how to do it."

From the way Simon stood tall, with his head up, Gabe could tell that his brother felt good about learning the task.

"Now I can fix the fence anytime the cows push it loose," said Simon.

"You can fix the wire part," Gabe said. "The fence posts—that part takes a little more time to learn." Gabe pushed against the post. It was solid and secure, but there were miles of fence around their farm. "I hope we don't need to replace any of the posts until spring. It's hard to dig in frozen dirt."

"Any more fixing you need?" Simon asked, holding up the pliers.

"We're done for today. It's time to head back."

Simon tucked the pliers in with the other tools in the saddlebag, then called to his horse. Shadow didn't come like a dog, but her ears perked up, and she lifted her head to eyeball Simon. The boy walked over to her and took the reins. "Hold still now." The horse stood like a statue as Simon put one foot in the stirrup and swung his small body high into the saddle.

"You've trained her well," Gabe said.

Simon nodded. "She's a smart horse."

As Gabe got on his own horse, he hid a smile. Sometimes Simon echoed things their dat used to say. He looked over at his brother. "Do you want to race?"

A mischievous look crossed Simon's face. "I'm just warning you, Shadow is fast."

Gabe nodded. "We'll see who gets to the barn first. Are you ready?"

Simon counted down, and they were off. At once they urged their horses ahead, pressing them to gallop over the damp grasses. The world sped past him below as Gabe's senses became alert to the pounding of Mercury's hooves, the rush of cool air on his skin, and the beating of his own heart. Gabe laughed out loud. He hadn't done this with his brothers for years!

His horse was ahead, but when he rose over the last hill and caught sight of the barn and the smaller outbuildings, he slowed Mercury, just in case someone was watching.

At that moment, Shadow pounded past him in a thundering blast. Gabe groaned, hating to lose, though he didn't mind giving Simon the sweet taste of victory.

His younger brother was waiting outside the barn. He had jumped down from the horse, and he stood beside Shadow, casually leaning against her withers and talking quietly. Simon looked up at him and grinned. "What took you so long?"

Gabe laughed. "You won, fair and square. But next time, I will show you what my horse can do when I let her."

"That was fun," Simon said as they led their horses into the barn. "I love galloping fast."

Gabe recognized the look in his younger brother's eyes. *The need for speed.* "Galloping can be exciting," he told Simon. "But it's nothing compared to racing motorbikes."

"Motorbikes?" Simon pushed his hat back on his head. "I've never done that."

"I have, and I can tell you, a motorbike is ten times more exciting than a horse."

Simon's eyes opened wide in an expression of wonder. "Where did you get the motorbike?" He turned toward the barn. "Is it here, in the shed?"

Gabe explained that he had only borrowed a bike from an English friend who had many.

Staring at him in awe, Simon rattled off a dozen questions. "Does it steer like a horse? Does it start with a key, like a car? Do you put gasoline into it? Is it hard to balance?"

As they unsaddled their horses, Gabe answered Simon's questions, glad to be talking about motorbikes with someone who understood the thrill.

"Can I come along and ride a motorbike, too?" Simon asked.

"No. It's too dangerous."

"But you're doing it."

"I'm older, and bigger, too. Your feet probably wouldn't reach the pedals."

"Folks said I was too small to ride a horse, but Dat let me do it," Simon pointed out.

"Simon, you can't do it now. You're too young, and it's forbidden by the Ordnung. Adam would never allow it, and he's in charge now."

Simon was quiet a moment. "But you're doing it," he said slowly.

"I'm older, and I'm in rumspringa. When you get to be my age, then you can ride a motorbike."

Simon frowned. "Okay. But can we still race horses?"

"Ya, we can race. But don't tell anyone about that—or about the motorbikes. If the bishop hears about it, he'll ride right over to give me a talking-to, just like the ministers did with Sadie."

Gabe still remembered how the ministers had come to their house to scold their sister Sadie, who had been caught singing in bars. The bishop had told her to stop being of this world and return to the Plain ways, but no amount of scolding could fix the unzufriede, the discontent she felt in her heart. That was probably why she was now many miles away, living among the Englishers.

"I miss Sadie. Are you going to go away and live with the Englishers, too?" Simon asked as he brushed down his horse.

"No." That was one thing Gabe was sure of. He didn't want a life away from the land and the animals he loved. Living on an Amish farm kept a body going. From what he'd seen of cars and televisions, he liked them just fine, but they took a person away from the important chores of life. He knew he would get antsy sitting in front of a picture screen all day long, just watching other people live. Englisher life wasn't for him.

Gabe knew that someday he would choose to get baptized. Amish was the only way he knew to live, and it suited him just fine. But he wasn't ready for that yet. And right now he couldn't change who he was. He was in rumspringa, and he'd found an adventure right here at home—a sport that challenged his balance and skills.

Ya, when he was on a speeding bike he felt like a man.

And he wished Emma could understand that. The last few days he had missed her. He wanted to court her, but she was the one who had broken it off.

All over a motorbike.

He would have galloped into a fire to save her, but with this demand she wanted too much from him. Right now, riding bikes was the one thing that made him feel powerful and independent. There was no way he would give this sport up for a girl.

TWENTY–SEVEN

*S*aturday morning, as soon as the milking was done, Jonah and Adam went to the barn to have a look. Working together, the two men pulled open one of the wide red doors and stepped into the shadowed space.

"We'll move most of the animals out," Adam said. "The children will sweep up. Uncle Nate is bringing the church wagon, and Abe and Ben will cart over the propane heater in case the weather turns."

So far the day had dawned sunny and cool, but dark clouds over the hills were headed their way. Jonah hoped they could get the benches loaded into the barn before the rain started.

"Mary has had the girls cleaning house for days already. And somebody's got to mow that lawn out front." Adam pushed his jacket back and put his hands on his hips, looking solid and strong. "What do you think?" he asked Jonah.

"I think we'd better eat a big breakfast," Jonah teased, "because we have a big chore ahead of us."

Adam clapped a hand on his shoulder as they headed toward the house. "A big chore, but we do it every year."

"And deep inside, I like it," Jonah admitted. "But don't tell anyone. They'll think I'm verhuddelt."

Jonah didn't mind when it was their turn to host. The duty fell on each family in the district every year or so, and Jonah always enjoyed the days of preparation. The house got a scrubbing from top to bottom. Windows were washed till they gleamed. Walls and floors were washed. The yard would be clipped and trimmed, and the women had already started cooking and baking enough to feed lunch to the entire district.

It was a mountainous task, but every year it brought the family together. That was the part Jonah liked most—everyone in the family pitching in.

Inside the kitchen, Remy stood at the counter slicing apples while Mary placed a platter of eggs on the table.

Adam sneaked up behind Remy. "If you're here for your baptism, you've come a day too early," he said.

She flinched, then swung toward him, a challenge in her green eyes. "You should know better, Adam King. Never sneak up on a woman with a knife in her hands."

Adam put a hand on her shoulder. "Especially an English woman who has watched horror movies."

"I'm not an English woman anymore," Remy said. "Or at least, after tomorrow I won't be. And I won't miss horror flicks either."

"So you've come to help us set up?" Jonah asked her.

"Of course! I want to know the inside skinny, all the dos and don'ts. I need to learn this stuff, right? We'll be doing the same thing next year." She sprinkled sugary crumbles over the apple slices, then popped the dish into the oven. "I can help until lunchtime, then I have to go into town for a meeting with

Deacon Moses. It's our last class—the wrap-up session before baptism."

Jonah remembered that last class. *This is your last chance to turn back,* the deacon had warned. The ministers made it clear that it was better to back out than to make a vow and later break it.

Jonah hung his hat on a hook, washed his hands, then took a seat at the far end of the table as the family assembled for breakfast. Susie helped Katie into a chair. Adam had stored the high chair in the shed ever since two-year-old Katie started climbing out of it on her own.

Remy took her place at Adam's right hand. From the far end of the table, Jonah observed the look that passed between Adam and his fiancée—a solid, steady love. Not the quick flame of attraction two people might feel at a singing, when people were cleaned up and having a good time. This was the kind of bond that would make it through hot summer days and long winter nights, through sorrow and joy.

Adam and Remy were a good match. He felt sure that they would be sitting together at that end of the table for the rest of their lives.

And where would Jonah be?

He knew he would always be welcome at this table, in this house, but a good Amish man was expected to find a wife and start a home of his own.

As everyone bowed their heads for a silent prayer of thanks before the meal, Jonah closed his eyes and tried to open his heart to Gott's plan for him. In these past weeks he had believed he was getting closer to Annie, but he'd been wrong. What would it take for him to simply accept that it wasn't his time?

Disappointment had darkened his mood for a while, but when he woke up this morning he'd cast it away like a snake in the grass. If he clung to bitterness, he would only become a bitter man, and that wouldn't do anyone any good.

To everything there is a season, and a time for every purpose under heaven. Autumn was not going to be his season to win over Annie's love. Apparently winter, spring, and summer hadn't worked that way either, but he couldn't complain. He would trust in Gott the Father . . . trust and pray that he wouldn't end up at this table in thirty years, old man Jonah who'd never found a wife.

As soon as the prayer ended, Adam began assigning tasks for the day. Ruthie and Simon would sweep the barn while Gabe moved the animals outside. All the men would meet Uncle Nate when he arrived with the bench wagon, and they would load the benches into the barn before setting up tables in the house. Susie and Leah would help Mary clean the walls and floors, then attend to the windows.

"Ben said that most of their family is coming to help," Gabe reminded Adam. "And Ruben Zook said they'd be here, too."

In past years, the Zook family, their closest Amish neighbors, had come around to help prepare the house for church.

"This is going to be a very special church service because *you're* getting baptized, Remy," Ruthie said.

"And then you'll be Amish?" Simon asked.

"She'll be a member of our community," Adam said.

"And Teacher Emma," Ruthie said brightly. "She's getting baptized, too."

And Hannah Stoltzfus, Jonah thought. Annie must have reminded him of that at least thirty times in the past week. He knew the hidden meaning: Hannah, or any girl who got baptized, became an adult member of the community. That meant she would be ready to marry and start a family. Only a man with a brain of wood could miss Annie's hint.

"What about your dress?" Susie asked Remy. "Is it ready for tomorrow?"

Remy nodded. "It's hanging on a hook in my room." She smiled across the table. "Denki for letting me borrow it, Mary."

"We'll keep it in the family," Mary said. "I'm not sure Sadie will be using it, but it should fit the other girls when the time comes."

"And if Susie and I get baptized in the same year?" Leah asked. "Who gets to wear the black dress?"

"You'll each get half of it." Mary cocked one eyebrow, but she didn't crack a smile. "Which half would you like, Leah? The front or back?"

Leah and Susie looked at each other, then burst out laughing.

"When the time comes, we'll have to make another dress, Mary," Susie said. "Half a dress would be very drafty."

The family joined in their laughter. All breakfasts weren't so spirited, but everyone seemed to share the excitement of tomorrow's big event. At least, everyone but Gabe. He had been distant lately, more quiet than usual, and Jonah had noticed that his brother did not look him in the eye. Something was going on with Gabe, and Jonah suspected it involved a girl. Jonah wasn't able to help his brother on that one; that was one skill he didn't carry in his toolbox.

As Jonah helped himself to a second baked egg, he was grateful for the banter that went on during the King family meals. If he did end up lingering at this table as an old man, at least he could look forward to lively conversation.

Jonah was finishing his second helping when the sound of a horse and carriage came from the lane. Simon popped up from the table and ran to the window.

"The church wagon is here!" he exclaimed. "And Ruthie and I haven't swept the barn yet!"

"All in good time," Jonah said, wiping his mouth with a napkin. "It will all get done."

Adam gestured Simon to come back to the table. "Sit. Say a prayer of thanks, and then you can run and greet Uncle Nate."

Outside, Nate was backing the church wagon up to the open barn doors with a precision born of practice and a well-trained horse. Sam was jumping up and down with excitement, and Katie copied her older brother, matching him jump for jump. A grin tugged at one corner of Jonah's lips. It was good to see these young children enjoying life again.

A gray carriage had arrived behind Nate, and the rest of his family climbed out. Betsy and her daughters Rachel and Rose carried baked goods straight to the kitchen, while Ben and Abe came around to flank their father.

"What have we here?" Hands on hips, Nate looked down at the children. "All this hopping around, I thought I was looking at popping corn."

"We're not popcorn!" Sam rolled his eyes.

"Not popcorn," Katie echoed.

"We want to see the benches," Sam said, running along the flat black side of the windowless wagon. "Are they inside the wagon?"

"I certainly hope so." Nate pushed his hat back to rub his brow. "Or else I'm going to have to go all the way back and get them!"

All the men pitched in to unload the benches and line them up in two separate sections inside the newly swept barn. The children wanted to help with the benches, and Jonah let them hold on to the sides a few times before sending them out to the yard to help Remy with the cleanup. While they were setting up, Dave and Joseph Zook arrived to lend a hand. One minute they were taking the first bench out of the wagon, the next there were two well-formed sections set up in the barn. *Many hands make chores go fast,* Jonah's mamm used to say.

As people moved in and out of the barn, Jonah listened for the patter of another carriage—Annie's carriage. Mary had mentioned that her friend was coming, and the thought of having Annie here on the farm magnified his joy of the day. He sincerely hoped she did not bring Hannah, but it would be good to see her here, in his familiar territory, in his world.

With the barn nearly finished, Jonah passed through the wide doorway, paused in the brisk, damp air, and listened. No sign of Annie's carriage yet.

Tipping his hat back, he scanned the yard and saw three figures down on the lawn. He recognized Simon and Ruthie moving along the far reaches of the yard, trimming along the fence line with gas-powered weed trimmers.

At the base of the hill Remy wrestled with the reel mower. It looked like she was wiggling the long handle more than pushing it over the grass, which wasn't getting cut. In a fit of consternation, she put her hands on her hips and stared at the mower as if it were a stubborn mule. Glancing up, she noticed Jonah on the ridge by the barn and waved him over.

He jogged down to her, mildly amused by her enthusiastic waving.

"I'm having a battle with this lawn mower, and so far the mower is winning." She gritted her teeth and gave a push, but the wheels turned only a few inches. "Who decided that it was women's work to mow the lawn?" she asked.

"I don't know the answer to that, but it was probably a wise Amish man," he teased.

"Exactly. I don't mean to wimp out, but I have to leave soon and I've gotten nothing done."

He stepped up and gave it a push. The mower squeaked, but it barely budged. "Ya, there's something wrong there." He squatted over the blades and gave it a quick assessment. "The wheels aren't turning properly. Let me sharpen the blades and add some oil to the wheels," he said, dragging it toward the toolshed.

"Denki. At the rate I was going, I wouldn't have finished the job until after Christmas."

Jonah was turned away from Remy, so he let himself smile. Had she always had this sense of humor, or had she been influenced by her time among the Amish?

"And that's another question," Remy said, struggling to keep pace with Jonah's long strides. "If the use of gas-powered mowers is forbidden, why are those screaming weed trimmers allowed?"

Jonah shot a look at Simon, who aimed the machine at tall weeds near a fence post. "Again, I have no answer for you. You're learning the riddle of Amish ways. The reason behind rules is not always logical or obvious. We follow rules because they are rules."

"I've got that part down," she said. "Rules are the real deal in the Amish world. I think I've managed to navigate the big rules. I'm good with the Ordnung. My big problem is the Pennsylvania Deutsch dialect."

"They say it's hard to understand if you didn't grow up with it."

"And I've studied the baptismal ceremony. If there was an exam on it, I'd ace it. But I'm still a little nervous about the baptism tomorrow."

Jonah turned to face her. "Not that I'm unsure," she said firmly. "I just don't want to goof up and announce myself as an outsider during the service."

He pursed his lips. In some ways, Remy McCallister would always be an outsider. Her fiery red hair announced it immediately. Then, once you spoke with her, any Amish person could tell she was Englisher by her choice of words and her attitudes. Within a minute or two of meeting her, most folk would know she wasn't raised Amish.

Still, he had to admit that Remy was a special person. She had jumped into this new life, taking on duties and chores that would send most Englishers running.

"Don't fret over the baptism," he said. "If you don't have the right words in German, speak English. Gott understands all languages."

Remy cocked her head, her eyes wide with wonder. "What a beautiful thing to say."

"Ya. And it's true, too."

"You are a man of few words, but they're well chosen."

"And you've come a long way from the girl who tried to milk a cow in my sister's nightgown."

She blinked. "Thank you, Jonah. It's nice to get an 'attagirl' now and then."

He nodded. "Attagirl."

TWENTY-EIGHT

*A*lthough it was cold and rainy outside, the carriage was warm from the loaves of bread in the back, some just out of the oven. Annie had started baking before breakfast, having promised Mary that she would contribute fresh-baked bread for tomorrow's church meal at the Kings'.

As Annie directed the horse down the lane toward the Kings' farm, she sensed something different about this visit. Was it her? She no longer felt the heavy cloak of dread on her shoulders at the thought of seeing Adam. Since Remy's mistake at the last church meal, Annie's attitude toward the Englisher girl had softened. If Gott intended Adam to marry someone else, at least that someone was a very nice girl.

She slowed the horse as they approached the farmhouse and barn, which were both buzzing with people, like bees on a busy hive. Annie pulled up beside a row of horseless carriages and hopped down to the ground.

Simon came running out of the barn, holding his hat against the wind. "Do you want me to unhitch your horse?" he asked.

"That would be good, but first, will you help me carry bread inside?"

"Sure. How much you got?"

When she told him there were eight loaves, he dashed back to the barn and returned with his brother Sam. Annie's heart melted at the sight of the little boy who trudged through the mud. He was a small version of his big brothers! Sam had grown so much since the last time Annie had visited with the family.

"Mind you don't drop them." Annie leaned down to place two foil-wrapped loaves in Sam's arms.

"I can do it," Sam said.

"Good." When she turned back to the carriage, Simon already had the heavy basket of warm bread in his arms.

"Smells good," he said.

"That batch is still cooling. Let's go right into the kitchen." Annie followed the boys in, amused at the way Sam walked slowly under the weight of the precious bread.

Even from the mud porch, Annie could hear the sounds of activity. Inside she found Mary sliding a tray into the oven. Remy washed dishes in the sink. Betsy King was rolling out dough at the kitchen table.

"We have bread!" Sam announced.

"Look at that! We'll need it for sandwiches," Remy said, with a friendly nod for Annie.

"Where do you want me to put this?" Simon asked.

"On the table." Annie patted a spot at the far end of the table. Simon hoisted up the heavy basket, then went off to tend to Annie's horse.

Mary clapped two oven mitts together and smiled in relief. "Denki, Annie. I knew I could count on you."

Annie squeezed her friend's arm. "You know I enjoy baking."

Sam climbed onto a chair, his curious gaze on the dough. "Are you making gmay cookies?" he asked Betsy with obvious interest. Gmay cookies, sometimes called church cookies, were a favorite among children. Platters of the cookies were handed out to little ones halfway through the service, and the rest were served to everyone at the meal afterward.

"Ya. Do you want to help?" When he nodded, she sent him off to wash his hands.

"What can I do to help?" Annie asked. "Anything you need, Mary. I saw Leah and Susie outside washing windows. Your house will be clean as a whistle when everyone is done."

"The house is good, but I'm worried about the barn. The children got a late start on the sweeping. Would you mind checking that it's fit for church?"

"I'll go along, if you don't mind." Remy wiped her hands on a dish towel. "I'm curious to see how everything will be set up for the baptism."

"Then we'll go check the barn together," Annie said.

Just then the porch door opened without warning and men began to stream in.

Jonah was in the lead, his dark eyes cool and confident. His sleeves were rolled up and he wore a black vest. Annie smiled a greeting, then stood back out of the way. He nodded, eyes narrowed as if he hadn't expected to see her here. Granted, she wasn't family, but Mary was her best friend, and how could one so young prepare a house for church without every friend and family member pitching in?

Jonah pointed to the daybed in the corner of the kitchen, and three men hoisted it off the floor and whisked it out the door.

"What's going on?" Remy asked, and Annie remembered that this would be the first church service she had seen in the King house.

"They're preparing the house for church," Annie said. "Or at least for the lunch after church."

"Ya." Mary kept her eyes on her chopping. "Church will be in the barn, but we can't trust this weather for the meal. The men will take down the wall and we'll set up tables in here."

"Hosting is such a major endeavor," Remy said, smiling as Adam traipsed through the kitchen with the rest of the men.

As Adam smiled back at his fiancée, Annie braced herself for the familiar sting of jealousy . . . but the glum feeling never came.

Instead she felt happy for them. Annie could see that Gott meant Adam and Remy to be together.

"This is all really amazing, when you think about it," Remy went on. "To think that every other week, a family goes through all of these preparations? From now on, I'll appreciate church a little more knowing all the work that's required to pull it off."

"At least the hosting only comes around once a year," Mary said.

While the women discussed the duty of hosting, Annie peeked into the living room. She was intrigued to see Jonah in charge. He knew what furniture had to be moved first, how to angle the pieces out the door, and where to store it. Adam, Nate, and a handful of other men and teenaged boys pitched in, but Jonah was clearly the boss.

Hannah should be here to see this, Annie thought. With his reputation for being the Quiet One, no one expected Jonah to be a leader. But here he was, the man in charge of church preparations. This was a side of Jonah that Annie wanted her sister to see.

"Should we head out to the barn?" Remy asked. There was such gentleness about her that Annie wondered how she could have ever felt cold toward this young woman.

"Ya." Annie headed toward the door, stopping to pat little Sam on the back and tell him what a good job he was doing. Jonah had been right; he and Levi would probably enjoy spending time together while Jonah was working at their farm.

Outside the rain was coming down harder now, dark lines slashing through the air. Annie and Remy gathered the skirts of their dresses and ran all the way to the barn. They arrived at the big barn doors, where they paused to wipe the rain from their faces and take in the sight.

"It's been transformed." Remy pressed her fingertips to her lips, awed by the sight.

Annie had seen many barns and homes set up for church, but something about the stillness of the Kings' barn amid the rustling storm made it seem like a blessed place. The gray day brought little sunlight into the barn, but the single kerosene lamp that hung from a pillar cast a golden light over the rows of wooden benches.

"I've never seen the barn so clean," Remy said.

"Ya, someone did a good job sweeping. And the benches are in nice, neat rows. Mary's got nothing to worry about here." Annie pointed to the section of benches on the left. "The men always sit on the left, and they can hang their hats on the granary there. Those two rows in the middle will be for you and Hannah and all the other young folk ready to be baptized."

"I can't believe it's really happening tomorrow." Remy walked up the aisle and paused at one of the center benches, lost in thought.

Annie followed her, wondering what could be going through this English girl's mind the day before her baptism. "Are you nervous about tomorrow?" she asked.

"A little," Remy admitted. "I'm very secure in my decision. This is where I want to be, and I'm committed to living Amish. But there's always the worry that I'll do the wrong thing at the wrong time. I had a nightmare that Bishop Samuel was speaking a language I didn't understand at all. It was Portuguese or Italian or something."

Annie laughed, amused by the thought of their bishop speaking a foreign language. "I don't mean to make light of your worry, but that is funny."

Remy sank down on the bench. "I can laugh now, but it was pretty scary in the dream."

"I think it would scare me, too." Annie took a seat on the bench facing Remy. "But you're a brave girl. You have to be, coming here from the big city and taking on the ways of Plain folk." Annie thought of her sister Sarah, moving to a very different Old Order district in New York. Sarah had her husband and child for comfort, but Remy had landed here alone—with no one.

"You came here on your own," Annie said. "That was a brave thing to do."

"Not so brave, really. I came here for my work." Remy shrugged. "I had no idea that I would end up staying forever."

"Gott's plan often surprises us," Annie said. "And do you know how unusual it is for an Englisher to join the Amish community?"

"I know that now," Remy said. "I didn't know it when I made my decision to become Amish."

"It must have taken a lot of courage to convince the ministers that you truly wanted to join us. They don't usually take to Englishers who are interested in our ways. A lot of times they turn Seekers away. They tell them to live Plain on their own and follow the Golden Rule, to be kind to others, treat people the way you would want to be treated. The Amish aren't looking to bring Englishers into the community."

"It's a good thing I charged ahead like a crazy bull," Remy said. "Bishop Samuel kept giving me that look he has, with those bushy eyebrows and concerned eyes, but I didn't back off. That look said I was one pebble short of a rock collection. But there was no stopping me when I made the decision to join the church."

Annie had seen that look from the bishop and it frightened her.

"Thank goodness the bishop is a very wise man. I think he could tell that I was ready for this. This family. This way of life." She leaned back and looked up toward the rafters. "This faith. But if you had told me a year ago that tomorrow I would be baptized into the Amish faith, that I would promise to spend the rest of my life living Plain, I would have said you were crazy. Verhuddelt!"

"But . . . here you are," Annie said brightly.

"Here I am, and I couldn't be happier. I've found a home here. Ironically, I stick out like a sore thumb in the place where I belong in the world, but I'm very happy." Remy touched the string of her prayer kapp. "Gott had this wonderful plan for me . . . a life more awesome than I could have ever imagined. A big family, a home, and so much to do! My days used to be so empty, but now they're full of love and laughter." Remy spread her arms in a burst of enthusiasm. "I know it sounds corny, but it's true. God did an Extreme Makeover of my life. The Amish Edition."

Annie didn't get that last part, but she did see the big picture. She saw it clearly now. Gott had brought Remy here to make her life whole, even as her marriage to Adam would make the King family whole again. Only the Heavenly Father in His great wisdom knew how to heal so many lives so completely.

In comparison, Annie's broken heart seemed to be a very small matter. Small as the birds fluttering and cooing in the rafters. Annie let her eyes go soft in the golden light, and the neat rows of benches resembled a ladder. *Jacob's ladder to heaven,* she thought.

Remy rose, hugging herself as she looked around. "They did a great job lining up all these benches."

"I was just thinking the same thing. But there's one problem." Annie wagged a finger at the wall of alfalfa bales that backed up to the benches on the women's side. "Those bales there."

Remy looked up to the top of the tall stack. "Are you afraid they'll fall?"

"No, they're not going anywhere. But the alfalfa is scratchy and rough. Folks will brush past it. You know, a person could get cut from the stubble. Or splinters." Annie walked to the end of the row, thinking of what to do. "We need to cover it."

Hands on her hips, Remy asked, "How do we do that?"

"Let's talk to Jonah," Annie said. With all the time they'd spent together at her family's farm, Annie was more comfortable talking with him than Adam, and he was good at solving problems.

Outside the rain had stopped but the sky was the steely gray of evening. A line of men trudged from the house to the woodshop, each man carrying a rocking chair on his head. Annie was reminded of ants, bearing loads twice their size as they filed toward the nest. Jonah led the line.

Remy started to follow them into the woodshop, but Annie stopped her with a gentle hand on her arm. "We'll wait until they come out," she said. Once again she realized that Remy still didn't know all the ways of the Amish. Women didn't mix with men in all situations, and while men breezed into a place without knocking, most women gave a knock before entering. Such simple ways, though Annie could see how it would be hard to learn a lifetime of small traditions in a few months.

Jonah immediately stepped out; he must have seen them coming. "Are you looking for me?" He held on to the wooden door cautiously, and Annie felt the urge to tease him that they wouldn't bite.

"I'm wondering about those bales of alfalfa near the women's section," Annie said. Jonah nodded with understanding as she explained how they were too rough to leave exposed. "Do you have something we can cover them with?"

Jonah rubbed his chin. "I'd pin a bedsheet up, but that might ruin it."

"You don't want a bedsheet in the barn," Annie said, looking past him to the silos, the horse barn, and a piece of harvesting equipment parked near the new milking barn. "What about some sacks?" she asked. "Do you have any old feed sacks we could use? We could pin them up, side by side."

He nodded. "That would work, and I think we have some burlap sacks in the barn." He started across the path. "Kumm."

Annie followed him, then turned back to link arms with Remy, who smiled as Annie tugged her forward. Gott did work in mysterious ways. In just weeks He had softened her heart and turned the person she dreaded most into a friend.

"Come along, and I'll show you how to cover the hay bales," she told the girl with a sprinkling of freckles and eyes the color of a cat's. When it came to the ways of the Amish, Remy had a lot to learn, and thanks to Gott's blessings, Annie had much to teach her.

PART THREE

Dawning Grace

For by grace are ye saved through faith;
And that not of yourselves;
It is the gift of God.
—Ephesians 2:8

*A*n iridescent green dragonfly zigzagged through the air as Gabe crossed the barn Sunday morning. Golden dust and tiny bits of chaff glittered in a shaft of sunlight as he went down the aisle, checking one more time to be sure that everything was in place. The barn was quiet now, but in an hour or so it would be bursting with people, echoing with voices in song.

Baptism today.

He knew that Emma would be here. He'd been thinking about that all week, and since she'd broken up with him, the thought of seeing her had weighed him down, as if he'd been harnessed to a boulder. It wasn't easy stepping around her feelings and his. He'd spent a lot of time thinking of how to avoid her.

But now that the day was here, his feet felt light, propelled by the excitement of hosting the church service. There was much to do over the next few hours.

Satisfied that everything was in order inside the barn, he stepped out into the bright September day and joined his older brothers, who waited on the knoll at the end of the lane. It wasn't even eight o'clock, and yet a line of gray carriages moved along the main road. The gentle clip-clop of hoofbeats filled the fields like a country song announcing that it was a church Sunday.

"Here come the carriages!" Simon's eyes were bright with excitement as Gabe joined his brothers. Today would mark the first time Simon helped handle horses and carriages, and the boy was quite pleased to be included with his older brothers in this hosting duty.

Gabe tagged his shoulder. "Are you sure you can handle these carriages?" he teased. "Folks don't take kindly to a runaway horse—especially when it's theirs."

"Horses aren't so hard to handle," Simon said, staring at the line of horse-drawn carriages coming down the lane. "But that is a lot of carriages to take care of."

"Give us a shout if you need a hand," Gabe called over his shoulder as he moved forward to take the first carriage from the Yoders. Gideon and Deborah climbed out, then turned to help their three little ones to the ground.

Gabe climbed into their carriage, took the reins, and directed the horse around the side of the barn. He let the horse have her head, and she was a little fast on the curve. The steel wheels popped over a ridge, and Gabe popped up in the seat. He grinned, hoping the Yoders hadn't seen that.

Around the back of the barn was an empty field where two horseless carriages were already lined up. Gabe waited as the carriage was pulled in line with the others. Then he reined the mare in and jumped down. Since the service and lunch would last a good five hours, the horses needed to be unhitched and given space to roam. Gabe released the chestnut mare from the rig, then led it over to the paddock, where it would be free to graze for the rest of the morning.

He hurried back on the footpath. So many aspects of Amish life were slow and easy, but on a church morning the horse hostlers had to move quickly, with so many carriages arriving at once. He came around the barn just in time to see Simon riding off to the field in an open buggy. Only Jonah was left standing at the edge of the lane.

"You're moving like the wind today," Jonah told Gabe.

Only as fast as a horse will go. Gabe wanted to tell Jonah that he knew of a way to truly ride as fast as the wind, but he kept to himself. It wouldn't do to talk of such things right before church. "This is the part of hosting I like the most," Gabe said as another carriage rolled to a stop.

Gabe and Jonah approached together.

"Leave this to me," Gabe said casually. "You can handle the next one."

Jonah nodded as Gabe moved forward and froze. Was that Emma in the carriage? But it was too small. He'd been expecting her to arrive with her father and stepmother and all her sisters and brothers.

Things seemed to happen all at once. Something popped out the side of the carriage. A plastic crate. As it toppled to the ground, Gabe realized that it was the crate Elsie used as a step to get out of the carriage since her short legs didn't reach the ground. Emma's brother Caleb came out from the other side.

Gabe's palms began to sweat as he backed away. He couldn't do this. He didn't want to see Emma. He wasn't ready to look in her eyes.

He turned away, facing his bewildered brother. "Please . . . you take the Lapps' carriage. I'll get the next one."

Jonah squinted in surprise, then quickly moved past Gabe to pick up the cockeyed crate and set it in place right under the carriage door. As Gabe strode up the lane to intercept the next carriage, he heard them talking behind him.

"There you go, Elsie." Jonah's voice was warm, and when Elsie thanked him, it tugged a sensitive cord deep inside Gabe. Elsie was a cheerful girl, who always had something kind to say, and though it hurt Gabe to turn away from her, it would have been ten times worse to come face-to-face with Emma. That was something he could not do right now.

Later, when the men were lining up to enter the barn, Gabe felt a broad hand on his shoulder. His older brother Jonah stood beside him, a question in his eyes.

"There must be a good reason for the way you treated Elsie Lapp," Jonah said quietly, "but I can't for the life of me imagine what it might be. Don't ever forget your manners like that again, Gabe. And I'm going to pray to Gott that you'll come to see that every person He created deserves your kindness, no matter how different that person looks."

Gabe's jaw dropped. "Are you saying that I . . ." *That I avoided Elsie because she's a little person?* The notion of such cruelty sent waves of nausea through his belly.

Jonah kept his voice steady, conscious of others who might be listening. "Ya, I'm sure there's a story."

"Jonah, you have to know that's not true. Look, there's no time to explain now." Any second, they would be filing into the barn. "But I don't judge folks by how they look, Jonah. Judge ye not—that's God's law. And I'd never do anything to hurt Elsie."

"You were rude. She needed help, and you walked away."

Growling to himself, Gabe rubbed his forehead, pushing back the brim of his hat. In trying to dodge Emma, he'd scorned Elsie—kind, good-natured Elsie, who always had a smile for everyone. Guilt throbbed, a raw ache that penetrated his soul.

"I didn't mean anything by it. I'll speak with her."

Gabe wanted to make things right with Elsie. He wanted to go to her now—right away—and beg her forgiveness. But this was not the time. The men were filing into the barn, and Jonah and Gabe followed in turn. They hung their hats along the granary and filled in the benches on the left side of the barn. The women and children would be coming in behind them. The service would start soon, and then it would be hours until the end—longer than usual on account of the baptism.

For now, all he could do was pray. Ask for Gott's forgiveness and pray that Elsie's forgiveness would follow.

As the *Vorsinger* began to lead the first song, the bishop, preachers, and deacons left the barn to meet with the baptismal applicants one last time. Gabe joined in the singing, letting his voice drain from his body. If only the heavy burden of guilt and anger could drain out, too. Such a tangled knot of pain from his parents' death, love for Emma, passion for motorbikes . . . and now he could add guilt to the crippling mountain of glowing embers.

It was probably a sin to come to church with such a heavy heart, but this was who he was now, and rumspringa or not, he knew he needed to keep coming to church. Even though he was enjoying his taste of the English world, it was good to be reminded of the faith he shared with his family and with the community. Motorbikes and loud music sparked excitement in his heart, but church brought him comfort. That was what he needed.

Peace in his heart.

The smell of the haymow was sweet. Insects buzzed around the open door and over in the women's section, children fussed. At times like this, Gabe wondered why he was leery of making a baptismal vow. This was where he belonged. But how could he make such a final choice when part of him was like a bird that had already flown away from the nest?

He wished he could talk to Emma about it. She had been the one person who would listen when he talked, without judging or teasing him. She tried to understand and she never told him how he should be feeling or thinking, like a lot of folks tried to do. Especially the older members of the congregation who seemed to think that everyone should act the same, never drawing attention to themselves. Maybe that was okay for them, but Gabe didn't mind rattling a few buggies now and then.

The second hymn was slow and thick as molasses, and Gabe's mind drifted to Emma. He had spent the past few days coming up with reasons why he and Emma didn't belong together. He wanted to be logical about it. If they didn't have enough in common, maybe Gott didn't intend for them to be together.

Reason number one: Emma was modest, and Gabe . . . not so much. He liked it when folks noticed how well he handled the family's herd. He knew that good Amish were modest. Modesty was something you needed to have *Gelassenheit* in your soul. Gelassenheit in your heart, too. Gabe wanted to yield to Gott's will—that was the Amish way—but he couldn't do that right now. Riding the bikes, he'd gotten a taste of power and speed. The bikes made him feel more like a man than any Amish custom. He needed to explore some more before he could clear the way for Gott. Baptism and gelassenheit would have to wait.

Reason number two why he and Emma shouldn't be together: Emma was quiet and calm, through and through, while Gabe was only quiet on the surface. She was Halfway's schoolteacher and he had always thought of school as a large pen that kept children corralled during the best hours of the day. Even in the dead of winter, Gabe would not have locked a cow or a horse into the stables for the day. Why was it done to children everywhere?

Reason number three . . .

The thought faded as the young people wanting to be baptized filed into the barn. They moved up the aisle in a line, heading toward the center section near the minister's bench.

Remy passed by, looking a little jittery as she smoothed her white apron. Next came David Fisher, followed by Gabe's cousin Abe.

Then he saw her, dressed in black, her eyes shining like a lantern in the dark.

Emma.

All the logic in the world couldn't keep him from loving her.

Black was such a solemn color, but Emma sparkled in it, her skin milky white against the dark fabric. A lump thickened in his throat when he recognized that it wasn't just the way she looked that made her so beautiful. It was Emma's spirit shining through that stole his heart over and over again.

A beacon in the night. How her eyes did shine!

With so much light inside, Emma would find her way. He had hoped they would find their way together, and it crushed him to think of her moving ahead without him. She would be a full-fledged member of the church now. A grown woman.

She would find her way, even if it meant leaving him behind.

THIRTY

*E*mma focused on a shaft of sunlight falling on the aisle in the crowded barn. As each candidate for baptism passed through it, she imagined that it was Gott's light shining down upon them. Stepping into the light herself, she pursed her lips and prayed for Gott's blessing.

Although the congregation was facing the ministers at the front of the room, there was no mistaking Gabe King from behind, with his broad shoulders, hair the color of wheat, and that casual way he tilted his head, as if he saw something no one else noticed.

That was one of the things she loved about Gabe—his very different view of things. His surprising comments made Emma laugh, and his slightly crooked view made him stand out from the other young men in the district. Gabe was very much an individual, his own man.

And at the same time, that quality was yet another reason to stay away from him.

Emma sucked in a tiny gasp of hope and nervousness and sadness when she passed by his row. Most girls would have taken offense to see their beau go running when she arrived, but Emma knew it was too hard for Gabe to face her. She wanted to think they still had a chance, that someday in the future Gabe would come to understand and accept the core values of their community. Gelassenheit was the foundation of Amish culture. It was all about submitting to a higher authority. Although it was rarely talked about, folks recognized it as the cornerstone of their faith.

Today, Emma would be asked to "give under" the authority of the church. *Unnergewwe* was what they called it in Pennsylvania German. Emma knew that it was a humble person who found fulfillment in serving the community. The qualities that she had nurtured in herself, submission, obedience, and simplicity, these were the values of their community. Sadly, she knew that Gabe didn't have much use for such things right now.

Had he always been that way?

As Emma took a seat on one of the benches in the center of the barn, she wondered if Gabe was nursing a secret wound—something deep in his heart, hidden from his family and friends. This was the time when a fella his age was moving from boyhood to the responsibilities of a man. Was Gabe being held back because he didn't have a father to show him the way, to lead by example, just as Emma did with her students? Emma had once talked with her sister Elsie about how Gabe must have suffered, losing his parents so tragically.

"It must have been a terrible shock," Elsie had said that night when they'd stayed up late talking after the lights were out. "All of a sudden, and to know that they were murdered . . ." Elsie's voice had trailed off on a wistful note. "Such a heartbreak. At least when our mamm died, we had some warning. She was sick for a long time."

"And to think you remember that," Emma had said. "You were barely seven when she died." Emma had been nine, a little more aware of the details of her mother's illness. Some memories were vivid in her mind. She had been picking strawberries the day Mamm came home from Doc Trueherz with the news that her heart wasn't working properly. And then there was the surgery at the hospital with its shiny floors and antiseptic smells. Everyone in the family had traveled there and stayed in the waiting room, for days, it seemed. Emma remembered falling asleep next to Elsie on the couch in the waiting room, her arm around her little sister as they huddled close.

"It's times like that—the darkest, saddest times—that's when Gott bonds people together," Elsie had told her. "Mamm's death brought us close."

"But Gabe didn't get close with anyone when his parents were killed," Emma had said. "He got real quiet . . . like a turtle pulling into his shell."

Elsie had agreed. "From what I can tell, you're the only person really close to him. Ya, he spends time with his cousins, but you're the person he talks with. You're his buddy."

Emma wanted to be Gabe's best friend, but she saw them moving farther and farther away from each other. Her students looked to her for a good example—faith in action—and she would not let them down. And now, with her baptism, she would go forth with a humble heart to serve her family, her students, and her community.

While Gabe sneaked off to ride motorbikes. Oh, why didn't he put those boyish things behind him and start thinking about their future?

Emma blinked back to attention in the warm air of the barn. Preacher Dave was beginning the *Anfang,* the opening sermon, and here she was wallowing in worry and memories. As she often told her scholars, it was time to open her eyes and ears to knowledge . . . and to the wonders of Gott's love.

THIRTY-ONE

*A*nnie was holding hands with her mother when Deacon Moses tipped the cup over Hannah's head, sending water running through her tightly bound blond hair and onto the white organdy cape Annie had worn for her own baptism.

Little Hannah was now a grown woman, a baptized member of the church. . . .

Annie turned to Lovina, whose eyes held a certain peace and contentment. Mamm lifted their joined hands to her heart and squeezed tight, and Annie smiled, sharing Mamm's joy.

It was a good thing to see the baby of the family taking this vow, though it did make Annie feel old to be watching her sister come of age while she herself was like a carriage with its wheels stuck in the mud of eternal courtship.

Lovina sniffed, then pulled her hand away to retrieve a hankie from the bib of her apron. They were tears of joy—Annie knew that—and yet, it made her want to cry, too.

Biting her lips together to hold back the wellspring of emotion,

Annie turned to her left, where little Levi sat sandwiched between her and Rebecca. His eyelids drooped and his head wavered from side to side on his shoulders. Rolling her eyes, Rebecca put an arm around his shoulders and pulled the child against her, and his eyelids drifted closed.

The sight of mother and child snuggled together warmed Annie's heart, and she tried to imagine herself sitting through church with a son or daughter at her side. How she longed to hold a babe in the crook of her arm or pull a little one close to give comfort! The yearning to be a mother had swelled inside her over the past year or so, and she had let the feelings of affection flow to her young nephews. Her sisters had been grateful to see their children loved and cared for. But now, with little Mark gone, she worried that she was coddling Levi too much. Smothering him. "Dear Annie, you need a babe of your own!" Rebecca had teased, not knowing how very true her words had been.

Annie let her gaze pass over each of the young people kneeling in the center section of the barn. Although it was a solemn moment, tears of joy filled Annie's eyes at the sight of these young people beginning their journey in the faith.

Bishop Samuel, Deacon Moses, and Mary Yoder, the deacon's wife, stood over Dave Fisher, whose head and face were now wet with baptismal water. The three moved on to Remy, who knelt next to Ben.

Annie saw that Remy's hands, pressed down against her dress, were trembling. The poor girl was nervous. Well, that was no wonder, with Remy being new to the community and new to the language, too. Annie wished she could place a gentle hand on Remy's shoulder—just a small bit of encouragement. But baptism was the time when young people had to stand on their own two feet and pledge their faith to Gott. This was Remy's moment to stand alone and make her promise.

The congregation was silent as Mary Yoder untied the ribbon of Remy's black head covering, revealing hair as bright and shiny as a new copper penny. Remy would always stand out among the Amish.

Laying his hands on Remy's head, Bishop Sam spoke. "Upon your faith, which you have confessed before Gott and these witnesses, you are baptized in the name of the Father, the Son, and the Holy Spirit. Amen." Mary Yoder helped Remy replace the head covering, then extended her hands to help Remy to her feet. There was a holy kiss, and then the ministers and the deacon's wife moved on to the next young person.

Annie dared a quick glance over to the men's section by the granary, where the men's broad-brimmed hats hung. This time her heart didn't ache at all when she spied Adam. Gott was healing her heart.

Her gaze landed on Jonah, who was looking intently toward the front. Was he watching the baptism, or admiring Hannah? With his dark hair and smoky dark eyes, Jonah King was a handsome man. Seeing him around the family farm, she had noticed how his eyes seemed to penetrate right to a person's heart. He was a good farmer, very handy to have around. And lately she had enjoyed talking with him. Jonah King was a very good match for her sister.

Elizabeth Mast was the last to be baptized. There was a quiet note of patience in the air as the bishop cupped his hands above her head, and the deacon poured water into them. As it brimmed over and trickled into her hair and face, Annie thought of how only Gott had the power to make a heart brim over with love. She wanted that for her younger sister and Jonah.

She wanted that for herself, too. Nothing would fill her heart more than a loving husband and a houseful of children who would be raised in the simple ways of the Amish, taught to be good Plain folk.

But that would have to come later, since there were no available young men in sight right now. Sometimes her heart ached with loneliness, but this was where Gott wanted her to be right now. Like Mamm always said, she was going to bloom where she was planted.

A little girl sitting in front of Annie yawned, and a wave of weariness came over her. Ya, the service was long, but the baptism ceremony was a good reminder of why they were all here—so many people working together to make up one community of faith. And now Hannah was a member, too. Mamm must be pleased. Annie looked at her mother beside her, praying that one day, she, too, might have a daughter who joined the faith.

THIRTY-TWO

*J*onah lifted the mallet and swung it down with all the force his muscles could conjure. Chopping wood helped to release the pent-up regret that stuck to him like a burr on a sock.

Each time he swung the mallet, he hit on a question.

Had he mishandled things?

Why didn't he go to Annie directly and tell her how he felt?

Should he have come forward years ago when she was pining for Adam, who was off during his rumspringa?

It was useless to drag all the questions and what-ifs through the mud again. It wouldn't change the way Annie felt toward him.

He swung the mallet, driving the steel wedge into the log. Another strike and the fat log split into three pieces. As he tossed the smaller logs into the bin, his sister Mary came round the side of the house with the wood scuttle.

"It's good that you're doing this. Now that it's cooler, I've been lighting the woodstove in the morning." In the hot summer months, they used only the gas stove in the kitchen, but this time of year,

Mary started a small early fire to take the chill from the air and percolate coffee.

"And we'll need some more wood split if we're going to burn a bonfire for the singing tonight." He put the mallet down and went to the woodpile to help Mary load the bin.

"About the singing." Mary paused, as if suddenly remembering something. "Annie told me that she and Hannah would be here tonight. She asked me if you ever spoke about Hannah at home, and from the way she was talking, it sounded like she's still got you and Hannah matched up."

Jonah groaned. "I don't really want to talk about it."

"I kept your secret, Jonah. I didn't say a word about it to Annie. But you didn't either." She shook her head, confusion clouding her eyes. "What's keeping you back? You go to work on their farm nearly five days a week. You'd think that somewhere between mending the roof and making hay you'd manage to spit out the truth."

"I've tried, really. In so many ways, I've told her the truth. But Annie can't seem to hear it, with all the notions swirling around in her head." He shook his head. "Matchmaking for her little sister, and somehow I got caught in the middle. And you know Annie. When she starts something, she doesn't let go until it's finished."

Mary sighed. "So Annie still doesn't know? Dear Jonah! You can't let this go on any longer."

"I want Annie to know the truth . . . how I feel. But every time I bring the conversation around to that, she goes right back to talk of Hannah. I'm not sure I can get her to hear me, short of telling her flat out that I don't favor her sister."

"If it's true, and it's not meant to be hurtful . . ." Mary shrugged. "Maybe that's what you need to say."

Jonah looked toward the heavens in dismay. "And Annie will never speak to me again."

"She'll forgive you eventually. But this has gone on long enough.

Annie needs to know the truth, and if it doesn't come from you, if she figures it out some other way, that would be even worse."

Mary was right. Jonah knew that, but it didn't make facing Annie any easier. Without speaking, he hauled a fat log onto the stump and tapped the wedge into a small crack. Most folks would have assumed the conversation was over, but Mary knew him well. She wrapped her bulky sweater tighter, giving him time.

Finally, Jonah pounded the wedge until the log split. "Maybe I've let it drag on, but Annie has become a friend. Many times she's started talking with me while I'm working, and she's easy to talk to."

Mary nodded. "And you don't want to lose that friendship. You're thinking she's going to be upset with you when she learns the truth."

"Ya."

"Most likely, she'll be angry, but I don't see a way around it, Jonah. And the longer you let this go, the worse it's going to get."

He nodded. "I'll do it tonight," he said. "I'll tell her. Even if I have to sing it across the table."

Mary's eyes opened wide. "Now, that would make for a singing folks would never forget."

The moon was a pale orange circle in the sky. As carriages began to arrive for the singing, Jonah lingered in the shadows outside the barn. It was a more public spot than he liked, and many couples and groups greeted him on their way into the barn. *They're probably thinking that I'm being a good host,* he thought. In truth, he was waiting for Annie to arrive. Mary had been right; he couldn't let this go on any longer.

At last he saw them—Annie and Hannah sat side by side in an open buggy that clopped down the lane. He stood his ground, a knot in his throat. He was sorely tempted to escape into the barn and take a seat, just like any other singing, but he stood his ground. It was time to get this over with.

He moved toward the buggy as it slowed. Young folks knew to take their rigs to a field around the side of the barn and tie them up to a wagon where the horses could graze. Jonah headed that way to confront Annie, but the buggy pulled to a stop and Hannah jumped down and hurried right smack toward him. He had no choice but to stop.

"Jonah . . . how are you this evening?"

He squinted at her, wondering if this was something Annie had told her to say. Most of Hannah's conversation seemed forced and stale, and he suspected that Annie fed her the words.

"Did you know I was baptized today?" she asked him, her pale brows lifting.

"Ya. Welcome to the congregation." He kept his tone even, though his patience was running out and his eyes were on the field behind her, watching the Stoltzfus buggy head over to the hay wagon.

"So now we're both baptized." Hannah's tone wasn't as enthusiastic as her words sounded. "That's one more thing you and I have in common." She tugged one of the strings of her prayer kapp, then began to wind her finger in it. "Annie says you and I have a lot in common."

He swallowed hard. "I know Annie thinks that way. But to tell you the truth, I think you'd be better off with a younger fella."

Her lower lip jutted out as her mouth formed a pout. "You don't think we'd be a good match . . . you and I?"

"What would you want with an old man like me?" He kept his voice steady, not wanting to ruffle her feathers but determined to speak his mind. "You're a good and kind girl, Hannah. Lots of fellas here would be happy to take you home in their buggies tonight. I'm just not one of them."

She squinted up at him. "So my sister doesn't always know best."

"You don't sound surprised."

"I never thought you favored me much. That's what I told Annie." He stared at her. "Is that so?"

"Ya, I told her that a few times. You and I have been tripping over each other, but that's all. Still, you have been spending a lot of time around the house. More than most hired hands. That's why, when Annie started to talk about you, I figured there was something to it."

"Well . . . it's not about you. Not to be mean or anything."

"It doesn't disappoint me one way or the other . . . but there's more to this, isn't there?" She put her hands on her hips, her pale eyes studying him. "You've been hanging around for a reason. If it's not me, there's got to be someone else." Jonah squirmed, and her eyes flared. "It's my sister, isn't it? You've got a hankering for Annie."

"Whoa. Pipe down." He looked around to see if anyone else had heard, but people were wrapped up in their own conversations.

"I had a feeling." Hannah grinned. "She doesn't have a clue, but I'll tell her if you want." She clapped a hand over her mouth, as if to keep excitement from bubbling right out of her. "I could match you two up!"

"No, please don't." Jonah was through with roundabout messages. "I'll tell her."

"Okay." She glanced back toward the side of the barn. "She'll be around in a minute. But I can't believe she doesn't know already. I guess she's been looking at you with her eyes closed."

"That's about right." Jonah had felt invisible to Annie for so many years; Hannah hit it on the nail.

"Don't forget to tell her," Hannah said as she fell into step with a group of girls headed into the barn, leaving Jonah alone in the moonlight.

The talk with Hannah had strengthened his resolve to tell Annie how he felt. Hannah didn't laugh or look at him cross-eyed when she got an inkling of his feelings for Annie.

She thought he had a chance.

Just then Annie emerged from the moon shadow of the beech trees. It was clear that she'd been watching his exchange with her sister.

"Jonah?" She hurried closer. "Why did Hannah go on without you? She was looking forward to seeing you tonight."

"We talked. She's inside with her friends."

A frown darkened Annie's face as she looked toward the light of the barn doors. "But I thought you two would be like two peas in a pod."

"No, Annie." Jonah felt truth in the air, steely and cold as the bite of autumn. "Hannah and I don't favor each other."

There. He had said it, plain and simple.

She bit her lower lip—those naturally rosy lips he couldn't take his eyes away from—and he felt a stab of regret. It would not be good to tell Annie he cared for her while she stared at him with fierce eyes, angry as a mother bird protecting her young.

"I mistook what you were saying the other day, and . . ." How could he spell it out without blaming Annie for jumping to conclusions? "Now I owe you the truth."

"And all along I thought you were telling me the truth. Don't you know a lie is a sin, Jonah?" Shock was evident in her blue eyes.

"It was more a misunderstanding than a lie," Jonah said, not wanting to get off track. "The truth is, I don't favor Hannah." The glimmer of betrayal in her eyes made him pause. "There's someone else I've had my eye on for a long time. A girl with freckles and hair the color of wheat and eyes like the summer sky. A stubborn girl who loves to laugh. A girl who's strong on the outside but gentle and caring inside."

She stared up at him, her expression slowly softening as recognition dawned. "Wait. Are you saying that you favor me?"

The thick knot in his throat threatened to choke away his words, but he pushed past it. Tonight, he was not going to be the Quiet One. Tonight he would speak his mind . . . and his heart.

"Annie, it's you I've always had eyes for. Only you. I counted my blessings when I got to sit beside you when we were children in the schoolhouse. I've gone to every singing just to hear your voice—to listen to you sing and laugh with your friends. Didn't you ever notice how I was always nearby when you came to visit Mary?"

She shook her head in disbelief. "No!"

The word hit him like a bucket of cold water. He wasn't sure just what she was saying no to, but it didn't matter. Her answer was no.

Annie put her hands up to cover her ears. "I don't want to hear this."

"But it's the truth, Annie. It needs to be said."

He wanted to tell her more. That her bright eyes made him feel alive and that he was sure he could chart the freckles on her nose as well as the stars in the sky. That her stubborn spirit and her tender heart set her apart from all the other girls. That her rollicking joy for life had taught him to laugh at himself. But as he tried to find the words, her face blushed pink and her eyes pinched with anger.

"You've already said too much." She lifted a hand to make him stop, backing away from him. "And you've got things all twisted around. You belong with Hannah. That's how it should be." She ran into Ruben Zook and David Fisher, who were coming up behind her, watching the exchange with wide, curious eyes.

"Easy, Annie," David said, catching her as she stumbled back.

She stepped away from him, rubbing her elbows protectively, before she shot a piercing look back at Jonah. "No." Her voice was quiet, but firm. The word hung in the air a moment, and this time Jonah took it as a warning.

He didn't move as she turned and ran around the side of the barn. Things like this were better mulled over in quiet or shared with a good friend, and Annie had plenty of friends at the singing.

Ruben and David nodded as they passed and headed into the barn.

A minute later, when a horse and buggy shot out from behind the barn, Jonah's jaw dropped. She was leaving the singing. No one left a singing this early—certainly not in a fit of anger.

But sure enough, it was Annie sitting alone in the front seat, her horse charging so fast that the buggy bounced over a bump in the lane. Jonah thought about going after her, but that would only make her race faster down the road and out of his life.

THIRTY-THREE

*H*orse and buggy flew over the road like a bat soaring through the darkness as Annie fled the King farm. She was running away, fleeing as fast as she could to escape the embarrassment and disappointment that burned straight through to her heart.

How could she have been so blind? And to think that it had been going on for so many years, while she had been waiting for Adam. . . .

Tears stung her eyes, but she dashed them away, trying to focus on the dark road. What had begun as a plan to help her sister had soured into a terrible stew. How silly she'd been, to think she could be a matchmaker. Such a fool! She wasn't even able to find a fella of her own; how did she think she'd make a suitable match for Hannah?

And to pick Jonah! Of all the young men, she had chosen a man who secretly favored her.

How had she missed the signals, all these years? She bit her lower lip, trying to think back to a time when Jonah had chatted with her or teased her as boys tended to do with a girl they liked. When she looked back to their school days, back to summer days in the row-boat with Mary or skating on the Kings' pond, she remembered nothing of Jonah aside from his steady silence. The Quiet One had been his nickname.

Too quiet to even talk to her back when they were children.

For her, hearing about it now, after so many years, was a slap in the face. She couldn't consider courting a man that her sister favored. It was as if the whole world was in on a joke that she knew nothing about. She couldn't have known Jonah's feelings all this time. They'd barely exchanged a word until he'd started working with Dat on the farm.

By the time the golden windows of home came into view, her tender emotions had drained to a sense of sadness. She slowed Dapple on the lane and guided him to the carriage house. She didn't need a light to unhitch the horse, having done it countless times, but she was so overwrought that her fingers fumbled in the darkness. At last, Dapple was free, and she released the horse to the pasture and plodded over to the house.

Weary to the bone, she didn't bother lighting a lantern downstairs. Leaning heavily on the handrail, she climbed the stairs and went straight to the room she shared with Hannah.

Of course, her sister was still at the singing, but without a fella now. Annie bit back tears at the thought of her sister all alone. She had failed Hannah.

Too weary to wash up, she sat on her bed and pulled her sweater closer around her. Without the chance to match up Hannah and Jonah, Annie had nothing to look forward to here.

No hope.

She sighed. That was wrong. She was making a mountain out of a molehill. She had a wonderful family and a good home. Loving parents and an adorable nephew who warmed her heart every day.

So many blessings . . . but no prospects for a beau.

There was a knock on the door. A moment later Mamm peeked in, a small lantern in her hand.

"Oh, Annie, it's you. I was wondering who it could be this early. The singing just barely started." Lovina stepped into the room. She wore a nightgown and her hair hung in one long braid down her back. "Why are you home so early? Are you sick?"

"No, Mamm." Annie felt the sting of embarrassment as her mother came over and pressed a hand to her forehead to check for a temperature. It was a loving gesture, but it reminded Annie that she was acting like a baby. Selfish and silly.

Mamm sat beside Annie on the bed and gently rubbed her shoulder. "What's the matter, honey girl?"

"I don't know, Mamm." Annie wasn't sure what to tell her mother, but she knew it would be silly to recount all the details of the mistaken matchmaking and the man who had admired her since he'd been a boy.

"I think you know exactly what the problem is," Lovina said. "Otherwise, you wouldn't be sitting here alone in the dark when all the other young people are off having fun singing songs and talking around a bonfire."

Annie looked down at her hands, small but capable. "I'm worried, Mamm. It probably sounds selfish, but I'm afraid that I'll never find a beau—and you know how much I want a family with little ones."

"Mmm. I can see how that's a worry. There aren't many young men your age left in our district. But we can never know Gott's plan. Have you thought about looking in the next district over the bridge? I know it's a long drive, but you could attend one of their youth events."

"I've been there already." Last summer she had gone to a volleyball game and picnic with a handful of girls from Halfway, all of them looking for beaus. The event had been lively enough, but Annie and her friends hadn't felt completely at ease with the group of young people who had known one another all their lives. "I reckon I could try it again," Annie said.

"It's so hard to know what the Heavenly Father intends for us," Lovina said. "But we have to trust in Him." She squeezed Annie's shoulder. "In my day, we had a lot of young men, but not so many women. Most girls could have their pick of beaus, but the boys, they had to drive here and there, to singings and bonfires and hayrides."

"And you picked Dat. What was it that made him stand out from all the others?" Annie asked her mother.

"He's always been a right good farmer. He was born here in this house. And you know me, growing up on a farm, it was the way I wanted to live."

"You married Dat for his farm skills?" Annie's voice squeaked.

Lovina chuckled. "More reasons than that. Most of all, he listened to me. Whether I was talking about keeping pests off tomatoes or the stars in the sky, your dat listened. Aaron wanted a wife who would be his partner, and that suited me just fine."

Annie sighed. "You made a good choice, Mamm." If only Annie had any choice at all!

In the muted lantern light the bedroom seemed small but cozy, the pale yellow walls warm and welcoming. Everything was tidy— the two beds neatly made, clothes hanging neatly on hooks. The only thing out of place was the folded paper of a letter Annie had received from her sister Sarah yesterday. The letter was short, but Sarah had made sure to write Annie soon after she'd attended last week's church in New York and seen for herself the large number of single men in the district.

"Maybe I need to go farther than the next district. Sarah says there are lots of young men my age in New York."

Lovina hugged her close. "Oh, honey girl, don't say that. I don't want to lose you, too!"

"But maybe that's Gott's plan for me. I must pray for His will to be done." Annie closed her eyes, losing herself in Mamm's softness for a moment. She didn't want to leave here, but maybe she was too attached to Halfway. Gott wanted His children to live on the earth, but not of it. Maybe she needed to separate herself from the earthly things she valued a little too much.

Leaving her home . . . that would be a bitter pill to swallow. But maybe it was like forgiveness; if she said the words, the acceptance would eventually come to her, a blessing from Gott.

Annie slipped out of her mother's grasp, but she took Lovina's hand and held it to her heart. Her mamm's eyes shone with tears in the dim light, and Annie couldn't deny the knot of emotion in her throat.

She felt as if she were about to jump off a cliff, but she had to trust that Gott in His infinite wisdom and mercy would take care of her.

"It's a choice that breaks my heart in two," Annie said, "but I'll never have a family of my own if I don't go to New York. I have to go, Mamm."

"Oh!" Lovina's small cry brought tears to Annie's eyes as her mother pulled her into her arms again.

"Promise me you'll think about it," Mamm said. "You don't have to rush, do you?"

"There's no rush," Annie said. "But I have to abide by Gott's plan for me and . . . I should go before the winter weather comes. That could make travel a problem."

"Wait till the end of fall, then." Lovina held her close, stroking her back. "Give it some thought."

Annie didn't tell her that she'd been mulling over this problem for months. Instead, she tried to push all thoughts of the future away and simply rest in the peace, comfort, and love of her mother's arms.

THIRTY-FOUR

*J*onah tossed one last piece of wood onto the bonfire and stirred the glowing embers with a long stick. Without Annie here he'd had plenty of time to move benches and build the fire—typical hosting duties.

The singing was winding down quickly. Only two couples were left sitting near the fire as, one after the other, carriages made their way up the lane to the main road. Over by the line of parked carriages that belonged to the Kings, Jonah saw someone hitching up a horse.

Who was that?

Jonah headed over as the man jumped into a buggy and called out to the horse. Gabe? Ya, it was Gabe, in his souped-up rig with fancy speakers. He guided Mercury over to the barn, where Hannah Stoltzfus stepped through the golden light of the open doors and climbed in beside Gabe.

Jonah cocked an eyebrow. Hannah and Gabe? Surely Hannah was not the girl his brother had been seeing in secret?

Just then Jonah noticed he wasn't the only one watching Gabe and Hannah ride off. He approached the tall woman in the shadows, recognizing Emma Lapp, the schoolteacher, just before she pressed a handkerchief to her eyes and sniffed.

"Emma?" He stopped a few yards away, a safe distance to give her space and time to compose herself. "Are you all right?"

"I . . . I'm just worried about how I'll get home." The tremble in her voice told him that she was worried about more than that. "My brother left with a girl, and . . . I guess Caleb and I should have come in two carriages."

This lost, sad girl was so unlike the confident, calm schoolteacher who had done so much to bring Simon around after their parents' death. "Do you want a ride home?" Jonah offered.

She swallowed. "Would you? Do you mind?"

"Wait here while I get a carriage."

In five minutes he was back at the barn door with Jigsaw hitched up to the big family carriage. Emma climbed in beside him, looking calm and composed now. He was grateful for that as they headed down the lane.

"Denki for the ride, Jonah. I don't mind walking, but tonight . . . tonight I just don't have the heart."

"My horse needed some exercise," he teased. "But isn't your house a bit far for walking at night? You live near town."

"Ya. It's . . . I usually get a ride."

He kept his eyes on the road. Sometimes listening was a better salve than too many kind words.

"I've never walked all the way." She turned toward him; he could feel her eyes upon him, and when he looked they were big and round, like a deer drinking from the river. "To be honest, I usually start walking home, and then your brother Gabe gives me a ride the rest of the way."

"Gabe?" So Emma was the mystery girl in Gabe's life.

"We've been seeing each other for more than a year now—all in secret. Gabe wanted to tell people, but I convinced him to wait. I need to be careful about whom I'm connected with socially. A schoolteacher needs to maintain a very good reputation. There is no teaching to compare with example."

"That's true." Teachers were closely watched by children and adults alike. But if Gabe and Emma were courting in secret, why did he take off with Hannah in his buggy? "So why didn't Gabe give you a ride home tonight?"

"Maybe I shouldn't have expected him to, but I came to the singing with high hopes. We broke up this week, but I thought we might patch things over. At least, I thought we could talk ... but he wouldn't even look at me. Did you see him this morning when we arrived for church? He ran the other way when our carriage arrived."

Jonah nodded. That explained a lot of things. Gabe hadn't been running away from Elsie Lapp; he'd been avoiding Emma.

"And now he's ridden off with Hannah Stoltzfus." Emma's voice trembled, and he saw the hankie being twisted in her hands.

Jonah hoped that she wouldn't cry. When girls cried, he felt so useless.

"I can't believe that he's moved on already," she added.

"Things aren't always as they seem." He should know that, having been set up as a suitor for Hannah for the past two weeks. "And I think you have probably been very good for Gabe. He's leveled out over the past year or so. There's peace in his heart. Contentment." He turned to Emma. "I'm wondering why you and Gabe called it quits."

His question brought a new flood of tears, and Jonah turned back toward the dark road, wanting to kick himself. "That was too personal. I'm sorry."

"It's okay." Emma sniffed and dabbed at her eyes, composing herself. "And it's good to hear that you think Gabe is calming down. I thought that was true, too. I thought he was settling down . . . that I could trust him . . . but I was wrong."

He rubbed his chin, wondering what sort of high jinks his brother was up to now. "Gabe has always had a secret wild streak," he said. "What did he do now?"

"Motorbikes. He's been spending his Sundays riding fancy bikes with some Englisher. Dirt bikes, he calls them."

"Mmm." It made sense to Jonah; he had sensed that Gabe was sneaking away from the farm for something, but he wasn't quite sure of the details.

"He knows he's breaking the rules . . . that it's against the Ordnung." She didn't try to mask the raw pain in her voice. "But he won't give it up."

"It makes things hard on you," he said sympathetically. "But you shouldn't worry so much. Worry is a sin, ya? Besides, most Amish boys try their hand at riding bikes or driving cars at one point during rumspringa."

Emma shook her head. "Why would anyone do that? I understand that people make mistakes, but to deliberately break the rules . . ."

"There's something about learning to drive a car or motor-cycle . . . it's something a man wants to try."

"But an Amish man isn't supposed to drive a car. That doesn't make sense."

"Because you're not a man, and you're trying to be logical. Ask your brother Caleb. If he's honest with you, he'll tell you he's done it."

Emma pulled her sweater closer around her. "Oh, Caleb would never admit anything to me. He thinks I'm a Goody Two-shoes."

Funny, but Jonah had always thought the same of Emma. He sensed that Gabe had come to know a different side of her. "Don't worry about Gabe. In the long run, he'll come around. He's not like

Zed Miller, with that Jeep that caused so much trouble. Gabe is having his fun, but you won't see him leaving the community the way Zed did."

"How can you be so sure?" she asked. "Your sister Sadie is gone, and your older brother left for years. He was gone for so long that people had given up praying that Adam King would ever come back. How do you know Gabe won't be lost to us, too?"

"Gabe is content in our ways, and he's got dairy farming in his blood. No one knows our livestock the way Gabe does. To leave the cows would be like abandoning children. That's not Gabe."

"I don't know anymore," Emma said. "I thought I knew him, but I was wrong."

Jonah didn't like the idea of her giving up on his brother. "Do you see the horse up there pulling our carriage? His name is Jigsaw, and he was a wild one when he came to our farm. He was a beast of a horse. He bit anyone who came near him. Dat used to joke that Jigsaw would buck and kick if he didn't like the way you looked at him."

Emma gazed ahead thoughtfully. "He's been well trained. Was it you who trained him?"

"With my dat's help. But before any training began, the horse needed to be calmed. Have you ever just stood with your hand on a creature, feeling it breathe, praying for calm and peace?"

"That's something I've never done, but growing up in town, I wasn't around animals much. Just the one horse we need to pull the carriage, and my brother takes care of him."

"Our dat taught us to respect all Gott's creatures, large and small. He taught us well. And after lots of calming and a summer of training, Jigsaw joined the team for harvest. When I turned sixteen and my parents let me choose an animal, everyone knew it would be this horse. I was the one who named him Jigsaw."

"Because he was like a puzzle. You needed patience. You had to wait and see how the pieces would come together." She sighed. "Patience is one thing I understand. Teaching my scholars is a process. No one learns everything overnight."

"Ya. That's very good. I guess it takes a smart one to be a teacher."

"So they say. But I'm not feeling very smart right now. Trusting Gabe wasn't the smartest thing I've ever done."

"But that's the point of my story about Jigsaw. The wildest ones, the ones with spirit, once they settle down they make the most reliable friends you could ever have."

"Jonah, I hope and pray that you're right." Sadness crossed her face as she stared at the horse leading their carriage. "I know they say boys will be boys, and Gabe is still in his rumspringa. . . ."

In Jonah's eyes, Emma was very mature for eighteen. But then, girls at that age were often more settled than boys.

"But men can't be tamed like horses," Emma said.

Jonah rubbed his chin, thinking of the similarities. No, a man wasn't trained. Gabe would come around; he knew that. But there were some things that book learning couldn't teach you. Some things, you just had to stumble through in the school of life.

THIRTY-FIVE

Gabe frowned up at the yellow moon shining like a round beacon in the sky. It would be a good night to court a girl on a nice long buggy ride.

But not for Gabe.

The girl he wanted to court was out on this dark road, walking home in the orange moonlight.

Emma was part of the reason he kept Mercury moving so slowly. He figured if he squinted into the darkness he might find Emma hiding behind a fence post or walking primly, shoulders back and head so high and even that she could balance a book on top of it.

He missed her. It hadn't even been a week since she'd ended everything with him, but watching her get baptized, and seeing her across the barn at the singing, felt wrong. And this was their time—late Sunday, after a singing. This was the time when he picked her up along the side of the road and they talked and laughed and sat close under the stars.

If he closed his eyes he could imagine the sweet, soapy smell of her neck and the luster of the soft moonlight on her lips. He could see the little crease that formed in her forehead when she was serious, and the dimples that appeared when she smiled. But he didn't want to close his eyes too long and take the chance of missing her walking alongside the road.

He let his horse poke along slowly, his eyes combing every tree, field, and sign for her as he headed home from the Stoltzfus farm. If he found her, he would find a way to make things right. Not that he'd give up the bikes. A man couldn't cut off his arm to please a woman. But they could get to a place where they could talk again. He could make things up to her and ease the guilt that burned inside him like a piece of bark curling in the fire. He felt bad about taking Hannah Stoltzfus home. She was a sweet girl, but he had to admit, he wasn't interested in Hannah. He had driven her home because she needed a ride and because he was hurt about Emma breaking things off with him.

Had he wanted to show Emma that he could socialize with other girls? Maybe. But the truth? There was no replacing the bond he had with Emma. And during the whole ride, Hannah had kept asking questions about his cousin Ben, so it was clear who she was really interested in.

As the family farm came into view, silos gleaming in the moonlight, he had to accept that he had spoiled things for Emma and himself today. From the start, when she had pulled up in the small carriage and he'd fled from her sister Elsie . . . Gabe winced. After today, he had some fences to mend.

As Mercury climbed the rising path to the barn, he saw that the wide doors were still open, the lanterns lit. The church wagon had been pushed close to the doors once again, and Simon and Adam were hauling a bench out of the light.

Eager to give them a hand, Gabe tied Mercury to a post and jogged to the barn.

"Need some help?" he called.

"Ya, help us finish," Adam said, motioning him over.

Gabe grabbed the end of a bench, opposite brother Simon. "I didn't see you at the singing," he teased the boy.

Simon laughed, his sleepy eyes glimmering. "No, but I got to stay up extra late to help clean up."

"It is late," Gabe agreed. "If you stay up a few more hours, the cows will be calling to be milked."

"I can't stay up all night," Simon said. "I have school in the morning."

"We'll get you to bed soon, but it's good experience, seeing how the benches go just so in the back of the cart," Adam said as they carried the bench past him. "Boy's got to learn how to load a church wagon."

"True." Gabe watched his younger brother's face as they carried the bench out into the darkness. He was glad that Simon was enjoying this, and a little surprised at how strict a "parent" Adam was becoming. Although Dat had expected his sons to do their chores, most times his easygoing nature had made work seem like play.

At the wagon, Jonah hopped down and helped them hoist the bench high so they could slide it onto the top.

"Almost full," Simon said.

They returned to the barn for the last of the benches, and in no time the job was done.

"Where does the church wagon go next?" Simon asked before dropping his jaw to yawn.

"Depends on where church is next." Jonah pulled the tarp down to cover the opening in the back. "The Fishers', I think."

"Kumm." Adam touched Simon's shoulder gently. "Let's get to bed."

"Good night," Simon called, heading back to the house with Adam.

"I'm glad that's done," Gabe said. "Less work for tomorrow."

Jonah nodded, watching as Gabe headed over to the fence to fetch his horse and send him out to pasture for the night.

"Where you going?" Jonah asked.

"I still have to unhitch Mercury."

"I'll help." Jonah met him at the line of horseless carriages. Gabe patted Mercury's withers as he began to unfasten the line.

Jonah worked from the opposite side. "It's been some night."

"Ya." *Not a good one,* Gabe thought, but he kept quiet.

"Full of surprises," Jonah said. "For the first time in years I left the singing with a girl in my buggy."

Gabe looked over Mercury's backside at his brother. "After all this time?" Jonah had faithfully attended singings but always left alone. For a long time everyone had been sure he'd had his eye on a certain girl, but Jonah kept things to himself. "Who is she?"

"Emma Lapp."

Gabe's jaw dropped as his fingers pressed into Mercury's bristly coat. "You . . ." He couldn't believe it. "Emma Lapp? Jonah, is Emma the girl you've been pining for all these years?"

Jonah circled in front of the horse to cuff Gabe on the shoulder. "Pining? I'm not a lovesick puppy. But no. Emma needed a ride home; that's all. I gave her a ride, and she talked my ear off on the way."

"Ya, girls do that." Gabe was relieved but cautious. What was Jonah getting at?

"She talked about you the whole time. At least now I understand why you ran from their carriage this morning. She's upset with you, Gabe. Something about racing motorbikes."

Gabe grunted. Why did she have to go and spill the beans? Emma had said too much and he didn't want to talk to Jonah about this.

"When I was your age, it was a Jeep," Jonah said. "Manual transmission. You know, switching gears and all. It takes more skill than driving a car that's automatic."

"You need to switch gears on the bikes, too," Gabe said as tension drained from his shoulders. "And when you want to go, you gun the throttle. Have you ever ridden a dirt bike?"

"Just a regular bike with pedals. So how did you get your hands on these motorbikes?"

"An Englisher guy owns them. Ben met him first, and now the three of us go riding together. Blake doesn't mind us using the bikes, as long as we help pay for the gasoline." Mercury was free from the harness now, and Gabe led him away from the buggy, rubbing his coat briskly, smoothing down the hair on his back. "Don't tell Adam. He won't understand."

"Adam probably doesn't want to know," Jonah said. "It's your rumspringa, and as head of the family he would probably look the other way . . . within limits. We're all still missing Sadie, and no one wants to lose you, too, Gabe."

"I'm not going anywhere." Gabe leaned into his horse, grateful that he didn't have to face Jonah in this conversation. He didn't want to be penned in by the rules, and he didn't need his older brothers pushing him toward the church. "So tell me. When did you learn to drive this Jeep?"

"When I was seventeen I used to go off with Zed Miller. It was my rumspringa. Zed was already in his twenties, but he hadn't joined the church on account of his Jeep. It's the one that sits along the road, for sale now—the one that got his father, Ira, into so much trouble."

Gabe smiled, imagining quiet, straight-arrow Jonah roaring along in a Jeep. "That's what happens when you're the Quiet One. No one notices when you're sneaking around."

"That's right. No one in the family noticed, unless Mamm and Dat figured it out. But they never said anything—none of the parents did. There were a bunch of us—five or six Amish boys who learned to drive in Zed Miller's Jeep."

"And was it like jumping through a window into a different world?" Gabe asked. "Because that's how I feel on a motorbike."

"I remember liking the power of the machine," Jonah said. "That rumble when I started the engine. And the way it leaped forward when you hit the gas pedal. That part got the blood going. But the battery was always dying, and the gasoline was expensive then, too. Come the winter months, most of us just gave it up."

"But a Jeep would have been good in the snow. I've heard that it can climb over a mound of snow—better winter transportation than the horses."

"Mmm. Our horses are probably more reliable, but that Jeep can cross a river. Which we did more than one time. Once, the water came up over the wheels and started seeping inside." Jonah chuckled. "Zed was a wild man with that Jeep."

"That's what I like about the motorbikes. The power." No longer feeling defensive, Gabe told Jonah about the dirt bikes, the track Blake built, and the fun of it all. "Once you get going, you feel like you're flying over the land. You should come along sometime."

Jonah grunted. "No, not me. I'm a baptized member of the church. You won't find me breaking that rule again."

"Do you miss it?"

"Not for all the bother and trouble. Besides, I grew out of it. That kind of excitement doesn't seem real to me anymore. It's sort of made-up noise and power. But not everyone gets past it. My friend Zed Miller left, you know. I hear he drives a truck now."

"Come on," Gabe teased. "You must miss it from time to time."

"Nay. Now I like the feel of a plow or harvester under me, and the excitement of working a team of draft horses. There's nothing quite as thrilling as real horsepower . . . the raw power of horses pulling across the earth. Besides, bikes break down. Horses foal. Gott sees to it that our horses make more horses. It's one of the many ways Gott provides for us."

Gabe saw the truth and wisdom in what his brother was saying. "Horses get the job done, all right," he admitted, "but I'm not ready to give up the dirt bikes. And Emma was being unfair to make me choose between her and the motorbikes."

Jonah gave a mock gasp. "She gave you a choice? And you chose the bikes?"

"You drove a Jeep."

"But I didn't have a fine young woman waiting for me," Jonah said.

"You think I made a mistake?"

"Mmm." Jonah tipped his hat back. "In ten years, will the dirt bikes matter to you? In ten years, will Emma matter to you? I'm thinking you might want to choose the thing that will last."

"But I don't want to look back with regret for the things I gave up. And it wouldn't do to be mad at Emma for making me give up something I love."

"A bike would be cold comfort in the night," Jonah said. "And the Bible says there are but three things that last: faith, hope, and charity. And the greatest of these is charity."

THIRTY-SIX

After a restless night, Annie got out of bed before sunrise, lit a small lantern, and decided she could sleep no more with this heavy heart. She washed, dressed, and then moved quietly down the stairs, trying not to wake Mamm, who always joked that she slept with one ear to the door.

Down in the kitchen she lit the big kerosene lamp, then opened the pantry door. The large plastic bins of sugar and flour and brown sugar were well stocked, thanks to Mamm's trip to the bulk-food store. She considered what recipe would be best. Being up this early, there was plenty of time for dough to rise, and while she was waiting she could start the fire in the woodstove and prepare breakfast.

It was a good morning to punch some dough. Annie had made a very tough decision last night, and though she believed it was the Almighty's will, she still had a few concerns to punch out. She put on a kitchen apron and turned on the spigot to get warm water for the yeast.

Whenever worry pressed upon her, baking was one thing that

eased her mind. The sweet smell of baking in the kitchen provided comfort for the saddest heart. Besides, she knew the steps of bread-making . . . when to knead the dough and when to let it sit. If only the rest of life could be so simple.

She decided to bake one of Dat's favorites, a loaf of nutty cinnamon bread. Levi had recently asked why a "nutty sinner man" had a bread named after him—a question that had prompted some good-natured chuckling in the house.

At the heart of the recipe was cinnamon, a spice that Annie believed could improve even the grouchiest mood. There was something about the clean, sharp taste that lifted the spirit. Mixed with plenty of butter and sugar, cinnamon reminded Annie of cozy winter mornings and holiday baking.

Cracking an egg into the big bowl of yeast mixture, she began to hum a song from the singing called "Somebody Cares." Her high-pitched voice had never prompted much attention at a singing, but she could carry a tune just fine. The lyrics spoke to her in a new way this morning.

> "Somebody knows when your heart aches,
> And everything seems to go wrong;
> Somebody knows when the shadows
> Need chasing away with a song;
> Somebody knows when you're lonely,
> Tired, discouraged, and blue;
> Somebody wants you to know Him,
> And know that He dearly loves you."

No matter what the problem or how bad she felt, she could take comfort in Gott's love. Her problems weren't so bad, and in some ways she had brought them on herself. She beat the ingredients, stirred with all her might, then paused to add flour.

Foolishness . . . she had been full of it, acting like a fool. She'd been so proud of her matchmaking skills, when the truth was, she'd made a bad match. She had pushed together two people who didn't have special feelings for each other. Hannah had tolerated her plan, but Jonah . . . that poor man had walked into a trap. It was a wonder that he didn't think she was verhuddelt.

But no, Jonah had made it clear that he didn't think she was crazy at all. In fact, it was just the opposite. He said he had a fond spot in his heart for her. How did he put it? He'd wanted to sit near her ever since grade school. He said something nice about her eyes and her hair . . . hair the color of wheat.

That was wonderful good—not at all what she'd expected to hear from Jonah King.

Dumping another cup of flour into the bowl, she stared through the cloud of powder. She needed to keep a clear view of things, and that meant realizing that Jonah had played along with her plan. Even if he did fancy her, he had let her make a fool of herself, and now . . . now she'd have to face him when he showed up to work.

As she set the dough on the warming stovetop and covered it with a dishcloth, she wondered how she would face Jonah King. Today was her day to mind Levi and feed the men lunch.

How she dreaded seeing Jonah.

Besides, there was Hannah to think about. Jonah had been her first real suitor, and Annie couldn't imagine her sister's disappointment when she learned that it was over almost before it started.

Poor Hannah! And here Annie had been feeling sorry for herself because she looked foolish. Hannah had lost her first fella.

Humming her song, Annie set to work preparing the kitchen for breakfast. She filled the scuttle with wood and started a fire in the potbelly stove. She ventured out to the henhouse to gather fresh eggs, then lit the fire under a fry pan of scrapple. She combined walnuts, brown sugar, almond extract, and cinnamon to make the filling for her nutty cinnamon bread.

Then came time to knead the risen dough. She punched it down a few times and divided it in half. She pressed half of the dough into the pan, sprinkled the sugary topping onto it, then patted the top layer of dough in place. Twenty minutes in the oven was all it took.

The house began to awaken with creaks overhead, and she heard Dat's footsteps on the stairs. Soon Daniel, Rebecca, and Levi would head over from the little cottage, which was cozy for sleeping but had no kitchen. Annie decided not to tell anyone of her decision just yet. Sarah and Perry would get their letter, but otherwise, Annie would keep it to herself.

"Good morning, Annie girl." Dat plodded into the kitchen, his face looking about as ashen as his graying hair.

"Morning, Dat. Your favorite bread is baking in the oven."

"Nutty sinner man bread?" He nodded. "I thought I smelled cinnamon."

Although his words were kind, his soft smile was missing, as was his energy. As soon as he poured himself a cup of coffee he went over to the corner rocking chair in the living room. A moment later he was settling in, staring down at an old copy of *The Budget,* a newspaper that covered happenings in Amish and Mennonite communities around the globe.

Dat stroked his beard as his eyes slid closed. When had her father become so gray, so tired . . . so old?

Had Annie had her eyes closed these past few years? Dat had aged. So had everyone. She herself would be twenty-one next year, an odd turning point for a single Amish girl. Although she still lived with her parents, she would be allowed to open her own bank account in town and keep her own money. Folks would be watching and wondering what was so wrong with Annie Stoltzfus that she couldn't find a fella to marry.

Frustrated, she ducked out to the storeroom, frowning in the dim light. She had to stop worrying about these things. Tiptoeing to reach the jars of fruit on the rough-hewn shelves, she hummed the song, remembering the words. *You are not lost from His sight; Somebody waits for your coming, And He'll drive the gloom from your night.*

Back in the kitchen, Hannah looked up from the coffee she was pouring. "You're baking cinnamon bread! Are we celebrating my baptism?"

"Why not? It's a wonderful good thing." Annie didn't want to admit the real reason she had started baking this morning—her sleeplessness over a mountain of troubles. How she wished she didn't have to be the bearer of such unfortunate tidings today. She hated to disappoint her sister, but she was not going to hide the truth. She had learned firsthand how that could sting.

"Dear Hannah . . ." She placed the jars on the counter. "There's some bad news that needs to be known. I was wrong to match you up with Jonah. It was . . . just a mistake—my mistake. But don't you worry. I'm going to put my mind to finding someone else for you. A right good match."

Hannah sipped her coffee, eyeing Annie curiously. "Are you trying to spare my feelings? Because I know that Jonah doesn't favor me. He told me, flat out."

"He did?" Annie blinked. "When was that?"

"Just last night when we talked." Hannah brought a stack of dishes to the table, as if this was any ordinary morning. She didn't seem the least bit upset about Jonah King. On her way to the silverware drawer, she paused near Annie to add in a lowered voice: "It didn't take long to figure out that Jonah favors you."

Annie was flabbergasted. Was she the last one to know about how Jonah King was holding a torch for her? And look at her little sister, not even caring! "He told you that? And you're not disappointed? After everything we planned . . ."

Hannah shrugged. "I don't mind at all, but I hope you won't break his heart. Jonah's a nice fella, just not for me. Besides, I got to talking with Ben King last night, and it was wonderful good. He's so easy to talk with, and I used your tips when things got quiet. Kept the conversation going by talking about the weather. I'm hoping he'll be at the next singing. Or I was thinking, if Mamm gives me more hours at the tea shop, maybe I'll see him in town."

It was not a bad plan, but Annie had trouble absorbing it with all the changes spinning around her. She broke the seal on a jar of peaches and poured them into a bowl, taking a moment to let her thoughts catch up.

"What's the matter, Annie?" Hannah was placing forks on the table. "You look a little shaken."

"Things are changing so fast. Here Jonah King is out and Ben King is in. You've learned your lessons well, and now you're talking on your own. Everyone around me is moving ahead. Seems like I'm going to be left behind, stuck in the mud."

"My head is spinning, too," Hannah admitted. "But I like the feeling. I miss Sarah and Mark and Perry, but the other changes are exciting. I've finally found a fella I like!"

Annie nodded, though something kept her from feeling glad for her sister. "I just wish I could have helped more."

"Don't be that way." Hannah put her hands on her hips, looking authoritative. "You've never been good with change, but you need to pick yourself up, dust yourself off, and move on."

"I've handled a few setbacks in my life," Annie said defensively. "I know how to move on."

Hannah shook her head. "You cling to the old ways, the old customs. It's your nature. You keep all the Christmas traditions. You make the same quilt pattern every time and you never change your recipes, even for a fruit in season. Some of the old ways are good, but you've got to learn to handle the things Gott sends your way. As Mamm says, bloom where you're planted."

Was her younger sister giving her advice now? Annie was glad for the need to turn away and remove the nutty bread from the oven, as she didn't want her sister to see the stubborn frown on her face.

"That's something I'm trying to learn," Annie said, thinking of the letter she'd written last night after her mother went back to bed. Annie had taken writing papers and a pen from the drawer of the dresser and sat down on the bed. *Dear Sarah,* she had written.

You may be surprised to hear this news from me so soon after you left. I know I told you that I would never leave Halfway, but I've had a change of heart.

She had wanted to tell her sister about her longing to have a family and her lonesomeness without a beau and her embarrassing mistake with Jonah King. She had almost written about how her world had come crashing down all around her in the past few hours.

Instead, she had kept the message simple: *If you will still have me, I will come to New York.*

THIRTY-SEVEN

*J*onah was oiling the wheels of the hay cart when the lunch bell rang, the sweet clang floating over the hills. He straightened and cast a look toward the house. Would anyone notice if he hitched up his horse and headed home now? Not that he was chickenhearted about facing Annie, but he wanted to delay the final rejection. Besides, he hadn't seen her all morning and he got the feeling she was avoiding him, too.

Just then Aaron came out of the tack room. The older man looked him up and down as he passed by. "Didn't you hear the lunch bell?" he asked. "Kumm."

And that was that. When it came to older men in the community, Jonah remained respectful.

He washed up in the mud sink, then stepped over the threshold and hung his hat on the hook with the others. There she was in the center of the kitchen, bright as the morning sun. Annie was all business, serving soup to Aaron and Daniel, who were already seated at the table. Annie kept her eyes on the floor, and her voice seemed flat as she spoke to the men.

"Where is Levi?" she asked, hands on her hips. "He was here five minutes ago."

"I'll get him," Jonah offered.

"No. Sit." Her eyes didn't meet his as she spoke, and he felt the chill of her voice travel all the way down his spine.

This was not the Annie he knew.

In the wintry silence he took his place at the table and waited as Annie went to the stove to ladle soup into a bowl for him. Daniel caught his eye and cocked one brow, as if to say: *I'm staying out of this.*

Annie turned away from the stove with a bowl of soup in hand. She was halfway across the kitchen when there was a commotion out back. Sunny barked and the porch door slammed and Levi shouted. "No, Fluffy! I told you not to go . . ."

In a white flash the lamb bolted in the kitchen door and skittered across the floor.

". . . inside!" Levi called, appearing at the door with a stricken expression and a shirt streaked with mud. "Come back!"

The lamb galloped to Annie, its spindly legs struggling to get a grip on the clean linoleum floor. As soon as it had surveyed the folks around the table, the playful lamb gallivanted around as if it were playtime.

Annie paused as the creature circled her skirt. "Fluffy, no!" She held the bowl high, her cheeks rosy with excitement now. "What are you doing in here, little lamb?"

"Get the animal out of here, boy," Aaron ordered his grandson in a gentle tone that hinted at amusement.

"I try and try, but she doesn't listen." Levi kept reaching for the lamb, even as it danced away in a game of chase. Fluffy meandered closer to the table and seemed about to leap onto Aaron's lap when the older man waved it off.

"This is why we should have gotten a dog instead," Daniel muttered.

Jonah grinned, enjoying the chaos. Fluffy had turned a strained lunch into an exciting calamity. He rose from the table and slipped toward the living room doorway, cutting off Fluffy's only other route of escape.

The lamb circled and headed toward Levi, who greeted it with open arms.

"Kumm, now," the boy said. He reached for the animal, but Fluffy wheeled and headed in the opposite direction. . . .

Dashing right into Jonah's arms.

"Got you!" He pulled the lamb against him and cradled the squirming critter in his arms.

"Good, Jonah! You saved the day," Annie cried.

With his back to her as he carried Fluffy to the porch, Jonah reckoned that she must have forgotten that she was angry with him. He smiled. Maybe he would have to send Fluffy into the house every day to cheer Annie up.

Lunch was much more lively after Fluffy's appearance.

"Your lamb is very eager to get into my house," Aaron told Levi. "If I don't watch it, she'll be sitting in a rocking chair, reading the paper."

Everyone chuckled, including Levi. "Doddy, she can't read. She's just a baby."

"But she's a smart one," Jonah teased. "She'll learn fast."

"She is a happy little thing," Annie said, pulling Levi's chair closer to the table. "She reminds me of you when you were a toddler."

"Except that I'm not a sheep," the boy said.

"How could I forget?" Annie's cheeks were pink with excitement now, her lips red as summer berries.

Jonah admired her simple beauty, created by Gott like a flower or a spectacular sunset. But he knew her smile and pretty eyes were just a small glimpse of the beauty within, and that was the girl he had fallen for so many years ago.

The girl inside.

She glanced over and caught Jonah stealing a look at her. Quickly, he looked down at his soup, smiling over Daniel's story of a dog he'd once had who always liked to ride on the seat of the buggy, like a big Amish man.

"One day my brother put a hat on him, and half the people in town were fooled," Daniel said. "Folks wanted to know if we had a relative visiting."

That brought another round of laughter to the table.

Lighthearted talk like this reminded Jonah of his own family gathered round the table for a meal. How easily Annie would fit in there, with her sense of humor and her easy laugh. He set his jaw, wondering if his earnest prayers were meant to be. In some ways, they were closer than they had ever been . . . but still so far away.

After lunch Annie followed Jonah out past the washroom.

"Wait," she called as he reached for the screen door. He turned to find her smoothing her apron down nervously. "Can we talk for a minute?"

He nodded, looking around. Daniel had left for the harness shop, but Aaron was still in the kitchen, having coffee while Levi cleared the table. "Outside?" he suggested, wanting some privacy.

She nodded, and he held the door open for her, noticing the slender curve of her neck as she passed close to him. Sunny stood up when he saw them, probably hoping for table scraps. Jonah scratched the dog's head, then followed Annie around the side of the porch, out of sight of the kitchen.

"I fled like a wild horse last night," Annie said. "That was mean, and I'm sorry."

He nodded. "I'm sorry, too. Truth is, I took this job to be near you, but now, with everything that's happened, I understand if you don't want me around here. I'll talk to your dat, and I can be gone from here soon as he finds someone else."

"No, please don't do that. Dat needs your help, and he's real picky about who he'll hire. He'll never find another man as good as you. He's been slowing down lately, and it eases his mind having a man with your experience around."

He frowned. "I don't want to be here if it makes you skittish."

"I'm not some jumpy colt." She put her hands on her hips. "I can manage with you being here."

"You manage just fine, but I won't stay around here if it's going to make you grumpy as a bullfrog."

"I am not grumpy," she said, scowling.

He rubbed his chin, hesitating. There was no denying the edge in her voice.

She looked down at the ground, then prodded a knot of grass with the toe of her shoe. "Okay, I'm grumpy, all right. But I'm not a bullfrog, and that's not the best thing to say to a girl you want to court. Just so you know, in the future."

In the future . . . *when I'm courting you?* He wondered, his heart leaping in his chest at the notion. "I'll remember that," he said. "Bullfrogs are off the list. Skittish colts, too."

She heaved a wistful sigh and looked up at him. Was that pain or amusement sparkling in her eyes? He couldn't be sure. "Oh, Jonah, you do have a sense of humor. I've enjoyed getting to know you these past weeks. It's just that . . . you took me by surprise."

But you like surprises. You like practical jokes and birthday cakes and snowstorms that blow in unexpectedly and paint the world white. He knew all these things about her, but he didn't want to gush and scare her.

"I never thought of you as someone to court," she said. "You were always just Mary's brother." Her blue eyes were a glimpse of summer sky and cornflowers in a meadow. "I didn't notice you that way but . . . I wasn't really looking at you."

"I'm invisible," he said, trying to keep the misery from his voice. "It's a problem. Folks can't see me. They run right over me with their horse and buggy."

She chuckled. "See that? You are so much funnier than anyone knows."

"There's humor in some very serious things."

"And you see it all. But that's something your family is big on—finding the joy and humor in things. Every time I had dinner at your house when I was growing up, we were laughing over something. Once, I laughed so hard I almost choked on my beets. I was so worried about what Adam would think when he saw me spit out a mouthful of beets."

Adam again. He gave a half smile, holding back his disappointment. He was a good listener, and Annie seemed to want to talk.

"When Mary and I were little, I used to love spending time with your family."

And I liked having you there.

"Even when I was a girl, I longed to marry into the King family. That probably sounds silly to you, but it's the truth. That's how I set my sights on Adam, and you know how long I held on to that dream."

The wind picked up, making one of the quilts hanging behind her flap, and Jonah thought of how ridiculous it was. All those years, Annie had waited for Adam, while Jonah was waiting for Annie. Such a waiting game, like two quilts hung out to dry, flapping alone in the wind.

"I waited so long for him. There was one last burst of hope when he finally came back from his rumspringa, but by the time I got his attention, he'd already fallen for Remy. That much I knew. And so I gave him up. And that meant giving up your family, too."

He wiped his palms on his pants. If he was ever going to ask, now was the time. "What about now? Would you ever consider courting me?"

"I can't," she said quickly.

Hope drained from Jonah's heart. "But you said you always wanted to be a part of my family."

"It's true, but I can't stay here in Halfway much longer. Please don't tell anyone, but I trust you, Jonah. You'll keep my secret, won't you?"

His mouth was suddenly too dry to form words, but he nodded. Yes, he would keep her secret. Hadn't he kept his own for most of his life?

"There are so many closed doors for me here." Her eyes sparked with something akin to pain as she looked over the rolling hills. "But I think the Heavenly Father has opened a window for me somewhere else." She smoothed her apron, nodding with resolve. "I'm going to New York."

The ground dropped away under his feet, as if he had fallen into a hole. "But Halfway is your home," he said. "Your family and friends are here. Your church is here, and you know half the town. You can't leave."

"Perry and Sarah are there. And an Old Order church, too. It's a scary thing, to move so far, but this is what I have to do."

He didn't see it. Why would she think Gott was sending her to New York?

But the ache clogging his throat kept him from asking any more questions, and Aaron was calling from behind him.

"Jonah?"

"You'd better go." When she took a breath and looked up at him, the flash of her blue eyes seared straight through to his aching heart. "Denki, Jonah. Thanks for listening and for keeping my secret."

Remember this moment . . . this day, he told himself. If she was moving away, it would have to be enough. Memories like this would have to be enough to last a lifetime.

That night, after dinner, he poured a box of jigsaw puzzle pieces onto the table and sat there staring at the chaotic mess that was his life. Everything in pieces . . . one thousand pieces.

Jonah ran his hand over the mound to level the pieces, then stopped. Suddenly, it was too much . . . too overwhelming.

"Are you starting a new puzzle?" Ruthie came over and picked up the box. "Such a pretty picture, but the little boat looks lonely."

"Let me see." Simon leaned over her shoulder to get a look at the picture. "That's not in America. See? It says Norway."

"Norway is in Europe." Susie sat down at the table beside Jonah and started turning over pieces, one by one, so that the colored side was facing up. "How many pieces are in this puzzle?"

"One thousand," Simon said. "That's what it says on the box."

"Can we help, Jonah?" Susie asked as she continued to flip pieces.

Dear Gott, I need all the help I can get. "Ya. The more the better," he said, looking up at Simon and Ruthie. "You, too?"

"Sure." Simon took a seat. "Did you ever go to Norway, Adam?" Simon asked their older brother, who was sitting in a rocking chair, reading *The Budget.*

"No. I only got as far as Rhode Island. It's a long way across the ocean to Europe."

Still studying the box, Ruthie wandered over to another chair at the table. "What's a fajord?"

"It's called a 'fiyord,' " Leah said, looking up from her book. "That's what they call it in Norway. It's a narrow blue sea with high land all around it."

"So many beautiful places that Gott created," Mary said as she came into the room. Katie was right behind her, dressed in footy pajamas. She crossed the room and paused by Jonah's side, where she peered up to the table. The little girl smelled of soap and her hair was still damp around the edges of her face.

"Bath night?" Jonah asked.

Katie nodded without smiling. She reached her arms up to him, and he pulled her into his lap so that she could have a perfect view of the scattered puzzle pieces.

Sam paused in the doorway, then hurried over when he caught sight of them. "I like puzzles."

Mary brought over two chairs for Sam and her. "This puzzle hasn't been out of the box for a long time," she said. "I think Jonah is the only one with the courage to take it on."

"Either courage or foolishness," he said, though he felt himself relaxing. He was no longer sinking in a hole; with his family around him, he was on solid ground, Gott's good earth. Jonah felt the bitter disappointment ease. His family was a good distraction, a true blessing.

"This is too many pieces," Simon said. "I don't even know how to start."

Jonah understood that feeling.

But he had always loved jigsaw puzzles. It was the reason he had chosen his horse, whose markings resembled puzzle pieces. Besides that, Jigsaw's bad temper was like a puzzle waiting to be solved—a wild horse who would find peace when all the chaos around him settled into place.

"You start by turning the puzzle pieces over." Susie's nimble fingers flipped and spread puzzle pieces as she spoke. "One piece at a time, that's what Dat used to say."

"I know that." Simon rubbed his chin, reminding Jonah of himself. "But so many pieces look alike. This one is blue. Maybe it's the sky, or maybe the water. How do you tell?"

"Mmm. You might not know where it goes until later," Jonah said. "But there are a few ways to set it up. First, find all the pieces with a straight edge, like this one." He held up a piece. "Put these around the edge of the table. Those will make the border."

Busy hands sorted and shifted puzzle pieces on the worn table. Jonah found two border pieces that matched, and he let Katie have the satisfaction of fitting them together.

"Good," she said, smiling up at him.

Jonah let his gaze skim over his dear family as they tried to match up the right pieces to make the border. Sometimes it took many tries to make things fit. All it took was patience, and he had plenty of that. Working together, they would build something out of these cardboard scraps.

One piece at a time.

THIRTY-EIGHT

Gabe let Mercury have plenty of line as he scowled at the road and gray skies looming above. He dreaded the chore ahead, but it had been hanging over him like a dark cloud, and he was eager to be rid of it.

He was headed into Halfway to apologize to Elsie Lapp. His excuse for coming into town was to bring his sisters to work, since he didn't want to open a can of worms by explaining everything to Adam.

He tried not to listen to Leah and Susie's chatter about their job at the tea shop, but Susie's voice was always so animated that it was hard to ignore.

"I hope Lovina wants me to work in the front today," Susie said. "Talking with customers is no work at all, and I like tending to the pastry case. Lovina lets me clean it each morning and set up the muffins and scones just so."

"You're a good worker in the tea shop," Leah told her twin. "The job suits you well."

"You're a good worker, too, but the tea shop isn't your favorite thing, is it?"

"It's a fine job, but I'm still hoping to be trained as a teacher. Remy said she would help me, but she doesn't know how things are done. Next time I see Emma Lapp, I'm going to ask her if I could be her assistant for a while."

Gabe felt a twinge of guilt at the mention of Emma's name. If things were right between them, he could have asked Emma about his sister. He could have been a big help in fixing Leah up with a position at the schoolhouse. But now Emma wasn't going to look at any of his notions too favorably.

The horse slowed as they came to the edge of town, passing the Zooks' old barn that was now used as a market, then coming up on the bank where Mammi liked to take the carriage through the drive-through. Next they passed the ice-cream parlor, where the picnic tables would be pulled inside soon to save them from winter weather. In the golden October sunshine with a brisk wind stirring leaves, it wasn't hard to believe that winter was around the next corner.

Would Blake let them ride the motorbikes in the winter? He hoped so. It would be a long, boring winter without the dirt bikes. The ice could be slippery and treacherous on a bike, but in Blake's magazines Gabe had seen pictures of riders flying over mounds of packed snow. He would like to try that.

There was a nudge on his shoulder. "Gabe! Are you dropping us at the tea shop or not?"

He jerked to attention just as the tea shop passed by. "Whoa!" Slowing the horse, he guided the carriage toward the right and turned down the next side street. "Sorry about that," he called back to his sisters as he reined Mercury in.

"Daydreaming again?" Leah teased. "If Susie didn't nudge you, we'd be on our way to Paradise."

The girls climbed out of the carriage and thanked him for the ride. Gabe watched them link arms and make their way toward the tea shop. They were so caught up in chatter that they wouldn't notice him tying up his horse to the hitching post and stopping in at the Country Store.

His shoes felt heavy as he stepped over the threshold and plodded toward the moment he dreaded.

The shop was brighter than he remembered it. Tourists moved down some of the aisles, hovering over displays of soap or apple butter like bees over flowers. He glanced toward the old cash register, looking for Elsie, but the tall chair was empty.

He took his hat off but hesitated by the hat rack. What if Elsie wasn't here today? Maybe her dat or her brother Caleb was working. That would be awkward, trying to explain himself to them.

Looking for Elsie, he moved up the candy aisle, where there were now displays of homemade candy—taffy, candy apples, and fudge made by Amish families in their district. The sight of butterscotch fudge made Gabe's mouth water. This was a lot more appetizing than the candy bars they'd been selling in the past few years. The shop was starting to reflect Amish folk again, the way it had when Emma and Elsie's mother ran it.

On the next aisle, he found Elsie with two Englisher ladies who didn't even spare him a look. They were riveted to her description of how apple butter was made. "I'll take three jars," one woman said, filling her basket. "It will make a wonderful gift."

Just then Elsie glanced up at Gabe with a look of surprise. "I'll help you at the register whenever you're ready," she told the women, then headed back to the counter, motioning Gabe to follow.

"What can I get you, Gabe?"

"I'm not here for buying," he said, glad to move away from the other customers. "I've come to ask your forgiveness." His throat was dry as autumn leaves.

Elsie eyed him curiously as she climbed onto her stool by the register. "For what?"

He turned his hat in his hands. "When you arrived at our house for church the other day. I'm sorry, Elsie. I . . . I never meant to be mean to you, and I was less than a man, running from your carriage. But I wasn't running from you. It was Emma. . . ." What kind of chickenhearted man ran away from a girl? It made his face flare with heat just to think of it.

"I didn't take offense," she said, her round eyes earnest. "Emma told me what had happened with the two of you. I knew."

"Something just snapped inside me when I saw that she was in the carriage." He pinched the brim of his hat, not wanting to say too much.

"It's sad, the things that are keeping you two apart. I wish there was something I could do to help."

He smacked his hat against his thigh. "There's nothing that can be done. Emma's a baptized member of the church now. She can't be seen with the likes of me." He knew that wasn't completely true. As a baptized member, Emma had promised to follow the rules and regulations, but she was allowed to court a fella who wasn't baptized. The problem was the things that Gabe was interested in . . . bike racing and a souped-up buggy. Emma couldn't get tangled up with a fella who broke the rules.

"You make it sound like there's no hope at all," Elsie said. "Don't tell me you're giving up on Emma."

Gabe swallowed back the knot of emotion in his throat. "It's Emma who's giving up. And I understand why. I think she's figured out that I'm no angel."

Elsie folded her arms across her chest and sighed. "She told me about the motorbikes."

Gabe rolled his eyes toward the heavens. "Ya, I figured."

"Don't tell her I talked to you, but she's heartbroken. Since you two parted, she hasn't had much appetite, and I haven't heard her laugh once. My sister has always been a serious person, but this is different. She looks like there's a bitter taste on her tongue all the time."

Gabe knew that taste. Like a sour lemon that brought tears to your eyes. Nothing was quite right without Emma. Food tasted flat, his bed seemed hard, and the sun had refused to shine for days. Even the cows were cranky. In his logical mind he knew the sun would shine again, but he wasn't so sure he would ever enjoy it in the same way.

But he couldn't tell Elsie any of this. Any fella would be hard-pressed to admit how much he'd fallen for a woman, and Gabe was no exception.

"Ya, Emma has been worrying me lately," Elsie said.

Gabe didn't want to think of Emma, so solemn and hurt and all because of him. The girl didn't have a spare ounce on her; it wasn't good that she wasn't eating. He put his hat on, ready to leave. "Give her my best," he said formally, then leaned forward to add: "I miss her, too."

Elsie nodded. Wisdom shone in her dark eyes as she looked up at him. "I'm not giving up on you two. I never give up on happiness."

Such a girlish thing, to believe in happy endings and true love. Gabe imagined that Elsie would get along well with his sisters, but as far as he was concerned, hope was a foolish thing. Light as birdsong, it could make you feel good, but it faded fast.

THIRTY-NINE

*W*ith a wire basket of eggs in one hand, Annie rounded the henhouse just as a wind gusted through, swirling orange and brown leaves around her. Just days ago October had blown in with blustery winds and more rain, a warning of the colder season to come.

Autumn was in the air, and as Annie buttoned her sweater at the neck she was struck by the changes all around her. Not just the fiery colors of the foliage, but the fact that her sister Sarah wasn't here to enjoy it. Sarah, Perry, and Mark were settling in up in New York, in a district that would soon be Annie's home, too.

The thought of leaving Halfway brought a flicker of worry to her heart, but she kept reminding herself that things were changing here, too. The earth seemed to be shifting beneath her feet. Her sister Hannah was baptized now and courting Ben King. Although Annie was happy for her, she was getting a little tired of hearing about Ben-this and Ben-that every single night as they lay in bed.

And then there was Mary, her very best friend. Mary would wed

Five soon and start her life as a young wife. Of course, Mary would stay nearby, but things would be changing. In the blink of an eye, she'd be pregnant, and starting her family with Five.

Annie bit her lower lip as regret tugged at her. Ah, well, there was nothing to do but look forward and make her plans for New York. She had promised Mamm she would wait until the end of the busy harvest season, another month or two, and then she would go. If everything was changing around her, she wasn't going to stand still like a stick-in-the-mud.

As she passed the barn, Annie was stopped by her father.

"I'm going to drop a broken harness off at Daniel's shop in Halfway," Aaron informed her. "Then I'll ride over to the seed shop in Paradise. There's a discount if we get our spring seed order in early."

"That'll take a few hours." Annie shifted the eggs to her other hand. "Do you want me to go with you, Dat?"

"Why would you do that? You're needed here, Annie girl." He looked a little pale, and since he had been slowing down lately, she worried that it wasn't only his age. He was just over fifty years old— not an old man—but lately he seemed tired most of the time and his skin was as gray as ashes. "Besides, a ride into town is nearly a nap— all that sitting."

"Well, don't be falling asleep in the carriage," Annie said as he continued into the barn. Heading into the house with the eggs, she looked back at her dat, recalling his reaction when she had told him she would be going to New York. "First, we must both sit," he'd said, finding a spot on a hay bale. "And now, tell me why you want to leave this wonderful good farm Gott has blessed us with."

Telling her dat had been one of the hardest things. It was important for Dat to know that she was grateful for Gott's bounty, for the farm and the home and the love that had always been here. "But I need to find a husband, Dat, and there's none left here in Halfway."

He had nodded sagely. "You missed the harvest season, Annie girl. I don't want you to go, but I understand if you need to move on and try another crop."

Those had been his exact words—another crop! Why did Amish men always compare things to farming and herding? His little joke had endeared him to her all the more. It would be hard to say good-bye to both her parents, but she reminded herself that there would be a new life to look forward to in New York.

Now, as she passed by the garden, the chirping voices of young boys caught her attention. Levi was playing with his new companion, Sam King, whom Jonah had brought to the house a few times. She slowed to watch their game.

"Look at this one!" Levi pointed to a weed that was half as tall as he was.

"That's a big one," Sam agreed. "Should I give it a pull and see what happens?" He held up his hands, which looked tiny under the large garden gloves he was using.

"Go on and try it," Levi said, stepping back to give him room.

Sam clasped the fat weed in his gloved hands. There was much show of grunting and pulling, but with some effort he pulled it out.

"Gut," Levi said. "We'll get a good price on that at the market."

"What are you talking about?" Annie said under her breath, amused.

Just then Jonah appeared around the side of the garden shed. "So . . . you see that I've put the weed pickers to work."

"I see that." Annie put her basket of eggs on the ground, glad to see Jonah. Now that they were past the awkwardness, she always felt happy to see him. There was something about having him around that reassured her; it warmed her to know that, sure as the sun would rise each morning, Jonah would appear at their farm, ready to lend a hand. With all the changes in her world, Jonah was steadfast and reliable. Solid as a rock.

"Who would think weeding the garden could be so much fun?" Jonah said.

She smiled. "You have a knack for making work fun for them." Every time Sam came to visit, both boys became captivated with chores and games.

"Nay, it's not me." He pointed a finger to his head. "They use their imaginations—and they make everything a game. Right now they're collecting weeds for the compost pile, but in the game, they pretend to bring them to the farmers' market to sell their wares. Thistle salesmen."

Annie laughed. "Thistle salesmen? And who will buy their weeds?"

One side of Jonah's mouth lifted in a subtle grin. "Imaginary customers, of course."

"They're very creative. It's all good experience for when they want to sell in the market," she said. "But if they could find a real market for weeds, now, that I'd like to know about."

"I'll get them working on it," Jonah teased. "Just as soon as we weed the garden and feed the horses."

"You get a lot done in one day, Jonah. I don't know what Dat would do without you."

"He'd find some other young Amish man to help him out," he said quietly.

"But none of them would make the chores go as fast as you do. I always tried to make work a joy when I was younger. The things I would do to get Hannah to stop being grumpy about chores! Singing to the cows and giving her little tastes of treats we baked." She laughed at the memory of Hannah's sour expression. "She was a hard one to please. She never quite took to farm chores."

"Is that why she usually goes into town to work at the tea shop?"

"I reckon the tea shop suits her better." She picked up her basket of eggs, though she was reluctant to end the conversation. "Did you always take a shine to farm work?"

"Ya. I never thought to do anything else. There are some, like Adam or Sadie, who look for their heart's desire down the road. Me, I did some looking but I never went too far. The farm, my family ..." He shrugged. "It's a good fit. I always knew I would stay here in Halfway."

"I always thought I would, too." The words were out before she realized how much they revealed. Ya, she'd been concerned about leaving home, but she still stood by her decision. "I mean, I would have liked to stay, but now my mind's made up, and all the plans are made. I got a letter from Sarah last week, and she's found me a place. There's a family in the district in need of help. The mamm is expecting and she needs to rest till her baby is born. I'll stay with them and mind their three small children." She glanced over at Sam and Levi, who were now pushing a wheelbarrow of weeds over to the compost heap. "That's what I do best—taking care of the little ones."

"You have a gift for it." It was no flowery compliment; he said it as a fact, and it made her heart glad that he saw her so clearly.

She glanced toward the house. "I'd better get back. Mamm wants these eggs for a dish she's making." Though she longed to linger and watch the little boys. There was also the temptation to stay and talk with Jonah, who made work a joy for her, too. Whether milking, shoveling, or grooming, he always managed a conversation that took her mind off the task. Such a talker he was when you got to know him! Hardly the Quiet One. Yesterday they had spent the afternoon together in the stables, tending to the horses. Normally, the process of scraping dung and clumps of mud from two dozen hooves was a task she dreaded, but Jonah's knowledge of the horses and his dry sense of humor had made the afternoon pass like the wind.

"And I'd better get these gardeners the tools they need." Jonah ducked into the shed and reappeared with two small spades. "Try these, boys. For the really deep weeds, you can dig down around the roots. Just don't disturb the sweet potatoes."

The boys let out a squeal of delight and came running toward Jonah. Glancing back at them on her way to the house, Annie smiled. He was good with the little ones, too, and that was a good thing for young Sam, who would grow up without a father.

At least he would always have Jonah.

Over in the garden, Jonah was lifting the boys into the wheelbarrow for a ride. Ya, he would always have his big brother.

That afternoon Annie was taking clothes down from the line, moving fast to stay ahead of the approaching storm. Black clouds billowed over the hills and the wind gusted around her, tearing at her skirt as she moved along the clothesline. Normally she would take time to fold the clothes, but today she dropped trousers and dresses into the basket willy-nilly. Better to have rumpled clothes than soaking wet laundry.

Sunny barked a warning, as Mamm called, "Hurry in!" Lovina waved with one hand, pressing the other to her prayer kapp to keep it in place in the wind.

"I'll be right there!" Annie shouted, though the wind seemed to sweep her voice away. She dropped both laundry and clothespins into the basket now. She could sort them later, safe in the house.

Just then a flash lit the sky and Annie saw an unnerving slash of lightning silhouetted against the dark hills. The quick crash of thunder let her know the storm was getting close . . . and she still had another line of clothes to bring in.

Rain was falling slowly now, fat drops that splatted on her head and shoulders. At this rate, she would be soaked before she got inside.

A dark figure crossed the lawn—it was Jonah, running toward her.

"Let me help," he said, nearly tearing two shirts from the rope line.

Annie felt a mixture of relief and amusement. She had never seen a man tend a clothesline, and Jonah was pulling pins off so fast they flew to the ground over his shoulder.

At last, they got everything down. Jonah grabbed one basket and Annie held the other to her chest. Head down against the driving rain, she held her breath and ran alongside him. The sky opened up, tossing down splattering rain just as Jonah pulled the porch door open. She felt giddy with excitement as they scurried inside.

"Where did that come from all of a sudden?" she asked, swiping at her wet cheeks with the back of one hand.

Jonah took off his hat and shook off the rain. "It came from clouds in the sky," he said with barely a grin, though amusement danced in his dark eyes. "That's how it looked to me."

"Oh, you're so funny." She picked up one of the baskets. "Kumm, help me bring these into the front room." The damp wind blowing through the mud porch chilled the air, so she would do the sorting and folding inside.

Mamm looked up from the cutting board, where peeled potatoes waited to be sliced. "That storm blew in fast, but you two moved faster. I was watching you through the window."

"We saved the dry clothes in the nick of time," Annie said. "Thanks to Jonah."

"It's a blessing to have you around, Jonah," Mamm said.

He nodded, holding up the basket. "And where do you want this?"

"The front room."

"And would you light a fire in there?" Lovina called after him. "There's a chill in the air."

The two little boys were glued to the window of the front room. "Did you see that lightning?" Levi asked.

"It's Gott's electricity," Sam advised.

"But I don't like those loud booms," Levi said wistfully.

Jonah placed a laundry basket on the floor. "That's just thunder. It's the noise made by the lightning."

"It makes me shiver," Levi said.

"But you're safe inside." Annie folded a towel under her chin and touched the boy's head consolingly. "Why don't you boys play a game or get the storybooks out?"

Sam moved away from the window. "Let's play a game."

"Is my dat afraid of those booms?" Levi asked, still focused on the window.

"Not the booms," Jonah said. "We all need to stay away from lightning but the thunder won't hurt you." He went back to the kitchen to fetch firewood.

As Annie folded a shirt, lightning zigzagged through the sky beyond the window, and Levi clapped his hands over his ears in anticipation of the noise.

"Kumm, dear one." She pulled him away from the window, hugging him with one arm. The poor thing was afraid of the storm and worried about his parents, too. "Do you want to help me fold?" When he shook his head, she brought him over to the shelf, where Sam was looking through games.

"Let's play jacks," Sam said.

Levi shook his head. "I don't know how."

"Jacks is a good game to learn." Jonah returned, carrying a scuttle full of wood. "I'll play a round with you if you promise to let me win."

"But I want to win," Sam insisted as Levi took the little ball and bounced it hard. The small red ball leaped high in the air, then dropped into the laundry basket.

Everyone laughed, and Levi's worries seemed to melt away. But as rain tapped against the window, Annie wondered about the folks in her family traveling in the blustery storm. Rebecca and Hannah were working at the tea shop. Daniel was also in Halfway, managing the harness shop. And Dat was probably on the road, heading home from the seed shop in Paradise.

Not a good day for travel.

As the dinner hour approached, rain and wind continued to batter the house. Annie began to share Levi's worry. Would their family make it home?

While the boys played in the front room, Jonah and Annie warmed up with hot tea. Annie kept expecting to hear the familiar sound of horses' hooves on the lane or Dat calling from the mudroom, but the only noise was the rush of wind and rain against the house.

"It's not letting up at all," Lovina said. "It's not safe to travel in this until it all blows over." She insisted that Jonah and Sam stay for dinner, and Jonah didn't argue. He thanked Lovina for her kindness, slipped on a plastic poncho, and went out to the barn to milk the family's three cows.

Mamm took the meat loaf from the oven. "That'll be cool enough in twenty minutes, but we're still missing a few." She glanced up at the clock.

"Nearly six," Annie said aloud. She had been watching the clock for the last hour. "I keep thinking their carriages will come down the lane any minute."

"Not if they're smart." Mamm took a deep breath, rubbing one temple. "Jonah knows it's not wise to go out in this. Your dat and your sister would know the same. If they got the same storm in town, maybe they decided to stay put?"

It was a good point. "There could be a message on the phone. I'll go to the shanty."

"You'll get soaked." Her mamm put a dish towel over the potatoes au gratin to keep them warm. "Have some dinner first. We'll eat as soon as Jonah finishes milking the cows."

Annie nodded and started setting the table, though if she'd had her choice she would have gladly skipped dinner and run to the phone shanty.

As Annie bowed her head in silent prayer, she asked Gott to keep her family safe from harm. Although she was grateful for the distraction of Levi and Sam, who enjoyed the novelty of having dinner together, she was anxious to finish. She couldn't relax until she knew everyone was safe.

Wary of the strong winds, Jonah warned that it wasn't a good idea to take a carriage. Better to walk the half mile. He would go along so that he could call his family's phone and leave a message for them not to expect Sam and him home tonight.

"This is an adventure for me," Annie said as they stepped out into the dark storm. The thunder and lightning had passed, but rain was falling steadily. She had secured the plastic poncho around her with a string at the waist, but the wind tugged at the bottom. "I've never deliberately walked into a storm."

"You're not missing anything," Jonah said.

With the patter of falling rain all around them, the farm seemed different—like a forest of rain.

"It's not so bad," she told Jonah. "I could have walked this by my—" The words weren't past her lips when the wind kicked up and knocked her back. She put her arms out to regain her balance, but that opened the poncho for the wind to catch it like a kite.

She wobbled and gasped and finally laughed as she was knocked back into Jonah's arms.

"Easy there," he said gently, his lips not far from her ear.

"That wind is like a giant fist!" Annie had never experienced anything quite like it, but somehow she was more amused than frightened. Was it because Jonah was by her side, here to save her?

"This storm has a lot of power. I've seen winds like that knock over carriages. It's a good thing we're walking." He eased her to her feet again, but he kept one hand behind her back, his fingers curling round her rib cage. "How about if I hold on to you, just in case it hits again?"

"That'd be good." She didn't mind the feel of his arm around her at all. In fact, there was something reassuring about the way her body fit against his. Something very natural about it. What a blessing that he was here tonight, when she and Mamm truly needed help.

As they walked together, arm in arm, their steps matched in the dark storm, she thought about what he said about how a carriage could topple in high winds.

"Do you think something happened to their carriage?" she asked, worrying aloud. "In the rain and wind . . ."

"I don't think Rebecca and Daniel would leave town in a storm like this," he said evenly. "And your dat has more experience with foul weather than all of us put together."

"That's true. I'm just all in knots about it. I think Mamm is worried, too, only she doesn't want to scare me."

"Let's just get to the phone shanty. One step at a time."

She looked up at him in admiration as he continued to guide her forward. Jonah's easy, steady approach was good at a time like this.

At last, the small shanty was in sight. Another gust of wind battered them as they reached the tiny hut, but Jonah held on to her tightly. She felt the wind tug at her dress, and she was sure she would have been swept away if it weren't for Jonah.

He opened the door and she stepped inside, wind whistling through the tiny building until he entered and closed the door behind them. The space was small, and Jonah stood close behind her, his hand between her shoulder blades as she checked the answering machine.

"The light's flashing! There's a message." She pressed the button, and relief washed over her at the sound of Rebecca's voice.

"Mr. Kraybill warned us that there's a bad storm coming with lots of rain and high winds, so we're all staying in town. We'll sleep in the office over the harness shop. Hannah is here, and Leah and Susie King, too."

Jonah rubbed his chin. "I'm glad to know my sisters are in good hands."

"Susie is very excited. She's calling it a storm bee," Becca went on.

"That sounds like Susie," he said.

When Rebecca's message ended, Annie checked the answering machine one more time. "Only one message," she said, looking up at Jonah, whose face was barely lit by the flash of the answering machine light. "Do you think Dat is trying to make his way home in the storm?"

"I don't know." There was a grave silence as they both considered the possibilities. "Is there someone else we can call? Maybe a friend in Paradise he might be staying with? Do you know anyone there, Amish or English?"

Annie took a deep breath, considering. "No one I can think of." She stared at the floor while Jonah quickly called his family's phone shanty and left a message there, saying he and Sam were fine and would stay the night at the Stoltzfus farm.

When he hung up, she stared at the phone. "Who can we call? We have to find Dat."

"You won't have much luck finding an Amish man with a telephone." Annie knew he was right, but she didn't want to leave the phone shanty without word from Dat. "I'm so worried for him."

"I know," Jonah said softly. "But we can't stay here all night." He touched her cheek gently. "You're a good daughter to worry for your dat, but Gott will take care of him."

His touch stirred something deep inside her even as it seemed pure as snow. Maybe it was because his words reminded her of a song refrain—*God will take care of you.* . . .

As they walked back to the house, Annie leaned heavily into Jonah. The excitement of their journey in the storm had faded to a dull fear that she could not ignore. Like a burr, it needled her and hindered her every movement as she worried about her dat. Was he out in this storm alone, in the cold, driving rain? Were the battery lights working on his carriage? Was he right now calling the phone shanty, leaving a message telling them not to worry?

Annie held tight to Jonah and tried to chase those dark thoughts from her mind. She imagined waking up in the morning and finding her dat in his usual chair, reading a newspaper while he sipped coffee.

Please, Gott, let that happen just as it has every other morning. . . .

Back at the house, they stepped into the mud porch, hung up the rain gear, and dried off. Inside, they found Lovina on the couch, sandwiched by two sleeping boys who leaned against her.

She held up the book in her lap. "I was reading them Bible stories, and suddenly, they got very quiet."

Jonah squatted down beside his brother. "They had a long day."

"Any news?" Mamm asked, her eyes alight with hope.

"Someone in town warned them about the storm," Jonah said.

"Rebecca, Daniel, and Hannah are going to stay in the office over the harness shop," Annie explained. "Susie and Leah are with them. They plan to stay through tomorrow's work and return home in the afternoon."

Lovina nodded. "I thought as much. Any word from Aaron?"

Annie shook her head. "No message from Dat."

"He must have taken cover somewhere along the way," Lovina said. "Maybe in Paradise, or at a friend's farmhouse."

Jonah lifted Sam into his arms and straightened, hitching the sleeping boy over his shoulder. "Where should I put this one?"

"Upstairs," Lovina said as Levi shifted and snuggled against her. "You and Sam can sleep in Sarah's old room."

"I'll show you," Annie offered.

"And I'll get this one to bed." Lovina rose from the couch and turned to scoop Levi into her arms. The small boy was lighter than Sam, so it was no problem for her.

"Kumm." Annie took a small lantern and led the way upstairs. Away from the fire of the living room there was a chill in the air. Autumn was here. Inside Sarah's old bedroom she turned down the quilt and stood back to watch as Jonah tucked his little brother in.

"He might want an extra blanket." She took a warm blanket from the closet and spread it over the sleeping boy's feet.

"That's good," Jonah said quietly.

When he bent over to kiss Sam on the forehead, she felt a pang of tenderness for this man who had lost his father but still knew how to care for a child. Jonah would be a fine father someday.

A wonderful good dat.

FORTY

*I*t was a vigil of sorts; waiting for Aaron's carriage to turn down the lane. Jonah knew Aaron would have looked for a place to stay the night, but not knowing that he was safe kept everyone on edge.

Annie stood at the front window, hugging herself as she stared into the darkness. Behind her, Jonah sat quietly, his fingertips pressed to his mouth as he considered distracting Annie.

"There's no need for all of us to stay up all night," Lovina said as she gathered the children's books into a neat stack and tucked them away on the shelf. "Why don't you two get some sleep? Jonah? Don't feel obliged to stay up waiting."

"Denki. When I'm tired, I'll go up."

"And you, too, Annie." She slid an arm around her daughter's shoulders. "He'll be along soon. Don't you worry."

Annie hugged her mamm. "I'll just feel so much better to see him arrive home."

"Well, if he's staying off the road at someone's place, you're going to be up all night." Lovina patted her daughter's shoulder and turned away. "But I don't think I can sleep a wink either. I'll make some cookies for the tea shop and kill two birds with one stone."

Jonah let his eyes follow Lovina as she disappeared into the kitchen. He wondered if Annie's mother knew how he felt about her daughter. Lovina was a woman who read people well, so he expected that she knew. If so, she would have realized that he would gladly stay up all night if it meant spending time alone with Annie.

Was that selfish? Here they were, at wit's end waiting for Aaron to come home, and Jonah couldn't help but notice the tilt of Annie's chin and the slenderness of her fingers as she pressed them against the windowsill. She had rejected him. She was leaving Halfway. She had said no to him in every way. And yet, he hadn't stopped loving her. He didn't know if he ever would.

"How can you stay so calm?" Annie asked.

"I have faith in Gott's plan," he said quietly.

"Do you think He's planning to send my dat home tonight?" she asked, still staring out the window.

"I can't say what will happen, Annie." He frowned. Annie wouldn't be consoled to hear that Gott didn't always deliver everything a person wanted.

He thought of another dark night, nearly two years ago, when he'd been waiting with his brothers and sisters for his parents to come home. Their simple waiting vigil had tumbled into a nightmare.

Suddenly Annie turned from the window, her face open, her blue eyes full of light. "Oh, Jonah, I'm sorry. You've been through this before with . . . with your parents." Biting her cherry red lips, she came and sat beside him. "Is that what you've been thinking?"

He nodded. He didn't want her pity, but he would not lie to her.

"Do you want to talk about it?"

"Do you really want to hear it? Because I don't want to scare you. This thing with your dat . . . it's a very different situation, I think."

"I know that. But tell me about that night. When did you hear the news?"

Strange how that night seemed so far away and yet so vivid in his memory. "I didn't hear it so much as I saw it."

He and Mary had been the oldest in the house, with Adam gone on his rumspringa. Jonah remembered talking with Mary about why their parents could have been running so late on their errands.

"When Mamm and Dat and Simon missed dinner, Gabe and I went looking for them while Sadie went to the shanty to call the police. We retraced their route to Halfway first, but didn't find anything. By the time we got back to the farm, we started circling toward the back lots. That was when we saw the flashing lights of the police cars."

The things he remembered about that night still surprised him. How the seat of the carriage was cold as a block of ice, the ground so frozen that the carriage bounced over small ruts in the road. The lights of the emergency vehicles, flashing red and blue and white like stars on the ground, had drawn his eyes and beckoned him. He could still remember that sinking feeling as if the earth were slipping away under his boots, dropping him into darkness.

"So you saw the carriage?" she asked softly.

Jonah shook his head. He could still see the creases at the corners of the sheriff's eyes as he stopped them. "Hank warned us not to get any closer. Traumatizing, that was what he called it. He brought us over to the ambulance, where the paramedics were taking care of Simon. Not a scratch on him, but he couldn't stop shivering. He couldn't speak. He was in shock."

Those had been dark days, just after they'd learned that Mamm and Dat had been shot and killed. Simon, who'd been traveling with them in the buggy, had been spared, but he'd been shocked into silence. Just eight years old and lost in the dark.

"Little Simon didn't talk to anyone for months," Annie said. "Mary talked to me about it all the time. She was heartbroken for him, but she couldn't get him to say more than a word here and there."

"Ya, and he had those terrible nightmares, too. We were all worried." Simon had remained silent for months after the murders. He had seen the killer, but the truth had been locked inside him.

"What brought him out of that bad way?" Annie asked.

"Adam spent a lot of time with him. And when Remy came along, she got Simon to open up more and more. We didn't know she was a reporter, but she dug into every bit of information she found. In the end, she helped the police find the man who had killed Mamm and Dat." Although the Amish believed that Gott brought His own justice to those who sinned, it had helped to find the man who killed their parents. Jonah had been relieved to know that a killer was no longer in their neighborhood. Simon had felt the same way.

The truth had lifted the cloak of darkness.

Jonah rubbed the back of his neck. "Those were dark days, but Gott has healed our family. The sorrow has faded, and Gott has eased our pain. Simon has come back to us with his love for the horses and plenty of words now. I was just talking to Teacher Emma about him, and she's seen a lot of progress."

"Gott heals in amazing ways." Annie's blue eyes sparkled with hope.

"It's true. We still miss our parents, of course, but now we're all beginning to remember more of the good things. When I'm walking around on our farm, I still feel my father there. It's as if Dat is just around the corner of the barn or leaning on the fence by the beech trees. And when I hear the birds chirping or see them circling the fields, I think of Dat listening to the birdsong that made him smile."

"Your dat was a wonderful man. He was always singing as he walked around the farm, and he used to tease me about my red lips, saying that I must have just eaten my way through a bowl of berries."

Jonah felt a smile tug at his mouth. "That sounds like Dat."

"And your mamm . . ." She looked toward the kitchen to be sure Lovina wasn't listening. "Don't tell Mamm, but Esther was the one who taught me how to make a good, flaky piecrust. And do you remember how she used to braid it on top? Such a nice touch. She could put a pie together, one-two-three, as if it was no trouble at all."

"I thought there was something familiar about your shoofly pie," he said, warmed by the memory of Mamm standing at the kitchen counter, pushing her rolling pin over dough. He still missed her. He missed them both. But he would not question Gott's will.

"Denki, Jonah." She pressed her hands to her heart, her voice earnest. "Thank you for sharing your story with me. Denki for staying with us now."

"No need to thank me." It was a man's duty to help in a situation like this, no matter what his feelings for Annie were.

No matter that he still loved her.

"You've been a pillar of strength through this terrible storm." Tears glimmered in her eyes, that blue of a soaring summer sky. "There's no one else I would rather have here, helping us, than you, Jonah."

He felt a twinge of satisfaction. So Annie cared for him in some way; she loved him like a brother. It was not what he'd planned, but a starving man had to take any crumb thrown his way.

He took her hand, so smooth against his rough, big paws. "Even in the darkest night, Gott won't leave you without a light."

She nodded, swiping at a tear.

Then, without warning, she pulled away her hand, reached up, and hugged him.

The breath froze in his lungs at the feel of her small, soft body clinging to his big, square frame.

A second later, his arms wrapped around her. Only a fool would refuse such a soft embrace. He held her close, wondering if she could feel the love burning inside him. Surely the thumping of his heart pounded through the wall of his chest.

A gentle sigh whispered from her throat as she relaxed in his arms, and he wished he could be with her always. He prayed to Gott that she would give up her plans to go to New York and stay here in Halfway.

Stay here with me.

He could not protect her from every sorrow, but he could stand by her side, her pillar of strength.

Jonah kept the fire going through the night, and Lovina brought blankets for the three of them to keep warm as they waited in the front room. Lovina settled into her favorite rocking chair, and he and Annie were at opposite ends of the sofa.

Once, when Jonah went back to the couch after tending the fire, Annie stirred. A sigh escaped her lips, and he paused, not wanting to disturb her. He watched as she shifted onto her side, curled her legs onto the couch, and rubbed her nose.

After all these weeks of seeing her nearly every day, Annie was still a wonder to him . . . a beautiful mystery he longed to unravel, one day at a time. What a blessing it would be to be able to sleep beside her like this every night of his life, to hear her sigh in her sleep, to feel her soft warm body beside his in bed.

He sat on the edge of the couch and pressed his face into his palms.

Father Gott, why do I keep wanting the one thing that will not be?

Try as he had to temper his love for Annie, his feelings for her never changed.

But she had come to appreciate his steady support. Maybe that was as good as it would get.

He drew in a deep breath, finishing his prayer by asking for Aaron Stoltzfus's safe return. That was why he was here now; Aaron's safety was what truly mattered.

Watch over him, Father, he prayed.

Jonah was adding a log to the fire in the murky gray of breaking dawn when two white lights came down the lane.

A car.

He reached over and touched Annie's shoulder. "I think your dat's home."

Her eyes opened slowly, then she jerked upright. "What?"

"Lovina?" He went to the window. "There's a car coming."

"Oh, glory be to Gott!" Lovina rose abruptly, dropping the blanket onto the rocking chair to join Jonah at the window. "Aaron must have hired a driver to bring him home."

There was a flurry of excitement as Jonah lit a lantern, Annie gathered up the blankets and Lovina fairly flew out the front door wearing only socks on her feet. She ran down the path, mindless of the wet stones.

"Aaron? Is that you?" Lovina called.

As Jonah stepped out the door behind her, he noticed that the car was a small SUV. The driver's door opened, and an Englisher man climbed out of the car. Jonah squinted, recognizing Doc Trueherz, from Paradise.

"It's Henry Trueherz, Lovina." The older man slammed the door of the Jeep and jogged up the path to the house.

"The doctor?" Annie said from behind them. She pressed a hand against Jonah's back, trying to peer around him. "Is Dat with him?"

"He's alone." Lovina's voice was cold as the damp morning air. "Doctor, do you have news of my husband?"

"I do." Dr. Trueherz paused on the top step, his eyes earnest as he faced Lovina. "Aaron is in the hospital in Lancaster County. He's had a heart attack."

"Oh, my dear Aaron!" Lovina gasped, her hand flying to cover her mouth.

"I know. It's hard news to hear, but he's hanging in there." The doctor patted Lovina's shoulder. "Can we step inside, out of the cold?"

"Of course."

As everyone moved inside, Jonah caught the look of panic in Annie's eyes. He wanted to reassure her, to be her pillar, but in the close space of the front room with the doctor and Annie's mother here, he could only stand by, his hands at his sides.

Lovina was plucking her wet socks off even as she rattled out questions for the doctor.

"I got a call late last night from an associate at the hospital in Lancaster. Aaron is there in the cardiac ward. He suffered the heart attack during the storm yesterday. Fortunately, he managed to make it to a merchant he knows in Paradise, who got him to the hospital."

"A heart attack!" Lovina winced. "Aaron hasn't been feeling well at all lately. He never complained, but I noticed he was slowing down. We all noticed. I asked him to go see you, get a checkup, but he said he was just tired. And it's hard to get enough sleep when there's a farm to take care of."

"Will he be all right?" Jonah asked.

"I'm optimistic but cautious," Dr. Trueherz said. "He's not out of the woods yet. It looks like he's going to need a coronary bypass—a major surgery. But we can't do that until he's stabilized. I'll let the cardiac specialist fill you in on the details. Right now, I imagine you want to see him at the hospital."

"I was just thinking that," Lovina said. "We've got to get to Lancaster. I'll run to the shanty and call a car service."

"No need." Doc Trueherz stopped her. "I'm happy to give you a ride. But I have a four-passenger limit, and no children. I know you'll want to bring the whole family, but I have a Jeep with no car seats." Doc Trueherz had worked with Plain folks long enough to know that when an Amish person was in the hospital, the entire family usually went to visit and provide support.

"Denki, Doctor," Lovina said, turning to Annie. "Who should go? Look at me, I can't even think straight. If Levi stays with Jonah, maybe we can go to town and—"

"No, Mamm," Annie interrupted her. "Jonah's going to have his hands full taking care of our farm."

Lovina pressed a hand to her cheek. "That's right. Will you mind the farm while we're gone, Jonah?"

He nodded. "Whatever it takes. I'll get my brothers to come lend a hand if I need it."

"Denki," Lovina said. "But what of Levi? He needs a car seat."

"I'll stay with him, Mamm," Annie said. "You go, and I'll arrange for a car this afternoon so that Levi and I can come. I'll finish the baking and drop it off at the tea shop, too. And that way Levi won't have as much time to get fidgety in the waiting room."

"If you don't mind," Lovina said. "I just want as much of the family as possible at the hospital."

"Maybe you can pick up the others in town," Jonah suggested.

"That's a good idea. Dr. Trueherz, can we stop in Halfway to pick up the rest of the family?" Lovina asked. "Our other two daughters and son-in-law Daniel will want to come, too."

He adjusted his glasses. "Fine with me. We've got to swing through town on the way."

"God bless you," Lovina said, slipping her coat on. "The thought of Aaron all alone in that hospital is too much to bear. I have to go now."

"Mamm?" Annie grasped her mother's shoulder as she headed for the door. "Don't forget your shoes."

Lovina looked down and threw up her hands. "Look at me!" she cried. "Going off to the city hospital with bare feet!"

Annie ran to Lovina's bedroom for socks and Sunday shoes, and Jonah suggested she bring money, so that the family could purchase food from the hospital cafeteria.

Five minutes later, Lovina was sitting in the passenger seat of Henry Trueherz's Jeep, trying to reach Daniel's harness shop on the doctor's cell phone.

Jonah and Annie watched from the front window as the Jeep pulled away.

"How will you ever manage?" Annie asked.

"I've been farming all my life. The work will get done. But I might need your help lifting a few bales into the hayloft."

"Don't tease me. There's a lot I can do to help you. I can milk the cows, and tend the sheep and horses."

"I know that." He had worked side by side with her these past few weeks. Annie was a capable worker. A strong woman, despite her small size. "But you've got the hardest job of all." When she lifted her eyes to his, he saw the storm of emotion threatening to overcome her. "You've got to keep those two boys upstairs out of trouble."

She shrugged. "They're easy enough to handle. But the farm . . . and Dat. Jonah, I'm so worried about him. Did you hear what the doctor said? He couldn't even assure us that Dat would be fine. He needs a surgery."

Jonah nodded. "But Aaron's in good hands. Henry Trueherz is a fine doctor. He saved our Susie's life. He might not be the one doing the surgery, but I know he'll make sure they take good care of your dat."

Annie bit her lower lip as tears welled in her eyes. "It's too much. It's just too much." Her sob tugged at his composure, and he took her into his arms, as if he had consoled her a hundred times before. As if holding Annie in his arms was the most natural thing in the world.

How easily his arms folded around her, and the way she fit against him . . . She was a perfect fit. They were like two pieces of a jigsaw puzzle. Only Annie couldn't see that. He'd spent a lifetime trying to open her eyes, but she couldn't see that the one thing she was missing in her life was right here in front of her.

FORTY-ONE

*I*n the unusual quiet of the kitchen Annie slid an applesauce cake into the oven and checked the clock to see when she would need to take it out. Humming a church song, she quickly rinsed the bowl and rotary hand mixer.

The rest of the house was neat as a pin, and she had at least an hour to spare before dinner had to be started. She pulled the kitchen apron off, grabbed a coat from the hook by the door, and set out to see if Jonah needed help with farm chores.

In the three days since Dat had been in the hospital, Annie and Jonah had worked together to keep the farm and house running, and thanks to Gott, it was working.

Of course, they'd had help from near and far.

The social workers at the hospital in Lancaster had found a place for Mamm and Hannah to stay so that they wouldn't have to make daily trips all the way into the city. After a full day at the hospital, Daniel and Rebecca came home. They went into Halfway to tend to the tea shop and harness shop each day, while Annie watched Levi here at home.

When it came time to gather up the last of the hay, Jonah had called on his brothers Adam and Gabe. Now that it was baled and stored in the barn, the heavy harvest work was over.

A good thing for Dat, who would have to rest in the house when he came home tomorrow. Because of a certain medication, Dat would need to wait a month or so for his coronary bypass surgery. Although the cardiologist preferred to keep him in the hospital on bed rest, Dr. Trueherz had intervened to get Dat released.

"A month in the hospital wouldn't be good for anyone," Dr. Trueherz had said when Annie had visited Dat in the hospital. "It's expensive, inconvenient, and quite frankly, a little unhealthy. Aaron is better off at home as long as you can keep him away from chores. Rest and reading should be his tasks of the day. He can walk to and from the table to eat—and that will be the extent of his exercise until we can get this surgery done. His coronary arteries are in a very vulnerable state."

Dat had agreed to be a good patient as long as he could go home and sleep in his own bed. "How does anyone sleep here with lights on all the time and machines beeping and whooshing all the time? I feel like a cow hooked up to a milking machine."

Annie wanted everything to be in good shape when Dat came home tomorrow. She had baked the applesauce cake following his new low-fat diet. Jonah had been chasing sheep and trimming their hooves. They didn't want Dat to see anything that would make him feel like the farm needed his attention.

If they did a good job, maybe Dat would stay put!

Annie didn't see any sign of Jonah and Levi over in the pastures, so she headed into the barn. As soon as she stepped in the door, the tall wall of hay stopped her short. With everything harvested, bundles of hay were everywhere. She reckoned Jonah and the other men must have been handy with the winch to load all of this hay. By spring, most of it would be used up.

Voices came from the area where the horses were stabled, and as Annie made her way over, she couldn't help but listen. Jonah's voice was so low and soothing, she edged closer, wanting to be reassured the way Levi was.

"I want to give my doddy a big hug when he comes home," Levi said. "Is he too sick for a hug if I go nice and gentle?"

"A gentle hug would be wonderful good," Jonah said.

"Is he going to get better?"

"Let's pray that he does. We know Gott is watching over your doddy. I think it was a guardian angel that got him to the hospital in Lancaster."

Up on tiptoe, Annie peered over the wall of the stall to see the two of them sitting on a bale together beside Dapple, the chestnut mare Annie favored. The sight of Levi, relaxed in the crook of Jonah's arm, made Annie's lower lip tremble. What a whirlwind week it had been for the five-year-old boy, from his fear of the thunderstorms to his worry over his grandfather. Everyone had been in a worried state, and the boy must have felt the fear swirling through all of them over Aaron's condition.

And through it all, Jonah had remained steadfast. Steady. Calm. And tender with little Levi.

Jonah had been here day and night, as faithful as the sun and moon.

She lowered herself from the rail and pressed a hand to her chest, sure that her heart had swelled to eight times its normal size. Why had she never noticed him before? How had she gone on all these years without seeing him, seeing the man he truly was? And these last weeks with him here on the farm, right under her nose . . . how could she have been so blind?

She was falling in love with Jonah King.

The next day dawned gray and damp with a mist clinging to the hills. But Annie didn't let the rainy day dampen her mood as she washed the breakfast dishes and tidied up. Dat was coming home today, and that was the first step in getting things back to normal around here.

But the man who was rolled out of the special van in a wheelchair did not look at all like Annie's father. Her dat was strong and robust, bold and tireless. But this man seemed small in the narrow chair that bumped along the path, pushed by a young man in a navy blue jacket. The man in the wheelchair was small and gray and light as a dry leaf in the wind.

Biting back her worries, Annie stepped down from the front porch and forced herself to smile. "Welcome home, Dat!"

The man in the chair lifted his head. His eyes found Annie, and he smiled Dat's big smile, the one that could melt the coldest heart.

Only then did she recognize the dear father she so loved. She ran to meet him, reaching out to squeeze his hand as the attendant pushed him along.

"It's good to be home, Annie girl." When the wheelchair reached the single step of the porch, she expected him to get out of the chair and walk, but he waited there. As if he had surrendered to the ailment that was eating away his energy.

Mamm and Jonah were suddenly behind her. Mamm stood by, looking tired as Jonah helped the attendant lift the wheelchair onto the porch.

Annie held the screen door open as her father was wheeled into the house. Annie fully expected him to go into the kitchen for some tea and applesauce cake, but Mamm directed the man to push Dat straight into their bedroom.

But when would she be able to visit with him . . . talk with him? She missed her dat.

Annie stood in the hallway, confused. "Do you think he's coming out?" she asked Jonah.

He shrugged.

A moment later, the door opened and Lovina emerged with the English man. "Thank you very much, Jerry. So we bring back the chair when he returns for surgery?"

Jerry nodded. "Make sure he uses it whenever possible. We don't want to tax his heart in any way."

Annie and Jonah watched as Lovina thanked the man again and saw him out. Once the door closed behind him, Annie turned to her mother. "Can I go in and talk to Dat?"

"Not right now, honey girl. He's very tired from the trip, and rest is the main thing right now. Leave him be. Maybe he'll come out for dinner. Maybe not until tomorrow."

Annie nodded as her mother disappeared back into the bedroom, closing the door firmly behind her. She felt foolishly disappointed. How she wanted to tell her dat all about how she and Jonah had managed the farm! She wanted to see him enjoy homemade food for the first time in days. She longed to spend just a few minutes with him . . . to hear a few words that would reassure her that everything would be all right.

"I'm so disappointed." She turned to Jonah. "And worried for Dat. The sickness has taken a toll on him. He's so . . . so small."

Like a withered branch.

It was as if autumn had come through and stripped him of life.

Seeing him this way frightened her more than the news of the heart attack. "Did you see him?" she whispered to Jonah.

He nodded. "He's in a bad way, Annie. Until he gets the surgery, he's going to need all our help and patience."

He was right, of course, but she couldn't forget the ghostly image of her father that had just passed by.

"Annie . . ." Jonah reached for her hand and held it tight. "Give him time, and pray for Gott's healing love."

She bit her lower lip, taking strength from the spark of determination in Jonah's dark eyes. Time and prayer . . . she had plenty of those to give.

FORTY-TWO

*J*onah sat at the kitchen table, his thoughts focused on a farm miles away, beyond the neat white frame of the kitchen window. Was Aaron taking it easy, as the doctor had instructed? He wondered when, exactly, Annie would be leaving for New York, though he didn't have the courage to ask her. And he wanted to be there when that pregnant cow freshed, which could be any day now.

Most of Jonah's brothers and sisters were gathered in the kitchen to listen in on the big discussion. Although Jonah enjoyed spending time with his family, he wished he didn't have to be a part of this talk.

Wedding preparations . . .

Jonah didn't have much interest in the details, but Adam had wanted him to be involved in the financial planning.

There was a nip in the air, but the potbelly stove kept the kitchen warm, as well as the gas stove that was heated up for baking. Remy had made hot cocoa for everyone. Jonah sipped from his mug, tuning out the talk of who would handle the horses for the bridal carriages and who would serve the meal.

The good thing about a family meeting was that it brought the family together. His grandmother sat beside him, taking notes on costs. Nell King had been the farm's bookkeeper for more than a decade, and no one knew the family finances as well as she did.

At the far end of the big table, Ruthie, Leah, and Susie sat, tending to some kind of embroidery project. Tonight he had a feeling each was more focused on the wedding details than the needle in hand. As much as he disliked wedding plans, the girls seemed to eat them up like candy.

"My father has offered to pay for the wedding, if that's okay," Remy said. "I told him he would not be allowed to meddle in the plans or break Amish wedding tradition, and he's agreed to that."

"That would be a lot of money for one father to pay," Mary said.

Remy lowered her mug. "In the English world, it's traditional for the father of the bride to pay for everything, and he's prepared to do that. He can afford it."

Mammi Nell tapped her pencil against her open book of accounts. "As your bookkeeper, I think that would be very good. But as Adam's grandmother, I have to say that it's too much."

"It is too much," Adam agreed. "It's not right for your father to pay for a double wedding with more than five hundred guests. Maybe you can calculate what one fourth of the cost would be, Mammi?"

"Ya, I can do that," Nell said.

"And the Beilers are going to help with money, and the preparations, of course," Mary said.

"Gut," Adam said. "And did you ask about the wedding wagon?"

"I got the information from the woman who runs it." Mary handed a folded piece of paper to Mammi. "For this price, we get the wagon a week before the wedding, so we can use it to start preparing."

"All those pots and pans . . . and five gas stoves?" Mammi said as she read over the letter. "That's gut. There's a lot of cooking involved for five hundred people."

"Lots of potatoes to be peeled," Remy said.

"How many potatoes will that take?" Susie said.

"If everyone eats two potatoes, that's one thousand," Leah said. "We're going to be peeling for many days and nights."

"And it comes with a giant coffeemaker," Mary said. "It brews a hundred and sixty cups of coffee at a time."

"Mmm." Nell tapped her pencil. "No waiting for a cup of coffee."

"The wedding wagon would make things go smoothly," Adam said. "What about the cost, Mammi?"

"It's good." Nell tapped Jonah on the arm, showing him the letter. "What do you think, Jonah?"

"Fine by me." Jonah shot a look down the table at his younger sisters. "I'm just wondering who's going to peel all those potatoes?"

"I'm a very fast peeler," Susie said.

"My fingers are getting tired just thinking about it," Leah said, stirring laughter at the table.

Flames curled around the log in the fireplace as Jonah sat still in a wooden rocker, staring at the dancing light. He had come down and built the small fire because he couldn't sleep.

All the wedding talk had led his thoughts to Annie.

She would be around for the wedding, now that she had decided to stay and help out until her dat recovered. There was a part of the wedding reception where all the single young people got paired off, and he wondered if Mary would pair Annie off with him. Hmm . . . He would like that, but Annie, not so much.

Or would Annie go along with it because of the friendship that had grown between them in the past few weeks?

Working with Annie on the Stoltzfus farm, he had seen her in many new ways. Talking to the horses. Tending the sheep. Nurturing the little ones. Humming as she hung clothes on the line. She had insights about the animals' behavior that could come only from growing up on a farm, and there was a certain way about her—sensitive, bubbly, but firm, too. She could be strict with a misbehaving sheep when she needed to be.

And when she was around Levi and Sam, Annie's loving instincts came alive. She enjoyed teaching them things, and she had a talent for getting them to mind without a scolding. Someday, she'd be a fine Amish mother to her own children.

The woman he'd come to know in the past few weeks was far different from the girl he'd watched from afar when they'd been growing up. But for every quality he'd recently discovered in Annie, he'd come to love her that much more. With her gift for children and her love of farm life, Annie was heading toward the same life that Jonah had always planned for himself.

At times, he thought to take her into his arms, kiss her, and tell her that they were meant to be together. It seemed simple.

But he would never do that to her. He respected her, and he would always abide by the things she had told him. Always. She had made it clear that she didn't favor him; he did not need to hear that again.

The stairs creaked, and Jonah looked away from the fire to find his brother Gabe in the doorway, his hair mussed, a blanket wrapped around his shoulders.

"What are you doing down here?" Gabe asked.

"I couldn't sleep. And you?"

"I just had a nightmare that made me want to go outside and

check the cows." Gabe went over to the fire and stood there a minute, warming.

Jonah shifted in the rocker, glad for the distraction. "What was the dream?"

"I dreamed that the cows had gone for days without milking while I slept in bed like a lazybones. When I realized the milking had been forgotten, I hurried out to the barn." Gabe shifted the blanket on his shoulders. "Wouldn't you know, Dat was out there waiting for me. 'What happened?' he asked. I felt so bad to let him down. But before I could explain, Emma popped out."

"Emma?" Jonah rubbed his bare chin. "This is getting good."

"She was standing there all proper in her sweater with her satchel. Emma said that she knew what happened. 'I know the terrible truth,' she said. I figured she'd tell Dat about the motorbikes, but instead, she took a stack of papers out of her satchel. 'These are Gabe's papers from all his school days, and they prove that he didn't learn anything.' That's what she said. And then she said I would have to return to school until I got everything right."

Jonah grinned. "That's a telling dream."

"You think it's funny." Gabe scowled as he sat down in the chair beside Jonah. "I'd laugh if it didn't bother me so much. I never dreamed about Dat before, and he seemed so disappointed with me. And then Emma . . . I never want a scolding like that."

"Teacher Emma can be very strict." Jonah knew that it was important for an Amish teacher to have the right balance of control and compassion. "So, is Emma still being strict with you?"

"She hasn't even spoken to me since we broke apart. She's making a big deal about me riding the motorbikes."

"Maybe you should give up the bikes."

"Ach! You sound like a father."

"Well. Dat's not here to tell you what you need to hear." Jonah rubbed his chin. "You know, those motorcycles are dangerous. People get killed on them."

Gabe scowled. "People get killed in farm accidents."

"Ya, but a plow brings bread to the table. It's a part of life. A motorbike? Not so much."

"But there's nothing like riding on a motorbike. You feel like a man. At the same time, you feel like you're flying, faster than any bird. Dat would understand that. He loved to watch the birds flying yonder."

Jonah sat for a moment as he pictured their dat watching the nightjars or jays circling over the wavering alfalfa. "Dat was a bird-watcher, all right. But he wouldn't expect you to be flying. You don't have wings, Gabe."

"Mmm." Gabe ran a hand through his untidy hair. "I'm tired but I don't want to go back to sleep and dream about Emma scolding me again."

"So . . . you and Emma are still stuck in the muck. Have you tried to talk to her?"

"What's the point?" Gabe shrugged. "She's through with me."

Jonah leaned forward and pointed to the back lot. "When you have a section of broken fence out there, do you just leave it be?"

Gabe frowned. "No."

"Then why would you ignore what's broken with Emma? Go talk to her. Step up and try to mend things."

"I guess I can try." Gabe rubbed the back of his neck. "And how come you know what to do when you don't even have a girl? Or do you?" He squinted at his brother. "Is that why you can't sleep?"

Jonah gave a nod. "Now you know my secret."

"But you didn't say who she is."

"It doesn't matter. She won't be around here much longer."

Gabe pursed his lips, nodding. "So it is Annie Stoltzfus. I thought so."

"Ach." Jonah pushed back in the rocking chair with a groan. "Don't tell me tongues are wagging about me favoring Annie."

"Don't worry. Nobody knows, except for the brother who's watched you go to that farm day after day. You've been downright cheerful about it, and that's not like you."

"The Quiet One."

"Not so quiet anymore," Gabe said. "So what are you going to do about Annie leaving for New York?"

"There's nothing to be done. She's made her choice, and I need to respect that."

A quiet growl pealed from Gabe's throat. "Come on. You can't mean that."

Jonah folded his arms across his chest. "It's the truth."

"What about mending your fences, like you told me?"

"There's nothing broken to fix. She doesn't favor me. She's leaving Halfway. It's not meant to be."

"I don't think that's true." Gabe squinted at him. "And you need to do something if you want to stop her from going. Hide her hope chest. Talk to her parents. Lovina and Aaron have both taken a liking to you."

"It's not so simple," Jonah said.

"Then get crafty." Gabe rose and tossed another log onto the fire. "Don't let her get away, Jonah. If she's the one for you, don't watch her slip away."

Jonah watched as the cinders popped and scattered in the fire-place. *Good advice,* he thought. *If only I could do something about it.*

FORTY-THREE

*F*alling back into a rocking chair with a sigh, Emma savored the silence. Dat, Fanny, and the children had just left to have dinner with Bishop Samuel and his wife, Lois; and Elsie and Caleb were working at the shop. That left Emma alone in the house—a rarity for her.

Everywhere she went, someone was talking around her. Her pupils at school, her spirited younger siblings, her sister Elsie in the room they shared. Sometimes she longed for a few minutes of blessed silence.

Time to clear her mind. Time to think about Gabe.

When she closed her eyes, she could see him: The hard jaw that lent defiance to his face. The amber eyes that seemed to read her deepest thoughts. And that half grin, a crooked smile that hinted at amusement lurking under his cool demeanor.

Oh, she really shouldn't love him so, but she couldn't help herself. The feeling hadn't faded at all, despite her anger with him for breaking the rules of the Ordnung. She had talked to Elsie about it—dear

Elsie, who had calmly listened and counseled Emma to be patient. Give the boy time and he would come around. She appreciated Elsie's advice, but she did not share her sister's patience or faith in Gabe.

How could she be sure Gabe would ever "come around" and follow the rules of their Amish community? There was always the chance that he would take a different path, like his older sister Sadie. Or he might even leave the community for years, as his brother Adam had done.

And where would that leave Emma?

Adrift in her own community. If she waited for Gabe to come around, there was a chance that she would be waiting alone for the rest of her life.

In her logical mind, Emma knew that it would not be smart to wait for Gabe. But in her heart, there was no room for any other beau. She loved Gabe, and no amount of logic was going to change that.

So . . . it was time to settle in for a long winter, and a long wait.

She got out of the chair to find her satchel. The rumpled stack of papers peered out at her, calling for attention, very much like her young scholars. But the afternoon sun on the window beckoned her.

"I'm going to work outside," she said, grabbing a sweater for when the sunlight faded.

The two-story house just outside town was built on a small lot, but there was a natural boundary of bushes on one side of the yard. When they had moved in to the house, Fanny had set out four chairs and a table that Emma and Elsie had covered with a mint-green rust-retardant paint. Surprisingly, the little table had become the hub of family activity in good weather. Some summer nights, when the weather was hot, they brought out dining room chairs and ate their dinner out here.

She took the top essay from the stack in her satchel and leaned into the last of the day's golden sunlight. Leaves shimmered in the hedge behind her, and she imagined that they were Gott's own wind chimes.

She was reading an essay about an afternoon of fishing when a whirring sound buzzed in the distance.

A large wasp?

She looked around, but saw no insects crossing the swath of sunlight. And yet the sound grew louder. It was some kind of vehicle. A vehicle on the road?

Sparked by curiosity, she stood up. Her papers ruffled in the breeze, and she quickly shoved them under the satchel so they wouldn't blow away. She moved closer to the hedge to peer through the bushes. A motorcycle was passing on the main road. A moment later, it turned down the lane, a whining beast.

The rider was dressed Amish in dark broadcloth trousers and blue shirt, suspenders . . . and a helmet that covered his whole face.

Gabe.

The breath caught in her throat. What was he thinking, coming around here, and on a motorbike? The boy didn't use the brain in his head.

She tended to her papers, shoving them back into her satchel as a strange mix of excitement and agitation brewed inside her. Her heart raced at the sight of him, and yet she knew he had brought trouble with him.

With a whir of the motor, he pulled off the driveway onto the grass and rolled to a stop beside the little table. Her fingers worried over the pins of her apron, as she watched him dismount.

He turned off the bike, swung his leg over the side, and rose to his full height. Why did her heart soar at the sight of him? He pushed a little spike down with the toe of his boot, and the bike stood on its own, all glinting metal in the sun.

Emma frowned. That bike might as well be cow manure, but

Gabe . . . he was still so handsome, lean and tall. There was no denying the glow she felt at the sight of him.

Still . . . she couldn't have him here like this. On a bike. Her conscience whispered, "No, no, no . . ." But standing this close to him was like stepping into the sunshine after a week of night.

He pulled the big black helmet off and shook his head as he came toward her. "Emma . . . Did you know it was me?"

"It wasn't so hard to figure out," she said. "What are you doing here?"

"I came to give you a ride. I brought one of the bigger bikes so that we can ride together."

"Gabe, are you verhuddelt? I can't be riding a motorbike."

"No one will know." He lifted the helmet toward her. "You can wear the helmet so no one will know it's you."

"I would never do that. It's against the rules."

"Can't you just stop worrying about the rules for once and try something new? I want you to see how much fun it is, Emma. Just see for yourself." He came toward her with the helmet, but she held up a hand, pressing it into his chest.

"Stop, just stop it! I don't want anything to do with your bike, Gabe." She pulled her hand back when she saw the forlorn look on his face. He seemed stunned . . . but how could he be surprised? She was standing by what she had told him all along. "Why are you looking at me that way? You know the rules as well as I do."

"I thought you would understand." The hurt in his eyes tugged on her conscience. "You've always tried to understand. When my parents were killed, you were the only one who talked to me about it . . . the only one who listened."

"This is different, Gabe."

"Is it? This is something good I'm trying to share with you. Something that makes me feel strong but light . . . like an eagle soaring over the land."

Torn between her desire to reach out to him and her faith that she had to stick to her beliefs, she studied his face, wished she could make him understand.

"I would love to soar with you, Gabe." She swallowed over the lump in her throat. It would be so easy to give in and go with him. Put on a helmet and pray that no one would recognize her so that she and Gabe could be close again. One small concession would mend their relationship.

But Emma could not go against her own promise. In her heart, she would always know of the sin she had committed, and that offense would fester like a wound.

"I wish I could share this with you, but I can't . . . I can't break my vow to the church just to have some fun with you. Someday, when you're baptized, you'll understand how important this is."

He scowled. "Maybe not. Maybe I won't get baptized, and I'll just keep on doing what I want, like Zed Miller."

"You don't mean that." She could tell that he was angry now; he was saying things out of bitterness.

"I can't really say. Who knows what will happen down the road?" He turned the helmet in his hands. "I guess the only person who can find out is the one who rides down that road. Like me."

"Don't do this, Gabe." Her voice was quiet now, quiet and cold as the shadows that had fallen over the small yard. She always tried so hard to be understanding. Why couldn't he see her side of this? That parents and ministers trusted her with the education of their children—a good Amish education. Her actions were under scrutiny. Her values were everything to her.

"I'm just a guy trying to take my girl for a ride on a fall after-noon," he said.

Emma bit her lips together, fighting back tears. How could he hurt her so?

Gathering her things, she allowed herself one last look at him. Oh, why did she care so much about him when he pulled stunts like this? She marched into the house and let the screen door slam behind her. It was an angry, heavy sound . . . a sound that signaled the end to a conversation, a beautiful day, a bittersweet love.

FORTY-FOUR

I got the joy, joy, joy, joy, down in my heart. Where?" Annie sang the quick song, clapping along with the other young people at the table. She didn't remember the last time she'd felt such bright joy at a singing, but then the very fact that she was here was one of the biggest surprises of all. Just a few weeks ago, she had thought she would be long gone from Halfway by now, the end of October. But here she was . . . and there was a smile on her face, as if the happy glow inside her was shining through.

And all because of Jonah King.

She turned her head to take a look at him down the table. He was singing along, but he did not clap or make silly faces like some of the other young people. That stoic, almost stern expression on his face . . . she liked that about him. There was no giddiness about Jonah King, but she had come to rely on his rock-solid patience and thoughtfulness in times of stress.

Ya, Jonah was the main reason she had wanted to stay. And she had never expected the odd twist of circumstances that had kept her here in Halfway long past the time she thought she would be moving away to New York.

Soon after Dat had returned, he and Mamm had asked her if she would consider staying in Halfway awhile to help out at the farm. "Just until I get through the operation and back on my feet," Dat had said. "I know you've got good reason to go, but we need you now, Annie girl."

Her answer had been yes, yes, and yes again. She told them she would stay as long as they wanted. She wouldn't think of going away when her family needed her. But secretly, she was thinking of staying on for good, and she had hinted at that in her letter to Sarah.

Please don't count on me coming anytime soon, she had written. *So much has changed here, not only on account of Dat's sickness, but some good things have sprung up like seedlings in the garden. There's a fella here that I've been getting to know—I won't say who, because it's all so very new—but it's given me a spark of hope that things might work out just fine here in Halfway.*

That spark of hope was now a flame dancing in her heart, fueled by the good conversations and silly jokes she had shared with Jonah as they worked side by side on the farm. Morning, noon, and night, she found herself drumming up excuses to spend time with him out in the barn. She scheduled chores so that she would cross his path and have a chance to talk with him. She didn't need to use the court- ship tricks she had tried to teach her sister Hannah because things flowed naturally between Jonah and her. Conversation was easy, his jokes made her laugh, and his dark eyes seemed to have the ability to see her fears. Jonah had a knack for easing her worries about Dat's health, about her sick horse, or about how hard it was to make tasty dishes that followed Dat's new low-cholesterol diet.

But despite the easy conversation between them, Annie had not had the nerve to turn the topic around to ask about his feelings for her. He had admitted to favoring her for years, but then she had pushed him away. She could kick herself for that . . . but it was water under the bridge. Right now she needed to know just where she stood with him. A simple question . . . an easy question if she could just summon the nerve to ask Jonah.

As they took a break from singing, Annie skimmed the room to locate Jonah. Maybe if they took a walk together outside, just maybe the bright glow of the moon would lend her the courage to ask her question.

She moved past her sister Hannah, who was already talking with her beau, Ben King. Elizabeth Mast blocked Annie's view for a moment. When the girl finally shifted, the sight of Jonah in the corner made her heart sink.

He was talking with Emma Lapp—Teacher Emma. Stunned, she stared at them a moment, then forced herself to look away. She had heard that Jonah gave Emma a ride home from a singing recently, but she hadn't thought much of it.

Now she tried to ignore the achy pain at the sight of the two of them together. Emma was a nice girl, but she didn't know Jonah the way Annie did. It wasn't possible for Emma to love him the way Annie did.

"What are you staring at with such a sad face?" Mary asked as she followed Annie's gaze across the barn.

When Annie tried to answer, the knot of emotion in her throat kept words from forming.

"Are you feeling okay?" Mary linked arms with her and cast a curious glance down at Annie. "Your face is pale and you look like someone just stole the last piece of pie right out from under your nose."

Annie snorted. "You know me too well."

"What's going on, Annie?"

Should she tell Mary—her very best friend who also happened to be Jonah's sister? "Will you promise not to tell anyone?"

Mary tilted her head. "You know I try not to gossip, and I certainly wouldn't do that to you."

Annie steeled herself, wanting to be honest with her friend. "The truth is, things have changed for me here. You know Mamm and Dat asked me to stay to help out with his recuperation. Well, I'm hoping to stay for good because there's a fella who's caught my eye."

A smile lit Mary's eyes. "Praise be to Gott! I'm so happy for you!"

"But he doesn't know yet. And right now, I'm watching him across the room, talking with someone else." Annie shifted so that she wouldn't be staring at Jonah and Emma. "I don't know what to do. I'm afraid I've waited too long to tell him how I feel."

"I think Jonah will still be happy to hear the news."

Mary's words eased Annie's heart; it was as if someone had lifted a heavy load from her shoulders.

She still had a chance with Jonah. . . .

Annie grabbed her friend's hands. "Do you think so? That would be the most wonderful good thing! I can't tell you how much I . . . But wait." She looked around to make sure no one was listening. "How did you know I was talking about Jonah?"

"Well, I saw you looking at him with so much love in your eyes. And to be honest, Jonah confided in me long ago that he favored you. More than that, really. I think he had a crush on you when we were kids and he never got over that. I promised him I wouldn't tell anyone, and I kept my promise. But now . . . well, the truth is out. He told you himself, so I don't think I'm breaking my word."

"He did tell me, and I turned him away," Annie admitted, still annoyed at her own blind foolishness. "You know that, don't you?"

Mary nodded. "I've heard bits and pieces along the way."

"But you think I still have a chance?" Annie glanced back at Jonah and Emma. Their faces were solemn, their heads lowered close together. "What about Emma?"

Mary snorted. "I'll tell you this: He doesn't spend every day at

Emma's house. Just talk to him. Tell him the truth. You know what the Bible says. The truth shall set you free."

Hope surged through Annie as she gathered her dear friend's hands and squeezed them. "Denki, Mary. You've given me the courage I need to talk to him."

Mary smiled. "Really? I can't imagine you in need of prodding to talk."

"I know. Hard to believe, isn't it?" As Annie gave her best friend a hug, she realized that love changed some things. Being in love had softened her impulsiveness. She wasn't so quick to let comments fly from her mouth unchecked.

Folks were starting to head out of the barn for the bonfire in a nearby field. Five came over to accompany Mary, and as Annie chatted with the two of them she kept checking on Jonah, who was still talking with the schoolteacher. How wonderful it would be to sit beside him at the big bonfire, chatting and sharing little jokes while more singing went on. And if she grew cold, maybe he would offer her his jacket, or put an arm around her shoulders to keep her warm. . . .

As Jonah and Emma walked out of the barn together, Annie realized that her plan wasn't very realistic—at least not for today. Jonah was going to maintain a respectful distance, as long as he thought that was what she wanted.

Outside, as everyone gathered around the big fire, Annie found a place beside some other single girls and let her gaze wander the circle of faces lit by firelight. Mary and Five were together, as were Remy and Adam. Hannah's face glowed with happiness as Ben King leaned close to whisper something into her ear.

And where were Jonah and Emma?

She flinched, noticing that Emma was standing nearby, in the same group of girls without beaus. And across the fire, Jonah and his brother Gabe joined a group of young men.

As Annie let her gaze rest on Jonah's face, flickering with firelight, she wished she could talk to him right now.

Someday, Gott willing, we'll be sitting beside each other, watching the dancing flames together.

Later that night, after Annie finished unhitching Dapple from the family carriage, she patted the horse vigorously before she brought him into the stables. Excitement bubbled inside her, and though she could barely wait until morning to talk with Jonah, a part of her savored this special time. Like a bird about to take flight, hope pulsed inside her, excited and strong and eager to soar.

The night was growing cold, with temperatures dipping into the forties, and as she wandered through the barn, Sunny followed her restlessly.

"What's the matter, girl?" She bent down to stroke the dog behind her ears, but she was too excited to stay still for long. "What are you trying to tell me?"

Since they weren't a dairy farm, they only had a handful of milk cows. When she went to check on them, she found that one was missing—Buttercup, the pregnant Dexter.

"That's it," she said as she went to the barn door, Sunny sticking to her side.

"Buttercup, where are you?" she asked aloud, looking out over the dark fields. She frowned as Sunny barked a call into the darkness. Their Dexter was ready to deliver any day now. Although Dat had repaired the calving shed, Annie knew that there was a good chance that once again, the cow had chosen another spot on the farm to fresh.

Returning to the horse stables, she saddled up Dapple, working quickly. The horse responded, prancing excitedly when she first got out of the stables. For safety's sake she kept Dapple on the path between the fields, but she let the horse trot freely as they searched for the errant cow. She prayed that she would find Buttercup safe and sound; it wouldn't help Dat's condition for him to be getting bad news now.

A pale half-moon cast a silvery glow over the cold landscape, lighting the path and the bulk of reddish cow perched on the ground up ahead.

"Buttercup," Annie said aloud as her horse closed the distance between them. She climbed down from the horse and walked alongside the cow that lay in a sprawling heap on the ground.

The Dexter cow was breathing heavily. Her eyes were wild, and as Annie watched she moaned and pushed her legs up in the air.

Buttercup was giving birth. From what Annie could see, she figured the cow was still in the first stage of labor. They had some time.

"You poor dear. We need to get you help." Although Annie had lived on a farm all her life, she'd never been in charge when any of the animals gave birth. There was no way she could disturb Dat, and Mamm didn't have any more experience with this than Annie did. Daniel would be willing to help, but he had been raised a harness-maker.

There was only one person who'd be ready and able to help Buttercup.

Jonah.

"I'm going to get help for you. You stay right there," Annie told the prone cow. As she climbed onto Dapple, she realized that wouldn't be a problem. In her condition, Buttercup wasn't going to wander off.

She called to her horse, and they galloped off along the silver landscape.

As it turned out, Annie didn't have to ride all the way out to the Kings' farm to get Jonah. Before she even reached the main road she came upon Ben King and Hannah, saying good night at the end of the lane. When she explained that the cow was freshing out near a ditch, Ben reassured her that it sometimes happened that way.

"Chances are, you won't have to do anything to help her along," he said. "But I'll go get Jonah, just in case. He's an old hand at this."

Hannah hopped down from the carriage and he took off, the red triangle on the back of the carriage quickly growing smaller as he sped down the road.

"Isn't he wonderful, helping us like that?" Hannah stared wistfully after him.

"Ya, he is," Annie said, thinking that Jonah did ten times as many favors for their family. Still, she was glad that Hannah had found someone who filled her heart with love. A person couldn't ask for a more precious gift than Gott's gift of love.

By the time Jonah arrived, it was nearly midnight. Annie had changed into her everyday dress and assembled blankets and a few other supplies she thought they might need.

As he drove down the lane, his horse moving at a quick trot, she felt her heart swell with relief to have him here. Jonah would know how to handle this. When he was around, everything turned out fine; she had learned that over these past few weeks, and now she was hanging on to the hope that Jonah would be in her life forever.

The sight of him jumping down from the carriage made her heart leap for joy. He'd changed out of his Sunday clothes and now wore a heavy black jacket and hat. "What's all this excitement you've got going on?"

"Buttercup sure knows how to choose her moments—and her spots. She's out there on the edge of one of the creek beds. And right now, with all this rain, there's a few feet of water in it."

"And how far out is she?"

"Probably a five-minute ride. I hitched a cart to Tully, thinking we can use him. And I packed some flashlights, a lantern, blankets, and a thermos of hot tea."

"And you're bringing tea for Buttercup?" he teased.

"For us. Aren't we going to be waiting around for a few hours?"

He nodded. "It will take a while, but Dexters are easy calvers. She might deliver in two to three hours, depending on how far along she is."

"Do we need anything else for her?"

He rubbed his chin. "Let me get a few things from the barn. She'll probably deliver fine on her own, but it wouldn't hurt to pack some iodine and rope. Some hay, too."

With a few other items in the cart, he swung up into the driver's seat. "Let's go check on her."

She climbed up beside him and lifted the big lantern into her lap. It was tight with two on the little seat, but she didn't mind sitting close to him. Even through his jacket, she could feel the warmth of his body against her shoulder, a shield against the cool wind that whipped along the open fields now and again. She should have thought to bring a warming brick or a plastic bottle of hot water, just to keep their feet warm, but as it was still autumn she wasn't really thinking of warding off the cold yet.

"Which field is she in?" Jonah asked.

"Down east." She pointed the way.

What a thrill this was, riding out in the night with Jonah to take care of a laboring animal. It was more proof that they made a good team.

"Did you tell your dat that the cow is in labor?" he asked.

"I didn't want to wake him. When I went into the house to heat up water, both he and Mamm were asleep."

"You did the right thing," he said. "Knowing your dat, he wouldn't have been able to stay in bed."

"That's what I was thinking, and I didn't want him up pacing the floor all night, or worse, coming out to the field to have a look. The doctor says he's getting stable. The medicine is working. If he keeps following the rules and resting, Doc Trueherz thinks he'll be able to go to the big wedding at your place next month."

"That's very good news. I know it's been hard for Aaron to sit still."

"Ya, but he's grateful to have you here, Jonah." When she turned to him, she couldn't help but notice how the lantern light outlined the planes of his face—his chin, forehead, and cheekbones. "We're all grateful, Jonah. Especially me."

He shot her a quick, curious look. This was not a speech he expected. "I'm glad I was able to help." Quickly, he turned his attention back to the path, where the cow was now up and staggering unsteadily on the edge of the embankment.

"Whoa!"

"She looks like she's trying to walk away," Annie said. "Is that normal?"

"The mother cow usually gets up between contractions." Jonah halted their horse a few yards away from the laboring cow. "We'll give her a little space." Buttercup didn't seem to notice them as she collapsed onto the ground, her legs kicking at the air.

Annie hopped down to the ground but stood back a bit as Jonah took the lantern and went over to check the cow.

"There's nothing coming out yet," he called over to her. "Looks like she's still in the early part of her labor. Right now we have to let nature take its course. But we can put some hay on the ground. A clean bed would be better for mother and calf." They made quick work of spreading hay from the cart around the moaning cow, who was back on her feet again, plodding around.

"Just stay away from that ditch," Jonah told the cow.

"She's too upset to answer you," Annie teased.

"It's a funny thing," he said, looking up at the sky. "So many cows give birth in the middle of the night. Why do you think that is?"

Annie shrugged. "They like the moooonlight?" she mooed.

They both laughed.

"Now we wait." He glanced back toward the cart. "How about some of that hot tea you brought?"

"Sure." As they climbed back into the cart and Annie poured the hot tea into a cup, a sense of calm washed over her. Here they were in the middle of one of Gott's miracles—a new calf about to be born. And amid all the excitement, Gott had given them this little quiet time together.

She handed Jonah the thermos cup. "We'll have to share. I only brought one cup."

"Fine with me." He took a cautious sip. "Still hot. That's good on a night like this." He took a deeper drink, then gave it to her.

"Is there anything we can do for Buttercup?" She took a sip, grateful for the warmth of the sweet tea.

"Not unless something goes wrong. Sometimes if the calf is in the wrong position—breech or maybe the head turned back—you have to position the calf before it comes out. That's not easy."

"Have you ever done that before?"

He nodded. "But most times, the mother just pushes it out, all on her own."

"It's amazing, when you think about it." She handed him the empty cup and reached for the thermos. "Gott takes care of most everything and a new life comes into the world."

"Gott takes care of everything," he said, watching as she poured. "Even the things that don't go our way. They're all part of Gott's plan. We just don't understand why."

She capped the thermos, staring at his eyes, so full of wisdom and gentleness. "Jonah, I'm sorry I was such a disappointment to you."

He squinted. "What was that?"

"Before . . . when you told me you wanted to court me and I said no. I know I hurt you and I'm sorry for that. It was foolish of me to—"

"Don't apologize," he said, interrupting. "You were just telling the truth."

"Maybe I was, but I was wrong. I was a fool not to see you—the real you. All I could see was that you were Adam's brother, that you looked a little bit like him, and that was reason enough to keep away."

His eyes studied her as he took a careful sip of the tea. "But it's been hard to keep your distance, with me working here."

She nodded. "Ya, and that was a good thing. With you here every day, I got to know you. We became friends." She paused, licking her dry lips. This was not an easy thing to say. "My thoughts and feelings have been jumbled for a long, long time, but now I see it all, clear as the sky above us, and I've just got to tell you that I've come to favor you, Jonah. I think we belong together."

His eyes opened wide. "Did I hear that right?"

She nodded, not wanting to stop before she spilled the whole truth. "I admire your patience and skill. I enjoy your sense of humor. I feel so alive when I'm with you, and when you're not around there's such emptiness inside that my heart aches."

"Annie." He looked at the mug in his hand, tossed the tea out onto the field, and then dropped the empty mug onto the seat to take her hands. "I know how you feel, because I've been there for the past few years."

He lifted their hands to her cheek. "Your mouth goes dry. Reasonable thoughts fly from your brain."

He let his hand slide to the crook of her neck, the trail of his fingertips sending shivers through her. "And the heart . . . it pounds in the chest like a galloping horse."

She nodded, her throat growing tight with emotion. "That's just how it is, Jonah. And I have to ask you if you . . . do you still feel the same way about me?" She was wound up so tight that her voice cracked during the most important question.

"I do." His dark eyes, just inches from hers, were solemn and yet filled with the light of hope. "I tried and tried to shake it off. I tried to get over you, but every time I turned around, there you were, sneaking into my dreams and laughing behind me at a singing. So eventually, I just came to accept that there would always be a place for you in my heart. Always."

"You waited for me to come to my senses." Tears stung her eyes. "You're so wonderful."

He lifted her chin, smiling. "I'm nothing so grand, Annie. But I will always love you." He leaned closer and their lips touched, gently at first.

With a burst of emotion Annie reached for Jonah's shoulders and swayed into his arms.

He caught her and held her close and deepened the kiss until all she could think of was Jonah and her under the great black sky, the moon and stars. Two people in love . . . so much in love.

FORTY-FIVE

*J*onah kissed her, loving the soft feel of her cheek, the smell of her skin, the taste of her. His heartbeat thundered in his ears.

Was this really happening? Annie so soft in his arms, saying the words he had longed to hear for so many years . . .

He ended the kiss and lifted his head with a sigh. Her lips, red and plump from kissing, held his gaze until her eyes slowly opened and he was lost in that beautiful blue of a summer sky.

His racing heart was no joke. Annie was really in his arms.

"I can't believe this," he said softly. "I keep thinking that, in a minute, I'm going to wake up from this dream, because it is a dream come true."

Annie's smile filled his heart. "But it is true. It took me long enough to sort it all out. I know. I've been a fool, thinking that my feelings for you were just friendship. Thinking that I had to go off to New York to find a husband, when the answer to my prayers was right here. My heart could just burst with joy when I think of it."

He felt one side of his mouth twitch into a grin. "Let's not have anything bursting now," he said, gently rubbing her smooth cheek. "Besides, we can't forget poor Buttercup calving at the edge of the creek."

"Buttercup!" Annie's hand flew to her mouth as she looked over at the heifer, which chose that moment to flop on the ground again for another contraction.

Jonah jumped down from the cart and went over to check the cow. Sure enough, there was a white sac beginning to push out of the cow's hind end. Good old Buttercup kept pushing, and a minute later, he could make out a small black hoof inside the sac.

"Attagirl," he said, reassuring her.

"The calf is coming, right?" Annie joined him. "Is there anything we should do?"

"I like to think that it helps to talk her through it, but what do I know?"

She laughed. "Well, I guess it's worked for you before. How are you doing, Buttercup?"

As if in answer, the heifer got to her feet, her tail distended over the two hooves that were poking out of her.

"Are those hooves?" Annie asked.

Jonah nodded. "And they're pointed in the right direction. That's a good sign. We can leave her be. It shouldn't be long now."

The cow dropped to the ground, moaning softly and sucking in air.

"Did you hear that, Buttercup?" Annie said, going toward the cow's head to look her in the eye. "Not too much longer."

Meanwhile, Jonah watched the rear to be sure the calf was in the right position. Just about thirty minutes after the hooves had emerged, he caught sight of the head.

"I see the calf's nose coming out . . . and its tongue." He laughed. "A lot of very pink tongue."

"That's good?"

"It's in the right position. A few pushes and it'll be out."

"Good." Annie clapped her hands together. "Okay, Buttercup. Your little one is coming. Just keep pushing! That's all you need to do."

He grinned, enjoying Annie's enthusiastic sermon for the cow.

The shiny black calf continued to emerge as Buttercup pushed. Within minutes Jonah saw the full head, the curved body, the long, slick back. "Almost done," he called to Annie. "Only the rear hooves are left."

With that, Buttercup lifted her big head, swung round to look behind her, and gave one final push. The black calf was completely out, sprawled on its side in the hay.

Another miracle.

Although Jonah had witnessed this process before, sheer amazement still overcame him at the sight of a new life coming awake in the hay.

Immediately, Buttercup got to her feet. Jonah stepped back as she came around and vigorously licked the calf.

"Such a sweet little thing. And look at how she's mothering it already," Annie said, touching his arm. He covered her hand with his, and together they watched as the mother cow very thoroughly licked her newborn calf.

Within a minute or two, the calf was trying to stand on its spindly legs.

"It's trying to walk," Annie said.

"They're quick learners. People, we take a year to learn what they do in three minutes." As Jonah spoke, the little calf walked and stumbled, moving dangerously close to the edge of the creek.

"Oh, stop him!" Annie cried. "What if he falls over the side?"

"Hey, little one. You don't want to go down there." Jonah hustled over to the edge of the ditch, making himself a barrier between the creek and the calf. "That water must be freezing tonight."

The calf came barreling his way, stumbling against his legs. He caught it firmly and carried it away from the edge, back to its mother.

"It should start on the teat now," he said, helping the calf find Buttercup's udder. "It's good to get them going in the first hour when the sucking instinct is strong, and the early milk is good for them."

While he helped guide the calf to nurse, Annie fetched the iodine and slathered it onto the cord. Then they both stood back and watched as the calf fed.

"It's a miracle," Annie said. "I've seen puppies and sheep born, and it's always a wonder."

Jonah nodded. "The second miracle tonight." He slipped an arm around Annie's shoulders and held her close. "You were the first one."

"Not me." She slid her arms around his waist and pressed her face to his chest. "Gott's love is the real miracle."

She was right. With a deep breath, he held her close, thanking the Heavenly Father with all his heart.

After a few minutes of contented feeding, the calf scampered away.

"We need to get this one in a pen before he takes a very cold swim," Jonah said, lifting the calf into his arms. "We can get them back to the calving shed now, out of the wind. If we take the calf in the cart, Buttercup will follow."

"How are we going to keep that little one from jumping right out of the cart?" Annie asked.

"I'll hold him."

The calf was probably only seventy pounds or so, but the spindly thing was awkward, as if it wasn't sure if it should nuzzle Jonah or squirm to escape. He lifted the creature into the back of the wagon, climbed up, then cradled it in his arms, making sure the hooves were up so that it couldn't get traction.

As he sat in the back of the cart, the newborn calf trembling in his arms, Jonah took in the farm and the night sky and the stars with a grateful sigh. The fields sparkled in the moonlight, as if the angels had painted each chopped stubble of hay with glittering silver paint. In this moment, with Annie driving them along the path and this baby creature in his arms, he felt sure that he was the happiest man on Gott's earth.

A Bible verse came to him, and it seemed a fitting prayer for the moment. *The Lord is my shepherd. I shall not want.*

Two miracles in one night.

Ya, he was a happy man. And with Annie by his side, he would never want again.

PART FOUR

Season of Love

What manner of man is this?
For he commandeth even the winds and water,
And they obey him.

— LUKE 8:25

The whir of bike engines screamed along the country road as Gabe and Blake headed toward a wooded area near the King farm. After weeks of riding on the course and the trails near Blake's house, Gabe was getting bored with that area.

"I'd like to try something different," he'd told Blake earlier as they'd rolled two motorcycles out of Blake's garage.

"You are, man. That new bike you're on has great tracking and improved linkage. I think you're going to like it."

"Yeah, it looks good." Gabe looked down at the new bike—a small motorcycle. With practice, he had worked his way up from the smaller bikes, and now he could handle the real thing. "But I was thinking of trying it out down the road, on a new trail."

"I'm up for something new. What are you thinking of?" Blake had asked. When Gabe told him about the wooded area in the back acres of his family's farm, Blake had been game.

It was an off Sunday in November, and Gabe had been eager to get away from the farm, where all the talk was about the preparation for the big double wedding. Gabe didn't mind doing his part, scrubbing down walls or clearing out the barn. But he didn't get too excited about all the fanfare . . . the details of how many different types of cookies to bake or where all the horses and carriages would be stored during the wedding.

Today, it was just Blake and him on the bikes. For the last few weeks, Ben had bowed out because of plans with his new girl, Hannah Stoltzfus. Henpecked, that was what Ben was, giving up motorbikes for a girl. Gabe understood the lure, but he was sticking to his choice. He loved Emma, but he wasn't about to let her make his decisions for him.

Even without Ben, Gabe enjoyed riding with Blake. Sometimes he got a laugh when he passed Amish buggies on the road . . . like the one up ahead. The couple in the front seat and the little children in the back turned and stared at him. They were probably surprised to see a young man dressed Plain on a bike. And with the red helmet covering his entire head, Gabe was pretty sure they didn't recognize him.

That made him grin—speeding past the carriage with ease as the folks in the carriage wondered who that Amish wild man was.

It was sort of strange, being on the road but so low to the ground. Still, he loved the speed of the motorbikes. Amish folk just didn't understand the powerful feeling of having a wailing engine between your legs. Gabe revved the engine and grinned as the bike shot forward.

This was how a man should get around.

When they got to the access road that led to the woods on his family's property, Gabe signaled to turn right and Blake followed. As they shifted gears, the two bikes let out dual whines that must have cut straight across the open fields to the Kings' farmhouse. It made Gabe feel like a real daredevil, riding so close to home. He wouldn't have dared to do this weeks ago, but back then it had been a thrill just to learn to ride the bikes.

Gabe rolled to a stop and pointed out the entrance to two different trails. Blake decided to take the one on the right, and Gabe decided to take the one on the left, knowing both trails met at the edge of the woods in one of the back fields. With a burst of the throttle, he was on his way.

The bright colors that had painted the trees when he had begun riding the motorbikes had given way to bare gray bones. Gray and brown were now the main colors of the woods.

Kind of glum.

Or maybe that was just his mood since Emma had chased him away from her house last weekend without even trying the motorbike. He hadn't been sure she would go for a ride, but he had expected her to be happy to see him.

He'd been wrong. Emma had been so furious about him bringing the motorbike, he wasn't sure she'd actually gotten a look at him at all.

All the rain had softened the hard-packed trail, and as Gabe hit a wet patch the rear wheel spun, sending mud splattering behind him. His pants would be pretty dirty by the time the afternoon was over.

Trying to keep out of the soft mud, he kept to the edges of the path, thinking that he probably hadn't been out in these woods in the last year.

He saw the dark figure coming before he heard it: a tall draft horse with a rider dressed in black. Gabe pulled off the path and waited behind a tree as the horse and rider approached.

An Amish man on a huge horse.

As it galloped closer, he recognized the rider—his brother Adam.

Thunder's hooves pounded the moist earth, sending dirt spraying in his wake. Adam was a seasoned rider, and he moved as if one with the horse.

Like one iron muscle.

Gabe felt like a small woodland creature as he looked up at the towering horse, the earth vibrating beneath his boots. The horse roared past.

Now, that was true power and strength.

Gabe looked down at the shiny motorcycle, then burst out laughing.

Really? Did he really think a small, whining bike made him look like a strong man? He had started riding bikes because he wanted to feel like a man. He wanted power and speed. The bikes gave him that, along with a sense that he was escaping from his life, tearing away from the strict, orderly rules of the Amish.

But today he had seen his brother moving down the trail with more speed and power than any of these little bikes could summon. There was no match for real horsepower.

He squeezed the handlebar grips, suddenly missing the feel of reins in his hands. His horse was waiting for him, along with his buggy.

This motorcycle, with its bright red paint and shiny silver pipes . . . this was not what Gott intended for a man. Why hadn't he seen that before? Still laughing, he turned the bike around on the trail and headed off to meet Blake.

And as he motored down the trail, he remembered the first time Dat had let him drive a buggy. He had been only five or six, coming home from a horse auction. Gabe remembered the excitement that fluttered in his belly when Dat let him hold the reins all by himself.

"Not too tight now. Give him a little slack. There you go." Dat's words had eased him through the moment, scary and exciting all at the same time. And Gabe had felt a new awareness of the movement of the buggy, the tug of the horse in front of him, the curve of the road ahead. Lots of things to think about, but he could do it. He wanted to learn to handle the horse like a man.

So many years ago, Dat had started him in the right direction. A knot of emotion grew in Gabe's throat at the memory of Dat's patient voice. He wondered how he could have forgotten his first lesson from Dat with a buggy. It worried him that Mamm and Dat were fading from their lives—gone before half the kids in the family had even gotten baptized.

But we're on the right path, Gabe thought. Mamm and Dat had made sure of that.

By the time he met Blake, Gabe was grateful for the tinted visor, glad to have something to mask the tears in his eyes.

FORTY-SEVEN

There was a chill in the night air, November's warning that autumn would end soon. Jonah took one last look at the barn and imagined all the folks who would come through here tomorrow. Hundreds of people would pass through these doors, all here to celebrate the weddings of Adam and Remy, Five and Mary.

Reassured that all was ready, he took the kerosene lamp down from its hook and closed the door. A silvery ring glistened around the moon. Up on the road, twin white lights moved slowly. When the car turned down their lane, he was curious for a second, then smiled.

It was probably sister Sadie, back for the wedding.

He quickened his pace, wanting to greet her before she walked into the dark house. The word was that she wouldn't arrive until morning, so everyone else was asleep.

As the car pulled up on the side of the house, Jonah hurried down the path from the barn. The passenger door opened, and two people stepped out. As the trunk of the little car popped open, Jonah recognized Sadie and her boyfriend, Mike Trueherz.

He held up the lantern. "Hello? Is that my long-lost sister?" he called.

Sadie whirled around, her loose brown hair swinging around her shoulders. "Jonah?" She dropped her satchel and came running to give him a hug.

"What are you doing sneaking back in the middle of the night?"

"I left as soon as my choir practice finished." She clapped him on the back, then stepped away for a long look. "I've missed you! You seem taller."

"Maybe I've grown since the last time you were here." He turned to nod to Mike. "Will you come in for some hot chocolate?"

"No, thanks, Jonah. I've got to get back to Philadelphia."

"We thought it would be better for Mike to drop me off tonight than in the morning."

"You're not staying in Halfway?" Jonah asked Mike. "Aren't you coming to the wedding?"

"I've got classes in the morning. Besides, the church leaders are already upset with Sadie about leaving. We figured it would only make things worse for her to have an English friend at an Amish event." He handed Sadie a duffel bag from the trunk. "But my father will be here."

Jonah nodded. "Adam and Mary will be glad to have the doc at the wedding." All the Kings were grateful for the help Mike's father had given them over the years.

"I'd better go." Mike smiled at Sadie. "Give my best to Adam and Mary. I guess things will be changing around here."

They already have, Jonah thought. Change had swept through the farm like an autumn wind, shifting things around while they were all sleeping. Sadie was now a visitor. Mary had moved her things to the carriage house at the Bielers', and Remy would be living here after today. Remy would be the one in charge of the baking and the washing. Katie and Sam would go to her with their bumps and bruises.

Ya, the winds of change were blowing through, and Jonah thanked Gott that he'd been touched by changes, too.

Gott had brought him the love of a good woman.

Inside, Jonah added wood to the fire as Sadie took off her coat and settled into a rocking chair. Jonah was curious about the way she'd changed. Not just her Englisher blue jeans and sweater, but her hair, loose and obviously cut. No Amish girl would take scissors to her hair.

"What are you staring at? Do I have food in my teeth?"

"I think you forgot your kapp," he teased.

"Oh, my hair." She scraped it back and began to braid it behind her head. "I still have my prayer kapp. I was thinking of wearing it tomorrow, out of respect, but I'm not going to dress Plain. I've made my decision, and I'm sticking to it. What do you think?"

"I think the bishop is going to want to give you a scolding whether you wear a kapp or not," he said. Even though Sadie hadn't been baptized, Bishop Samuel had made it clear that she was not welcome to drop in and out of the community at will. One of the conditions of her attending the wedding was that she would not be in the bridal party or sit at the dinner table with a baptized member. "Bishop Samuel will be putting the squeeze on for you to come back. He wants you back for good. We all do."

"I might have to spend most of the reception hiding from Bishop Samuel." With her hair braided behind her, she looked more like her old self. She scooted her rocker closer to the fire and reached out to squeeze Jonah's arm. "It's good to be home, even if it's just for two days. I have to get back Thursday for afternoon classes."

"It sounds like you're very busy in the city."

"You know me. . . . I'm not so good at sitting around. But I get a lot of joy out of everything I'm doing. My school hours, and singing with the choir, and being Katherine's caretaker . . ."

He listened as she shared some stories of her life in the city. Now that he saw Sadie with her new haircut and clothes, it wasn't hard to imagine her living among the English.

"The strangest thing is the way people have to plan to get their exercise," Sadie said. "They pay money to go to these little gyms and use machines. If they would just walk instead of riding in their cars, they would save a lot of money."

He smiled. "How's Mike's grandmother?"

"Good. Katherine and Mike are teaching me about good nutrition. I do miss cooking for eleven people. Sometimes, when I go to make mashed potatoes for Mike and Gram, they have to stop me from peeling the whole five-pound bag."

"Old habits die hard."

She nodded. "But I reckon I'll get my chance to do plenty of cooking in a few hours. Mary said the girls are getting up at four in the morning to get the fryers going. Three hundred pounds of chicken takes a while."

He glanced at the clock. Almost nine-thirty. "You'd better get to bed if you're going to be up for the cooking."

"I don't mind missing sleep for the chance to talk with you. I do miss times like this."

He caught a glimmer of sadness in her amber eyes. "The little ones still think you might come back."

She bit her lower lip and looked down at the floor. "I hate to disappoint them, but I'm not coming back. I'm not an Amish girl anymore."

When she looked up, tears glistened in her round eyes. "I've moved on, Jonah, but I'll always love the family I've left behind."

"And we'll always love our sister Sadie, no matter what the bishop says."

She wiped the tears from her eyes with the back of her hands. "Look at me, a regular crybaby."

He looked back toward the fire. "Don't worry. I won't tell any-one."

"It's good to be home, but it's difficult, too."

He nodded. "I know the good and bad. You followed your dream, but you miss your home. And we miss you, too. No one mucks out the stables as well as you did."

She laughed through her tears. "I miss you, but I don't miss *that*."

His mouth twisted sideways at the memory of Sadie shoveling away in the stables, singing her songs to the cows and horses in that beautiful voice Gott gave her. It seemed like yesterday.

"I'm glad you're happy, but I don't want to think of you so far from home."

"When you have a car, Philly isn't so far. And I'll always visit. At least, as long as the bishop allows it."

Jonah nodded. Whatever Sadie decided, he would always love his younger sister. In his heart, she would always be welcome.

"And I've got news." She put her hands on her hips. "Don't say anything, but Mike asked me to marry him."

She looked so pleased, her eyes shining bright, that Jonah couldn't help but grin. "And I take it you said yes," he teased.

"Of course I did. I can't imagine living without him. We're going to wait a year or so until he finishes school. And that'll give me a chance to get further along with my school and music lessons. I'm making the most of the gift that Gott gave me, and it feels right for me."

"Good." That would make three of his siblings married. He hoped to make it four once wedding time came around next fall. "Mike's a lucky fella."

Sadie stopped rocking. "And what about you? Why do you look so different to me?"

"Because you've been away too long?" he asked. "Or maybe because I have a secret of my own." He hadn't planned on telling her about Annie, but then he didn't know when he would see her again.

She gasped. "What's your secret? Now you have to tell me for sure."

Jonah got up to tend the fire. It was a little awkward talking to a sister about these things. "I'm hoping to get married next year, too."

"Praise be to Gott! You've found someone."

He nodded. "Annie Stoltzfus."

Sadie clapped her hands together. "I always thought you had your eye on Annie. Does Mary know? She'll be so glad to have her best friend in the family."

"Mary and Gabe know. No one else . . . unless they're all guessing, the way you did." He looked up from the fire. "Am I that easy to read?"

"To your sisters? Ya. But don't you worry. I'll keep your secret as long as you want."

"Maybe it won't be so long. Mary has me paired off with Annie for the wedding."

"So people will start to notice tomorrow." Sadie grinned. "I'm so very happy for you. Where do you think you and Annie will live?"

He laughed. "Well, first we've got to get married, of course, and I haven't asked her yet. But I reckon we would live with Annie's parents. I've been helping out with the sheep and the harvest ever since Aaron had that heart attack. There's plenty of work to be done there." He hadn't really thought about it, but he would be very comfortable living on Stoltzfus land and continuing to run the farm. He and Aaron had developed a good rapport. He felt needed there.

"Mike was right," Sadie said. "So many changes going on here."

"Ya, but good changes." He gave the fire one last jab as he thought of the months ahead. This time next year, Gott willing, he would be getting married himself. " 'To everything there is a season,' " he said, thinking aloud.

"'And a time for every purpose under heaven,'" Sadie answered.

"I used to worry that I'd grow old alone," he confessed. "Old man Jonah, too old to go to the singings anymore."

"See how you worried for nothing? Gott has a plan for us. Just as He brings every new season, He's brought a season of love for us."

Jonah would always think of autumn as Gott's season of love.

FORTY-EIGHT

*R*ain beat against the windshield of the King carriage the morning of the wedding, as Jonah drove Annie and her parents there. The ceremony would be in the Beilers' barn, then everyone would move down the road to the Kings' place, as no single farm could accommodate both events for five hundred people.

"Another gray day," Annie said brightly. She didn't mind the bad weather one bit when Jonah was beside her. "Good thing we'll all be snug inside at the wedding."

"Only you can make a rainy day sound cozy," Jonah said, one brow lifting in a wry expression.

"How you doing back there, Dat?" Annie asked.

"I'm good, Annie girl. Grateful to Gott that I can go along today." Dat was allowed to attend the festivities as long as he took it easy, stayed off his feet for most of the time. Although the doctor had warned Aaron to get medical attention at the slightest twinge of pain, the slow improvement Annie had seen in the past weeks had reassured everyone in the family.

Still, driving was out of the question, so Jonah had offered to take care of that, and Lovina had agreed that the family would be better off in two carriages so that Aaron could rest in quiet if he needed to. Annie was glad her dat could attend, and ever so grateful to Jonah for driving them. Since they were both attendants and Jonah's family was hosting the reception, Annie knew that he had many extra chores to see to—including clearing out all the furniture downstairs so that dining tables could be set up in the bedroom, kitchen, and living room.

Humming, Annie looked past the droplets of rain wiggling down the window to the river that ran parallel to this section of the road. "Look at that," she said. "I've never seen the river so swollen."

"Good thing we don't have to go across the covered bridge," Mamm said from the back. "People have been talking about it at the tea shop. They say the water level is almost up to the bottom of the bridge."

"It's no surprise, with all the rain we've been having," Dat said.

"I was crossing the bridge last week on the way back from Paradise, and I saw some inspectors from the county checking it over." Jonah's voice was soothing, but Annie noted the undercurrent of concern. "They said they were worried about the stability of the structure when the river crests."

"I pray it doesn't get damaged," Mamm said. "It's such an old bridge."

Jonah nodded. "But all this rain, it's got to go somewhere. Our pond at home has grown so high that it's taken over the marshes. Have you ever seen such a rainy season, Aaron?"

"Not that I can remember. But it's not just the rain. Remember how the wind took part of our roof at the end of the summer?"

"That crazy storm!" Annie smiled; that was the storm that had brought Jonah to their house to lend a hand on repairs. "I thought I was going to take off like a kite in the sky!"

Her parents chuckled behind her. "And no wonder," Lovina said. "You're such a wisp of a girl."

"Wisp or not, no wind should be strong enough to send a girl flying through the air," Annie insisted.

"Let's hope not," Jonah said. He lowered his voice, adding, "I had a hard enough time catching you on the ground."

Annie giggled.

"What was that?" Dat called from the back.

"Jonah's just trying to make me laugh again," Annie answered.

"He does a good job of that," Aaron said.

"Ya, he does." Annie turned to Jonah, thinking how blessed she was to have found a man who loved to make her laugh. Mamm always said that laughter was the closest distance between two people. Now, at last, she understood what Mamm meant.

It was customary for the bridal couple and their attendants to be seated a full two hours before the ceremony because everyone wanted to come by and shake hands with the wedding party before sitting down.

So many faces, Annie thought, as Amish folks filed past. Tall and short, blond and dark.

As friends and neighbors walked by, emotion swelled in her chest. These were the faces of her life, past, present, and, thank the Heavenly Father, future. So many different people, but like a fine cloth, they were woven together into a tight community, bonded by love. What a blessing it was to live here.

When the ceremony started, Annie listened with a new ear to the words of the vows. The service suddenly seemed so personal, partly because her best friend, Mary, was the bride.

"Do you also promise your wedded wife, before the Lord and His church, that you will nevermore depart from her, but will care for her and cherish her?" the bishop asked Five. "If bodily sickness comes to her, or in any circumstance which a Christian husband is responsible to care for, until the dear Gott will again separate you from each other?"

"I do promise," Five said solemnly.

Annie let her gaze wander to Jonah, and wouldn't you know it, he was looking at her! Was he thinking the same thing?

She closed her eyes and resolved herself to think only of the two blessed couples now. This was their wedding day, and she was here to attend to them.

Those other sweet hopes and dreams . . . there would be time for that later.

When they arrived at the King house for the reception, all the carriages had to file around a white stretch limousine parked in the lane.

"What's that fancy car?" Aaron asked.

"That's Herb McCallister's car—Remy's father," Jonah explained. "She wasn't sure that he would come, but I'm glad he did. I think it means a lot to her."

"Of course it does. A girl wants her dat at her wedding," Annie said. She thought of her own dat and said a little prayer of thanks that the doctors had been able to help him. Gott willing, his medicine would keep him going until he was ready for the triple bypass surgery he needed.

As their carriage rolled up to the barn, they were greeted by a group of young men who had been assigned to park the carriages and tend the horses.

Jonah jumped out quickly and helped Dat from the carriage. "I'm good to walk in with my wife by my side," Aaron said. He looked toward the door of the house, as if measuring the steps. "Lovina hasn't let me down in thirty-two years. I trust she'll get me to a chair inside."

Annie and Jonah watched as Dat made slow but steady progress toward the front door, where Nate King stood, ready to receive and seat guests. Mary and Adam's uncle was performing the duties usually handled by the father of the bride. Nate would turn away folks who were not in the first seating, and he would assign each guest a table, usually based on kinship. Guests waiting for a later seating would socialize in the barn, where benches had been set up.

"We'd better get inside, too," Jonah said. As attendants, they would be expected to sit with the bridal party through all of the seatings, which suited Annie just fine. They wouldn't miss one minute of the celebration.

Inside the living room, tables were set up in a U shape, with the two corners, the *Ecks,* specially decorated for the two bridal couples. Those parts of the big long line of tables were laden with bowls of sweets, candies, fruits, and handcrafted cakes made by friends.

"So many cakes!" Annie said.

"So many mouths to feed." Jonah cocked an eyebrow as he looked down at her. "But yours is my favorite. It looks like a white cloud."

She was pleased that he had been paying attention when she'd dropped off the pineapple sheet cake last night. She had covered it with vanilla icing and piped puffs of frosting in the shape of a heart in the center.

"Denki. The ecks look beautiful," Annie said. "And you're a lucky man. You get to sit with me since we're both in the bridal party."

"I'm guessing Mary had something to do with pairing us off?" Jonah said wryly. "Because I thought I'd be sitting beside Adam."

"It's the bride's choice. Well, at least one of the brides. And you don't want to argue with a bride on her wedding day."

"Mmm. Never argue with a bride." Jonah tipped his head toward the side, studying her. "You look happy."

"I am." She squeezed her eyes shut, then looked up at him with a heart full of love. "Jonah, when we were sitting there, before the ceremony, and all those folks came by to shake hands, I felt such an outpouring of love." She hugged herself. "It gives me goose bumps just talking about it. We're so blessed to live here in Halfway, to be part of this community."

There was a golden light in his eyes as he thought about that. "It's true. I wouldn't want to live anywhere else."

"I just wanted to share that. So many times we're praying about our worries and fears. It's good to have a prayer of thanks bubble inside you that way."

He nodded.

"Kumm, you two," Mary called. "Time to sit."

Annie took her seat next to Mary, facing the room, and Jonah sat opposite her.

When everyone was seated, the bishop called for the silent prayer. "If the tables are full, let us pray."

Heads bowed throughout the house, and in the sweet silence Annie thanked Gott for the many blessings He had showered upon everyone here. For Dat's mending heart. For the blessed union of her four good friends.

And for Jonah.

She was so grateful to have found Jonah King, who was right under her nose all along. *Thank you, Heavenly Father, for giving me eyes to see.*

FORTY-NINE

I should have stayed home," Emma whispered as she and Elsie stayed close to each other in the Kings' barn. "It hurts me to look at him. What am I going to do when it's time for us to go inside and eat?" Emma would have loved to stay home from the wedding just to avoid seeing Gabe, but she couldn't deny her young scholars, Ruthie and Simon, the support they deserved. So here she was, trying not to look his way, trying to deny the vibrations that quivered through her whenever he was near.

"If you see him coming toward you, look down at the floor," Elsie suggested softly. "Chances are, they'll put us at a table out in the kitchen, anyway. We're not close kin."

"It gives me that nervous butterfly feeling," Emma said. "Butterflies that won't fly away."

Elsie closed her hand around her sister's wrist and looked up at her. "You stand up in front of dozens of children nearly every day. You keep them quiet and orderly and teach them reading, writing, and arithmetic. You can do this, Emma. Do it for your scholars. Didn't you say Ruthie and Simon so wanted you to be here?"

Emma pressed the palm of one hand to her flat belly. "They did, and I'm happy to please them. It's just that—"

"I know. Gabe is a thorn in your side right now. That's why you have to think about the good things that could come of you being here: Ruthie and Simon. You're a helper, Emma. Go help your students."

Emma took a deep breath, trying to ease the tight feeling in her chest. "You're right. But I don't want to leave you alone." She knew that Elsie felt uncomfortable in social environments beyond the shop.

"I see Fanny over there talking to Nancy Briggs. I'll go join them." Elsie put a hand on the small of Emma's back and pushed. "Now go. Do a good deed. It'll take your mind off your worries."

"How did you get so wise? Most of the time you have more common sense than me, and I'm two years older."

Elsie smiled, her widely spaced teeth showing. "Gott blessed me with wisdom. Now go find them."

As Elsie moved off, Emma glanced around the barn in search of the children, but most of the guests in here were young people of courting age. She stepped outside the wide barn doors, a little relieved to be away from the crowd of young people. Ever since she and Gabe had parted, Emma had found it difficult to be at singings or where she had to face young people. Her heart filled with envy at the sight of other couples, and hearing other girls talk of their beaus reminded her of the one she had lost.

The sight of three children running out the back door of the mud porch caught her attention, and she recognized Simon and Ruthie, along with one of their older sisters.

"Simon!" She quickened her step, dodging two waiters who were carrying trays of food from the wedding wagon.

Simon turned to look back, then stopped running. "Teacher Emma." He grinned from ear to ear. "You came!"

"How could I miss such a wonderful celebration?" As Emma drew closer she recognized the taller sister as one of the twins who had finished eighth grade last year. Leah—a wonderful good student.

"Ruthie . . . and Leah, we miss you in class this year. Have you read any good books lately?" Emma asked Leah.

"She's been too busy cooking and cleaning for the wedding," Ruthie answered for her.

"But I always find time to read," Leah said.

Ruthie trotted over and took Emma's hand. "Come with us! Nate and Betsy gave us a job to do. They need more Nothings for the next round of guests. Did you try them yet?"

"I haven't been inside yet, but I'm sure they're delicious." Nothings were fried cookies that were traditional fare at weddings. So large they covered a dinner plate, the cookies were usually left in a stack on each table so that guests could break off a piece when they wanted.

"Betsy said there's a big bin in the cold storage cellar," Simon said, a sense of purpose in his stride. They were all moving quickly, as the drizzling rain was starting to come down harder now.

"I know where they are," Ruthie said. "I helped store the other cookies in there." She looked up at Emma. "Did you know that we have four kinds of cookies to choose from?"

"I'll have to remember to save my appetite." Emma felt her nervousness drain as she accompanied them to the cellar. Spending time with the Kings was always a delight. Gabe was blessed to have a loving family, and such a large one, at that.

Down in the cellar, Ruthie was quick to find the proper bin of cookies. "I can carry this myself," Ruthie said. "It's light. Why don't you two show Teacher Emma the study room you set up above the workshop? The one you used when Simon couldn't go to school last year."

Leah perked up. "Do you want to see it?"

"Just show me the way." In truth, Emma didn't mind missing out on some of the festivities if it meant she could avoid Gabe.

"And if the rain lets up you can visit with my horse, Shadow," Simon said. "You've met her before. Do you remember?"

"Of course. She's the one you spent the summer training, ya?" Emma recalled that Simon had written his essay about her.

"That's the one, over there in the field. She's a quick learner. We were able to put her on the team to help with the harvest this year."

"Wow." Emma nodded. "I'd like to have such a good student in my class," she teased.

They showed her the little room above the woodshop where Leah had tried her hand at homeschooling Simon during the difficult times last winter.

"This is his arithmetic book," Leah said. "He doesn't like long division."

Simon's face puckered at the thought.

"But he learned his times tables. And this is his writing notebook." Leah handed her a marble notebook. "Writing is his best subject, I think."

"And reading," Simon said. "I used to like it when you read to me."

Emma leafed through the notebook, smiling at the progression of Simon's handwriting from wobbly, oddly spaced letters to better formed words. "It's good to see your hard work, Simon. And yours, too." She held the open notebook to show Leah. "See how his hand-writing is rough and hard to read here in the beginning? And then, after you worked with him, there was good improvement."

Leah beamed when she showed her some examples from the back of the notebook.

"Have you ever thought of being a schoolteacher?" she asked. "You have a good start with your first pupil here."

"It's a dream of mine," Leah said quietly.

"But, Leah, you already have a job at the tea shop," Simon pointed out.

"The tea shop, I'm not so good at that," Leah admitted. "But reading and writing, I could do that all day and night."

"Then we have to get you back into the classroom," Emma said. Why hadn't she thought of this last spring, when Leah completed her schooling? "If you like, I can talk to the school board and see if you can be my teacher's helper. If they'll approve it, you can work with me at the schoolhouse. It would be an apprenticeship of sorts."

"I would love that," Leah said earnestly. "I've been wanting to do it for a long, long time." She pressed her fingertips to her mouth. "Do you think the board would allow it? I would work ever so hard for you. I don't mind making alphabet posters for the wall or grading papers."

Emma smiled. "I know you're a hard worker, and the board will keep that in mind when they make their decision. I'll talk to them first thing tomorrow. Or . . . maybe today. I think some of the members are here for the wedding."

"Denki!" Leah clapped her hands together and gave Emma a hug.

Emma smiled, patting her back. "Don't thank me! You would be making my job much easier."

"Hey, up there?" Ruthie called. "I need your help. Betsy wants us to bring out the other cookies."

"We have to go!" Simon dashed for the stairs.

"Do you need my help?" Emma asked as she followed them down the narrow staircase.

"You're a guest. You must go back to the wedding and celebrate," Leah said merrily. "Make sure you get a taste of the Nothings. And the Ranger Cookies; I helped bake those."

Now that the children had lifted her spirits, Emma felt ready to enjoy the festivities. Rain was falling harder now, and she walked briskly. *Run between the raindrops,* Mamm used to say.

She was on her way back to the main house when a hand reached from the darkness and pulled her out of the light of the porch lantern.

"What . . . ?"

"I got you now." Gabe gripped her hand and he was tugging her around the corner, to the open nook used to split wood.

"Gabe?" She gasped, even as her heart leaped in her chest. Ya, she was happy to see him—thrilled—but she couldn't let him know that. She had to stay calm and in control. "I can't be alone with you here or . . . or anywhere."

"Emma, the truth is, you can't be without me." He released her hand, but she still felt the warmth of his touch on her palm. "And I don't want to be without you. I'm sorry. I . . . I was doing what boys do. But that's no excuse. I hurt you. I didn't honor your vow. I won't do that again."

"You . . . you won't?" Emma had to remind herself to breathe, but her chest felt so tight—a fist of emotion—and she couldn't look away from Gabe's lovely amber eyes. "What about the motorbikes?"

"I'm done with that. I liked the speed and power, but a motor-cycle is nothing compared to what my own horse can do. I'm giving up the bikes."

Emma took a grateful breath. "I'm so happy to hear that."

"And you don't have to worry about me getting you into trouble with the school council. I've been thinking on that, and an Amish schoolteacher deserves a good Amish beau. So I'm getting baptized next fall. I'll start the training in the spring."

She could hardly believe what she was hearing. "Are you sure you're ready, Gabe? This is a big decision, you know. Don't be taking a vow on my account."

"This is my choice." He looked away, and when his eyes returned to hers, she saw a tenderness there that made her knees sink. "I've been thinking about my dat a lot . . . about what he would have wanted me to do."

She bit her lower lip. "I know it's hard for you, not having him here."

"Sometimes I still expect to see him tinkering beside the barn or walking in the back fields." He rubbed his knuckles over his jaw. "I knew he would have wanted me to step up and take on responsibilities. I fooled myself thinking that riding a bike made me a man. I was wrong. A real man finds peace in here." He pressed a fist to his chest. "That's what my dat would say."

Emma nodded. "Your father was wise."

"He was." Gabe caught her gaze, his amber eyes flickering with gentleness. "So, I'm done with the bikes and the boom box. From now on, it's just you and me, Emma. And a gray stallion named Mercury." He reached for her, and Emma felt likely to melt under his touch.

"Gabe, I can't do this here. Someone will see. . . ."

"Let them see. I'm going down the right path, and it's time we let people know we're courting. I don't want to keep it a secret anymore." He turned and cast his arm out toward the darkness. "Hello, out there! I'm courting Emma Lapp."

She laughed and tugged him back into the shadows. "Gabe, quiet now! There's a wedding going on. We'll tell people soon enough, but right now we need to get out of the rain."

"The rain will dry, but the love I feel for you will never run dry."

Her heart leaped at the mention of love . . . and in such a sweet way.

Like a poem.

And suddenly she didn't care who saw them together here. Let folks talk about Gabe and her. They were a couple now . . . officially courting.

Two young people in love.

"I've missed you." Emma rose onto her toes and kissed him, so happy to be Gabe's girl once again.

FIFTY

Near the end of the wedding, Lovina came up to the eck and leaned between Annie and Jonah.

"Your dat is all tuckered out." She covered Annie's hand with hers. "Do you mind if we go home now?"

"That's fine." Jonah stood up. "I'll go get the carriage."

While Annie went to check on her father, Jonah found Mary and told her that he was leaving to take Aaron home.

She nodded. "So, big brother, you seem to like the one I paired you off with."

"Who?" he teased. "Oh, you mean Annie."

"Ya, Annie. It looks like you two talked."

"We've been doing a lot of that."

Mary could no longer restrain her grin. "So the ice is broken?"

He nodded. "Broken and melted. We're courting now."

She pressed a palm to her mouth. "Two of the people I love so dearly, together. Maybe I should do some more matchmaking."

"I wouldn't go that far." He didn't want to admit that everything had really come together over the birth of Buttercup's calf. For now, it was nice for Mary to think that she'd had a hand in bringing Annie and him together; in a way, she had.

A quick look through the room revealed that Remy and Adam were standing near the other eck, talking with Remy's father. He went over and clapped Adam on the back.

"Time for me to get Aaron back. It was a wonderful day."

Adam's smile caused little creases at the outer corners of his eyes—just like Dat's. "It was a fine day." He opened his arms and the two men embraced. "Denki for all your help . . . for everything."

Jonah hugged his brother hard. For him, all the hectic chores of the past few days had been a true labor of love. At last, Mary was able to wed the man she had loved for years. And beyond all expectations, Adam's girl, an Englisher, had changed her life to become Amish. Remy was a quick learner, and she had plenty of love for the younger children, who still needed a mamm.

"I think you found a very good wife," Jonah said.

Adam leaned back and looked over at his bride. "She's the only woman for me. I thank Gott every day for her."

Remy glanced up as if she sensed that they were talking about her. "Jonah, did you meet my father, Herb?"

"We did meet," Herb said. "Jonah's the farming/mechanical expert of the operation, right? I think I've got this figured out."

Jonah nodded. "Usually we all pitch in, but I would like to be called a mechanical expert. It sounds very important." He turned to Remy. "I'm sorry I can't stay to help clean up. I need to see Aaron home."

"How kind of you to take care of Aaron." Remy hugged Jonah, then stepped back to Adam's side. "There'll be plenty of time to clean up tomorrow."

As Jonah turned away, an image of Mamm and Dat came to him,

taking him by surprise. They would have been happy to see their oldest son and daughter marrying today. It was a very good day.

When Jonah pulled the carriage up in front of the path to the house, he could tell that something was wrong from the pinched expression on Annie's face.

"What is it?" he asked.

She shook her head, nodding toward her father, who was making his way down the path on Lovina's arm. Drops of water fell from the corner of the porch roof as Jonah stood beside Annie, waiting until her parents were out of hearing range.

"One of the Englisher guests just told me the bad news. The covered bridge collapsed. The river crested and came up over the platform. It will be unusable until it's repaired."

Jonah frowned. "Sad news. Was anyone hurt?"

"No, thank Gott. But no one can get across."

"Mmm. From now on we'll have to take the main road into Paradise. Some of the folks here will have to detour to get home tonight."

She nodded. "And we'll need to hire a car to get Dat to his doctor visits. That would just be too long in the carriage."

He touched her arm. "We'll figure it out. It's bad news about the bridge, but eventually this rain will stop and the river will go down, and I'll help rebuild the bridge myself if the highway folk will let me."

She took a deep breath, nodding. "You're right. It's just sad to think of the old thing falling apart after all these years. If that bridge could talk, it would have so many stories to tell!"

He slid a hand over her shoulder and pulled her close. Annie could give a personality to a bridge or a voice to a newborn calf. It was one thing he loved about her. Down the path, Lovina and Aaron had just reached his carriage. "We'd better go help."

"Ya. Just don't tell Dat. I don't want anything worrying him right now."

He nodded. "You know me—the Quiet One."

The carriage was quiet on the trip back to the Stoltzfus farm. Jonah suspected that Aaron was tired, and rightly so. The wedding ceremony was long, and the celebration afterward had been a boisterous, social event, chock-full of food, laughter, and song.

Looking back on the day, Jonah felt as if he'd grown taller and wiser through seeing his brother and sister off into married life. The next few years would bring many changes, with babies and baptisms and more weddings.

This time next year, Gott willing, he and Annie would take their vows. They had a whole year to be sure of their commitment, but he knew his heart was steady and true.

Annie had always been the girl for him. Now that he knew her better, it only confirmed his love.

They were about a mile from the Stoltzfus farm when Jonah heard rustling in the back of the carriage. Lovina and Aaron were speaking in hushed tones that held a whisper of anxiety.

"Jonah." Lovina's voice held alarm. "Don't turn in at the farm. Just keep going into Paradise. We need to get Aaron to Dr. Trueherz's clinic."

"What?" Annie turned around. "What's going on?"

"He's not feeling well," Lovina said. "It's been going on awhile . . . through dinner."

"At first I thought it was indigestion from the coleslaw," Aaron admitted in a scratchy voice. "But this is no simple bellyache. My chest feels like a horse is trampling it."

"Dat, why didn't you say something to Dr. Trueherz?" Annie asked.

"He wasn't at the reception, and I felt okay during the wedding."

But Jonah's mind was caught up thinking what to do next. *Immediate medical attention.* That was what the doctor had ordered at the first glimmer of pain or discomfort. Jonah frowned, wishing that Aaron and Lovina had said something earlier. Back at the wedding, there had been a few Englishers with cars who could have driven them to the hospital in Lancaster.

"A heart attack?" Annie's whisper was laced with fear as she turned to Jonah. "What are we going to do?"

"Just keep going," Lovina said. "The doctor will know how to help him."

"Mamm, we can't." Annie's cheeks flashed pink. "We can't get to Paradise that way. The rain took out the covered bridge this morning."

"Oh, what a terrible time for this to happen . . . ," Lovina agonized.

"We'll have to take the main road." Annie's voice cracked as she tried to contain her panic.

"But that will take too long," Lovina said as Aaron let out a moan of pain. "Even if we push the horse, it will be an hour at least. Your dat can't take that."

"What choice do we have?" Annie asked.

"Go to the phone shanty," Lovina said. "We'll call for an ambulance. Or better yet, an airlift. I've seen them take patients off in helicopters from fields around here."

"I've seen that, too," Jonah said, weighing in for the first time, "but in this storm, they won't be able to get here. It's not safe to fly."

"Aaron, dear one, lean this way. I think your head is supposed to be higher than your heart," Lovina said. "We've got to get you there. . . . Jonah, the phone shanty it is. I know it could take half an hour for an ambulance to get here, but what choice do we have?"

As Aaron sighed in the back, Jonah tried to picture the river in his mind. They had to get across.

"What about the pass?" he asked. It was a narrow part of the river where the riverbed was naturally higher than the rest of the river. In the summer, the water was so shallow at the pass that it cascaded down the sides, like a trickling waterfall. Needless to say, horses and vehicles sometimes used it as a crossing.

"But the river is so high," Annie said. "Do you think it will be safe?"

"We can only go and give it a try . . . if it's all right with you, Lovina."

"Ya, go," agreed Lovina. "It's a good idea, and that's what we're in need of right now. That or a miracle."

Jonah urged Jigsaw to a faster trot in that direction. The horse was fast, but still his pace was maddeningly slow in light of the crisis. As they passed a car for sale along the roadside, Jonah looked on with a sigh. It was Zed Miller's old four-by-four Jeep, put up for sale by his father. He wished Zed were here now to drive them into town.

The pass was ten minutes away, but as they approached, the sight of two carriages stopped at the riverbank made Jonah's heart sink.

"It looks like they can't get across." Jonah felt the tense quiet of the carriage as he pulled close to one of the rigs parked on the road, handed Annie the reins, and jumped out.

Rain tapped the top of his hat as he slogged through the mud to the nearby carriage and looked in the open door to the driver. It was an Amish man he did not recognize, but the faces that peered back at him were full of concern.

"Have you tried the crossing?" Jonah asked.

"I haven't, but Amos over there started in. It's deeper than I've ever seen, and the current is strong. The horse lost its footing, and it was by the grace of Gott that Amos got the carriage backed up and out of there safe and sound."

"It's good that he's safe," Jonah said. "Will you head up to the main road?"

The man shook his head. "It's too much for the horses. We're going to wait here an hour or two. The river should draw back by then."

The man was right, but Aaron did not have an hour or two to spare. Jonah rubbed his chin as he looked toward the pass, where water churned over the smooth rise in the river. "Have you seen any cars here?"

The man frowned. "I expect most of them are taking the main road. But I did see one four-wheeler drive through. Made it straight across without a problem."

A four-wheeler.

Jonah flashed back to his youth, when he had learned to drive the Jeep with Zed Miller. How many times had they forded the river in it, right at this spot? He thanked the man for the information and hurried back to the carriage. "The horses can't make it across here," Jonah said as he turned the carriage and started back down the road. "But we can make it in a Jeep."

"That would be helpful if we had a driver with a Jeep," Annie said quietly.

"I think I know where we can get one."

He looked over at Annie, not wanting to explain the worst part of his plan. He knew that this would be an action that would ban him from the community they both loved. He didn't want to break the rule or disappoint her.

Dear Gott, I don't want to be another King who falls away.

But he couldn't let Aaron die when there was a way to get him help. They reached Ira Miller's property within minutes, and Jonah pulled over into the lane.

"Let me check this first." He ran up the hill to the parked Jeep and opened the door.

The key was plugged into the ignition, with another one dangling.

He climbed in and closed the door on the rain. Knowing he was breaking many rules, stealing and driving a car among them, he started the vehicle. The engine roared to life, and Jonah felt a glimmer of hope. The gas tank was almost full, and the wipers swished across the windshield.

This was going to work.

It had to work.

Although the gears were a little stiff, he managed to pop it into first and roll down the hill to the carriage. "This will be our ride," he announced.

Annie's eyes were round with amazement and shock, but Lovina said nothing as she and Jonah hoisted Aaron into the backseat. The man was pale and weak—almost in a sleepy state.

Jonah prayed to Gott that they would get to the doctor in time. Annie drove the carriage down to the hitching post by the Millers' house and tied off Jigsaw. Jonah followed in the Jeep, his heart beating loudly as she climbed into the passenger seat.

There was no time to leave a note for the Millers; they would have to explain later.

They rode in silence as the Jeep bumped down the lane. Jonah could feel Annie watching him as he worked the gearshift with his right hand, his feet on the brake and clutch pedal. He stopped at the end of the main road, jolted the vehicle into first gear, then quickly picked up speed, moving up to fourth gear.

"Looks complicated," Annie said. "How did you learn to drive like that?"

"I did some playing around during my rumspringa," he said. "Most of it in this Jeep. Zed was older, but he liked to teach guys to drive."

"I would have never thought that of you," Annie said.

"Those days are over." Or at least he had thought they were when he took his baptismal vow. Despite the damp cold, Jonah's hands began to sweat as they approached the pass for the second time. Although he had made this crossing half a dozen times in this Jeep, he had never done it with the river so high.

And on top of that, darkness was beginning to fall, dropping a soft cover of gray around them. Jonah found the switch for the lights and pulled it to the on position. The stream of light ahead was stronger than the lights on any carriage, and he was grateful for the beacon lighting their path.

The two carriages still waited at the pass, sprawled at the side of the river like forgotten toys. Jonah wove around them and pressed the brakes just short of the churning water. The headlights shone on the roiling river.

"I can see that the current is strong, but there's no telling how deep it is in this light," Jonah said, thinking aloud.

Annie turned to him, her voice so even that he could feel her trust in him. "Can we make it?"

"Gott willing." He eased off the brake, clutched, and put the car in first gear. As soon as the wheels touched the water he could feel the pull of the current. The car seemed to sway toward the right, and he steered left, pressing the gas pedal steadily.

Jonah had always felt in tune with nature, but this was a battle. It was Jeep against river, man against storm.

Outside the vehicle, water swirled against their doors.

"It's seeping in," Annie said, staring down at the door.

"We're almost through," Jonah said with a calm he didn't feel. He knew he would have to pay for damage to the vehicle. Water was not good for pipes and mechanical things.

But the tires were gripping the road—and the water's edge was now just a few feet away.

He kept his foot steady on the gas, even as the front tires dug into the mud, caught, and pulled them to safety.

"Praise be to Gott!" Lovina cried from the backseat.

Annie patted Jonah's shoulder as the cloak of dread lifted from his shoulders. He felt lighter, as if they were soaring now . . . flying Aaron to the help he needed.

"We'll have you at the clinic soon, Aaron," Jonah called behind him as he pushed the Jeep to a higher gear, holding tight to the wheel with his left hand. "Just stay with us."

Stay with us. . . .

FIFTY-ONE

*T*he false quiet of the hospital waiting room was enough to drive a man crazy. Jonah longed for the noises of home: voices and laughter, songs and jokes, clanging dishes and the inevitable cow mooing in the background.

Jonah shifted in the plastic chair of the hospital waiting room and took Annie's hand. Her small fingers wove through his and he gave a squeeze, wishing he could protect her from harm and fear and sorrow. Of course, that wasn't possible, but that was his desire.

"I wish someone would come out with an update," Annie said. Lovina was filling out forms with a nurse inside one of the hospital offices. And somewhere inside the cardiac ward, Aaron was being treated by Henry Trueherz and a handful of other doctors and nurses. Aaron's wife had been allowed to ride in the front of the ambulance that had transported him to this hospital in Lancaster, once Dr. Trueherz had "stabilized" him in his office.

In an attempt to get word back to her family, Annie had called the phone shanty and left a message. Daniel, Rebecca, Hannah, and Levi were probably already home from the wedding, but just in case, Annie had also left a message on the answering machine at the phone shanty the Kings shared with the Zooks.

"What if they don't think to check the answering machine?" Annie had asked, concerned.

"What about your English neighbors?" Jonah suggested. "I've seen Clem O'Boyle with his tractor on the road. Do you think he would ride over to the farm to deliver an emergency message?" Jonah asked.

Annie picked up the phone they'd been told to use at the nurses' station. "We won't know unless we ask."

The nurse had shown them how to get a phone number from directory assistance. When Annie had called, Clem's wife, Hattie, had answered and clucked with sympathy. "She said she doesn't mind driving over to tell them the news," Annie had reported. "And she said we must be sure to call her if there's anything else she can do for us."

"That's a good neighbor you have," Jonah had told her.

Now the ticking clock on the wall was beginning to get under his skin. The sound of footsteps on the shiny tile floor caught their attention, and he and Annie rose as Lovina came down the hall with Dr. Trueherz and a small woman in navy scrubs.

"He's going into surgery," Lovina said, her eyes shiny with tears. "They can't put it off any longer."

"But we knew the surgery was inevitable," Henry Trueherz reminded them.

"Aaron needs a triple bypass." The woman in scrubs who introduced herself as Dr. Patton didn't look to be much older than Annie, but she spoke with authority. "It's the only viable course right now. If all goes well, the prognosis is good." She looked at her watch. "I need to get scrubbed." She faced Lovina. "I'll talk with you when the surgery is done."

After the surgeon left, Henry Trueherz tried to talk them into going to the hospital cafeteria. "It's going to be a few hours, and a change of scenery might do you good."

"No." Lovina pulled her jacket tighter around her. "I want to stay here, close as I can. But thank you for everything, Doctor. Thank you for saving Aaron's life."

"It was quick thinking on Jonah's part that saved him." Dr. True-herz nodded toward Jonah. "You didn't let that river stop you, did you?"

Jonah didn't mind the teasing, but he couldn't summon a smile. Not while Aaron was in surgery and the consequences of his actions weighed him down.

Hours passed, slow as molasses. Jonah now understood why Aaron had wanted to get out of the hospital weeks ago. Besides the expense, a hospital was not a good place for people. The cold, long corridors, the noise of beeping monitors and machines, the smell of floor wax, and so many people wandering around, pushing carts or trash cans or wheelchairs. It was hard to believe people were healing in this cold, strange place.

The sound of footsteps in the corridor was not unusual, but the young child's voice caught Annie and Jonah's attention.

"Is that Levi?" Annie sprang to her feet and scurried to the hall-way. "It is! I'm so glad to see you all!"

Levi jumped into her arms as Rebecca, Daniel, and Hannah filed into the little waiting area.

"We came as soon as we heard!" Rebecca hugged her mother. "How's Dat?"

"Still in surgery." Lovina repeated everything the doctors had told them, including the part about how Jonah's quick thinking had saved Aaron's life.

Suddenly, three different conversations were going on at once, and Jonah was grateful for the way Annie's family had breathed new life into this very dull waiting room. Rebecca had been worried since they returned home to an empty house, and they were grateful for Hattie coming by with the message. Don, their usual hired driver, had gotten out of bed to make this emergency trip for them.

"Is it true that you drove Aaron to the clinic in a Jeep?" Daniel asked in a low voice.

Jonah nodded. "There was no other way. The horses couldn't make it across the river, and he had to get to the doctor right away."

Daniel clapped a hand on his shoulder. "Don't be so glum. The doctor says you saved Aaron's life."

"It's true." Annie's eyes were pools of pale blue.

"That was all I could think about," Jonah said. He realized the possible consequences of his actions—he could be shunned for driving the Jeep. He swallowed, his throat dry as a bone. It was necessary to save Aaron's life, but in that moment he might have severed himself from his community, from his church, from the people he loved.

"You're a hero," Daniel said.

"No. A hero would have figured out a way to save Aaron without going against the Ordnung."

"Still . . . you saved a man." Daniel pointed down the hospital corridor. "Aaron is alive in there because of your brave move. You did a good thing, Jonah."

In his heart, Jonah knew that was true. But he still couldn't reconcile the fact that he had gone against the Ordnung. There would be consequences. He might be shunned. Ya, there were levels of shunning, but even the most meager punishment before the community would sting.

Jonah sank back in the chair and closed his eyes. He had always been so sure of walking the right path. Not so much anymore.

A few minutes later, Jonah and Annie were going through all the snack items in a vending machine when the surgeon came down the hall with two other staff members in scrubs. Conversation stopped as everyone got up to face the doctors.

"Mrs. Stoltzfus?" Dr. Patton looked through the group and stepped forward once she found Lovina. "Good news. The surgery went well. Your husband is a very lucky man. . . ."

Not a lucky man, Jonah thought as relief washed over him. *A man blessed by Gott.*

FIFTY-TWO

*J*onah said good-bye to Ira Miller, then climbed into the carriage and turned Jigsaw down the lane. After the emergency of the last day and night, the fear and the waiting and the hope, he was glad to be alone with his thoughts. He had thanked Ira for taking care of his horse and carriage, which he'd left here when he'd "borrowed" the Jeep. The older man agreed they would settle up later on the Jeep, which still sat in the clinic parking lot.

"Maybe someone will see it there and buy it," Ira had said. "I'll be glad to have that thing out of my hair." Jonah understood how he felt, though he couldn't forget how the Jeep had helped them yesterday.

The hired driver had taken Jonah to Ira's place after dropping Annie and her sisters, Daniel, and Levi off at the Stoltzfus farm. They had waited at the hospital until Aaron came out of recovery and was resting in a hospital bed, Lovina tucked into a chair beside him. Although the nurses warned that he was still medicated and resting, they had filed into the room for reassurance. Despite the tubes running down to his arm, Aaron had looked like Aaron again, his face pink and peaceful. Annie had touched his hand. Rebecca had told Levi to blow his doddy a kiss. Daniel had reassured him that the morning milking would be taken care of by their neighbor. Jonah had not spoken, but he had made his promise long ago to keep the farm running, and Aaron knew he could count on him.

Now, as Jonah passed the Stoltzfus farm, he stretched as much as he could in the seat of the carriage. He was weary to the bone, but rest would be impossible. The incident with the Jeep pained him, a burr inside him.

He had to make it right.

He reined Jigsaw in at a stop sign and considered how to get to Bishop Samuel's house from here. Instead of taking a left toward home, he turned right.

At Samuel Mast's farm, he found the bishop out behind the barn, mending the latch on a fence.

Samuel straightened as Jonah approached. "I thought you'd be coming by to see me."

"And I knew you would have heard what happened." Word traveled fast in a tight-knit community like theirs.

"I don't listen to rumors. But I did hear the story of how you got Aaron to the hospital. He's going to be all right?"

Jonah nodded.

"Good." Samuel closed the gate and removed his gloves. "So you drove an automobile." His eyes, cold as ice, were magnified by the lenses of his glasses.

"I did. All the way to Paradise. The Halfway Mill Covered Bridge was damaged by the rising river, and a horse and buggy couldn't make it across the pass.

"When we got to Doc Trueherz's clinic, an ambulance came and took Aaron to the hospital in Lancaster."

"Why didn't you call an ambulance in the first place?"

"There wasn't time to wait for one. Aaron needed help." He explained how the doctors had warned them that Aaron needed to get medical help at the first sign of pain or discomfort.

"So you broke a rule." There was a raspy sound as the bishop let out a deep breath. "We can't have that, Jonah."

"I know it was wrong, Bishop. But it was the only way I saw to get Aaron to the doctor. His heart was in bad shape. He could have died."

"Don't get me wrong. I'm grateful that you saved Aaron's life. That was a courageous thing to do, getting the Jeep to ford the river at the pass. But we need to deal with the fact that you have broken a rule. You drove a car, and that can't be tolerated. No exceptions. If one person can drive without any consequence, soon everyone will be driving a car now and again. I have to talk with the other ministers about this, but I can tell you now, it must be dealt with. There will be a punishment."

"I understand." Jonah closed his eyes as a cold wave of dread slapped over him.

He was going to be shunned.

When the two familiar silos of the farmhouse came into view, Jonah gritted his teeth. He had never thought he would return home a broken man like this. The bann was something that happened to other people, not faithful, careful men like him.

He hung his head, wondering what Annie would think of all this. She loved living in Halfway. She felt a sense of belonging in the

Amish community here. And now, she was courting a man who would be shunned. Even after the bann ended, the memory of it would hang over Jonah like a dark shadow. Annie wouldn't want to be connected to such a person of disgrace.

As his horse clopped down the lane, he saw the children moving furniture from the storehouse to the main house. The wedding cleanup . . . he had almost forgotten. The process of tidying and moving everything back into place would take another day or so.

"Jonah!" Simon and Ruthie put the rocking chair they were carrying onto the ground to run over to meet him.

"Jonah!" Katie and Sam, little copycats, scampered over behind their older siblings.

The sight of the four of them running to greet him melted the ice in his heart. They loved him unconditionally, and no sin against the Ordnung or bann from the church would change that. He stopped the carriage and jumped down. Joy was in the air as Ruthie and Sam hugged him, Simon patted his back, and Katie grabbed his leg.

"You saved Annie's dat!" Simon said. "You're a hero, Jonah."

"Not a hero," Jonah said. "Gott saved Aaron."

"But you helped," Simon insisted.

"And you're home at last," Ruthie said, sounding like a grown-up girl. "We were all so worried."

"And now you can help in the cleanup," Simon said.

"We're helping!" Sam held up a sponge to prove it.

"It's good to be home." Jonah swallowed past the tight knot in his throat. After what he'd been through in the past day, cleanup sounded like a picnic. "How's it going?"

"The house is clean." Simon motioned to the chair, and Ruthie picked up the other end. "We're just starting to put the furniture back."

He looked up to see a line of people carrying furniture from the storage shed to the house: Adam and Gabe on either end of the day-bed; Mary and Five carrying the sofa; Leah, Susie, and Sadie toting chairs and a small stool.

"You made it back!" Mary called to him.

"Just in time to help with the heavy lifting," her husband added.

Jonah strode toward them, relieved to be home. "Looks like I should have stayed away a bit longer, give you a chance to finish."

"There's always more work to be done around here," Adam said.

"I'll join in, just as soon as I take care of Jigsaw."

Jonah unhitched the buggy and turned his horse out. Walking up the path to the house, he was grateful for the sights and sounds of home. The fences that wound down the hillside to outline the golden fields. Birds circling the pasture, landing, then circling again. The murmur of cows in the distance and the smell of fresh-baked bread coming from the kitchen.

Leah held the door for him as he brought a bench inside. Adam took the far end, and together they lowered the bench to the ground. Remy was setting a platter on the kitchen table.

"Are you hungry?" Remy asked. "Mary baked two loaves of bread, and I'm carving up leftover chicken for sandwiches."

He hadn't eaten all day. "I think I could polish off a whole chicken by myself."

She smiled. "Then you'd better get washed up, before your brothers beat you to it."

Jonah was quiet during the simple meal. He knew there would be time to talk of Aaron and the Jeep and his punishment in the coming days. Exhaustion pressed upon his warring thoughts. Part of him craved more meals like this, with everyone gathered around the table. The other part looked forward to the family branching out and growing . . . though right now he couldn't see how that might happen. Most of all, he was grateful to be home, where he knew his family accepted him no matter what fate the ministers decided.

Home . . . where the family sat together for a good meal.

Where Ruthie worried that he looked tired, Simon talked about his horse, and Leah shared her dream of becoming Emma's teaching assistant. Where everyone pitched in to make sure the cows were milked and the chickens tended.

And at the end of the day—a very long day—there was no comfort that could compare with stretching out on his own bed.

Although Jonah awoke the next morning with a clear head, worry shadowed him throughout the day as he did his chores at home. He had never been in trouble with the clergy before. Even during his rumspringa, no one had needed to say a word to him about staying in line.

But now trouble was brewing like storm clouds in the sky as he headed over to the Stoltzfus farm. As the horse's hooves clattered rhythmically on the road, the hammer of judgment pounded on his back.

And I don't deserve to be punished.

He had always been careful to choose the right path. Careful and obedient. He had a perfect record . . . a reputation any man could be proud of.

He tipped back his hat as realization dawned. Ya, he'd been proud of his good reputation in the church. Proud to call himself a faithful Amish man.

And that was wrong. Pride in any form was wrong. Hochmut, they called it.

Maybe it was time to let go of the reputation he valued so dearly and begin to see himself in a new light: a simple man who worked a simple land.

With the rest of the family working in town or still at the hospital with Aaron, there was no avoiding Annie. She popped out the side door, her cherry lips curled in a content smile.

"Good news!" she said. "Dat woke up and was talking last night. He even joked with Mamm and the doctors."

"Back to his old self." Hearing the news about Aaron made his worries seem small. It was time to step up and be a man, take the punishment handed out and move on. Time spent worrying about what other people thought about him would be wasted time.

She tilted her head, studying him. "Something's wrong. What is it?"

She had come to know him well. He rubbed his jaw. "I talked with Bishop Samuel yesterday, and there's going to be a price to pay for me driving that Jeep. I might have to make a public confession, and there's a good chance I'll be shunned."

She shook her head. "That seems unfair."

"It's what happens when you go against the Ordnung. We both know that. So if you want to distance yourself from me, I understand. You don't deserve to be connected to the kind of disgrace that'll be coming down on my head."

"That's crazy talk." Annie shook her head, her blue eyes flashing with indignation. "Jonah King, there is no better man for me than you, and you know it."

He tipped back his hat and rubbed his temple in weary frustration. "I'm a sinner now."

"How could I hold that against you? I was there and . . . do you want to know what I think? I think the Heavenly Father made sure you were with us, because you are the only Amish man I know who could think so clearly in a crisis and put us in that Jeep and get us across the river. You are the only one, Jonah. Gott sent us a miracle, and it's you."

He shook his head. "It's probably wrong to say those things. I went against the Ordnung, Annie."

"That's right. And that you would be willing to pay that price of repentance . . . to be shunned so that you could save my dat . . ." She frowned. "I'm sorry for the shame you feel, but if you'll stop beating yourself up and listen, you'll hear that I love you. No matter what the ministers decide. I will always love you. In good times and bad."

Her words stopped him in his tracks.

Annie loved him.

Unconditional love . . . like the love of his brothers and sisters. Like the love of the Heavenly Father.

It was Gott's greatest gift, but his heart was too troubled to accept it.

Gently, he put his hands on Annie's shoulders and faced those eyes that seemed to see right into his soul. "You know that I love you," he said. "I always have, and I always will. But right now, I'm stuck in this muck alone, and I don't want to drag you into it."

Her blue eyes flared wide. "Drag me in. I was there with you. I'm just as guilty. I would have driven the Jeep if I knew how."

The thought of Annie trying to drive eased the weight on his shoulders. "I think I'll have to confess before the congregation on Sunday," he said. "After that, after the punishment, you can decide how you feel about me." He dropped his hands from her shoulders and tore himself away, walking quickly toward the barn.

"This doesn't change anything!" she called after him. "It makes me love you even more."

Her bold words, shouted over the farm—typical of Annie. That courage was one of the many things he loved about her.

Although the words were a salve to his wounds, he kept walking. He was a practical man, and there were many chores to be done.

An hour or so later he heard the horses before he saw the carriages—three of them—coming toward the Stoltzfus farm. He continued pushing the wheelbarrow along the path, which gave him a vantage point that allowed him to watch the carriages pull up near the farmhouse. The three bearded men were their ministers, Bishop Samuel, Preacher Dave, and Deacon Moses. When Annie came out of the house and pointed toward the barn, he knew they'd come for him.

Hmm. Was his sin so great that it couldn't wait until Sunday for further discussion?

He parked the wheelbarrow and started down the path to meet the three men, who held on to their hats against a gust of wind.

"Jonah." Dave nodded. "We were at the hospital this morning, the three of us."

"Aaron was up and walking already," said Moses. "He looks mighty healthy for a man who had surgery yesterday."

Jonah let himself smile. "I'm glad to hear that. He was still recovering when I left the hospital yesterday."

"We heard more of the story from Lovina." Bishop Samuel's eyes were stern, magnified by the lenses of his glasses. "She told us how you came up with the idea to use the Jeep."

The breath froze in Jonah's chest. "I'm ready to confess on Sunday. Whatever you say, I will do."

"Ya. We've been talking about that." Dave tugged lightly on the tendrils of his beard. "Such a night! The covered bridge collapsed. The river flooded its banks. With all those things, how could you get Aaron to the doctor? It was a good thing to save him."

"But a sin to drive that Jeep," Moses added.

"A sin that must be confessed, of course," Samuel said. "But with all that was going on, we ruled that you won't have to confess before the congregation. You can do it now, to the brethren."

Jonah blinked. They were easing his punishment. "And the bann?"

Moses's mouth twisted around. "You won't be shunned, as long as you confess now."

"I will." Jonah sank to his knees on the cold earth. "I do confess. . . ." Relief washed over him as he lowered his head and spoke of his sin before the three men.

The men talked about the Ordnung and the importance of following church rules. "A car can take a man far from his family," the bishop added. "It makes a person part of the world, and we must remain separate, living on this earth but not of it."

Jonah was still kneeling when he saw a flash of white from the corner of his eyes. Fluffy bounded over, dashed behind the three ministers and circled back. The lamb scampered closer and nuzzled Jonah's shoulder.

Keeping his head bowed, he pushed the lamb away.

At once, the three ministers went silent, then laughed.

"This reminds me of the Lamb of God in the Bible." Of the three brethren, Moses knew the most about the Bible. " 'Behold the Lamb of God, which taketh away the sin of the world.' That lamb was Jesus."

"Then it's very fitting," the bishop said. "You've confessed your sin, and Gott the Father forgives you."

"But I think this is just an ordinary lamb," said Dave, always the practical one.

Jonah smiled as Fluffy came at him again, butting against his shoulder.

"You can get back on your feet," Dave said, "before this one knocks you over."

Jonah rose with ease as his burden slipped from his shoulders. He stood tall as the conversation turned to questions about Aaron's sheep and the running of the farm while the man was ill.

"I'm not a farmer," Dave said, "but I know that any farm needs many hands to succeed. And Gott saw fit to bless Aaron with all girls."

"Annie and her sisters know their way around the farm," Jonah said. "But it does take a handful of people to keep it running."

"Help is on the way," Moses said. "But you're doing a right fine job, Jonah."

The man's words brought Jonah back to a busy fall day, many years ago. His first day spent making hay with the men, from sunup to nearly sundown. "You did a good job today," Dat had said, his dark eyes twinkling. "You're a right fine worker, Jonah."

He swallowed back the knot of emotion in his throat. Now when he thought of Dat, it was the good memories that came to him: the gentle lessons, the jokes, the moments when his father had challenged him to take on the work of a man.

Looking over the fields and outbuildings, the barn and the farmhouse with smoke rising from the chimney, Jonah knew that time had come.

By the grace of Gott's blessings, he would carry on the traditions and faith followed by his family for hundreds of years.

After the men left, he turned to Annie, who had come out of the kitchen to say her good-byes to the clergy.

"They allowed me to confess, so I don't have to go through it in front of the congregation on Sunday." He explained it all, ending with Fluffy's intrusion on the proceedings.

Annie laughed, then turned to him, her blue eyes full of tenderness. "Good thing for Fluffy! Otherwise, you might still be out there listening to Bible stories from Deacon Moses."

He smiled. "You're right." He stood tall, feeling so light now that his burden had been lifted.

She pressed her small hands to his chest as she looked up at him. "I know this has been hard for you, but someday it will be a magnificent story to tell our grandchildren."

"Grandchildren?" Annie was always a few steps ahead of him. "Isn't that putting the cart before the horse?"

"It's good to plan ahead."

"Right now, I don't even have a plan for today."

"Sure you do. Some of the men are coming over this afternoon to help you finish off the winter shelter for the sheep."

Jonah nodded. "I can use the help." With a few men on the task, they might get the work done before sunset.

"But first, there's lunch. Three people dropped by with casseroles and bread this morning. Everyone who heard about Dat wants to help."

It was the Amish way. Jonah glanced out over the golden brown fields and purple hills, grateful to live in a community of kindness.

"But right now you need to wash up." She patted his chest. "And that's the plan. How does it sound?"

"Good." The weariness and strain of the past day and night slid away. His heart was so full, but he couldn't find the words.

"But first, before any of that, you need to kiss me." She curled her fingers over his shoulders, lifting her face to his. "That's part of *my* plan."

He folded her into his arms and held her against his heart. "You're a good planner." When his lips touched hers, he thanked Gott for the blessings in his life, especially the love of this woman in his arms. In his days on this farm Annie had become his best friend. Come next wedding season, he hoped to make her his wife.

Thank you, Father.

He imagined his small prayer circling around Annie and him, binding them close together before swooping over the golden fields like a flock of nightjars and rising to the wide blue heavens.

RECIPES FROM THE SEASONS
OF LANCASTER NOVELS

NUTTY CINNAMON BREAD

This is the nutty bread that Annie Stoltzfus bakes in *A Simple Autumn*. It's her dat's favorite. Some Amish bake this with walnuts from their own trees. Feel free to use fresh, but be advised that wild walnuts are really hard to crack . . . some tough nuts!

Preheat oven to 350 degrees F.

Combine:
- *1 tablespoon active dry yeast (dissolved in ¹/₄ cup warm water)*
- *³/₄ cup milk*
- *4 tablespoons butter (melted)*

Beat in:
- *1 egg*
- *¹/₂ teaspoon salt*

- *3 tablespoons sugar*
- *1 teaspoon almond extract*

Gradually stir in:
- *3 cups flour*

When the flour has been mixed in, place dough in an ungreased bowl and put a damp towel over the top. Let it rise for an hour, until doubled in size. Punch the dough and divide into two sections. Press half of it into the bottom of a 9-inch round buttered pan. Stretch the dough so that it covers the pan.

For the filling, in a separate bowl, combine:
- *4 tablespoons softened butter*
- *½ cup brown sugar*
- *½ cup chopped walnuts*
- *1 teaspoon vanilla*
- *1 teaspoon cinnamon*

When the filling is creamy, spread it over the flattened dough. Lightly grease your hand with butter, then stretch the second half of the dough over the filling, pressing down only at the edges. Bake for 20 minutes or until golden brown. Take the bread from the pan to let it cool before cutting.

GMAY OR CHURCH COOKIES

These large, soft sugar cookies are passed around for small children halfway through an Amish church service. The idea is to give the little ones a break during the very long service. Long after Amish children are too old to take the cookies, some still long for them when they see the platter go by on Sunday. The rest of the cookies are served to everyone as part of the meal after the service. These may have become the traditional church cookie recipe because they actually taste better when they are made in advance. This recipe makes ten dozen cookies, but you can cut it in half if you are not serving a congregation of a hundred or more. Sam King and his aunt Betsy make these in *A Simple Autumn*.

Preheat oven to 375 degrees F.

In a big bowl, combine:

- *3 cups lard*
- *5 cups sugar*

Add:

- *5 eggs*

Beat well. Add:

- *2¹/₂ cups milk*
- *3 teaspoons vanilla extract*

Stir in:

- *2 teaspoons baking soda*
- *5 teaspoons baking powder*
- *1 teaspoon salt*
- *11–12 cups all-purpose flour*

Stir until a soft dough forms. Lightly flour a surface and roll out the dough to approximately ¹/₂-inch thickness. Cut out shapes with cookie cutters or make round cookies with a drinking glass. Bake on an ungreased cookie sheet for ten minutes or until golden brown.

SAWDUST PIE

The name of this pie and the fact that it contains lots of coconut won me over right away. I find that adults like it more than children, and because it's so sweet, a little piece goes a long way. It probably got its name because of the filling's resemblance to the sawdust on the floors of Amish mills and woodshops. In *A Simple Spring,* Remy makes it for Adam, her woodworking beau.

Preheat oven to 350 degrees F.

Have your piecrust ready in a 9-inch pan. The crust should be crimped on the edges.

In a medium bowl, combine:
- *1½ cups shredded coconut*
- *1½ cups graham cracker crumbs*
- *1½ cups chopped pecans*
- *1½ cups sugar*

Mix in:
- *1 cup unbeaten egg whites (from 4–5 eggs)*

Pour the filling into the unbaked pie shell. You may want to cover the edges with foil if you don't like a browned crust. Bake for 35–40 minutes. Don't worry if the pie seems moist inside when you take it out. Cool for at least 45 minutes to give the pie a chance to set.

NO-BAKE OATMEAL TURTLES OR
AMISH FUNERAL COOKIES

Although I wasn't raised Amish, I loved making these cookies as a child—probably because I didn't have to wait around for them to bake and could lick the spoon. Some Amish folk came to call them funeral cookies because they could be prepared quickly and brought over to the grieving family. For me, turtles are a cross between fudge and a cookie. I like to think they're almost healthful with all that oatmeal. In *A Simple Winter,* Mary mentions these cookies to Remy while she is baking.

In a medium saucepan, combine:
+ *¹/₂ cup butter*
+ *1³/₄ cups sugar*
+ *¹/₂ cup milk*
+ *5 tablespoons unsweetened cocoa powder*

Bring to a light simmer, stirring constantly for one minute.

Remove from heat and stir in:
+ *¹/₂ cup peanut butter*
+ *1 teaspoon vanilla*
+ *¹/₈ teaspoon salt*
+ *3 cups rolled oats (or quick-cooking oatmeal)*

Mix quickly and drop by teaspoons onto waxed paper. Let the cookies cool outside the fridge for one hour. Makes about 3 dozen turtles.

ACKNOWLEDGMENTS

With the publication of this third Seasons of Lancaster novel, I am grateful to the many fans who have expressed the joy they have received from these books and encouragement to keep the King family going. Thank you, dear readers, for brightening my day with your warm reception of my characters and their stories.

No one can surpass Dr. Violet Dutcher's eye for story detail, Amish detail, and the nuances of Amish living. Your corrections gave this book authenticity, and your personal anecdotes inspired me to let Jonah have his story. I can't thank you enough. I would sign up for one of your classes in a heartbeat!

To my editor, Junessa Viloria, I can't tell you how fortunate I am to have found an editor who seems to love and understand these characters as much as I do. You have a wonderful sense of how to mingle authentic truths and entertaining fiction. I hope that you and I will have many more adventures together in Halfway, Pennsylvania.

Many thanks to the excellent staff at Ballantine Books, who took great care with this book in every stage. Denki!

ABOUT THE AUTHOR

ROSALIND LAUER grew up in a large family in Maryland and began visiting Lancaster County's Amish community as a child. She attended Wagner College in New York City and worked as an editor for Simon & Schuster and Harlequin Books. She currently lives with her family in Oregon, where she writes in the shade of some towering two-hundred-year-old Douglas fir trees.

2/14